The Death of All Things

Other Anthologies Edited by

Patricia Bray & Joshua Palmatier
After Hours: Tales from the Ur-Bar
The Modern Fae's Guide to Surviving Humanity
Clockwork Universe: Steampunk vs Aliens
Temporally Out of Order
Alien Artifacts
Were-
All Hail Our Robot Conquerors!

S.C. Butler & Joshua Palmatier
Submerged

The Death of All Things

Edited by
Laura Anne Gilman
&
Kat Richardson

Zombies Need Brains LLC
www.zombiesneedbrains.com

Interior Design (ebook): April Steenburgh
Interior Design (print): C. Lennox Graphics, LLC
Cover Design by C. Lennox Graphics, LLC
Cover Art "The Death of All Things" by Justin Adams

ZNB Book Collectors #10

Kickstarter Edition Printing, August 2017
First Printing, September 2017

Print ISBN-10: 1940709164
Print ISBN-13: 978-1940709161

Ebook ISBN-10: 1940709172
Ebook ISBN-13: 978-1940709178

Printed in the U.S.A.

Copyrights

TABLE OF CONTENTS

SIGNATURE PAGE

Laura Anne Gilman, editor:

_____

Kat Richardson, editor:

_____

K. M. Laney:

_____

Andrea Mullen:

_____

Faith Hunter:

_____

Kendra Leigh Speedling:

_____

Jason M. Hough:

_____

Julie Pitzel:

_____

Shaun Avery:

_____

Christie Golden:

_____

Leah Cutter:

_____

Aliette de Bodard:

_____

Andrew Dunlop:

Juliet E. McKenna

_____

A. Merc Rustad:

_____

Ville Meriläinen:

_____

Amanda Kespohl:

_____

Mack Moyer:

_____

Fran Wilde:

_____

Kathryn McBride:

_____

Andrija Popovic:

_____

Jim C. Hines:

_____

Stephen Blackmoore:

_____

Kiya Nicoll:

_____

Justin Adams, artist:

_____

INTRODUCTION
Laura Anne Gilman & Kat Richardson

Death is, as all the jokes go, universal. So we knew we'd get a lot of submissions, once the anthology was announced. What we weren't expecting was how good they would be.

We should have expected that Death, when you engage with it, pulls everything out and puts it on the table. And so did these stories.

Whatever the genre—and we saw them all—each story brought some fresh aspect to the portrait of Death, the Universal. Here you will find heroes and villains, as well as those who aren't quite either, and those who are a bit of both; there are tales of vengeance, trickery, and loss, but also stories of joy, duty, triumph—even love—as well as the divine, and the ridiculous. From so many great offerings, it was difficult to choose only a few, but we have selected the pieces we feel best illustrate a range of ideas and feeling, as well as a range of artists. So, from the minds and hands of bestsellers, seasoned storytellers, and fresh new writers, we're pleased to bring you twenty-two original views of the Death of All Things.

RAVELING
K. M. Laney

Alex eased the door closed behind him, shutting out the noise from the younger kids. His face brightened in a smile. Freedom!

He looked around at the gym lobby. A tennis match played on the big TV. The sound was off. Nobody was watching it. All the magazines on the coffee table were about sports or health or news. No comics or books to read. He looked through the windows to the pool room. Mom was there, along with all the other pregnant ladies in her water aerobics class. Boring. Even if he'd brought a suit he was only allowed to swim during his Tadpole class. Freedom, but nothing to do.

An older woman sitting quiet by the windows caught his eye. She wore one of those exercise outfits like Gramma did. A purple one. And a purple ribbon in her curly white hair. He only knew Gramma from pictures, but she always matched, too. He and Mom had gone through all the albums the other day. His favorites were the ones where Mom was a kid, like he was.

A purple gym bag leaned against the woman's left leg. Alex glimpsed fluffy gray stuff through the open zipper. She held a wad of the same stuff in her hand. Pulling at it and twisting it through her fingers, she fed a narrow strand to a top spinning in the air by her other ankle. Maybe it was a game?

Curious, Alex took a step toward her, then stopped. Mom said he wasn't supposed to talk to strangers. He glanced over at the front desk. The check-in girl sat on her stool, reading. Everyone in the pool could see him through the windows. He wasn't all by himself. Alex screwed up his courage and approached her. "Hi," he said.

The old woman looked up at him. "Hello there," she said. Her hands never stopped, the gray fluff flowing through her fingers like a stream of fog. "How are you?" she asked.

"I'm fine, how are you?" he answered. That's how Mom always answered when people asked her. "What are you doing?" he asked before she could answer his first question.

The old woman chuckled. "I'm very well, young man, thank you for asking," she said with a twinkle in her eye. "I don't think we've been introduced. My name is Nora. What's yours?"

"I'm Alex," he said. "Pleased to meet you." He stuck out his hand, remembering his manners.

Nora let the top touch the floor and it spiraled to a stop, trailing gray string. She took his hand and shook it. "Pleased to meet you as well, Alex. You have very nice manners."

Alex brightened. "Thanks!" he said. The other kids thought he was weird.

Nora picked up her top by the tall stick and gave it a quick twist. It began spinning rapidly. She teased fluff from the bundle and let the top wind it up. "I'm spinning. I bet you've never seen anyone spin yarn before," she said, watching him and not the yarn.

"Spinning?" Alex asked.

The old woman nodded. "Spinning. Making yarn."

"Is that like the spinning wheel in Sleeping Beauty?" Alex asked. "I saw a spinning wheel at the Heritage Museum once." He eyed Nora's top. "It was bigger."

She chuckled. "People made yarn on drop spindles like this for ages before they invented spinning wheels. Have a seat, Alex." She patted the seat beside her as the spindle ran down and gave it another twist while Alex settled. "Are you supposed to be out here?" she asked.

Alex scuffed his feet on the short blue carpet. "I'm supposed to be in there with the other kids," he said, pointing his chin toward the closed door labeled "Fun Space" in bright crayon colors. "But they're all little. All they want to do is run around and scream and stuff. There's no one for me to play with."

"I see," said Nora, a gentle smile in her brown eyes. "It's hard, being between worlds, isn't it?"

Alex looked at her. Nora understood. He nodded. "So how come you're here? You're not exercising like the other grown-ups. Are you waiting for someone?"

"I am," she said. She gave the slowing spindle another twist. "He's a little late. No matter, though. I like being near all the young people. Everyone is so energetic and full of life."

Alex giggled. Maybe Nora didn't fit in either. She was probably supposed to be with all the old people. He bent in to look more closely at the fluff winding as yarn on the spindle. "Why don't you just buy yarn at the store?"

"Oh, I can't use ordinary yarn," Nora said. "Made from sheep's wool or nasty plastic acrylic? Spun by the mile on machines, lined up with hundreds of identical skeins and sold for pennies by people who don't care? Never touched by warm, feeling hands? What kind of yarn is that? Good for socks and scarves, maybe," Nora caressed the soft fibers as the spindle imparted twist and wound them around its shaft, "not for what I'm making."

"Sorry," Alex apologized.

"Don't be sorry," Nora said. "It's a good question. I didn't mean to sound so snippy. I'm quite particular about my yarn."

Now that he was close, Alex realized the fluff wasn't gray at all. It was all colors mixed together. He had modeling clay like that came in a lot of colors in the beginning, but the more he played with it the more it got mixed up. Now it was all gray. Nora's fluff reminded him of that ball of gray clay that was really all the colors mixed up together. "So what are you going to make with it?" he asked.

"With my yarn?" Nora asked.

"Yes!" Alex pressed.

Nora smiled and leaned toward him. "A soul," she said in a conspiratorial whisper.

Alex sat upright. He must have heard wrong. "A soul?" he asked.

"That's right," Nora said, straightening and twisting the spindle again. She pulled more of the not-gray fluff from the bundle and let it twine between her fingers.

Alex crossed his arms. "You're making fun," he pouted.

"Not at all," Nora said. She let the spindle come to a rest on the floor and pulled a handful of fuzz from the purple exercise bag. She pulled and stretched the fibers a bit, making a loose bundle in her hand. When she started the spindle up again the fluff twined into smooth, neat thread.

"You can't make a soul," Alex said.

Nora's fingers moved with precision, feeding the fibers into the spindle. "Everyone needs a soul, and where do they come from if they're not made?"

Alex puzzled over her question for a bit. They talked about souls a lot in Sunday school, but not about where they came from. God, he guessed, but he never thought about where God got them. Or how He might make them, either. It suddenly seemed important to know. "God makes them?" he suggested, which really wasn't an answer. He hoped Nora would tell him more.

"Perhaps," Nora said. "Soulstuff is complicated indeed." Her clever, swift fingers kept twisting the spindle, twisting the gray fibers. The fluff in her hand drew down, quickly converted into soft usable yarn. Alex watched, fascinated, while the odd, all-colors thread built up in neat coils on the spindle. At last satisfied with the amount, she wound off the end. She bent down and retrieved a pair of sticks from her bag. They were shiny and smooth, a pale color not quite white.

"Are those chopsticks?" Alex asked. They looked almost like the chopsticks from the nearby Chinese restaurant. Alex liked their food.

"Knitting needles," Nora said. She slipped the skein off the spindle, formed a loose knot in the end of the yarn, then slipped one of the needles through and pulled the knot tight.

"Are they bamboo, like chopsticks?" Alex asked.

Nora smiled and tapped the side of her nose. "I can't say. Trade secret, you know."

He leaned in closer, marveling at the fine lines almost invisible on one of the needles' smooth surface. "Can I touch one?" he asked. His hand was already reaching toward the needle.

"You might fall asleep," Nora said. Alex yanked his hand back and Nora laughed, a fresh sound like a waterfall. "Like in Sleeping Beauty? I was making fun that time, Alex. You can touch them."

Alex's eager fingers reached out again. The needle was warm, not cool like he expected. Warm and smooth but with a little drag when he ran his fingers the wrong way. No splinters. He imagined he almost felt a heartbeat, a kind of pitpattery flutter in them. It might have been scary except for Nora's gentle smile. "So you're going to make a soul now?"

"Mmm-hmm," Nora agreed with a nod. She threw a loop over the needle and began knitting, the loops quickly building up on the shaft.

"Who's it for?" Alex asked.

"This one?" Nora asked.

"Yes," Alex said.

"For your sister," Nora said.

"Sister?" Alex asked.

"She's coming soon, isn't she?" Nora asked. Her quick fingers started another row and the piece traveled down the other needle.

"Well, yeah …" Alex admitted. Mom was a lot more excited about the baby than he was. He kind of liked the idea of being big brother, though.

"So she needs a soul, doesn't she?" Nora asked.

Alex pondered for a moment. "I guess," he answered.

Nora laughed again. "I guess!" she said. Her fingers never paused. "I guess. Spoken like a true child." She giggled. "I guess. She does need a soul. So this one is hers."

"Oh." Alex smiled despite himself. "How will she get it?" he asked, watching the loops build up on Nora's needles.

"I'll make sure she gets it, don't worry," Nora said. "That's part of making a soul."

"Did you make my soul?" he asked.

"Of course," Nora replied.

He peered at the emerging gray swatch, "Did it look like this one?"

"Not quite," Nora said, still working. "Every soul is different. They may have the same stitches, but the pattern is never the same."

"How do you know what to make?"

"I just do," she said. For the first time since she began knitting, she stopped. She set the piece down in her lap, her age-spotted fingers frozen before completing the next stitch. "I never really thought about it before, Alex. I always let my fingers decide. My fingers and the yarn and the needles."

"It isn't very even," Alex said, peering at the mass of gray in her lap. If Nora's spinning made perfect yarn, her knitting was terrible. It had long loops and short ones and tight spots and loose spots. He had a knitted hat and it was the same all over. "Is it supposed to be like that?"

Nora resumed her lightning-fast knitting. "A soul isn't like a hat or a sweater or socks," Nora said, as though she'd read Alex's mind. "It has to fit a person on the inside. And it has to have room to grow and stretch."

She stopped again. The soul was already the size of the littlest clothes Mom took out of storage and put in the baby's closet. Nora pulled at the gray-not-gray swatch and it stretched, first one way and then the other. Alex watched the complicated yarn loops tighten or slide past each other. Holes closed and new ones opened. Dropped stitches bound back up while other stitches fell. It was so much more than just fabric. "Wow," he whispered.

Nora smiled at him. "A soul has to grow and change with the person. With their choices and decisions, good and bad. Big ones and little ones. To follow rules or break them or make new ones. To live up to expectations or defy them. To be adventurous," and she winked at him, "or to stay with the little kids."

Alex grinned back, a gap-toothed smile. Nora was cool. He watched as the yarn unwound from the skein and she knitted it into fabric. Into a soul. The soft fluffiness beckoned.

"May I touch it?" he asked at last. He itched to feel it.

"Better yet," Nora said, "you can hold it." The last of the yarn worked its way into the soul, the tail end vanishing into the piece. She slipped it off the needle and into Alex's outstretched hands.

So soft! It felt like nothing, light as air. Springy and forgiving. Fine spun as cotton candy from the fair. Soft and gentle like his favorite blanket. He scrunched it in his fingers. Gave it a little tug and watched the threads move. Watched as the colors twinkled on the surface. He gave Nora a sideways glance to see if she disapproved, but she was smiling wide. Feeling a little guilty, he petted the soul until it flattened out and held it toward her. "Thank you," he said.

Nora closed his fingers back over it. "How about I let you give it to your sister?" she asked.

Alex's eyes went wide. "I can't do that. I'm just a kid."

"I trust you," Nora said.

He looked at the scrap of fabric in his hands. It felt warm. Magical. Special, like her knitting needles. "What if I forget?" he asked.

"You won't forget," she replied.

"But I'm just a kid," Alex said again, looking up and meeting Nora's eyes.

She pushed the soul back toward him. Firm, but not in a mean way. Like insisting he keep a gift. "I trust you," she repeated.

Alex felt her hands fall away. The soul was warm and soft. Alive. Alive and waiting for its body. Alex didn't know how he knew this, but he did.

"Isn't that your mother?" Nora asked.

Alex turned around. Waddling down the hall from the changing room was his mom, her wet hair bound up in a bright yellow towel like a turban. "Mom!" he called. He waved at her while she squinted in his direction. "Mom!" he repeated, and ran off to greet her.

"Hi there," she said.

Alex wrapped his arms around her waist, being careful not to squeeze too hard. "Hi, Mom," he said.

She hugged his shoulders. "Aren't you supposed to stay in the Fun Space until I come get you?" she asked, but she was more amused than angry.

"I got bored," Alex said. He stepped back, holding the gray scrap. "Look what I have!" he said.

Mom headed for the front counter. "That's quite the dust kitten. Where did you find it?" she asked.

"It's not a dust kitten. It's a soul." Alex looked at the soul. Now that Mom mentioned it, it did look a lot like a dust kitten.

"Uh-huh," Mom said. "Whose?"

"My sister's," Alex answered.

Mom laughed. "So it's a sister now? Yesterday you were sure it was a brother. Where did you get it?" she asked again.

Alex kept up with her. "From Nora. She makes them."

"She does? Well, I suppose someone has to," Mom replied. "Can I meet her?"

"Sure!" Alex said. "She's right over there." He pointed to the lounge area outside the pool. It was empty apart from the silent TV and the magazines.

Mom looked over. "Uh huh," she said, the way she did when she didn't really believe him. "Are you sure?"

Alex blinked. Where did she go? "She was right there!" he insisted. "She was in a purple tracksuit and had a bag the same color. All matching, like Gramma in our pictures."

"And she made you a soul," Mom prompted.

"She said I already had one and this one was for my sister," Alex said. He fingered the soul. It still felt magical, even if it looked like dryer lint.

"Uh huh," Mom repeated, still not believing him. "You have a great imagination. I'll ask at the desk, okay?"

"She was there," Alex insisted.

Mom tousled his dark hair. "I'll ask at the desk. Come on, we'll be late for my appointment. Oooh, kick. Really jumping today," she said, putting a hand on her stomach. She grinned at Alex. "Want to feel?"

Wide-eyed, Alex nodded yes. Mom took his hand and guided it to a spot at the top of the extra-round part of her stomach. In a moment he felt a push against his hand. It retreated, then two more in quick succession. In his other hand, the soul felt warm and soft and light as air. "Wow," he whispered. "It really doesn't hurt?

"It does feel a little funny," Mom admitted, "but it doesn't hurt." She enclosed his hand in hers. "Come on. We'll be late for my appointment."

"Okay," Alex beamed. As he approached the lobby desk with Mom he glanced over toward the waiting area. The magazines were still there. The silent TV, too, showing the endless tennis match. He didn't see Nora.

* * *

Nora smiled. With his mother, Alex was back in the adult world. No longer between. He had chosen a side and could no longer see her. She turned her head as an elderly man came in from outdoors. His back was bent, his face lined from the sun. A stained, wide-brimmed hat crowned his head and a pair of heavy hedge trimmers hung from his belt.

"I'm glad you're late," she said.

The old man shrugged.

Nora patted the seat beside her. "I had a visitor."

The old man raised one white eyebrow. He lowered himself onto the chair's pilled upholstery and slipped a coarse canvas sack from his shoulder.

"Children pierce the veil more easily than adults. You know that," she said. "Besides, he's related. Alex, up there with this mother." She pointed at the front desk.

The man's gaze followed her finger. Up at the lobby check-in Alex risked another glance in their direction. His mother, one arm wrapped around the boy's shoulders, gestured at the furniture outside the pool room. The attendant glanced at the empty sofas and the unwatched TV before returning her attention to the pair. Her lips formed the word "No" accompanied by shake of her head in the negative. She frowned and began going over the names on her sign-in sheet. Alex looked again at the soul in his hand, gray like rainbows in fog.

The old man turned his attention back to Nora. He tipped his head a fraction of a degree, the wide-brimmed hat exaggerating his movement.

"He'll remember. He's a perceptive child," Nora answered.

The old man raised an eyebrow. The hat's angle became steeper as the tip became a decided tilt.

"Yes he will," she countered. "Did I not knit his soul? Can I not see the patterns in its weave?"

He frowned, his white wiry eyebrows merging together.

"Pshaw, rules. Rules can be broken when required. You don't always keep your rules, either. Why were you late, anyway?" Nora accused.

A sheepish grin replaced his scowl and his bent shoulders rolled in a shrug. He refused to meet her shining eyes with his own coal-dark ones.

"Mmm hmm," Nora muttered. "We'll see. What do you have for me?"

The old man reached one gnarled hand into the sack and produced a scrap of multicolored knitted fabric. One single strand of yarn trailed from a corner, its end neatly clipped. He handed it to Nora and waited for her reaction.

She ran her fingertips over the fabric, lingering on the tight knots of sunny yellow. "Oh, look what she made. All this happiness. Even with dark times she found happiness." Nora traced the complex patterns and varied colors. "So resilient. Here at the end, too," she said, twisting the final, unraveled strand, gold and emerald together. "So short, their lives. To grant a little more, just a little, for a final goodbye. I see why you were late."

The old man shook his head no. He took a deep breath and reached into the sack again, this time withdrawing a large lump of fur, all shades of brown and black. It buried its head into the old man's elbow and clung to his arm, striped tail curled protectively around its body.

Nora blinked twice. "That's not a soul, dear."

The old man shook his head no. He ran his fingers down the animal's bony spine.

"We're not responsible for animals, love," Nora said.

The old man stroked the animal's back again. Its tail switched.

"Cat, then," Nora acquiesced. "It's still an animal. How did you get it?"

The old man bent his head and concentrated on the creature in his arms. He scratched at the gaunt neck with his rough fingers.

It was Nora's turn to frown. "Her. Get her. You're avoiding the question, dear."

The cat finally withdrew her head from the old man's elbow and huddled against him. She opened eyes as orange as an autumn moon and yawned wide. She looked around, stretched stiffly and rose on arthritic legs. She spotted Nora's tantalizing bag lying open on the floor and jumped down. A few shaky steps and she was inside. Only her tiger-striped tail remained visible. The old man tipped his head the other way and he gave a slight shrug.

Nora sighed and watched the cat's tail disappear slowly into the opening. "I'm sorry she was suffering. But even if she did see you, we can't keep everything that wanders between worlds. You know she has to go back."

The old man ran a finger over the edge of his shears.

"Well, yes, die," Nora said. "All things in their time. As Alex will die in his and his sister in hers. People understand what your arrival means. Animals don't. They can't." She took the old man's hand from his shears and squeezed it tightly. "I'm sorry, love, but you know it's true."

The cat emerged from the bag and shook herself. She cleaned a bit of wayward soulstuff from her whiskers and set about grooming. Her fur grew shinier and fuller and her body more sleek and well-muscled with every pass of the pink tongue. Finished, she dipped her forelegs in a deep stretch then reversed it. She bunted up against Nora's leg and sniffed the trailing end of the soul in her lap. The cat turned back to her benefactor and sprang to his knee, then his shoulder. She crept around the back of his neck and perched on the opposite side. The old man reached up with his free hand and scratched her chin. The cat rubbed against his grizzled cheek and settled down.

The old man raised his wiry eyebrows.

Nora sighed again in mock irritation. "Just because she remembered her younger self doesn't make her special." She reached over to scratch behind the cat's ear and the animal began purring. Her claws dug into the rough cloth of his shirt then relaxed, alternating paws. Her pumpkin-colored eyes narrowed in pleasure. Nora withdrew her hand but the cat continued purring. "I suppose if it's just the one," Nora said.

The old man smiled and squeezed her hand back.

"Ravens or owls are more traditional, you know," she giggled.

The old man's only answer was to tap the cat's salmon-colored nose and then Nora's.

"Well, rules can be broken when required," Nora said with a smile. "Best get to work." She took one of her needles and slipped it through the final knot in the soul she held. It loosened and she pulled the yarn free. In short order she reduced the piece to a tangle of multicolored yarn in her lap. Starting at the end, she untwisted it. Yarn became fiber, lost its distinct colors and became shimmering gray fluff. She added more from the bag. Carefully selecting her fiber, she teased off a lump of unformed soulstuff and replaced the remainder. Clever fingers twisted and pulled a thread from the bundle. She wound the end around the spindle and sent it spinning. The cat watched the process with interest.

"One life ends and another begins," Nora said. She looked up from her spinning with a smile. "Changes are good. Even for us." She scratched the cat's chin in between keeping the spindle turning. "Even for us.

DEATH AND MRS. MORRISON
Andrea Mullen

The chainsaw was still running, but there was no way to turn it off now. Blood spattered the grass and brush she had been trying to clear as Mrs. Morrison held her jacket over her wounded left hand. She hadn't seen much before she'd had the presence of mind to try to close the wound, but she was sure that she'd caught a flash of bone. This ridiculous little thicket shouldn't have been this much of a problem, wouldn't have been if she had dealt with the overgrowth on this side of the farm last year like she should have. But she got to meet her first great-grandchild last year, which took time, as did the weddings and graduations she was obligated to attend. Funerals too, which there were more of every year. Perhaps she should have taken her daughter's suggestion and hired help, or been a little more proactive in culling the herd. She was eighty five years old, after all. That was old enough to scowl rather than panic when the figure appeared in front of her. "You, again?"

The first time Mrs. Morrison had seen Death, she was not yet Mrs. Morrison. She was ten year old Mary Jane Dalton, lying in a breathless heap on the dirt floor after a startled milk cow had kicked her squarely in the chest. He had looked exactly like he did in the Halloween decorations and scary stories her brother read, with a black robe and a skeletal face, and a bony hand resting on his scythe. She was frightened and could feel her heart skipping in her chest, but knew she couldn't leave her family to do all of her chores by themselves. He had followed her around while she carried the pails to the cistern, dumped them in, and returned to the cows, concentrating hard on breathing regularly while she continued with the task at hand. As the fluttering in her chest had faded, so did the apparition.

* * *

Death visited her again and again throughout the years, but the incident with the milk cow had taught her that she could fight back, and win. He'd come to collect her during her bout with a particularly bad strain of influenza that claimed several of her classmates. She was pale and shaking with fever, but she waved him off in favor of her mathematics homework. He'd come again when the car accident had happened, and shook an hourglass that was nearly out of sand at her as she fought through the dizzy nausea from her head injury to pull her best friend out of the mangled vehicle. She'd seen him when her blood pressure dropped precipitously during labor with her daughter, and refused to make her an orphan. Ten years ago, when the heart attack gripped her chest in the middle of church, she learned that he could be frightened off. The memory of how quickly he had backed off when she'd shouted about how death had no place in the Kingdom of God kept her warm during cold nights for years.

The last time she saw him was in the hospital with her darling husband Felix. She held his hand while his lungs filled with fluid, singing him his favorite songs just a little out of key. She had no idea how long Death had been in the shadows in the corner—maybe it was from the very beginning, before she'd even heard the word "ventilator"—but he was impossible to ignore as the numbers on the glowing monitor got smaller and smaller, and Felix's breathing became shakier. The doctors evicted her from the room when the alarms sounded. "Take me!" she demanded of Death as they were ushering her out. "Take me instead! Or take me, too!" He did not extend his hand to her then, and did not follow, even after the somber doctor walked out shaking his head to offer his condolences. She left that hospital with her children at her side, but more alone and adrift in the world than she had ever been.

* * *

Mrs. Morrison glared through cataract-glazed eyes. "You always look the same. Seventy five years, and you haven't changed at all. Why is that?" Death said nothing, as usual, but extended his hand. Mrs. Morrison shook her head. "You had your chance at that," she snapped. "Five years ago, or is your memory worse than mine? You should have done it then. I have too much to do right now, and both you and this—" she nodded to the idling chainsaw resting on the grass amid the out-of-control multiflora rosebushes and black locust trees "—are going to have to wait!" She set her jaw and turned towards her tractor, parked on a flat spot a short distance up the hill. Somehow, Death was in front of her again, waiting for her to reach out and accept his hand. It would have been so easy to accept it.

But Mrs. Morrison did not forget easily, and did not forget a perceived slight at all. She stepped around him and hoisted herself into the seat of the tractor. The venerable Farmall had seen better days but still ran well with a little lubrication and proper rest, much like its owner. Mrs. Morrison stuck her tongue out in concentration as she worked out how to steer and shift at the same time with one hand. She'd keep the injured hand elevated and wrapped of course, and it would take time, but if she kept it in first gear all the way up the hill, she would never have to take her hand off the steering wheel.

She heard a tiny rattle of brass and couldn't stop herself from looking. The hourglass Death was shaking at her was down to a thin film of sand in the upper bulb. She glared at him as the Farmall's engine sputtered then roared and shouted, "Well good—I still have time to put the tractor away." Death's skeletal face could hardly be considered expressive, but Mrs. Morrison had seen him enough times to catch a hint of exasperation in the clench of the bony jaw. The tractor lurched as the transmission caught first gear, and she was off.

The terrain felt rougher than normal, but the Farmall made it to the open barn door. Mrs. Morrison drove it inside and killed the engine before she noticed her visitor. He stood by the sliding door, shaking the hourglass at her so hard that it clanked. There was less sand in the top than ever before. She sidestepped him again and began pulling at the sliding barn door with her good hand. "Shouldn't leave the door open. Kids will get in. You know as well as I do that won't end well." The barn door shut with a thud, and Mrs. Morrison turned to see Death just behind her, again extending a hand. She simply scoffed at this and marched off toward the fences.

She had a brief dizzy spell as she reached the gate. Perhaps she was losing a bit more blood than was healthy. She leaned on the fence for support until the spots cleared from her eyes and gave the gate a solid push. Death was again in front of her, apparently puzzled. "Well, this *is* a working farm!" she said, gesturing at the fenced-off pasture with her good hand. "I can't just let the herd go anywhere, can I?" Mrs. Morrison was gratified to learn that empty eye sockets can indeed roll.

Another dizzy spell struck her as she reached the door to her house. She forced the spots from her eyes and pressed on through the kitchen door. She reached for the cordless phone that hung on the wall, one of those large-button models that her son had given her when her cataracts began to cloud her vision, and hit the first button on speed dial. Death looked on as Mrs. Morrison listened to the phone ringing on the other end.

"Hello, Susan? Yes, dear! I'm well, but I've had a little bit of an accident. Do you think you could come over and—it was the chainsaw. I hurt my hand. Well, I might need stitches, but you—all right, if you insist. I really think you could put them in, though, I won't need that many. All right, dear. I'll see you soon. Love you, too."

Mrs. Morrison hung up the phone and muttered through gritted teeth. "She said she was calling an ambulance. I really don't understand why she can't just do it herself on the table here—she is a nurse, after all." Death gestured insistently with the hourglass. Only a few grains of sand remained. Her eyes stubbornly shot away from it, and widened when she saw the awful mess that she'd tracked right into her kitchen. The blood had finally soaked through the thick canvas jacket, and was dripping on the floor, and here and there on the walls were smears from where she'd leaned to keep her balance.

"Oh dear, this won't do," she said, shaking her head. "This won't do at all!"

Mrs. Morrison took a clean dishtowel from the drawer and packed it onto the jacket. She covered it with a plastic grocery bag to keep it from dripping more, and reached for the roll of paper towels stowed neatly above the sink. "My mother would have a fit if she saw this on her spotless kitchen floor. You know her, don't you? I assume you were there when the stroke happened." Mrs. Morrison stopped scrubbing. "She didn't suffer, did she? I mean, I never asked...I always assumed that it was too quick for her to even realize what was happening, but no one was there to know. So. I'm asking now." Mrs. Morrison looked up at the apparition. "Did she suffer?"

Death stood silent for a moment, cocking his head to one side, and regarded Mrs. Morrison. Then the skeletal head moved—left, right, left, right.

Mrs. Morrison closed her eyes and exhaled. "Good. Thank you." Death reached out to her again, but she waved him off and returned to her work on the floor. "No. Not now. I've done it for five years on my own, so you can wait until I'm ready." She got to one knee to wipe a spot where her jacket must have grazed the wall, bracing herself with her left shoulder to ward off the dizzy spell. "I've left such a mess here, and with company on the way!"

The last few grains of sand bounced into the neck of the hourglass as the knock came at the door. "Mrs. Morrison?" a man's voice rang through the open window. "Are you in there?"

"Come in!" she shouted, rising to her feet again. "The kitchen door's open!" A matter of seconds later, two paramedics opened the appointed door. She recognized one as a former classmate of her son's but couldn't place a name to the face—John Something? Maybe James? "So I suppose my daughter called you," she said as she lifted her arm up to show them. "I apologize for the mess, I tried to clean." Her son's classmate rushed to her side as his eyes went wide, and the other paramedic immediately moved to get a chair for her.

Mrs. Morrison smiled—she'd finally remembered. "Jeremy, is it? You were in my son's graduating class." The man nodded as he unwrapped her makeshift bandages. "So, I think I just need a few stitches. Can you do it here?" she asked. Jeremy shot a meaningful glance to the other paramedic.

Mrs. Morrison looked away from the two men for a moment as she sunk down into the kitchen chair that the paramedic had offered her. Death was still in the room, but was getting harder for her to see. The impulse to offer her own hand was strong. Her mother, the rest of her family, and her dear Felix were all there in that place of rest and refreshment she was promised, and she had the chance to join them. But here, there were grandchildren and great-grandchildren to spoil on their birthdays, and graduations and weddings to attend. There were cattle to sell and calves to raise, and no one else would clear those awful multiflora rosebushes in the western pasture. All that aside, Jeremy was trying to tell her something important, and it seemed rude to leave as he was talking to her. She pressed her lips together in a smile and slowly shook her head in the direction of the skeletal figure in the corner.

The skeletal hand now held an hourglass in which the sand was flowing upwards. Death stowed it in his voluminous black robe, and with a heavy soundless sigh, faded away.

DEATH AND THE FASHIONISTA

Faith Hunt₣r

The sun was setting when I slipped out of the house and over to the pile of boulders jutting on the crest of the hill. Sitting on the boulders gave me a clear view of the skyline in every direction, of the mountains that arched high and the valley that fell low, bright with the lights of Asheville. Of the sickle moon rising and the few early stars glittering, of the last of the sunset in the west, a scarlet reminder of the day.

If I turned my head, I could see inside my home, the lights glimmering through the windows, my children at the table with their father. The TV's muted laugh track sounded, stagnant and repetitive.

I ran my hands through the herbs planted around the boulders in the rock garden, releasing the scent of rosemary, basil, thyme, and chives, and pulled my ratty house sweater close against the autumn chill. Night birds called. Something crashed in the underbrush. But I was paying attention to one thing only—the forest I had killed.

I stared at the bare trees, bark sloughing off, revealing the pale wood beneath, limbs broken and pointing at the sky. Pointing at me as if in judgment. The accusation of death. Everything alive there had given itself to the pull of my new and unwanted death magics; the cursed gift had destroyed every blade of grass, every tree, vine, bird, lizard, snake, deer, squirrel. *Everything.*

With my native earth magics I had blessed and nursed that woods for years, bringing the trees from saplings to full grown and healthy, and then I had killed it all in a slow attrition of leaking Death. Since that time I had managed to encourage a honeysuckle vine to grow there. One vine. A few blades of scrub grass. Nothing else.

I came out here often to remind myself of the dangers of my cursed magics. To remember that if I didn't tamp down my curse-gift, strangle it, I might kill something more precious than the woods. If I let go, I might kill my husband. *My children.*

The power was seductive, forbidden. With it I would curse and kill, withering the land and bringing death to the ones I loved.

I massaged my belly and the baby who resided there, a magic user of undisputed power but unidentified future abilities, and I shivered. Night in the heights of the Appalachian Mountains was cold. Or maybe fear made me tremble. That was always possible. Death and fear rode the same horse and, for witches, pregnancy came with the likelihood of peril and sorrow.

As if in answer to my thoughts, the baby kicked. At the same instant, I heard the clop of hooves, two horses, iron shoes on the asphalt road. I pulled on a *seeing working.* The outer ward was still active, still in place, a pale reddish ring of protection around the house and grounds. A stronger one surrounded just the house. Double wards were difficult to maintain, but with Big Evan's and my magic combined, not impossible.

The back door opened and Angie poked out her head. "Mama!" she whispered, the word magically amplified by her will and desire. "Company's coming."

At her side, EJ, her little brother, stuck out his head. "Com'pee com'n."

They couldn't have heard the horses' hooves, not with the TV on, but Angie was a dangerously strong witch. The clopping grew louder. Closer. I climbed to the ground. "Who?"

"Don't know *his* name," Angie said. "But the lady is Sally."

"Sauwee," EJ repeated.

"My angel says she's a 'piece a work.' What's a piece a work? And he says, 'Death is the Truth and the Lie. And Death can be cheated.' My angel's confusing, mama."

Confusing. Yeah. And the warning made about as much sense as anything else ever said to me by a supposedly celestial being—which was no sense at all. I clenched my sweater tighter across my chest and rounded belly. "That's it?"

Angie tilted her head. "Yep. Cheating's wrong, right mama?"

"Right. Take EJ back inside. Tell Daddy what you told me." Angie took her brother's hand and closed the door. I walked around the house to the front, to the darkness at the edge of the driveway, and the sound of horse hooves, getting closer. Cue scary music, I thought.

The outer ward dinged smartly and juddered as horses turned into the drive and stopped.

The security lights came on, illuminating a man on a...a yellow horse. A heavy warhorse in daffodil yellow, its coat gleaming, its feathers, mane, and tail a brilliant white. The man atop the gelding wore black: a leather jacket and pants, Western boots, black saddle, while his flowing hair matched the horse's white mane. The man was gorgeous and color coordinated, like something out of an airbrushed Ralph Lauren ad.

Beside the yellow horse was a blood bay mare, a woman on the mare's back, her clothing matching the red horse: scarlet moto jacket, leather pants, boots that came to mid-thigh, matching riding gloves, and lipstick. Her scarlet hair was piled high in an eighties style. She carried a red leather handbag slung over the Western saddle horn, the kind of pricey handbag my sisters loved. Sally and the man were improbable, ill matched, and doing a poor job of aping human. When paranormals came calling, it meant trouble.

Something gleamed on the sole of the man's boot, darkly glowing, reflecting the silver moon. A taint of hellfire and brimstone. The man had been walking where he shouldn't. These two were far more dangerous than they looked.

When she saw me, the woman on the blood bay mare laughed. It was the sound of bones dancing, of dead bodies floating on still water, of ravens on a battlefield, laughter that ruined her harmless eighties style statement. Terror skittered up and down my spine at the sound and the thoughts stimulated by her laughter. I dropped my arms and put back my shoulders. Holding my comfy, shabby sweater closed was not saying good things about my self confidence.

The woman in red looked me over and lifted her eyebrows, mocking. "You're not what I expected, Molly Megan Everhart-Trueblood." She had a caustic high-class Southern accent, maybe Georgia. Rich, old-money-Atlanta. Servants, cotillions, and finishing school money. "Such a tacky cardigan."

"What's it to you, *Sally*?" I said.

The woman's gaze razored in on me, and when she spoke, the words went rough and sharp, like broken glass, her silly eighties façade cracking. "How do you know my name?"

I didn't answer. "What do you want, Sally? And who's your pal?" I glanced at the man. His face was pale, his eyes the bright white of the moon.

I heard the front door open, and Big Evan's air sorcery lifted my hair. We had created the wards to allow him access to air currents and weather outside the magical protections. He whistled a long note and the security lights brightened about a hundred percent. The two uninvited visitors turned aside, blinking. "I asked you a question," I said to the woman.

"Two," the man said. "You asked her two questions. Specificity is vital to such as we."

I tilted my head slightly. "Fine. I asked two questions. I still haven't received replies."

Behind me, Big Evan's whistling trilled. A harsh wind sprang up and blew back Sally's scarlet locks, whirling, playing havoc with the mounts' manes and tails, wrapping the man's hair around his face. The chilled breeze fluffed my own red curls. The heavy animals danced from hoof-to-hoof.

The woman sniffed, scenting the magic, and focused on my hubby standing on the porch. "You know *my* name," Sally said, sitting forward in the saddle and gathering her reins into one hand, "but you don't know his?" She flicked a thumb at the man.

Her question and change in posture sent more fear skittering across me, and I had no idea why. She swirled the fingers of her free hand, amassing power, curling it into her palm. In response, Evan started to hum. The ward began to glow a pale red at the corner of my witchy-eyed vision. My eardrums fluttered as if the barometric pressure had changed with a fast-moving weather front. Sally's magic spread around her in a slow spiral. I had no idea what she was, or what her gift was, but she was powerful. Fear skittered up my spine like baby spiders hunting.

I wanted to gather my own power, my earth magics, which were still available to me, but Death magics taunted, whispering of the brimstone on the man's boot. So easy to blast these unwelcome visitors and be done. *So easy,* it whispered. *Just reach and out crush the threat.*

But death magic was powerful, a nuclear arsenal compared to the slow, life-giving energies of my earth magics. I might use it—but at the risk of destroying everything. My earth magics were weaker, but came with a much lower price.

I shoved down the desire to rip the visitors apart and said, "All I know about you two is that Death is the Truth and the Lie. And you are a piece of work, Sally."

The magic in Sally's hand tangled, fell to the ground, a reaction I felt as much as saw. Eyeing me the way a cat eyed a goldfish in its bowl, Sally said, "No one insults a Death."

"It isn't an insult if it's the truth." I pressed my small advantage, repeating, very carefully, as if in some mild warning or threat, "What. Do you want. Sally. And who is your pal?"

The pretty man smiled. "I am Death come riding, one of Seven am I. Not youngest nor eldest, Death of Magic, I cry. Untested, unconquered, waiting beyond the veil. Till a ruby haired lass calls, 'Death Magic, Avail!'"

Riddles. I hated riddles.

Sally said, "You know what your sister thinks about prophecies."

"Death of War is tired," the man said, his eyes on me. "What she wants will soon be unimportant. It's my time to rule."

I narrowed my eyes at the two, absorbing and dissecting the riddle and the banter. I had red hair; so did my child. There was no way I'd *avail* myself of death magics. "Death of Magic. Death of War. Titles, not a names." It wasn't sneering, it was stalling so Evan could finish whistling up his *working.* I added, poking the bear only a little, "Death of Magic sounds like a Marvel comic character." Evan chortled on a breath and went back to whistling softly. In the sky clouds started to build. "Do you kill all magic or everyone who has magic? Either way, you die, too, and no one left alive likes you much."

Sally said, "Death of Magic has come to offer you a bargain and assistance."

I said, "Not interested. Not now, not ever." A cat interrogative sounded. KitKit mewled, winding around my ankles, her tail looping, a steady caress.

"A pet," Sally sneered. "I expected more of you."

KitKit leaped at the ward, claws spread, ears back, fangs showing. She hit and screamed a challenge, sticking to the magics for just a moment. The blood bay bolted. The yellow gelding sat back on his haunches, nearly unseating the man. Sally used her entire body to regain control of her mount and Death lunged forward, his arms around his horse's neck. KitKit slid and dropped to the ground. I laughed as my non-familiar cat sat, lifting her back leg to clean her nether regions, bored. "Name," I said, taking my cue from the cat and sounding jaded. When neither answered, I said, "Come," to the cat and turned my back on the uninvited visitors. The man growled at my pointed insult. I kept walking, KitKit loping in front of me. Big Evan's eyes were on me, my husband not questioning my decision to toy with predators, but offering support and protection. In the distance, I heard the howl of wind. KitKit raced inside.

I climbed the steps and stood beside Big Evan, his bulk and height dwarfing me. I took his hand, his magic surrounding me, surrounding us. Rising, humming with power. My earth magics responded and the ward, the upgraded *hedge of thorns 2.0*, was glowing so brightly red now that any witch could have seen it even without a *seeing working*. Even a human could have seen it.

"Tell me," Big Evan said.

"Brimstone on his boot."

My husband muttered an imprecation. The two looked a bit silly. They weren't. Outside, the wind grew stronger.

The man had dismounted and was standing before the ward, hair and clothing blowing in Evan's wind, his arm up, his palm open, flat. He placed it on the ward. A single loud dong rang, the warning of protection. He pressed, his power creating a prism of hues, iridescent blacks, like oil on ink. The ward gonged again, deeper, heavier. The wind whipped. The black iridescence of his attack spread, the shape of the hand growing, as if he claimed the ward.

Behind him, the horses moved restively, hooves dancing in distress. The wind blasted across them. Sally fought to keep control and slid to the ground, to hold the reins close to their heads.

I watched as *hedge of thorns'* energies coalesced at the bottom boundary, where they entered the ground. The red haze of the ward grew thick and bisected the black energies with a sizzle of power, like scarlet lightning. Death's attack fractured across the dome of energies and fell apart.

Death jumped back, eyes wide. The wind fell, leaving the world silent and still. Death studied the *working*. I turned my back on him again and slipped past Big Evan, almost into the house.

Death of Magics shouted, "Sam! My name is Sam! And your children are in danger!"

My belly twisted and the baby kicked. Right on my spine. I nearly fell to my knees, but there was no way I was going to appear weak in front of an enemy. I caught myself on the jamb and turned around slowly. "What *threatens* my family?" I growled—the tone of a mother when her child is endangered.

Death said, "A demon newly freed from the inner circle of Hell has scented you and your bloodline. Your children have gifts too strong to be contained in mere mortal bodies. They will die at the hands of the demon and it will eat the children's souls. I know this. I am Death of Magic. But I can save them from the demon's attack. For a price. A *small* price."

Death of Magic was either a very bad negotiator or he wasn't the brightest bulb in the chandelier. Or both. But stupid people could be dangerous. Deadly even.

"Save us for a price? Did you think an earth witch might miss the brimstone on your boots? You set this deception in play to barter for your own needs." He had said it was his time to rule. He wanted power. I stepped back to the lawn and began to pull the energies of the earth up through the ground. Taking just a fraction-of-a-fraction of life force from every living thing for a hundred miles.

"Oh shit," Sally said. "I told you this wasn't going to work."

"Molly," Evan said, a gentle warning in his tone. "Be careful. His name is Death. What if this is what he wants?" Meaning, what if they wanted me to get mad, lose my temper, and pull on death magics. Right.

"I've got this," I whispered, thinking, *all life. Only life*. But I broke out in a sweat, hot and stinking in the night air, straining to hold onto my earth magics and keep the death magics at bay. But … death magics would destroy this threat *so easily*.

Sam vaulted into the saddle, watching me across the intervening space.

"Sam?" Sally warned.

"Molly?" Evan asked, in nearly the same tone.

"They need to know we're not without claws." I shaped the magic of life into a spear point, a knapped and wicked-sharp weapon. I pulled Evan's magic behind it, like a shaft, to give it distance and force. And I focused on the being that threatened my children. "Now," I whispered.

Big Evan dropped the outer ward. In the same instant I threw the gift of life. It shot through the air. Toward Death. The point pierced Death's chest.

Sam fell off his horse.

Through the hole in the ward, something entered. Something dark and cold and seeking destruction. It saw me. It saw my death magics. It saw my blood. The blood demon spread its claws, a cobra hood expanding around its blacklight face. It snapped the hood closed, opened its mouth, rocketed at me. Aiming for my belly and the child within.

"Sam!" Sally shouted. "Don't!"

"Stop," Sam said from the ground, a hand out.

The demon stopped, hanging in midair, a foot from me. I backed slowly up the stairs, and through the inner ward on the house itself. The magics composed of the life force of Evan and me, woven together, slid around me and snapped into place.

Evan followed. The magics sealed behind him, too, leaving the demon just beyond our door. Evan turned out the inside lights and we fell together, holding each other. I was shaking, sweating a greasy film of fear, sick to my stomach, pressing gently on the baby with both hands. We stood in the dark, Evan's arms around me, and watched through the windows. I lay my head against my husband. "I messed up," I whispered, my voice barely a breath of fear. "I just wanted to make him go away. Mess with his pride a little."

"I agreed with showing a little power. Get him to back off," he said. "I didn't sense the blood demon either."

"Sam?" Sally asked, leaning around the yellow horse. "You okay, Sammy Boy?"

"I'm hurt."

"What kind of hurt?" Sally asked.

"I'm green."

"Gre—" Sally interrupted herself as Sam walked around his mount and up to the *hedge of thorns*. "Shit, Sam." She pulled a cell phone from her big purse, aimed it, and took a couple of shots of her partner.

"Stop that!" he yelled at her, just as a toddler might to his nanny. To the house, he shouted, "What have you done to me, witch?" He was still pretty, but now he had green scales, like a snake, and brown hair like dried vines. There were leaves unfurling from his hairline, darker than his scales, and daffodils bloomed from one arm and the right side of his head. Earth magics at work, though the working wasn't designed to last long. "Make it stop!" he shouted to me, panic in his voice. Yeah. A child. Death of Magic was a grown up child, pampered, spoiled, and not overly bright.

Sally put away her cell, giving me a glimpse of a silver zippered kit of some kind and what I could have sworn was a hair dryer in the red bag. "Sorry Sam. But it's part of my job. Your daddy will be pissed."

"You tell Death of Flood about this and I'll rip out your eyeballs."

"Yeah, yeah, yeah, whatever. We talked about the demon getting free but you said you could hold it. I told you this was a stupid plan to get close to the witch. Can you get the demon back?"

"No. My gift is…wrong, now."

"How wrong?" Her tone went jagged again.

"When I call the demon nothing happens."

"And if you just let it go?" she asked.

"It'll kill all the Everhart-Truebloods and steal their magic. And then it'll come after me."

My shaking worsened.

"Well shit. You *really* screwed up. Again."

Death of Magic stared at the snakelike blood demon hanging in the air. "I… I…"

Sally shook her head and to the house shouted, "Little problem out here."

Little problem. The idiot went to the circles of hell, let lose a blood demon, attacked my house, and set the blood demon on my family. If the demon got free, the result would be even worse than if I had used my death magics—everyone I loved would be dead, their souls sucked into the demon, giving him power. And I still didn't know what Death wanted. I'd have cried except that the demon whipped his head to me and writhed in the air. Sam, if he ever had control of the demon he had summoned, was about to lose it.

"Sam…" Sally warned.

"I—I—I—" He stopped, swallowed.

My Hubby whistled, the note low and vibrating, like air blowing over a jug. The demon's motion stuttered to a stop.

I risked a look around and spotted the children on the sofa, sound asleep. In a *seeing working*, I followed Evan's blue magics tying our babies into slumber with a rope of our own gifts. It was hasty but powerful work, their own bourgeoning magics reinforcing the working. Death wanted to use them for some purpose of his own, but if we died, our magics would augment the bindings and the tiny ward around them. The demon could get to them through their blood, but Death could never get to the children now. Half the threat beaten. "Good work. What should we do about flower boy, his nanny, and his demon?"

"Fear," Evan said, his lips scarcely moving, his long red beard shaking slightly. "That's Sally's job, Sally's title. For which info you may thank your sisters."

I spotted my cell phone in his shirt pocket. "Is it on speaker?"

Evan whistled a soft note. "Two way speaker now."

Cia said from Evan's pocket, "We're both here. And we're on the way, ETA seven minutes. Faster if Liz wasn't a wuss driver."

"Not a wuss. Just want to arrive in one piece on mountain roads," Liz said.

Boadicea and Elizabeth Everhart—Cia and Liz—were twins, and excellent researchers of witch oral tradition. The twins were the babies of the family, fearless, gorgeous, and always trying spells they shouldn't.

Cia was a moon witch, nearly powerless at the young sickle moon; Liz was a stone witch, weak from nearly dying, crushed beneath a boulder in a fight with a demon. "Okay. What can you tell us?" I asked.

"The Deaths are an obscure legend tied into oral witch history," Liz said, her voice tinny over the cell. "There was the first death, Death of Eden and his only son, the second Death—Death of Floods. The legends say Death of Floods has seven children: Death of Starvation, Death of Plague, Death of Childbirth, Death of Age, Death of Misfortune, Death of War, and Death of Magic, who hasn't used his power since the end of the Burning Times."

The Burning Times was also called the Roman Catholic Inquisition. So many witches had been killed that our race nearly died out. I stared into the dark and the two standing before the outer ward.

"The Deaths each rule over a form of human death," Cia said, "except the Death of Eden and the Death of Floods, both of whom retired after they harvested millions all at once. In Flood's case, according to oral tradition, only eight people escaped."

"Noah, his family, and his animals," Liz said.

"So what do we do?" I asked.

Outside, the demon quivered. What might have been a tail whipped hard, hitting the outer ward. The ward emitted a deep and panicked dong, before Death of Magic got the demon in hand again. At the moment we were fine. But if that thing got lose, this could go bad, fast.

"I think we have to invite Death of Magic inside the outer ward," Evan said, "and use his power to help bind the demon. Then we have to kick Death's ass."

I shook my head, not liking that idea at all. But not seeing any alternatives.

"Do we have time to draw up a contract?" Cia asked.

"Would a Death honor a contract?" Liz asked.

"Death can be cheated," I whispered. "That's what Angie said."

"If a witch cheats on a contract the three fold repercussions are bad. So instead of a contract, we plan on cheating Death and just fly it," Evan whispered back, miming throwing a paper airplane.

"Good by me," I muttered. Raising my voice, I called out, "Death of Magic, and Fear. If you come in peace, you are welcome inside the outer ward."

"We come in peace," Sally said. "Can I come in and use your powder room? That wind played havoc with my hairdo."

"Hairdo?" Cia said. "What century is she from?"

"The eighties, from the looks of her," Liz said. "Evan sent us pics."

"She has a Hermès bag," I said.

"Oh. My new best bud, then."

I called back to Fear. "Pee in the woods. We'll drop the outer ward and you'll walk in. Leave the horses on the other side. "

Fear blew out a breath and pulled hobbles from her bag. She strapped each of the horses' front legs together, leaving the mounts unable to travel far.

I contemplated the demon again. It had big teeth, gleaming talons, a long tail and scales, but without the dragon charm. And mad, mad eyes in a shade of burning purple tinged with emerald. There was no bargaining with demons. No negotiation. There was also no way to kill them. They were immortal. We'd bind it back to hell or die trying. Even a Death couldn't kill a demon.

Sally and daffodil-blooming-Death stood at the edge of the outer ward, Sam staring at the demon, his brow covered with sweat, his hands trembling. The demon shifted, and a stench of burning sulfur trailed into the air.

Evan said, "I'll handle the inner ward. Liz, Cia, when you get here, take over the temporary bindings on the demon. Molly, you figure out how to bind that thing."

I nodded, the gesture shaky. My sisters agreed. I heard the hum of a Subaru climbing the hill and caught a flash of car lights through the trees.

"Offer them tea. Put the kettle on," Evan said, giving me something to do to keep me from worrying as I tried to figure out how to save us. Busy hands and all that.

I went to the kitchen and started the electric kettle because it was faster than regular heat on the AGA stove. I heard them still talking as I worked, getting out a teapot filter and a good strong black tea. There would be no nodding off tonight.

"A tea party," Liz said, "with Death and Fear and a demon, oh my…"

"Alice in Wonderland meets the Wizard of Oz," Cia said.

Liz said, "Evan, your house wards are sparking."

"I see your car," Evan said.

As I put tea together, I also gathered necessities from my kitchen: the silver spoon *working* I kept in the kitchen for emergencies, quickly powering it with the rosemary plant I'd killed and then brought back to life. Long story. But the important thing was that now the plant seemed to be able to store a lot more earth power than it should. And … the solution came to me. I broke off one needle-shaped leaf and tucked it into a pocket. "Thank you," I murmured to the plant.

"Getting ready to drop the outer ward, ladies," Evan said. "You drive straight in. On three. One. Two. Three."

I felt the ward fall, the magics lashing back through the ground and through my bones. It stole my breath and froze my chest. The magics twisted and curled into the inner ward, reinforcing it. It was so heavy now, that air and weather wouldn't pass through. Once I got out of the house, there might be no getting back inside until Evan dropped the ward.

Putting a hand on my baby bump, I said a protective working over my unborn child. Though I didn't pray often, I added a prayer to seal the working and then whispered, "Hayyel, I could use some backup on this one." Angie's angel didn't respond. I heard the Subaru rolling into the drive, over the lawn, and up to the door. My sisters had gotten between the unwanted visitors and us. *Smart.* The car engine died and the doors opened. I forced myself to keep moving, keep thinking, and got out mugs.

Cia's voice called out, "I got it, *Lasso working* is in place on my end."

Liz said, "*Lasso* on my end. We need something stronger for its teeth and claws." Louder she added, "Hey, Death. Get off your ass and lend a hand here."

Cia shouted, "Fear, pull something out of that fancy bag and tie off its tail. It's getting free."

"I don't do magic," Sally said. "I do hair and fashion and terror. And Fear of Death."

"Well the fashion is seriously out of date," Cia said. "Big hair hasn't been around since the eighties and Peg Bundy. If you can't help, then get the hell out of my way."

"Witches. So snarky," Sally said. But her eyes hinted at her ire and fear. They coiled together on the night wind like asps, stinging. She was attacking us all. I fought the fear she caused and breathed my way through it.

"Liz, can you pull from the earth?" Cia asked.

"We can try. But it didn't work so well last time."

I poured water over tea leaves. The aroma of tea rose, soothing. I stirred the leaves with the silver spoon, the stored working moving from spoon to the tea. Softly, Evan said, "Mol? You need to see this."

I set the oversized teapot on the tray with mugs, linens, silver, sugar and cream, and carried it to the front. I felt better having done something, even something so simple as tea. I placed the tray on the table near the door and took Evan's hand. The ward on the house zinged through me, and I realized he had it looping through his own body. It was a dangerous tactic, but it also gave him total control over the energies and the maths of the ward, allowing me in and out more easily than I had feared. It wasn't something I could do while pregnant without harming my child. I squeezed his hand.

His voice rumbled in his barrel chest. "You know I'd never let you out of this house if I could do it myself," he said. "I'm good but I can't protect the kids, hold the wards, *and* dispose of a demon that wants your blood."

"I know. Of the two jobs, the one you left for me is safer for the kicker." I patted my belly. "And Cia and Liz and I can work a triangle inside the existing outer circle. What did you want me to see?"

"Their *lasso working*."

I did a small *seeing working* and focused on the magics they were using to bind the demon. "Ohhh," I breathed. "It's tinted with the same shade of energies as the stuff on Sam's boots."

"Yeah. They've been messing with something dark. Not enough to coat their souls or tint their auras, but enough to bring them more power than they ever had before. You be careful." He paused before adding, "I love you to the moon and back."

"I love you most of all," I said. It was a way of saying goodbye. I lay my head on his arm for a moment, took a deep breath, and stood away. Giving him a mug, I picked up the tray, took a steadying breath, and pushed though the ward. The magics coated my body and hair and pulled through me like electric taffy. The energies were attuned to me, and usually walking though wasn't a problem, but there was so much energy coiling through it now, far more than it was designed to hold. And it all looped through Big Evan, which was the only reason I could get through. Dangerous for my husband, but we'd deal with any repercussions later.

I opened the back hatch of the Subaru and set the tray down inside. Poured tea into mugs. Carried mugs to each of my sisters, then to Death of Magic, who looked like he needed the entire pot. Sam was shaking with exertion, and drained the mug in a single gulp. I studied the shape and form of his *snare working,* the incantation holding the demon. It was vastly different from a witch lasso working, but there were enough similarities for me to harness my workings to it. "Stabilize your working and then get out of the way," I said. "And I'll need your

Tony Lamas."

"I'm not giving you my boots."

"I'll buy you another pair, Sammy-pie," Sally said. She was standing at the back of the Subaru, drinking a cup of tea, one I hadn't offered her. I gave her a sunny smile, which seemed to startle her. "Just give the little witch what she wants. I have to be back across the veil by dawn. I'm doing one of the Waters' hair at ten, and I need at least *some* beauty sleep."

"Hope you don't give her broccoli hair like yours," Liz snarked.

Sally snarled and stared daggers at my sisters, but nothing happened. A look of surprise and then horror crossed Sally's face. My lips twitched as she looked down into the mug she had drained. Looked back at my sisters. She snapped her fingers. Neither witch sister showed the slightest bit of fear. I felt my own lingering terror lift too, and my smile took on a measure of satisfaction. The scarlet-haired sidekick's power had been neutered. Well, that's what you get when you take a mug that was never offered you. The quick little happiness working from the silver spoon had been for me, Evan, my sisters, and Death, to negate our fears. That same working had stopped it at the source. Sally wasn't used to being happy.

Fear-Fettered slammed her expensive bag on the back of the Subaru and pulled out a makeup kit, a brush, a mirror that was way too large to actually fit within the confines of the bag, and started to make herself presentable after all the wind. I got a good look inside and there were also three knives with crosshatched hilts and two semiautomatic handguns. The brush was spelled and the mirror was a scrying surface. Sally, the Fear of Death, was a fashionista killer. I hadn't forgotten they were here after my children. I gave Evan a significant look, mimed putting a purse over my shoulder and mouthed, "Her bag." He nodded.

"Boots," I said to Sam holding out a hand.

Death of Magic sat on the ground and pulled off his boots, the smell of the sweat of Death strong on the air. As he was yanking off the expensive footwear, I took over his working and wove the threads of my own earth magics into it. And into my sisters' *lasso working.* Death's magics felt warm, slippery, unstable in my hands. Foreign. The power in the magics skidded up my hands and wrists to my arms, enveloping my own cursed gift. It was a yearning, a wooing, a siren song of desire to join my gift with his magics. To...to become a Death myself.

Not Death of Magic. But Death of All. All humans. All plants. All animals. To do to the entire world what I had done to the hillside nearby. My mouth went dry with fear. If I lost control...if I let it ride me...I'd kill. I'd be a Death and my own fear would have won.

Sally looked at me and then at Death. "Oh, Sam. It wasn't the kids. It was her."

I understood. This was what Sam had wanted. Death magics. Not my children. They had thought the kids were the carriers. They had intended to trick us into helping them trap the demon, allowing them in close, so they could get at the death magics.

But my daughter's guardian angel had said I could trick Death. I shook my head, trying to force my earth magics to the forefront of my mind, to satisfy my magical needs. I accepted Death's boots, the brimstone and darkness on his sole shining bright. Brighter than the moon. The brimstone picked up my own curse. Pulled on my curse. The boots glowed.

"Mol?" Cia asked. "What's happening?"

"Nothing," I lied, jerking my attention away from the evidence of darkness. I had to end this quickly. "Binding?"

"*Blood of angels*," Liz said, naming the working. "Places, everyone." Holding the temporary bindings, I moved to the north. Cia walked to a position sixty degrees to my left, close beneath the sickle moon, now high in the sky. Liz took the place between us. We spread the energies we were working into the full one-hundred-eighty degrees of the equilateral triangle. Then we backed away, spinning the magics out until we touched the permanent circle of the outer trench, and sat—not so easy when a baby was in the way.

I pulled out the rosemary needle-leaf and placed it between my knees. Cia and Liz each placed their elemental focal between their knees. Cia invoked the circle, "*Dùin*." It was Scottish Gaelic. The circle rose around us, enclosing the half-bound demon, Death and Fear, and three Everhart sisters, but excluding my home, husband, children. Everything I held dear was safe. Except my sisters. I mouthed my thanks to them and got a wink from Cia and a nod from Liz.

"*Faoi dhraíocht*," Cia said. *Bound by a spell*. Her hands braided the energies, twisting, pulling, sliding them through her fingers.

"*Hhí ceangal na gcúig gcaol air*," Liz said. *He is bound hand and foot*. She plaited the energies she held with her twin's. They grew bright, a lovely blue and lavender tinted with paler pinks. The demon screamed, his howl full of anger and pathos and thwarted desire.

A cheangal, I thought, calling on my daughter's angel. I wove my death energies—*no*. I wove my *earth* energies and Death's own energies in with my sisters'. *You said I could cheat death*, I thought to Hayyel.

I gathered Death's magics, magic he had passed to me freely with his boots, into my own and tied them to the single rosemary leaf. I scraped the brimstone off Death's boot; at the same time I wiped sweat from the inside, onto my fingertips. I rubbed the darkness and the sweat together and took up the weaving, letting the magics pull through the mixture. I wove the dark energies and the sweat of Death's foot into the binding mix. Softly, I said the words, "*Mallachd dha! Mallachd dha! Mallachd dha!*" three times. *Curse him, to hell with him* in the language of my mother's, mother's people.

Death stood up fast. His eyes blazed with golden light. He glowed. Ravens began to call, the crowing of blackbirds out of place at this hour, screeching, screaming.

Fear reached into her Hermès bag and pulled two weapons, the slides *schnicking* into place as she chambered rounds. She aimed the weapons at me. Big Evan laughed, the sound all wrong, too deep, too heavy. The *hedge of thorns* on the house shivered and flashed a nearly black and sapphire blue. The weapons didn't fire.

Sam stretched out his hand to me. To the death magics he had come for. The death magics he wanted to steal to rule. I said a final time, "*Mallachd dha!*"

Death screamed, his cry like that of the ravens. Sally, Fear of Death, screamed with him. Their wails rose, a crescendo that cracked across the air and made the boulders out back shift and slide in a grinding tumble. Fear and Death both vanished.

The demon wailed and screeched, writhing against the bindings. It began to stretch and twist and pull, the power of brimstone dragging the demon after them in a long twirling trail of dark energies. With it went all the power in the equilateral triangle, then in the outer circle. Our own magics snapped back painfully. Liz and Cia swore at the sting.

There was only the final echo of the ravens. Silence settled upon the night.

I slid sideways and lay on the chilled ground.

Cia stood. So did Liz. Big Evan dropped the house ward and was by my side faster than he should have been able to move. He picked me up as if I weighed no more than his daughter and carried me inside. Liz and Cia gathered up the Hermès bag, the weapons, and led the horses to the backyard and grass to eat.

* * *

My sisters and my husband fed me tea and microwaved soup while they drank Evan's best single malt. The Everharts helped Evan unwind my babies from the *sleepy time working* and put them to bed. It was too late for the girls to make the trek back down the mountain, so they crashed on the oversized couches in Evan's man cave. I curled up in my husband's arms in the bed we shared.

"Your magic is different," Big Evan said. "It's cooler. Less barbed than before."

"I think...I think I figured out that death magics belong in hell," I said. "I think I channeled them, well, most of them, there."

"Temptation to use them is gone?" he rumbled.

I let my mouth pull into a wide smile. "Yeah. Your turn. Your magics feel different too. Hotter. More barbed."

Evan nodded, his beard tickling my shoulder. "I never *wanted* to kill anything before, not with my magic. But this time, with you and the baby and the kids..." He stopped, his breathing ragged. "This time I wanted to hurt them. I wanted them to be dead and gone forever. It's still roiling under my skin."

I nestled closer. "Part of that is the nature of Fear of Death. It'll go away soon enough. But if you can't sleep, the baby's nursery needs another coat of paint."

Evan chuckled. "Later. Tonight, I just want to hold you." He kissed the top of my head.

"Cia and Liz got Sally's bag and everything in it."

Evan sighed. "More trouble. But that's a problem for another day."

"We cheated Death," I said.

"And Fear. Nothing wrong with cheating the bastards. It's what life does every day."

That's my hubs. Full of wisdom. And strength. And all good things. "Night," I whispered.

"Good health and happiness. From now on," Evan whispered. I smiled into the dark. It was the Everhart blessing. And it was good.

AWAKE, AWAKE
Kendra Leigh Speedling

The basement repose-rooms of the temple of Rivni were drafty once the weather chilled. The dead occupants hardly minded; the living were generally too focused on their work to pay attention. Idenna Beravnis, junior priest, was no exception.

Her needle made a few final, deft strokes in the dead man's chest. She tied off the thread and removed her jade priest-ring, pressing its signet briefly into his forehead as she whispered a prayer. The stitching across the knife wound slashed from sternum to collarbone was as delicate as an embroidery sampler. When it came time to display the body at services, no one would see anything amiss. His face was peaceful; had it not been for the stillness of his form, and the line of blood-red thread across his skin, he might have been asleep.

A draft wafted through the grate over the dust-coated window, sending a sudden chill through the room. The gaslamp on the wall flickered. Idenna replaced her ring, murmuring the final words of the incantation. Her fingers only trembled slightly as she set the needle aside. She carefully dipped her forefinger in the cup of white tea next to her and splashed one, two, three drops on each of his eyelids. With the ritual complete, the only sound in the room besides the whistling of the wind outside came from the steady ticking of the clock in the corner.

It was done. Acanthus Moreva would not walk again.

Poor soul, Tirya, one of the temple acolytes, had said when the body had arrived. Successful businessman, generous to charity, eligible Society bachelor—Moreva had been well-known and well-loved throughout the city. *I wonder if they'll ever find who did it.*

Idenna certainly hoped not.

* * *

The temple was all but invisible once she had crossed the street, fading into the fog. Winter in Irdall was not cold so much as clammy. Sharp chills and bitter winds were for the northern islands; the feel of winter on an Irdalli street was that of a tendril of fog working its way under one's skin, blotting out the gleam of the gas streetlamps and making the citizens on the sidewalks appear nothing more than sinister shadows. Those hurrying past Idenna paid the temple no mind. The evening was chilly, and growing dark, and it was not a festival day; piety has its limits, even for a god of something as omnipresent as death.

Idenna stopped at the fishmonger's on her way home, as she did every Verday. One salmon fillet for her supper and one small sardine as a treat for her cat Palka.

Arden Vail, the fishmonger, made a quick gesture as she approached the counter. A piece of twine leaped up obligingly to wrap around her parcel. Vail was from the mainland, the southern portion like her father, and as such Idenna felt a sort of kinship with the man.

"Finally stitched up poor Moreva, have you?" he asked, offering her the wrapped parcel.

"How did you know?"

The words came out sharper than she had intended, but he didn't take her tone amiss. "Tirya stopped by earlier. She said you were working late to finish things."

"Well," she said, "it wouldn't do to have him get back up."

"Indeed not," he said, and clucked his tongue. "Are you doing all right? First your father, and now this."

"I'm fine," she said, and held out her coins.

He waved them away. "This one's on me. You've had a rough enough time of it."

Idenna's throat tightened. She took a few quick breaths, hoping that Vail wouldn't notice, or if he did, that he would attribute it to grief alone.

It was not enough; she had to turn away. Tightening her cloak around her, she waved a hand in thanks as she opened the door.

Outside, the fog had thickened. The carriages on the other side of the street were now eerie silhouettes. She held her skirt out of the half-frozen muck. It was the sort of day her father had always called *adhak*—bad atmosphere, in his native Elikan. Bad omen. Now that she was grown, Idenna was not a superstitious woman; she knew Rivni would take you when and where he wanted to and it would make no difference whether there was fog in the air or not.

But old superstitions die hard, and she found her steps quickening even so.

* * *

The night was quiet. Idenna cooked her dinner on the small gas hob in her kitchen, gifted Palka with her sardine, and settled down next to the fire with the latest R. Mairis pirate novel. The only sound in her snug townhome was the crackling of the fire and the ticking of the grandfather clock in the corner; the neighbors seemed to have resolved the familial quarrel that had been Idenna's unwelcome companion for the past several nights.

When the clock struck eleven, she closed her book, deposited Palka from her lap to the floor, and headed to bed.

She did not expect to wake in the middle of the night.

She wasn't immediately sure of what had woken her. Squinting in the dark, she managed to make out what appeared to be a shadowy figure standing in her bedroom doorway.

She banished a silly thought of vengeful pirate ghosts and fumbled for the box of matches on her bedside table. Finagling one free, she struck it and lit the lamp.

Acanthus Moreva was standing in her bedroom, shirtless, her carefully stitched blood-red thread slashed across his chest.

A dream, she thought, but she could think of no reason why she would dream of him. She was no stranger to death and certainly did not find it disturbing, and she felt her conscience was clear. The only other alternative—that she had done the ritual incorrectly, that Moreva had awoken once more to walk the earth—was unthinkable. She had done that ritual a thousand times. No one stitched down by a Rivni-priest got back up again.

He smiled. "Good evening, dear Idenna."

She did not bother pulling her bedsheets over her chest. Nightgown or no, there was no reason to dither with modesty in front of the dead.

"You're dead," she told him—foolishly; he knew that.

"Rather," he agreed. "It hurt. Thank you for that. I *was* enjoying my life."

"Too much," she snapped. The fire in the other room must have burnt down to embers; a chill was working its way through the cracks around her window. She resisted the urge to wrap herself more tightly in her quilt. In the old tales, showing fear to the dead meant showing weakness. Especially for a priest of Rivni, this would not do. "You were meant to stay dead."

"The dead don't stay dead when they're stitched down by their killer," he said, teeth flashing in a grin. "Didn't you pay attention to the nursery stories?"

"Superstition."

He sat down on the edge of her bed. She was tempted to throw the lamp at him, but she didn't want to risk burning down the entire building. Though if word got out that dead Moreva was still walking around, her reputation would be ruined. In more ways than one.

"Superstition, says the Rivni-priest of the walking dead."

"That's different."

"Is it?" He eyed her for a moment, head tilted to one side just a bit too far to seem natural. His movements were abrupt, but still graceful, the quick dart of a bird snatching a fish from the river.

"What do you want?" she demanded, setting her lamp down on her bedside table. "Revenge?" *You deserve no revenge*, she wanted to say, but that was intemperate, far too uncontrolled. She had thought the feeling had all drained out of her, weeks ago, but the sight of Moreva—dead Moreva, violating Rivni's Strictures as well as her father's memory—

Idenna took a deep breath, hoping that the sudden swirl of emotion hadn't shown on her face.

"Well," he said, tracing the line of thread on his chest with a finger, "you *did* kill me."

"You killed my father." Slowly, so he would not notice the movement, she edged a hand toward her nightstand, where she'd set her priest-ring when she'd taken it off for the evening. The marker of her position was mostly ceremonial— no priest in living memory had needed to bind the walking dead. But she trusted it would still serve.

"Your father put a small pistol to his temple and pulled the trigger." The words were dispassionate, neutral. No sign of remorse for the fate of his onetime business partner—were the dead even capable of such things?

"Because *you* ruined him!" She took a deep breath, trying to wait out the white-hot flash of rage. Wasn't killing the faithless bastard once enough; wasn't stitching him down enough? Did he have to reappear to torment her?

"I have a job for you."

"The dead have no jobs to offer. Especially not *you*." Her hand closed around the ring. Before Moreva could react, she squeezed her eyes shut and uttered the traditional incantation, one she'd heard used a hundred times in ritual, but never for its original purpose. The stitchings had kept the Rivni-blessed dead down for thousands of years.

When she opened her eyes again, he was gone, leaving behind only the scent of white tea.

* * *

In the light of day, it was easy to convince herself that Moreva's visit had been a dream after all, or if not, that she'd successfully bound the blasphemous aberration. Idenna went about her routine; she knew well enough how to keep up appearances. Her duties at the temple were uneventful—morning prayers, offering some words of comfort to those with departed loved ones, three more stitchings of the recently deceased. She was tempted to avoid these in favor of other tasks, let one of the other priests take her place, but rejected this as foolishness. If something had gone wrong, it hadn't been with the ritual itself; besides, shirking her duties would be shameful. Her father would not have wanted it.

She did not think about dead Moreva.

Her final task for the evening was preparing the small chapel for a mourning ceremony. Neve, the senior priest, would be presiding; Idenna's duties were only to consecrate the room and light the candles before making herself scarce. It was a simple duty, one she could perform in her sleep.

Dusk was falling, the sunset gleaming blue and gold through the chapel windows. Idenna dipped a candle in the altar flame, using it to light the others one at a time.

Awake, Idenna Beravnis.

She spun around, the flame flickering out at the sudden breeze. She was alone, but she had felt a definite presence next to her. And that had been Moreva's voice.

This is a sacred place, she told herself. *Here, the dead stay down as they should.*

There was no motion from the stairs behind her, leading up to the altar, no sound from the empty mourner-benches. No sign of anything at all, living or dead.

Idenna allowed herself a small sigh and turned to light the candle again. She caught a glimpse of her reflection in the mirror atop the altar and nearly dropped the candle in the fire.

Moreva was standing behind her.

She whirled, clenching the candle like a weapon, to find that there was no one there.

* * *

Idenna retired to bed at her usual time, forcing herself to return her book to her nightstand and avoid the temptation to wait out the night by reading. She had often read past her bedtime when she was small, hurriedly covering the lamp whenever she heard her father's footsteps near her door—but that had been years ago. She shook off the memory and turned to blow out the lamp, allowing herself only a brief hesitation.

She awoke not to noise, nor to movement, but to the scent of white tea wafting through the room. A silhouette stood at her door.

"I have a job for you," he said.

She lit the lamp, wishing she had bought some juniper branches on her way home. The notion had crossed her mind, but doing so would have felt as though she were acknowledging something.

"I don't take jobs from the dead," she snapped.

"You have only yourself to blame for that series of events." The way the shadows danced across his face made him look hawk-like, predatory, an unexpected impression from Moreva's boyish features. Though nearly her father's age, he had worn his years much more lightly.

"I did what was necessary to let my father rest." Anger rose to her throat again, choking off further reproof. Moreva knew very well what he had done, and even at the last, he had offered nothing but excuses.

"Your father was resting already," he said. "Fate ties us each with our own strand, awaiting shining Rivni and his scythe to return us to our natural state. The body is a temporary thing—"

"—for we are born of starlight and earth, a mixture which by nature cannot last," Idenna finished. "Do you truly mean to lecture a Rivni-priest on the Strictures?"

He chuckled. "Do you mean to lecture the dead on the nature of death?"

"You earned your fate!" The words burst from her before she could consider whether it was wise to provoke him. *Wise, not wise, what does it matter now? The only one who would miss you is gone.*

He stepped forward, far more quickly and fluidly than was natural, and was in front of her before she could blink.

"I was going to earn it back," he said. "I needed money. I needed time." His eyes, in this light, were hardly recognizable as Moreva's, which had been a piercing bright green. Now they were black, with no trace of either white or iris.

Was it the light?

"So you swindled him out of his fortune and stole his life! No apology, no remorse—"

"I did not make his choices for him!" The words were almost a snarl; he drew himself up to his full height—then, just as suddenly, he calmed. "We light our own fires, *viyane*. It is time you took up your torch."

Dear one, in her father's tongue. He was the only one who had ever called her that.

Idenna closed her eyes for a moment, letting the emotion pass. When she opened them again, she said, "You aren't Moreva."

He smiled.

"What are you, some sort of spirit possessing his form?"

"I am Moreva," he said. "After a fashion. At the moment, we are, for lack of a better term, sharing."

Was it her imagination, or were the dark pits of his eyes growing?

"It's a mutually beneficial arrangement," he said. "He gets to cling to a semblance of life for now—your sort always want that, regardless of whether it actually benefits you."

"And what do you get?"

His smile widened, too much; it looked feral and wrong. "I get the chance to talk to you, Idenna Beravnis."

"Why?" The word came out in a whisper, and she loathed herself for it. "What are you?"

He extended a hand, one long finger a hairsbreadth away from her face. "I'll give you a hint," he said, and brushed the finger against her forehead.

Idenna had almost drowned once, as a child. She'd fallen in the river while playing and the current had swept her away before her friends could reach her. She remembered the crush of the rapids, the waves cresting relentlessly over her head until all there was to breathe was water.

The sensation crashed into her like drowning; she had no sight, no air. She was not sure if the room around her was gone or if it was she who had left. In her ears echoed a choir, a chant—one she had performed at the temple a thousand times, but sounding like no human voice imaginable.

Bright spots began pulsing in her vision, different colors and sizes; they seemed to form a tapestry across an unimaginable distance. She could sense each and every one of them—their lives, their emotions, their deaths. She knew when all of them would meet their end—

The chant reached a crescendo. Her vision flared bright, and then there was darkness.

When Idenna opened her eyes again, she was on the floor. Moreva's silhouette was standing above her.

"You—" she gasped, once she'd gotten her breath.

"It's overwhelming the first time," said Rivni, shining Rivni in Acanthus Moreva's body. "One adapts."

"Rivni," she said. She didn't know if there was a proper obeisance to make to a god clad in flesh—anyway, she couldn't have moved if she wanted to.

"Your people call me by that name," he agreed, offering her a hand. "There have been others, eons worth. In the end, they all mean Death."

Idenna took his hand. It was cool, smooth, like marble. He pulled her up effortlessly; it felt as though she were floating to her feet.

She took a deep breath, dressing herself in her usual composure as if putting on a robe. Even if she couldn't make sense of what was going on, there was no need to seem like a fool.

"In the old tales," she said dryly, "you all just send visions."

Death-Rivni-Moreva flung his head back and laughed, the sound making the walls shake. Idenna was too disquieted to spare a thought for her neighbors.

"Unfortunately," he said, sobering as quickly as he'd been amused, "we have our own rules to follow."

"Why are you here?" she asked, meeting his eerie black gaze. "And why in Moreva's form?"

"I told you," he said. "To speak to you."

"Why?"

"You killed me." He laid a hand across the red line of thread on his chest. "It was unanticipated."

A weft of doubt curled through Idenna's mind; yes, that vision had seemed fairly conclusive, but a death unanticipated by Rivni could not be. Perhaps he was a spirit after all, possessing Moreva's form to lead her astray. Or perhaps it *was* simply dead Moreva, seeking vengeance.

"Rivni sees all fates," she countered.

"Yes," he agreed, tilting his head to the left, unnaturally far. "I see all fates, *viyane*, except Acanthus Moreva's, and except yours. Your thread gleams, and yet I cannot grasp it; you killed this man unbidden. It was not part of the pattern, and that tells me one thing."

As ludicrous as the notion was, a chill stole over Idenna. A death Rivni could not foresee would have been blasphemy—had it not been impossible.

"And what is that?" she asked, keeping her voice steady.

He regarded the wall clock in the corner, staying silent so long that she was tempted to repeat the question. She did not; she knew he had heard her. Rivni, spirit, dead Moreva—it would not benefit her to antagonize any of them. The steady ticking of the clock filled the room, though it was only the press of her own thoughts that made it deafening.

"It is time," he said. "Time to awaken once more. I have been Death for more millennia than you can imagine, yet I was not the first, and I will not be the last."

"I have no skill with riddles."

"Because you have always done as you were told." He extended a hand out, as if to touch her forehead again, then stopped. "Schooling, priesthood, dutiful daughter, day-to-day life repeating and repeating as if you had modeled it after that clock—"

"Until I killed Acanthus Moreva," she said, unmoved by his critical tone. She knew what her life had been, and she didn't see why it should be an object of reproach. She had always, always done her duty.

"Until you killed Acanthus Moreva," he agreed. "One moment of fury in a life regulated by routine. You say your prayers; you repeat the words and do your duty and keep the dead in their place. Do you feel it, I wonder?"

"Is that not enough?" she demanded, anger flashing through her tone. She was no mystic. Her faith may not have been as deep as that of some of the others, as Tirya with her visions or Neve with the prayers tattooed on her arms—but she had done her duty. Why couldn't he haunt one of *them*? "I followed your path, as my father wanted."

"I do not mind," he said. "But it cannot be easy to live while stitching your feelings down."

"I am no corpse." She could not quite hold back the venom from the words. Was haunting her not enough? He had to mock her as well?

He made a noncommittal gesture. "Moreva's death was a beacon, Idenna Beravnis. You caused a death I did not plan. Your fate has been decided."

Idenna glanced away, at his elongated silhouette cast upon the wall by the lamp. It was less unsettling than looking at his face, so familiar and yet completely alien. She realized her hand was knotted in her nightgown and made herself unclench it.

"If you're here to kill me, you could have done that the first night and saved us both a lot of trouble," she grumbled. She knew she should be afraid, but she had always expected Rivni to claim her one day; she just hadn't expected he'd do it personally. She had no remaining relations, no close friends, and no further unfinished business—save, perhaps, for making sure someone found Palka. She feared neither death nor Death.

"Equanimity," he said, regarding her through half-lowered eyelids. On someone else, the expression might have appeared lazy. "Surprising."

"Are you…reading my thoughts?"

He laughed. "I am not my magic-attuned sister; I do not possess the power. Your demeanor speaks clearly enough."

She supposed that was some sort of accomplishment.

"I am not here to kill you," he said. "Not exactly."

"What does that—"

"Your soul." He held out a hand expectantly, as though she could set it in his palm. "It is already in motion. If you planned the death of Acanthus Moreva and I did not, that means it is time. You will agree to unite; I will fade into the background; you will be scythe-bearing Rivni in the tower; it will fall to you to claim the mortal souls."

Idenna opened her mouth and closed it again three times before she arrived at a reply she considered suitably non-inane.

"You want me," she said, very slowly, "to…*become* Rivni."

"I told you," he said. "I was not the first. I will not be the last."

"Impossible. The Strictures—"

"The Strictures are made by mortal hands. Subject to certain…omissions."

She let that be, for now. "So we *unite*, and you leave behind Moreva's corpse—"

"I leave behind Moreva."

He stressed the word enough that it was clear he was trying to make a distinction.

"Moreva," Idenna repeated flatly.

"Alive," he said. "It is how things work."

She spun on her heel, paced a few steps toward the wall, and stared at the painting there—a landscape that had hung in that same spot as long as she could remember.

"I refuse," she said.

"I don't think you understand the gravity of the—"

"Do you know what it took to kill him?" she demanded, spinning to face him again.

"A knife," he said, with something like humor. "Probably a sharp one."

"You're asking me to return to life the man who caused my father's death."

"I am asking you," he said, "to fix what has gone awry. If you seek justice, you're talking to the wrong god."

Idenna took a deep breath. "Get out."

He extended a hand. "If you believe in me as you've preached over these years—"

"Get. Out."

Rivni regarded her a moment more, then turned to the door. "I will be waiting," he said, and faded into the shadows.

* * *

She could not sleep.

She made a cup of tea—green tea, not white—and sat at the kitchen table, thinking.

It could not have been Rivni. It must have been Rivni.

Palka meowed, rubbing up against her legs, and Idenna absently let a hand drift down to scratch the cat's head. Outside the window, the fog was still thick, swirling in face-like patterns—no, that was only her imagination.

Becoming Rivni. Impossible—wasn't it? But that vision, that feeling of those life-lights surrounding her…it sounded like ravings from a wild-haired mystic on a street corner, but it had *felt* real.

If she allowed that becoming Rivni was possible, that would be one thing. But allowing Moreva to return to life?

Palka jumped up into her lap, which Idenna normally discouraged when she was in the kitchen—the habit tended to lead to the theft of whatever was on her plate. She reached down to push the cat away, but was met with a paw pushing back against her hand.

"The stitchings will fail."

Startled, Idenna looked down. Palka was sitting upright, eyeing her expectantly.

That had been Moreva's voice.

"The stitchings will fail. The dead will rise. Those meant to die will live five hundred years. Those meant to live to ninety will collapse in the streets. Chaos. Destruction—"

Idenna leapt to her feet, tossing Palka to the floor. "You leave my cat be!"

Palka glanced over her shoulder, sneezed, and shook herself, then headed off to the living room with the offended dignity only a cat could muster.

Idenna reached for her cup of tea, more to have something to hold onto than to drink—and nearly dropped it on the floor.

Her green tea had turned to white, a delicate floral aroma wafting up at her.

* * *

Rivni was right. Within days, the stitchings had grown harder. Priests long accomplished in such matters needed their work checked two, three, four times. The temple of Rivni in Irdall heard similar tales from their brethren across the continent. The stitchings were not taking as easily as they had, and no one save Idenna knew why.

She said nothing. Even had she wanted to, she knew the politics of the temple. Her words would be dismissed as raving; no one spoke to Rivni directly, nor any of the gods. Not since the era of myth.

Other tales, too, spread: sightings of spirits and haunts and strange shapes in the fog. Some could be dismissed as superstition. Others seemed more plausible. The temple attempted to keep the latter sort of stories under wraps. No sense in causing a panic.

Idenna no longer slept well. Her dreams dwelled on that brief fragment of Rivni's consciousness he'd shown her, each new glimpse connected to the last like the facet on a gem. Of dead Moreva, she saw nothing, though often she felt something watching her.

She had begun to smell of white tea. Palka avoided her, as though the cat could sense the encroachment of death.

I will not let Moreva live. I will not let Moreva live. She chanted it in her head like a refrain, whenever she sensed her resolve beginning to waver.

Two weeks after Rivni's last visit, she stayed late at the temple. She lit the taper candles in the chapel and waited by the altar, keeping her gaze on the carved marble ceiling above her and not on the mirror.

"In the old tales," she said out loud, "there are bargains."

"I am not a vengeful hedgewitch." Motion in the mirror caught her eye; dead Moreva's body was standing behind her. Despite the passage of time, the corpse seemed to be as pristine as it had been when she'd stitched it down.

She turned. "Then stop this."

"You mistake me," he said. The pools of shadow filling his eye sockets had grown. "I could not stop this, even if I wished. It is not under my control."

"You're a *god*."

"Would *you* be able to stop a hurricane, if the people of Irdall wished? It is the same."

"The world is dying."

"Yes," he said, trailing a finger idly along the row of candles.

He did not speak further. Idenna suspected he was trying to leave her to think. How could she think, when every time she closed her eyes, she saw her father sprawled dead on the floor, blood leaking from the hole in his skull? How could she think, when dead Moreva still walked, taunting her at every turn?

He had not apologized. He had equivocated, pleaded, but he had not apologized. *I didn't kill him*, he'd said, more than once, as though that made a difference. It was true, but only in the most technical terms.

I was going to make it better, he'd said, and that was when she'd slashed him with the knife.

Had she meant to kill him? It had not been the planned end of that confrontation, but she'd interpreted it as fate. As the hand of shining Rivni, judging her father's killer. That *had* to be right, because if not—Oram Beravnis would receive no justice. No court in the land would convict Acanthus Moreva of irresponsibility, of talking his friend into a terrible investment as a personal favor.

"I will not let him live," she said finally, one hand clenched in her robes.

"And you would let the world die?"

"Bring someone else back," she snapped. "Anyone. I don't care who. Why not save my father, if someone has to return?"

"It is not the way."

She swung a hand toward his face, not thinking, aiming for a slap—*this is* **Rivni**, *not truly dead Moreva*—

She froze, her breathing harsh in her ears.

Slowly, he reached out and brushed a finger across her cheek, eyeing the collected moisture with bemusement.

Idenna was no less surprised. She was not a crier.

"Would he want the world to die for his sake?" Rivni asked.

"Don't you *dare*—"

"These are threads mortals cannot touch." He laid a hand on the red stitching across his chest.

"Moreva deserves no resurrection."

"It's not about deserving. Moreva needs to live because perhaps in five generations a daughter of his bloodline will play a vital role in saving a nation far away. Perhaps he needs to live because he invents something crucial to humanity's survival three hundred years from now. Or perhaps he needs to live in order to die in another way, at a later date. He is an infinitesimally small part of a larger pattern, like each one of you, and it cannot be broken. The world will rip itself apart trying to repair things."

It ripped me apart first, Idenna almost said. *Ripped me apart and remade me into what I was supposed to be, then did it again and expects me to accept it with a smile.*

"I cannot force you into this," Rivni said. He gestured toward the ceiling reliefs, one hand trailing through the candle flames. He did not appear to mind. "But you must understand."

"You want me to sacrifice the only thing I ever did of my own accord." It was, it had been. She had thought over and over, trying to find something else, and gods, was that what her life had amounted to?

"I want you," he said, "to save everything."

Idenna sat down on the altar stairs, trying to pass it off as a controlled movement. "Do I have a choice?"

"Yes." He did not elaborate, nor remind her of the stakes.

She looked at him for a moment, seeing not dead Moreva but *Rivni*, ancient and unfathomable. "Do you know what I decide?"

"No," he said. "My sight ended when you killed Acanthus Moreva."

"Then you don't know what will happen—"

He glanced over his shoulder, at the blue glass windows along the chapel wall. The message was clear enough.

* * *

On the way home, Idenna did not stop at Arden Vail's; she did not tarry on the foggy streets. A light snow was beginning to fall, swirling around the glowing gaslamps in miniature clouds. A peaceful winter scene.

When she returned, she put the kettle on the hob to boil, then thought the better of it.

She wasn't in the mood for tea anyway.

The halls of her house seemed emptier than normal, the wood paneling oppressive rather than cozy. Idenna paced around each room several times, trying to find the most comfortable spot, like Palka circling on the bed.

Palka herself was nowhere to be found. No doubt she had gone to see the neighbor woman, the housewife with the nice dried anchovies.

Idenna finally found herself in her father's study, regarding the bookshelves stacked precariously along the walls. He'd always loved reading; when she was small, he'd read her a chapter of a book every night. So many of those books had been gifts from Moreva, a personal inscription in each one. He and her father had met on the boat to Irdall; they had been inseparable from that point on.

The world is dying.

She heard the floorboards creak behind her and whirled around, expecting dead Moreva, expecting Rivni.

Her father stood in the doorway.

Idenna's breath rushed out in a hiss.

"You're gone," she said. "You were stitched down."

"Things are changing," he said. "There is a new breeze through the world. Do you feel it?"

"Rivni. This is one of your tricks." She wasn't sure if the knot in her chest was compelling her toward laughter or tears.

He smiled. It was too wide, unsettling. "Rivni has no power anymore." He walked past her, perusing the bookshelves. The hole in the side of his head was clean and empty. "How many of those would you say we read?"

"Almost all of them." She took a breath. "You shouldn't be here."

He tilted his head to one side, frowning. "Do you not want me around, *viyane*?"

"It's not you," she said, trying to keep her voice even. "Not really."

"No," he agreed. He held up a hand and studied it in the gaslight, veins standing out from the skin. "But it's better than nothing."

"It's *not!*" The words burst from her. This was a mockery, a false life; the Strictures told that nothing could truly bring back the dead, not all the way. To see him in this state—

"Do you remember?" he asked. "We used to have dinner on Aildays, you and Acanthus and I, and he'd bring you candied walnuts and ask you about your schooling "

"It's his fault you're gone!"

"You blame him because you cannot blame me," he said. He glanced away, ran a finger along the spine of his copy of the Strictures. "I understand. I am sorry, *viyane*."

Idenna swiped a hand across her eyes. "I killed Moreva so you could rest!"

"No rest," he said. "Not anymore."

She turned on her heel and ran, out the door, onto the street, toward the temple. His words followed her—*no rest, no rest, no rest…*

It's not going to fix itself.

* * *

The temple courtyard was deserted, cloaked in the hush of newly fallen snow. Idenna shivered. She hadn't stopped to grab her overcoat.

She had always been quiet, courteous, reserved. She abandoned that habit now.

"Rivni!" she shouted into the snowstorm. "Where are you?"

There was no reply.

"*Rivni!*"

You did this, she almost added, but—well.

Idenna sank to her knees, shaking, and closed her eyes.

"Do you have an answer?" dead Moreva's voice came from behind her.

She stood up, gathering herself, and looked him in the eye. "I want to fix this."

"Then break the stitching," he said, gesturing to his chest. The slash of red thread stood out in sharp relief against his pale skin.

Idenna reached into her skirt pocket for her penknife. A small, delicate thing compared to the instrument of Moreva's demise, but it would do.

"What will happen?" she asked, gripping the knife in her hand. "After."

"We will unite," he said. "Gradually, your influence will increase, and mine will…wane."

Something in his tone made her pause. "It's a sort of death for you, isn't it?"

"In a way," he said. "But I have been Death a long time."

"And the rest of it—the dead, the stitchings—it goes back to the way it was?"

"It does." He spread his arms, inviting her in. "It is time."

Idenna looked down at the enameled handle of her penknife. A gift from her father. He'd said it had belonged to the mother she'd never known.

She tightened her grasp on the handle and slashed, slicing through the red thread, opening the gash across Moreva's chest.

The world *roared*, or perhaps it was only the snowstorm whipping up again; everything went dark and cold and empty.

Idenna took a breath.

Then another.

It was done, she could tell.

It was done.

Slowly, the darkness around her seemed to warm; spots of light appeared in her vision, coalescing into bunches that spread out in tangles as far as she could see. She *understood* them, those people, each and every one, their wishes and dreams and fears and their appointed time, and oh, her own vengeance seemed small and unimportant and hugely essential all at once—

It had been part of the pattern after all. Rivni was right; it *was* time.

Welcome, a voice said within her head. It wasn't like dead Moreva's voice, but there was enough similarity in the intonation for Idenna to recognize it.

One of the spots of light danced up, just out of reach. She recognized that, too.

She almost pushed the emotion aside, but then thought the better of it. How long had it been since she had truly let herself feel something?

"Rest well," she murmured.

Come, Rivni-herself said. *We have work to do.*

THE END

Jason M. Hough

You tried to save me, Emily, and I love you for it.

We were walking along that path that winds down to the river, and you said you're always amazed how the sounds of the city fade away there below the old bridge. A place where we could get some solitude. "If our project is a success," I say, "peace and quiet is going to become a rare commodity for us."

Then there was a noise above, and you tugged at me, and then...nothing.

I wouldn't even call it a fade to black. It was as if even colors ceased to exist. No sound, no smells, no anything. I died.

Death is here. The Angel of Death. Flowing, tattered black robes that ripple as if underwater. The hooded head with only the barest hint of a skeletal something hidden in the shadows. One hand and arm, just bones, protrude from the sleeve, the fingers coiled loosely around the shaft of a sort of comically oversized scythe. Basically it looks like something off an Iron Maiden album cover, as if this is all a manifestation wrought from my own head. Maybe that's what the afterlife is: whatever you imagined it would be, made real. This thought is somehow more terrifying than the figure sitting across from me.

Death doesn't seem to be in any hurry to explain, so I take a minute to let the terror run its course. It does so surprisingly fast, replaced by something worse: despair. Sadness. I'm overcome with the simple truth that I'll never get to know if our experiment worked.

Death and I are on top of a low hill. There's a craggy rock with a murder of crows all perched atop it, squabbling at one another and dripping the occasional white shit. One flaps its wings, perhaps nervous under my gaze. It hops to regain its balance and they all jostle around for a bit and then settle back down.

There's an ancient tree that looks like it's been dead as long as it had been alive. Just gray smooth bark vaulting up into a crooked mess of spiny branches.

No leaves, but plenty of spiders. They crawl along the branches like ants, and their webs are everywhere, shifting despite the total lack of breeze with that same languid motion that waggles Death's robes.

"What," I begin, but there's a crack in my voice and I stop to swallow. "What happens now?"

This earns no reaction from Death. The immortal is not impressed.

Beyond the hill are more hills. The ground is as bleak as the First World War's western front, just mud and the occasional dead twig poking up. Here and there another craggy stone propping up another murder of crows.

Fine by me. The longer I can sit here, the more I can get my thoughts in order. I'm not thirsty or hungry, not in any pain. I feel my skull, wondering if my demise was due to some falling chunk of the old stone bridge, or perhaps I was the landing pad for the year's first jumper. If that was the case, the damage has been repaired here in the middling afterlife.

My knowledge of Death with a capital D is minimal. I recall something about the river Styx, but I see no river here. Death is supposed to ferry me to the afterlife. Or maybe I do the rowing and Death just makes sure I go in the right direction.

The sky is pure dull gray. Against it, more goddamn crows circle and swoop.

The continued silence fills me with a sudden irrational anger. "Say something, for fuck's sake. Whatever this is, just…get it over with."

"Jacob Oliver Crydon," Death says, "you are ready to cross over?"

His voice is like two smooth stones being rubbed together in your hand. A soft scraping that shouldn't form coherent syllables but somehow does. It unnerves the hell out of me. My whole body trembles with a sudden chill, cooling even my hot ears, and for a time I'm compelled to silence.

In a weird way that answers his question.

Death rises to his full impressive height. Ten feet tall at least. His bone fingers stretch and then curl again around the scythe. With that he turns and begins to walk down the hill. There is a river below, now. It wasn't there a minute ago. I see a small decrepit wooden boat and a hurricane lantern hanging from a hook on the bow.

I feel…a sudden urge to be defiant. One last little rebellion. So I remain firmly seated and watch him go. Part of me expects to lose control over my own free will, to be compelled to obedience. Another part thinks this is a test, that Death will turn and swing his scythe and that will be that.

Neither of these things happens.

Halfway down the slope the entity turns and stares at me. Really stares, eyes flaring like embers in the shadows of his hood. This moment drags on for almost a full minute before, as if with great reluctance, he takes a step back up the hill. Then another. Soon he's back to where he started, his gaze never leaving me.

His teeth clack together once. A horrible sound. He lifts his chin toward me. "I have guided billions to their final, eternal existence. I have witnessed and suffered every imaginable reaction to my appearance and all it entails. Fear, mostly. Sadness. Remorse. Those who plead at my feet and even those who worship there. Countless examples of all." He rushes forward with unnatural speed, in an instant he is at arm's length, filling my view. I can see little glowing universes in the deepest shadows of his eye sockets. Black scarab beetles by the thousands crawl around on the inside of his hooded robe. My nostrils fill with death and rot and ash. Death says, "But never this, Jacob Oliver Crydon. Never has any mortal soul simply remained. They always follow. Always. *Explain yourself.*"

That's when I know it worked. Our experiment. Our life's labor, built on hard work and countless hours of research and coding and tooling. And, okay, a bit of industrial espionage, but goddammit who cares, *it worked!*

The knowledge floods me with a sudden smug confidence, because I know what it means. Not just for reality, which is monumental, change-the-course-of-history kind of stuff, but what it means *here*. What it's going to mean for the being before me.

I inhale deeply, puffing up and meeting that horrifying gaze with something equal and opposite.

"That's just it," I say. "I'm not mortal."

Death actually tilts his head to one side. "You are here. Where mortals come when they die."

"True, but you see, I'm not the only instance of me."

His reaction to that is a low, impatient growl.

I go on. "I am apparently the first person in human history to become a *digi*. To upload." Impossible to keep the pride out of my voice. "Going digi." The term you came up with for our process. Ours, for the most part. We did cheat a bit, but that's a secret we'll take to our graves. But, I suppose I have already. Your turn will come someday, Emily. Then there's my digi, of course. No grave for a digi, is there? Don't worry, he'll know what to do. Keeping a secret can't be harder than deleting a file, for him.

The crows began to flutter and squawk, becoming a writhing mess of wings and beaks. Their little beady black eyes glisten as Death looms even closer.

"Do go on," he rasps.

"My entire mind was captured. Data, mapped into a computer. I wasn't sure if it worked, but this proves it has. I'm not following you because I'm not dead. Not really."

The ramifications of this start to settle like the placed pieces of a jigsaw puzzle. The end of death as we know it. You and I had never considered that. Not in the supernatural context, anyway.

Lost in my thoughts, I only now notice that Death is right up in my face. One skeletal hand comes up and the bony tip of the index finger touches my forehead. It's cold as ice, that fingertip, and presses painfully hard.

I feel something new inside me then. A softness, like a blanket has been wrapped around my thoughts. It quickly becomes a shroud. A mummification.

I'm spun about, mentally, and I become aware of something spiraling into that maelstrom of thought. Another mind. Death's mind.

He's searching for something, and I know at once it's the truth of my words he seeks to verify, and perhaps also to understand. An immortal entity or not, Death perhaps isn't up to speed on the nuances of neural networks and qubit arrays.

He rummages through my mind for concept and context like a hungry teen might raid a refrigerator and I'm powerless to stop him.

Death's presence changes. Becomes a pressure. I find myself shrinking, as if I'm in some carnival haunted house room where the walls are closing in. Only these walls are mine. More than that, they're *me*.

I'm shunted into a corner of myself. I can still see, and hear. I can feel and smell. I have no sense of touch, though, and that's odd, isn't it? I mean, all of this is odd, but why touch?

"What the hell is going on here?" I ask.

The words go unvoiced. I'm not in control of that particular function. Death has moved in. My hands raise in front of me and flop back and forth, seen for the first time. They clench into fists and then extend out again. I take several hops on my toes, then stand.

The crows take flight. They must have sensed this change, this transference. They're gathering. They're staring at me. At Death.

"Rabbettttty," my mouth says, sounding like I'm three sheets to the wind. My feet are stamping the ground now, as if I'm cold. I'm not cold. I'm terrified. "Rahh...Rab...Red...*Ready*."

This last with conviction. With more purpose and sinister mojo than I think I've ever put into any word when I controlled that voice. Ready for what? I want to ask, but then the word wasn't for me, was it?

It was for the crows.

And the crows react.

They swarm on my body. A black cloud of noise and feather, of those beady little eyes. They're clawing at my skin, my clothing. Sinking their little spiky talons into my flesh.

I can see it, I want to feel it, but I can't, so I wait. I watch. I listen.

We're airborne, heading for the gray sky.

* * *

I wake to gray, but it's no sky. It's a ceiling and there are humming fluorescent lights in uniform vertical lines.

I'm back. The real world. But Death is still with me. I've brought him here. He was supposed to ferry me to the afterlife but instead the opposite has happened.

My body starts to flop about. Skin against cool metal. Then my fingers are up and clawing at the edges of a table.

The wide-eyed face of a woman in her later years appears above me. She wears the uniform of cleaning staff.

She whispers something in a language I don't know and makes a rapid hand gesture—forehead to sternum, shoulder to shoulder.

Bad move, I think.

Death ignores it. He sits my body up and looks around. A morgue, of course. Stainless steel tables with bodies on some. Tags attached to toes.

No other living souls, though. Just the cleaning lady, and me trapped in my mental cage. Death looks back at her and she faints. Dead weight, dropping to the floor.

She'll forget this, I think. Chalk it up to a dream, until she realizes she's being asked a thousand questions about why there's a missing body. They'll ask this because Death has me up and walking now. A lumber, really. I'm a fucking zombie. This makes me laugh mentally and, to my surprise, my body laughs, too. Death gets the joke. Revels in it.

"Why are we here?" I ask, mentally. "What do you intend to do?"

"I must see this for myself," he says, using my mouth. The answer is aloud.

I find myself guiding Death through the streets, like an annoying suit trying to tell his cabbie the fastest route in a city well known. It's very late at night, a huge plus as hardly anyone is about to wonder at the naked man with the toe tag flopping in the wind with each step.

Part of me wants to guide Death to the police, but then I wonder, what's the point? I can't actually use my own mouth. I couldn't explain if I wanted to. And as of yet I have no idea what powers this immortal being can wield here in the realm of the real. Perhaps that woman in the morgue hadn't fainted at all. So I silence this part of me that wants to sabotage Death's wishes here. The rules are not exactly clear to me, but I suspect limiting how many people encounter Death is probably the wise move.

Best to take him to what he wants to see. I'm rather curious myself, if I'm honest.

Our route takes us toward the old bridge, and on a whim I guide Death down the path that leads to that quiet place you loved so much. It occurs to me then that you probably don't love it anymore. It will be a cursed place to you now.

I sort of hope to see flowers and some kind of improvised memorial blanketing the cobblestones where I met my end. But perhaps not enough time has passed. It could even be the same evening, because all Death and I find is some yellow police tape cordoning off the area.

We step under it and approach the spot. I'm hesitant to look suddenly, but I'm not in control of this so I'm forced to approach at Death's rather confident pace. I can't control what my eyes look at either, so I see the crimson staining the old stone pathway. My blood, soaked into those old rocks.

Anguish grips me, but I cannot look away. I cannot leave. You'd think Death would be long cured of a morbid fascination for this kind of thing but *noooo*, he's downright fascinated. Poring over the whole place, bit by bit.

I tell myself not to let it bother me. I'm not truly dead. I'm still around, elsewhere, in the machine that now houses me.

"Murder," Death rasps through my throat.

My hand points. There's a little flag on the ground, a white one with a number. Several others, on the edge of my vision.

Murder.

Not crows.

Murder as in the crime of killing.

The killing of me.

And then I'm wondering if all that blood is just mine, or if the killer got you, too. Perhaps you met Death, too, only…only you hadn't become a digi yet, had you, Emily. We'd flipped a coin for that and I went first. Even now you may be on the river, your lovely face lit by that dim lantern, a skeletal shadow in black robes behind you.

Who could have done it? We'd made our share of enemies in recent months. Nutjobs came out of the woodwork when we announced. And that doctor in Malaysia who claimed we'd stolen his process. He certainly has motive.

We're on the move again. With urgency. Up the path, down two streets and through an alley. Across a park, where an early morning jogger shrieks at the sight of me. I want to explain, to plead for information, but Death says, "Crazy night!" and in those two words the perfect cover story is laid out. The jogger somehow manages an embarrassed laugh and continues on their run.

My flat. Police tape across it. Death ducks under it and tries the keypad at the door. It bleats, a red light flashes. My door code has already been removed. Before I can even think it, Death mines my head and finds your code, Emily. That still works, and we're in.

Death enters my living room and there it is on the coffee table: the glasses without lenses, opaque and sleek gray. He sits my body down beside it and pulls on the thin device, powers it up. Darkness for a second, then a floating prompt appears before me.

I hesitate. Not because I wish to keep my password from the grim reaper, but because I'm suddenly irrationally afraid to talk to myself. It goes against the rules we agreed on. Death doesn't care. He mines my brain and finds the information he needs. Username, password, and of course he already has access to my fingerprint.

I want to swallow, I can feel the cold confused terror building in me and Death seems to understand this because I do gulp it back.

We're in.

But my fear was in vain. We cannot talk to the digital me.

Because there is no me in there. There's nothing at all.

"Entity capture deleted," with a time and date, the logs say. Just minutes ago.

What the fu—

There's a crash and door behind me slams open. Death turns my head enough to see two detectives, guns and badges in view, shouting. "Emily Jones! On the ground! Hands behind your fucking head!" Death does not obey. I'm not sure I would have if I'd been in control. I'm too confused. Why are they shouting your name?

Of course. We used your code to open the door.

Pounding footsteps across the carpet, beams of flashlights blinding as the two officers rush in. En route the lead cop roars, "Emily Jones you are under arrest for the murder of Jacob Crydon and the deletion of a digitized sentience! Do not—"

"It's not her, it's not her!" the other is shouting. "It's…holy fuck it's—"

And then Death reaches out and taps the closer one in the center of his forehead. There's a change in those eyes and I feel everything drain from me. Death, departing. Moving to a new body.

I'm dying again, more or less.

One last thought rolls through my head as I drop lifeless to the floor.

It was you. You did this.

And then I'm back with the crows.

Only this time, I'm alone, and I don't know what happens next, Emily.

We wanted to make Death irrelevant. What we did instead was unleash him upon the world.

And Emily…he's looking for you.

THE DANCE

Julie Pitzel

The torch at the door served as a beacon in the dying twilight. Or was it a warning?

Two dozen paces lay between the village and the feast hall, a squat hut carved from dull stones. Pitted and scored by desert winds, the hall melted into the low crag at its back. I stood watching, waiting. Dread washed over me. Dread, coupled with a dangerous eagerness.

Once the last rays of sun vanished and stars pierced the sky, I pushed aside the camelhair rug over the doorway and slipped inside. Fetid air, reeking of sweat and roasted meat, greeted me. Smoke from the torches hung under the low ceiling, making the room dimmer and closer than I liked.

A dozen Elders lounged against saddles or reclined on carpets and goatshair cushions, their fine linens and silks muted in the haze. Three gray and stooped village women carried platters of lamb, trays of grapes and figs, and jugs of wine. A musician playing a reed-pipe stood in the corner to the right of the door. The low light shadowed his features and briefly transformed his face into a jeering skull. The sight stopped my heart. Then a torch flared, revealing his lips, short beard, and the keen attention in his eyes. I dismissed the vision. Death sat too heavy on my mind.

One of the elderly servers, and the piper, were the only ones to notice my entrance. That would soon change. I unwrapped my scarf and hung it with my robe on an empty peg.

My costume chafed, exposing my belly beneath fringe the color of midnight. It had been Esme's, worn with pride until the material became fragile from too many washings. I resisted the urge to tug on the bra, filled out with small sacks of seed and grain to enhance my breasts. The skirt, cinched in at the hips, still threatened to slide off and land in an inky puddle. Esme had always teased that she got the body and I got the brains. It wasn't true. I'd studied the wise arts—healing the wounded and tending the sick—while my sister had learned to dance. She'd been both smart and beautiful, the heart of our family. I filled that role less successfully than I filled her dance costume.

We'd lost her barely a week ago. The sorrow was still so fresh my chest ached from swallowing the tears. But this was not the time to mourn. The Elders demanded entertainment. We'd been brought to this village because of Esme's talent, and now that she was dead—raped, beaten, and buried in the dunes—the task fell to me.

I walked to the empty corner of the room, opposite the musician. He stopped playing as I passed, and the rattling of my beads and light chains drew the crowd's attention. The servants abandoned their platters and jugs and scurried out the door, heads down and eyes averted.

The men paid no attention to the old women. These pillars of society with crumbs in their beards, wine stains on their fine robes, and greasy hands reaching for another piece of meat? They grabbed for me. Leered. And found me lacking.

"Not as pretty as the other."

"She has boy hips."

They discussed me as if debating the merits of a camel at market. There were more comments, darker, uglier words that I ignored.

The piper trilled an introduction to Esme's song and I froze, not sure if I could do this. I knew the steps. I'd practiced the forms. But I feared I wouldn't do her justice.

Grumbling started among the watchers. I glanced toward the door, briefly considering an escape. I had no choice. Surrounded by the leaders of this small village, I would not be allowed to leave until I'd performed. But I couldn't leave even if I had the choice.

I thought of Esme's battered body and shuddered. Shifting sands and luck had revealed her to me. Which of these men had killed her? Which carved out pieces of her flesh, sliced lines in her face, and hit her hard enough to dislodge teeth and jaw? I wanted answers, but they would be hard won and I wouldn't get them by running.

I looked to the piper. Another trick of light hid all but his gleaming smile and transformed his pipe into a blade, wicked and sharp.

Then the illusion dropped. He held his instrument up and canted his head in question. I nodded for him to start again and centered myself with a deep breath. Then I began to dance.

Not my sister's dance or any they'd seen before. *My* dance. I turned and twisted, feeling the connection with the packed earth beneath my feet. With each step, I sprinkled strands of Esme's hair. Calling her with her essence and with the dance.

Shouts and gasps rose from the crowd when she appeared, thin as smoke.

I continued the spell, pulling her further into this world, giving her solid form. Esme, who'd never stopped moving when music filled the air, stood still as stone. Her bright new costume, stained and ripped. She looked out at those men and smiled. I saw it briefly as I turned. She'd never worn that smile in life. The broken jaw and mutilations made it ghastly. The madness in her eyes made it so much worse.

Could I continue? I didn't want this to be my last memory of her.

Another twirl, my skirt fluttering like raven wings, and another woman formed ghostlike next to my sister. She wore green, with gruesome holes where her breasts belonged. I stumbled, shocked. Who was she? The spell needed hair, blood, or bone to link to a spirit and give them shape. The only way she could appear was if her blood had spilled here and soaked into the dirt beneath my feet.

A third woman appeared as I repeated the spell, followed swiftly by three more. Six women, including Esme, stood in my circle scowling at the men. Six women in a rainbow of dance costumes, who shared a certain beauty, a similarity of feature and form. And they all bore the wounds they'd died from. How much blood saturated this cold earth?

Esme's blood! She died here! The realization stole my breath. Her death and the death of these other women…Gods and Goddesses! They'd been part of the entertainment. How long had this been happening? Rage filled me, the heat of it rushing through my veins. Is that what these men planned for me? New energy, fueled by fury, spurred my steps.

"What trickery is this?" a man shouted.

And I changed the pattern of my dance in answer, unleashing Esme and her sisters-in-death—their forms now as solid as mine.

Esme stepped up to the fattest, ugliest gray-beard and dragged him from his couch by the hair. He punched her but she didn't cringe or waver beneath the blows. When she had him on his feet, she cradled his head, hands against his temples and squeezed. He wailed, screaming until his head caved in with a liquid crack.

Men scrambled to escape, but the woman with missing breasts blocked the door.

"We killed you," a man in the lead shouted and slashed at her with a short dagger. The blade carved another awful scar into her abdomen. No blood oozed from the dead gray flesh. "You're dead," he screeched, then gaped at the closing wound.

She took his knife, plunged it into his groin, and ripped it up his body until it became lodged in his ribs. I looked away as she tore out his entrails. It did me no good. Every turn revealed more blood and gore.

I had hoped Esme would point out the guilty and a magistrate would mete out justice. But the magistrate was here, meeting a different justice at the hands of the silent women. My stomach churned and I fought the rising bile. What had I let loose? Were innocent men being butchered? No. They had participated in rape and murder, even if only as avid spectators.

My dance gave power to these women that they hadn't had in their last hours. I couldn't stop dancing. I couldn't stop watching the slaughter. And I couldn't tune out the men's tortured howls mixed with the snap of bone and the moist sounds of rending flesh.

The chaos ended when the last Elder expelled his final, gurgled breath. The piper no longer played. I expected to find him cowering in his corner. Instead, Death watched from the shadows. He bowed.

And I understood. My studies had touched on darker magics. I hadn't used them, but they can't be avoided. Books and diaries filled with experiments and observations contained a blend of light and dark, helpful and destructive. I found the spells I'd used today in a slim journal picked up at a bazaar only a month ago.

Luck hadn't led me to my sister's body. Death had presented her to me as an invitation. This had become his house, binding him as surely as it bound these ghosts. Spirits of the women, tortured and killed for the pleasure of men who operated above the law.

I slowed my movements and changed the pattern once more, this time releasing the women from any earthly hold. As I completed my ritual, they became whole again. The visible scars disappeared and the madness left their eyes. They regained their stolen beauty. Each bowed her thanks to me before fading, finally finding their way to peace. Helping them, giving them this freedom, brought me a modicum of peace as well.

Esme remained. The sight of her, whole and unmarred, made me ache. This would be the last time I'd see her smile. I wanted to hold her, keep her with me. Run with her into the desert until we both turned to brittle bone.

Esme knew me too well. She shook her head and wiped a tear from my face. Her touch was warm, not the cold withered flesh I expected. Then she kissed my cheek and faded, leaving me alone.

The dance finished and the ghosts freed, I started shaking. The shivering began in my shoulders and moved through me. It made my hands tremble and weakened my knees. Charnel smells had my gorge rising and I forced myself to take shallow breaths until my stomach and limbs were once again in my control.

I weaved around the worst of the carnage, my feet leaden from exhaustion. The Reaper waited near the door. Thanking him didn't seem appropriate. I met his gaze, or what would have been his gaze had eyes still rested in his sockets. Staring into those bleak, dark cavities, souls stared back at me. Hundreds. Thousands. The longer I looked the more I saw: anger, pain, despair—

He broke the connection, pulling back and hiding his face in the shadow of his cowl. I don't think he meant to give me that vision. I must've gotten closer to the other side than either of us realized. No wonder he's considered grim, if the souls he carries only hold negative emotions.

Sorrow, grief, and the events of this day will haunt me until I'm as bent as the old village women. I'd wanted to find answers and accountability. I found them wrapped in more questions without answers. I wanted peace, but I don't think that's possible yet. I didn't expect to find compassion and pity for Death. But I'd stared him in the face and that...changed me. Again, I considered saying something to him, this time to express my sympathy. But I sensed he would not want that.

In the end, I nodded my respect, collected my robe and scarf, and lifted the rug to leave. One more glance over my shoulder and I witnessed Death begin his own dance. Graceful, beautiful in its own way.

I left to the hum of his scythe cutting the air as he collected the newly departed souls.

THE LEGEND OF JOHN BARRETT

Shaun Avery

His prisoner saw the strange town first.

Or perhaps it was more accurate to say that Gary the Torso felt it. Hanging from the side of Barrett's horse, tied to the saddle with a rope that looped tight around his waist, he suddenly went stiff, tense, saying, "Hey, what the hell is that?"

Barrett, never the pleasantest of people but feeling especially short-tempered and weary following this last bounty hunt, shot back, "What's what?"

"That. On the horizon."

Barrett pretended to look, peering through the trees of this dense forest. "Nope, can't see anything," he said. Then grinned to himself. "Why don't you point to it, whatever it is?"

Gary the Torso seemed to be considering these words. Before replying, "Barrett, you bastard, you think that's funny?"

Actually, Barrett did. In fact, he had been laughing when he first took this job, back at the Furthest Reach Agency a few weeks ago. The Agency specialized in the apprehension of supernatural criminals, employing bounty hunters to track them down and bring them in, so it dealt with all sorts of beings. Still, Barrett had been forced to ask the question, "How dangerous can a torso be?"

"Hey," had come the reply from Fingers, one of his fellow bounty hunters. "Guy's a Level Two."

This was the sliding scale they worked on at the Agency, the one they used to determine an offender's level of supernatural skills. It went all the way up to five, but few people had taken down many of those. Except Barrett, of course, though he suspected that some might think his methods had been…questionable.

"So?" he'd said to Fingers.

"So he's taken down a few of us already," Fingers had replied, then gone on to describe all the painful things that Gary the Torso had done to bounty hunters, bestowing injuries that would, at one time, have been invariably fatal. But Fingers was a sissy. And now the job was done, Gary the Torso safely apprehended, magic skills neutralized with a deadening dart, and Barrett should have been on his way back to a nice juicy payday, no complications needed along the way. But now he looked off into the distance and through the darkness of the night, through the thickness of the trees, he did indeed see what looked like the glow of a town.

He brought the horse to a stop, and dug around inside his trench coat for the map he had been using these past few weeks. Just one glance confirmed what he already knew—there wasn't supposed to be a town this far out in the countryside, miles away from anything. Still, what those damn fool mapmakers back at the Agency thought they knew about the world, and what was actually true were two very different things. He wanted to call them up and tear them a new set of orifices. But there was no mobile phone signal out here, so even that simple pleasure was denied him.

The thought made him focus further on the distant town.

Could they get a signal out here? he wondered. Whoever lived in this odd town, that did not seem to be on the map? Could people reach them? And if they could, how come?

It was enough to make him curious.

So he dismounted the horse and undid the rope around Gary the Torso's waist, letting his prisoner drop to the ground.

"Bastard," the prisoner said once again. "When we get back to the Agency I'm going to complain about you."

Barrett reached inside his trench coat again, this time coming out with a knife. "You might not make it back to the Agency yet, pal."

Then he turned back to the horse, letting his words sink in.

When he turned back, he had the length of rope in his hands. Within minutes he had Gary the Torso tied to a tree and was eager to leave him there and do some investigating.

But Gary the Torso was suddenly sweating, a scared look on his face.

"Barrett," he said. "Hey, Barrett. Don't leave me alone out here, man."

"You won't be alone." Barrett smiled, nodded towards the horse. "He'll be with you."

This seemed to make the prisoner sweat even more.

Barrett took a second to look the animal over—the sharp teeth, the dark eyes. The sense it gave was that this was not just any horse. It made him feel something a bit like ownership. But not quite.

"Yeah," he said, swinging his eyes back to Gary the Torso. "My friend here will look after you."

Then he walked off into the woods and towards the town.

* * *

Barrett wasn't really expecting much. Sure, he supposed, a place out in the wilds like this was strange. But in his job, he'd seen a lot stranger.

Then he saw the watchtower and his perspective changed.

Barrett squinted up at it, wishing he still had his binoculars. But Gary the Torso had used magic to smash them over his head during their struggle a few days ago, so he had to rely on his eyes. Which, given the darkness of the night and the fact he'd not slept for in a while, weren't too helpful.

Still, though…

He was pretty sure he saw a sentry up there.

His curiosity grew, making him wonder: Why did a place in the middle of nowhere have a watchtower and a sentry looking out over it?

* * *

"So what was it?"

Barrett untied his prisoner, let the man drop roughly to the floor. "Nothing," he said. Then he wandered over to his dark steed, ran a hand along its flank, caressed it lovingly.

"Come get your rope back on," he commanded the other man. "Move it. We've got a long journey ahead of us."

Outrage flashed across Gary the Torso's face. "What the hell are you talking about?" he said. "I can't levitate! You took my magic, remember?"

"So shuffle."

"Man, your manners are the pits," Gary the Torso said, looking up from the ground at him. "When I get back, I'm still making that complaint."

That comment finally wore the last of Barrett's limited patience.

"Yeah," he said, "about that," and he pulled his knife back out.

* * *

"Yeah, Chief, it was the weirdest thing," Barrett was saying a few days later. "Guy just bit off his own tongue."

Agency Chief Walker bent down and checked the mouth of the bound, heavily tranquilized Gary the Torso. "Looks more like it was severed to me."

"He was almost choking on bits that were only partially torn, sir," Barrett replied. "Had to cut those out for his own protection."

"Quite." Walker drew himself back to his full height. "Good work, John."

"Thank you, sir," Barrett said, while thinking, let's see the bastard make a complaint with no tongue.

The pair left the cells and wandered down the hallways of the Furthest Reach Detective Agency towards the Chief's office. Once there the older man sank into the seat behind his table and said, "Let me just sort out your fees, John. Anything interesting to report from your travels?"

Barrett thought of the strange town. "No, sir."

Walker rooted around in a drawer until he found the Agency checkbook and then began to write it out. "What you planning on doing now?"

"Probably take some downtime, sir," he replied. Though this, of course, was a lie. Downtime didn't pay the debts, and between hookers, gambling, and boozing Barrett was always running up plenty of those.

This thought prompted him to ask, "Anyone been around here looking for me?"

"No," the Chief replied. "Should there have been?"

The question seemed friendly enough. But beneath the words, Barrett detected suspicion. He cursed himself for having asked the question, knowing that the Chief liked to run a nice, simple organization here, did not want people's personal lives interfering in any way. So he brought the conversation back around to work, saying, "Old cases, old foes." And smiled, meeting the Chief's eyes. "You never know."

Apparently satisfied with this explanation, Walker went to hand over Barrett's check. But then paused as a third party entered the room.

* * *

Linda, the Chief's wife.

Barrett made his apologies and left them to it—after pocketing his check for bringing in Gary the Torso, of course. But he didn't go far, and when she exited the room and headed for the canteen, he dropped into step beside her.

"My fair lady," he said. "Care to get a room with me somewhere tonight?" He pulled the check out of his pocket, waved it around. "I got me some money to spend."

"You disgust me, Barrett," she replied, face suggesting that she meant every word.

"Disgust just turns me on, baby."

She looked over at him. "You know, my husband would stop giving you work if he knew you were harassing me like this."

He grinned. "Sweetheart, please—me and Walker go way back. I saved his ass in that Wild Weird Witch case. Think he's going to believe I would do the dirty on him?"

"He might."

"You're dreaming," he replied. "Besides, I'm the best hunter he's got."

She nodded, almost involuntarily, and he knew she saw the truth in these words.

Still she was defiant, saying, "Clever guy, aren't you?" Then she paused in the doorway of the canteen. "But what if I was wearing a wire and had recorded everything you just said?"

"You're not that clever," he told her, smiling at her back as she headed into the canteen.

Then, just as he put the check back inside his pocket, a hand fell on his shoulder.

* * *

"Should be an easy one," Fingers was saying a short while later. "We know exactly where he is, just a case of going in there and getting him."

"So why do you need me?" Barrett asked.

Fingers shrugged. "Travelling alone sucks."

"Right."

"One condition, though."

"Yeah?" This amused Barrett. "What is it?"

"We go by car," Fingers said. "I don't want you taking that...thing." And he pointed to the stable in which Barrett's horse was tied up.

"You don't like my ride?"

"Nope." Fingers shivered. "Thing gives me the creeps."

Barrett smiled. "That's not all he does."

* * *

Fingers' car was a piece of shit, which meant he'd probably not scored any good fees lately. It further explained why he'd come to him for help—Barrett's reputation was well-established among the other hunters at the Furthest Reach Agency.

"How'd you know where this guy is, anyway?" Barrett asked, getting into the passenger seat of the vehicle.

Fingers sat down at the wheel. "Got word from a source of mine."

"Oh yeah? Anyone I know?"

"I doubt it." Fingers held something out to him. "Here."

Barrett took the file containing all the information on their prey. He read it as his colleague started up the car.

Seemed their prey's name was William Black-stone—a pretty fitting name, Barrett thought, for one versed in the dark arts. And he was indeed versed in them; the guy was wanted for Human Sacrifice and Illicit Worship Rituals. But, like Gary the Torso, he was only a Level Two, so Barrett wasn't too worried about the job.

But he began to change his mind when they reached their destination.

It had once been a dusty desert town—remote but warm and welcoming. Now, as Fingers pulled the car to a stop and they both stepped out, they saw things had changed considerably.

On each house hung a dead body. All nailed to the walls through hands, heads, and feet. And they were all singing. Chanting. Repeating the words, "Praise William, worship His name."

Barrett checked his arsenal, reaching deep inside the huge, deep pockets of his trusty trench coat. Then he and Fingers headed towards the nearest hanging body—an obese woman with too much makeup on her dead face.

"Ma'am," Barrett said, greeting her.

She hissed back at him.

They all did, the dead bodies, straining at the walls to get at the two hunters.

Technically, this case belonged to Fingers; Barrett was just there as back-up, plus, of course, a split of the fee. But he was in the mood to hurt somebody, so he said to the hanging woman, "Care to point us in the direction of the great and mighty William?"

She hissed again. Snarled.

"I'm guessing she doesn't count as fully human anymore," Barrett told Fingers, pulling something from within his coat. "Which means it's perfectly acceptable to do this."

He flung the vial from his hands. Saw the glass shatter against the dead woman's face. Heard the sizzle and smelt the burn as the holy water burnt away what was left of her skin.

"The church!" she screamed, sounding a lot more human now. "He's waiting in the church!"

"Much obliged, ma'am," Barrett said, grinning up at her. Then he looked back to Fingers. "Your show," he said. "After you."

* * *

There was a throne inside the church. It was made of human skin, and a figure—sort of—sat on it.

At the figure's feet lay a disturbing sight: a skeleton that still possessed a human face, the rest of its skin removed via methods arcane and now making up, Barrett guessed, the bulk of the throne.

When he saw the mostly skinless body, Fingers gasped and said, "Paulo!"

So, Barrett thought, this is the "source."

The figure on the throne, meanwhile, had no face and no hands—at least none that could be seen. The rest of his body was encased in a dark cloak, and he spoke with a deep croak. "My dear hunters," William Blackstone said, "I've been waiting."

"We're taking you in," Fingers said, walking up the aisle towards the figure. "Dead or alive, up to you."

"Too late." And here, Barrett was sure that Blackstone's invisible eyes turned to him. "Can't you see I've already broken bread with Death?"

Barrett started following Fingers, heading towards their prey and not liking what the guy might be about to say.

"Yes," Blackstone went on, "come for me. Take me in. I might be able to tell you all some interesting facts about—"

That was when a shot rang out, cutting off the man's words.

Blackstone fell from his throne, tripping over Paulo's skeleton and landing loudly on his back.

Fingers gasped, then looked down and saw a gleaming silver bullet in the nothingness where the man's face should have been.

Behind him, Barrett lowered his gun. "Go call the Agency for a cleanup crew," he said. "I'll watch the body."

"But why did you...he was coming quietly..."

"Call the Agency," he repeated, putting a hand on his colleague's arm. "Now."

Fingers did as he was told, running back to his car to grab his phone.

Then it was just Barrett and the body. He looked down at it for a few seconds, waiting, wondering. But nothing happened.

This one was dead.

* * *

He accepted a thirty percent share of the fee on William Blackstone—less than he would have usually taken, to be sure, but he thought it best to keep Fingers sweet. The guy was still sore about what he saw as an unjustifiable killing.

Barrett could have explained it in some way, but he decided it would be better to let his reputation do the job for him. He was known for being a dirty and uncompromising hunter—that should be enough to answer any questions about his conduct. And anyway, since the warrant on Blackstone had said dead or alive, what the hell was Fingers complaining about? Barrett didn't know. Or care.

The "dead or alive" clause was an interesting one, though—since, these days, death was not at all assured. Death came and went as he pleased, letting some people live until they were two hundred, leaving some—like Gary the Torso—in a state that once, many years ago, would have always led to death. You saw it all the time—men and women shuffling around with wounds that should have killed them, massive gaping things, leaking pus and blood everywhere. In fact, the only time death was completely reliable now was when it came to violent death, specifically murder. And there was always plenty of that when Barrett was around. Still, though...

Blackstone's words had him worried.

Many people—like Barrett himself, and certainly like Chief Walker—were quite happy with the way things were in this strange new world. But many weren't, and some of them weren't the sort of people you wanted on your tail. So if Barrett's part in helping create this situation ever became public knowledge, he knew he'd spend the rest of his life watching his back. Even more than he did now. And he didn't want that.

He needed time to think, to plan. So as soon as he cashed his share of the fee he took off on his horse and rode, just rode. And soon found himself heading for the unmapped town again.

* * *

He'd contemplated mentioning the place to Walker, but unless it was filled with ghosts and demons, the Chief would know nothing about the town, let alone be interested in it. Plus, Barrett was already thinking this place might be useful to him.

He watched it now from a distance, back out in the woods, peering through binoculars, focusing in on the watchtower.

Barrett grinned. The guy up there was a bonny fucker. Tattoos, scars, a sneer that a rock star would die for—not to mention a great big rifle in his hands.

Barrett pondered taking him out—just a single shot in the dark and the guy wouldn't have a throat anymore. But that would put the town on red alert, wouldn't it? It might even make them move on.

But who were they? Why were they here? Why did they need an armed guard? Barrett needed to figure these things out—they could be useful to him in some way. The smallest trace of a plan started to form in his mind.

"What do you think, boy?" he asked the horse, dropping the binoculars. "What do you think I should do?"

Its dark eyes stared back at him, as if seeing what lay at the back of his mind. As if approving of it.

* * *

The riders came out the next morning.

Barrett had made a camp in the woods and had woken up early to watch. Now his surveillance routine was paying off, as four men set forth from the town on horseback.

His own steed seemed eager to give chase, perhaps sensing how such a pursuit would end. But if he wanted to get some answers, Barrett knew he would have to be stealthy, tail them discreetly.

As it turned out, they didn't go far. They went to the stream.

They left their houses high on the hill overlooking the water and headed down towards it. Barrett saw that they were armed. Sort of.

They had sharpened sticks, which they began to jab into the stream.

"I'm sick of eating fish," one of them, a man with a beard that seemed to be chewing its way across and around his face, said.

"Head to the next town, then, wherever it is," another of them replied—this one with his back to Barrett. "See how long it takes them to organize a necktie party, just for you."

The other two laughed at this.

"Eat shit, Collins," the bearded man said.

"Make me."

"That's enough," said the last of the quartet. This one was older, white of hair but bright blue of eye. Barrett could sense that this was the man in charge, the man that he needed to talk to. "Let's just do our job and get on home."

"Some home," the bearded man commented.

"It's the only one we've got," the old man told him, sounding so sad and weary that Barrett almost felt sorry for him. But pity wouldn't stop him from beating some answers out of the old guy.

As if sensing this thought, as if drawn by violence, the steed came up silently behind him.

The four men were pulling fish out of the water now, stuck to the end of their sharpened sticks, and throwing them to the ground, where Collins quickly gutted them and placed them all in a big pile. A messy business, to be sure, but the situation was actually starting to make some sense to Barrett.

Is the whole town a sanctuary for criminals? Does that lone sentry stand on guard against the forces of law and order?

Had Barrett worked for a regular bounty hunting agency, he could have been sitting on a goldmine here. But since the Furthest Reach only dealt with supernatural criminals, Walker wouldn't give a shit about this place.

Still, though...

There was other business in his life, was there not? Yes, indeed. And his plan was becoming clearer all the time.

Barrett went to take care of the quartet's horses.

* * *

They came back up the hill and Barrett didn't even give them a chance—he just drew his gun and dropped the three younger men. Leaving just the old guy.

Barrett was hoping he would piss himself with fear, but he was disappointed. The man, instead, threw his sharpened stick at Barrett.

The bounty hunter threw himself to the ground, firing instinctively and hitting the ground just as a bullet tore out the man's throat.

The old guy collapsed backwards, meeting the ground with a crash, sprawling beside the bloody carcasses of the torn-open horses.

"Shit," Barrett said, holstering his gun, walking over to the body. "Wanted you alive, you old fart."

Still, he thought, looking around, four dead horses and four dead people, all within a matter of minutes, was pretty good work, even if there wasn't any money in it.

He looked towards the town in the distance.

That was when the dead old man spoke.

"Bounty hunter," the voice said. "Thief. I've been looking for you."

Barrett looked down. His horse looked up. Both of them recognized the voice.

A voice that, quite clearly, did not belong to the dead man. It was not even a voice that belonged to this world, yet Barrett knew to whom it belonged.

"Tonight," it said, "I come for you."

Then it spoke no more. The corpse was just a corpse, but Barrett knew he was working now to a deadline.

* * *

He still couldn't get a signal in this godforsaken place, so he had to backtrack quite significantly before he could use his phone. When he finally found some coverage, though, there was only one call he could make.

"Furthest Reach Detective Agency."

"Linda! They got you manning the desk now?"

"Oh, hell. What do you want, Barrett?"

Just in case the calls were recorded, he decided he'd best be all business. "Get me Fingers, please."

She did so.

"Got some business for you, Fingers," he said, and then gave his colleague directions.

* * *

He didn't know how long the four fishermen normally took on their travels, wasn't sure how much time he had before someone in the town might get suspicious. But Barrett didn't suppose it mattered too much; either his plan would work tonight, or he would be fresh out of tomorrows.

Fingers arrived just as evening was settling in, parking his shit-mobile near the entrance to the woods. "This better be worth it," he said, exiting the vehicle.

"Oh, it will be."

Fingers leant back against the car. "So what's this 'business' you were talking about?"

"The best kind, Fingers," Barrett replied. "How'd you like to take down some bad guys?"

Fingers looked uneasy. "Any hunting activity has to go through Chief Walker."

"Only if it's supernatural crooks we're chasing, Fingers." Barrett shook his head. "That's not what we'd be doing."

"It isn't?"

"No," Barrett said, and told Fingers what he thought they would find in the strange town up ahead.

"I checked the ID on the guys I shot," he concluded. "In self-defense, of course. They're all known criminals, Fingers." This was true—well, apart from the self-defense bit. But here he deviated slightly from the truth, adding, "And one of them, just before he died, he told me that's what the whole village is. A safe haven for criminals." Playing to his colleague's sense of justice, he added, "You willing to let them get away with that?"

Fingers wasn't.

As Barrett had known he wouldn't be.

"So what do you want me to do?" Fingers asked.

Barrett smiled, and pointed towards the watchtower.

* * *

7:22p.m.

The night was drawing in.

Barrett had made his way around to the other side of town and he was unsurprised to find they had a guard there, too. This one, though, didn't have anything as fancy as a watchtower to hide in; he was just patrolling the street, rifle in hand.

Barrett attached the silencer to his gun, waited until the sentry was turned away from him, and shot the guy in the back of the head.

Then he crept over to the body and dragged it into a dusty back alley, out of sight.

Fingers would be taking out the other sentry, the one in the watchtower, soon. He knew this was a necessity to keep the element of surprise on their side.

But the fool also thought that they would be taking some of the fugitives in alive.

Wrong. So very wrong.

Barrett checked his gun, smiling.

* * *

7:40p.m.

Barrett was creeping through the town.

There wasn't much sense of a community here; there weren't many people on the streets. He guessed that was what happened when you were surrounded by criminals; it would be hard to open up and trust anyone. But he would take care of that.

He knocked on the first door he came to, gun held out in front of him, ready and waiting to be used.

Seconds later, the door swung open, revealing a heavily-tattooed woman with an eye-patch and a sneer. "Yeah?" she said.

Barrett answered with his gun, a single, well-placed shot taking away most of the girl's face. She fell back into the house.

It had begun.

* * *

The insular and unfriendly nature of the town worked to his favor—everyone kept to themselves, no one had visitors, and Barrett was able to slaughter his way through dozens of households before he was spotted.

It was a thin, weedy guy in a jogging suit—pedophile, Barrett would have said, if he'd had to guess a crime—that saw him, and he immediately shouted, "Hey, hey, intruder!"

The guy got a bullet through his teeth as reward for his big mouth.

But now doors were opening and people were emerging from houses with guns, and Barrett knew he was in trouble.

* * *

He leapt through the window of a dusty, derelict building as a barrage of bullets swept over him.

He returned fire, but there was a veritable posse out there. He needed a vast number of corpses to save his own skin, but he'd been hoping to catch them all unaware and alone, not have them ganging up on him like this.

They were pressing close to the building. And now more people were joining them. He needed a miracle, but God had long since abandoned him. Ever since he had committed the crime that had brought him here, to this moment.

Fuck it, he thought, and jumped to his feet, ready to make his last stand.

But that was when two members of the posse fell. Shot down. The shots come from far away.

Some of the posse turned away from him, firing back in the direction that the other shots had come from. Some leapt for cover, but it was too late. The element of surprise had not left them enough time to mount an adequate defense, and soon they all lay dead.

That was when Barrett's savior arrived: Fingers. Walking towards the scene with gun in hand, the weapon still smoking.

"Boy, am I glad to see you," Barrett said, but he couldn't help noticing that Fingers hadn't lowered the gun, that it was now pointed at him. "Hey," he said, "you can put that thing away now."

"Everyone is dead, Barrett," Fingers said.

"Self-defense. I don't know if you noticed, Fingers, but they were trying to kill me."

"Not them," Fingers replied. "I just took a walk around the place—you murdered people in their homes, Barrett. They were all unarmed."

"Would you believe they were resisting arrest?"

"No," Fingers replied. "Now tell me what's been going on."

Barrett shrugged, a chill in his bones telling him that the guest he'd been expecting had arrived.

Fingers felt it, too.

"You never liked my horse, did you?" Barrett suddenly said.

"What?"

"Well, here's a fact for you, Fingers old boy: it's not really my horse."

As if on cue, the steed walked down the street towards them. It stopped to sniff at the pile of dead bodies, then came to stand behind Barrett. "I stole it," he told Fingers. The chill was growing stronger now. "I stole it from Death himself."

"Death?"

"That's right. Why do you think so many people can't be killed? Death's not as powerful as he once was. Some of the power is in him, some of it is in his horse. They need each other to do the job right. And I…I sort of ruined that."

Barrett gripped his gun tighter, feeling as close to fear as he had ever felt in his life.

"That's why I had to shoot William Blackstone," he continued. "Once I knew he'd talked with Death. I didn't want him letting my secrets out to you."

"You expect me to believe that?" Fingers said.

Barrett shrugged. "If you don't believe me, ask him." And he pointed.

Fingers looked around.

Standing there behind him, black of cape and skeletal of face, was the form of Death himself.

Barrett looked at its blank white face. "I know you're angry, Death," he said. "But we can work this out. We can do a deal, Death."

The figure said nothing. Yet its empty eyes seemed to scream a million threats of vengeance into Barrett's mind. But he knew what he was doing, knew one important fact about Death. The guy was greedy.

All those deaths he'd been deprived of over these last few years, not being able to fully operate without his horse that must have meant a pretty hungry stomach. And Barrett knew just how to fill it.

"We've killed a whole town here for you," he went on. "And there's much more where that came from."

Death came closer.

"Haven't I proven that to you tonight?" Barrett asked. "Haven't I just sent hundreds of dead souls your way?" He smiled. "And I know you get these ones, can feel them, Death. You always can, with murders."

Fingers looked back towards him. Mouth hanging open, eyes wide, looking shocked that he'd been played this way.

"If you let me escape," Barrett told Death, "I'll send even more, whole towns full of souls your way." He grinned. "A feast of dead bodies."

"Oh, you bastard," Fingers said, "you're not using me." And he raised his gun.

But Barrett shot first.

Fingers' head exploded, cascading over Death's cape.

"Consider that a starter," Barrett said. Then he walked out into the street, towards Death. "So, big guy, what do you say?" He motioned around the massacred town. "Plenty here to keep you busy."

Death looked around, too. It was impossible to tell what he was thinking. There were no eyes to peer in to, no soul to investigate. All Barrett could do was stand there, feeling the power of this ageless being, diminished though it was, wash over him, and hope that he had laid enough temptation in Death's way.

And finally Death looked back at him. "Deal."

This close to that voice, even Barrett shivered. The imposing figure began to turn.

"Oh, and one more thing."

Death looked back, to see Barrett's gun at the horse's head.

"I like this world just the way it is," the bounty hunter said. "I'm not ready for you and the rest of your Horsemen yet." He smiled. "So I keep the horse."

There was almost a smirk in Death's voice. "Don't you trust me, human?"

Barrett shrugged. "Does anyone trust you?"

Death did laugh at this. Then he walked over to the pile of bodies, crouched down over them.

Not too keen to see what happened next, Barrett turned away, but Death's voice called him back.

"Many people you've sent my way," he said. "Even before you took that which was mine. Keep up the good work—but know that one day, I will come for you."

Barrett nodded.

Much like the rest of the world—except those taken from it by murder, many of those at his future hands—he guessed he could live with that.

He climbed back onto the horse and set out for the Furthest Reach Agency, hoping to find a few more towns along the way.

THE WOLVES OF LADY DEATH

Christie Golden

"That is a happy audience tonight," Lev said, listening to the crowd from the shadows.

"Yes, they are," agreed his wife, slipping an arm around his waist. "I wish we had audiences like this every night!"

"The Man No Lock Could Hold" could seemingly escape from everything—except for his wife's loving embrace. Lev pulled Dava close and kissed the top of her dark head, while their daughter Gillien watched fondly.

"I warmed them up for you, Gilly," her brother Kellien Steadyhand said airily. "No rotting fruit will be thrown at you tonight."

Gillien, known as Songespynner, rolled her eyes. "I'm the one who opened the show," she reminded him. "I warmed them up for you, and Mama, and Papa…and no one's ever thrown rotting fruit at me."

"That's all beside the point," Kellien said, and then, "Ow!" as his twin sister gave him a pinch.

The performing family had an established routine. Gillien introduced each act with a song or a story, and now, she was to provide the final performance of the evening. Every time she'd stepped out before the audience tonight, she'd told them to prepare. *I will close the evening with a special challenge! See if you can find something that I can't make a story or song about!*

Thus far, over the last few years she'd been issuing the challenge, no one had bested her. Gillien knew a song about almost anything—and if by some odd chance she didn't, it wasn't hard for her to make something up with a moment or two of thought. Many in the audience came back night after night when the performers were in town, eager to find out what the new challenge would be.

Now, Gillien caught snatches of excited conversation. A fire had been burning at the center of the encampment all evening, providing sufficient light for the performers to be clearly seen for appropriate appreciation. Gillien took a breath and stepped out, tall and self-assured.

For the finale, she had changed into her most expensive outfit: a wine-colored skirt and matching bodice made of the finest linen her family could afford. Her mother had even embroidered the bodice with golden thread, which now glinted in the firelight. The crowd really was one of the best the family had entertained and Gillien's smile was wide and real. She carried her mandolin in one hand and waved with the other, coaxing forth cheers and applause.

"So," she called, "are you ready for tonight's challenge?" Another round of clapping and whoops of delight. "Wonderful! I hope you've all been thinking very carefully about what you want to hear!"

Gillien lifted her instrument. Long fingers with short nails plucked a jaunty little tune and she gazed out at the crowd.

"You have seen my father's escapes," the young bard said, "and the astounding grace of Dava the Bird. Some of you almost got your beards shaved by my twin's knife throwing!"

The crowd laughed at that. While Kellien's hands were indeed steady, he loved to rattle those brave enough to stand up and permit themselves to have very real, very sharp blades thrown at them.

"But you know, and I know, that this is what you've been waiting for. Am I right?"

Good-natured choruses of variants on yes and more applause greeted her. "Now…who shall I pick? Someone who wants a love story?" The melody she played turned sweet and slow and soft. "Or someone who yearns for a bold tale of adventure?" A tune that was urgent and excited was coaxed from the instrument. "Perhaps someone wants a story about magic and elven enchantments?" The notes now were haunting and dreamy. Gillien was well aware that songs and tales about elves were usually very popular with crowds. People liked things they both feared and dreamed of.

"I've got a challenge!" came a young voice.

Gillien turned, seeking the speaker. It was a young man, only a few years older than she was, with a short, neatly trimmed beard. His eyes were bright and his face flushed from partaking of the now-limp wine sack on the ground beside him. His clothes, Gillien noticed at once, were quite fine. If she met this fellow's challenge, she'd likely get a tidy sum.

A young woman with a fall of blond hair snuggled into his side. The firelight was enough to reveal the soft curve of a belly rounded with the first few months of pregnancy. The man was grinning, and the girl playfully shoved him and murmured, "Love, don't!"

"Oho!" Gillien exclaimed. "My good sir, don't ask me to do any challenge that will drive apart such a happy couple!"

The pair giggled and drew closer. With his arm around his wife, the husband said, "I want you to make my wife like wolves!"

Gillien blinked, keeping a pleasant expression on her face. This ... was odd. In response to her husband's comment, the woman frowned, shaking her head as if to say *that's never going to happen.* "I know they prey on livestock," the husband continued, "but they're also very fierce and strong. Noble creatures. I'm a Davynn, and it's our house sigil, and I can't get my beautiful and otherwise perfect lady to love them as much as she loves me."

Gillien's heart leaped. She'd been right about the fine clothes. She curtseyed, deeply.

"I did not know we had nobility among us! You are most welcome, sir!" The man was obviously not the shire's liege lord—who would certainly not find his way to a humble bard's circle far from his comfortable ancestral home—but some lesser cousin. Nonetheless, this Davynn's coin would likely be yellower than most she usually received.

But it was a challenge indeed. Wolves could ruin a shepherd's livelihood, and their howls chilled the blood as they sang to—

Gillien's gaze was drawn by the movement of the lady's hand, dropping to caress the mound of her belly.

And just like that, Gillien knew what she would do.

"I accept your challenge. By the end of my story, if your lady wife can say truly that her opinion of wolves has not changed for the better, then you, sir, will have the honor of victory."

"I'd rather she'd not fear wolves," the young noble said, and everyone laughed.

"Me, too," Gillien said, and they laughed louder. She lifted a hand for their attention, and the crowd settled down expectantly. Gillien placed her mandolin down, clasped her hands in front of her and began to walk a slow path around the blazing fire, allowing them another moment to grow attentive, and then she began.

"There is a story, about one of the Seven Gods of Mortal-Kind," Gillien began. The fire crackled and a twig popped. "This is not a tale of the blessed Health, nor of the strange but kindly Traveler, or of beautiful, gentle Love. It is a tale of one of the darker deities. One whom, one day, we must all meet."

They were quiet, now. Listening.

"This is a tale," said Gillien Songespynner, "of Lady Death."

* * *

I am not cruel.

She stood regarding the elderly man in the sweat-stained sheets. His eyes darted beneath closed eyelids, and his body was knobby and twisted from joints swollen and aflame with agony. He was so thin, Lady Death could count each one of his ribs. She knew, for it was her task to know such things, that there was a mass growing inside him, hard and lethal.

His family sat with him in the small room. Death's gaze settled on them each in turn: the young grandchildren and their softly sobbing mother, the stoic son, and the soon-to-be widow. Some had love in their hearts. Some had hatred or, perhaps worse at such a moment, disinterest.

Lady Death knew these things, too.

Then there was the sound. The man's breathing became less a labored inspiration than a rattle; the somber declaration that soon, soon, there would be an end. She leaned forward and pressed warm, soft lips tenderly upon the salty, heated, pain-furrowed brow.

I am not cruel, she thought again. *I am kind.*

The man's restlessness eased. His body relaxed, the deep furrows in his forehead fading to simple lines. He breathed in, and breathed out.

Something else left his lips other than air: a tendril of what looked like sunlight, or spun gold, or the petal of that flower of many names which turns its face upward to the light.

This golden mist, too, sought the Light. It curled on itself, until it became a gentle orb of radiance, and floated to settle into the cupped palm of Lady Death's alabaster hand.

The man in the bed had been gentle and full of humor in life. He had cared for his family, his friends, and even strangers. He had loved his wife, the thin-lipped woman whose eyes were dry as she watched her husband's passing.

Lady Death could be both heard and seen when she desired. She did not choose to be either now. The family knew well enough they were in the presence of death.

She passed by the weeping daughter and the son struggling not to weep, past the confused, sad, frightened grandchildren, and paused next to this world's newest widow.

"I will come for you, too, soon enough," she said quietly. The woman tensed, sensing Death nearby, and shivered, but her darting gaze fell upon nothing. "And your soul will wait much, much longer in the darkness than this one ere it moves to the Light."

* * *

Lady Death had sprung into being the moment the first living thing had died, and nothing crossed from this world to the Light that waited to embrace it without her. Creatures so small that they passed unseen; insects that hatched, lived, mated, and died; plants and animals and humans—even elves, who lived so very long indeed, though they perceived her as an aspect of their goddess, the Lady—all were gathered by her. All were equal in death. Time and distance were her playthings; else no single entity could shepherd the dying.

It was that solitary state which weighed upon her.

She was not frightening to look upon. After all, was she not the sister of the goddesses Love and Health? Some said she was the shadow of that honored deity, but it was not so. Sisters they were, each with their own duties, and tenderness was between them.

Lady Death could appear as whatever she wished, but most often, those who beheld her saw a young human woman, with pale skin and long, flowing white hair. She was dressed in a black gown, and bore a rosewood staff with inlaid jewels. The just, good, and kind received a kiss and easeful passing. The rosewood staff struck down the wicked.

Or so it was said, at any rate.

Once, in one of the moments out of time, Lady Death went to Health and flung herself into her sister's arms, weeping.

"I am so alone," she said in a thick, broken voice. "They all fear me; all but a few. They beg me not to come, they curse my name, and only the darkest souls ask for my blessing for their shadowy deeds.

"All I will touch, but none will touch me. All will come with me, but none will walk beside me and see the beauty in passing that I do. I will know all that lives, but they do not wish to know me."

Her sister held her, comforting and soothing. "Death is your realm," she said. "You are its queen, its lady. Perhaps you are alone because you choose to be."

"No, I would have companions if I could. But the souls have their own destiny that is not mine to determine."

"This is true," Health agreed, her beautiful eyes kind as she stroked her sister's moonlight hair. It was soft and smelled pleasant. "But how you take those souls...whose sovereignty is that?"

For a thousand years, or an instant, Death pondered the words of her loving sister. But she had no answer.

Then, one cold winter night, she came for a child, as she had time without number before.

The girl was beautiful. Soft-eyed, bright with bubbly laughter, she was only three when Death appeared at her bedside as the girl burned with fever. Gently, Death regarded her. Such a bright spirit. She would move to the Light like a bird on the wing, swiftly and joyfully. Lady Death bent down to kiss the girl's dry, hot forehead, then paused when she heard words.

"Please...Lady Death...do not take her!"

Death turned to regard the woman who sat beside the child's bed, clinging to the tiny hand. She was unkempt, having tended to her daughter and not herself for so very long. Wild, but calm. And despair wrapped her like an aura.

So often, Death had heard these words. Those who were about to be left behind as their loved one went on begged, pleaded, threatened. But there was something about this woman that struck her. And so, as the wind sighed softly in the trees, Lady Death stood in the moonlight coming through the window, gazing sadly at the mother. And the mother saw.

"I do what I must," Lady Death said.

"Do you? This little girl, only a child, so sweet and funny and bright—you must take her?"

Lady Death nodded her white head.

"You must have a soul tonight?"

"I must have many souls tonight," Death said, regretful that her words caused the mother to wince.

"Then take mine."

It was not the first time the offer had been made. But now, after her conversation with her sister, Lady Death paused. The death of all that lived was inevitable…but was the hour of it? If it was, then how was it that Health could bring the dead back if she chose? Or prevent them from departing by allowing her priestess Blessers to heal?

None could cheat Lady Death. She would have her due.

But must she harvest the precious fruit at the first moment of ripeness?

Her heart, which was warm despite what many thought, swelled with hope. Still, she was kind, and wished to make certain the woman understood the nature of her request.

"If I take your daughter now," Lady Death said, "her pain will cease. She will never have her heart broken. She will never have her dreams destroyed, or know unkindness or violence or cruelty. She will not hunger or thirst, or mistrust, or fear. She will move swiftly to the Light, tasting only joy from the moment my lips press against her brow."

It gave the woman pause, but only for a moment. Then, with a sad smile, the mother replied. "But she will also never know a lover's touch, nor a full heart. She will never learn a skill, nor comfort someone less strong than she. She will never again laugh with a human voice, touch with a human hand, taste good food or drink sweet liquids. There will be no more songs or laughter, and Lady Death, even our tears are marks of having loved."

"You speak the truth," Lady Death said, and then made her offer. She clasped her hands in front of her to still their trembling; she, the reaper of souls, found herself shy, and excited, and a little afraid.

"The choice is yours. I would have a companion. One to walk with me, as I pluck souls as human girls do roses. Who would witness deaths uncountable. Who would help me to direct the souls along their paths, for not all are like your daughter, who is pure and ready to speed to the Light. Some must earn their way.

"I will turn from your child tonight, if you will turn to me."

The woman did not hesitate. "I will walk with you." Her eyes blazed with determination and joy. "For the life of my little one, I will do these things you speak of."

Again, Lady Death regarded the child, whose smooth forehead furrowed in a sleep that was more than sleep. Silently, Lady Death asked for her sister's blessing, if what she was about to do was right.

The little girl sighed. Lady Death watched the illness inside her depart with that breath, a sickly green-black of not-rightness, puff after puff, and then—a long pause.

With a gasp, the girl breathed in again, and exhaled only air.

The mother stared, her tears of grief and fear now those of utter joy and disbelief. "She...how long will she live?"

Lady Death waved that aside. "A moment. A hundred years. Time means nothing to me, and now, it means nothing to you. You offered. I have accepted."

Fear flickered across the mortal's face for just an instant. Then, she rose, brushing at her hair in an unconscious effort to look more presentable. The motion warmed Lady Death's heart as she found her own fingers patting at her hair. The two women locked eyes.

And then, they both smiled.

"I am...dead?" the mother asked.

"You are dying."

"May I kiss her goodbye?"

"Yes. But only once. A second time, and she must come with you, and neither of us wishes that."

"You are not cruel," the mother said. She sounded surprised. Her gaze traveled back to her daughter, breathing easily, deeply now. She bent and pressed cooling lips to the slumbering child's forehead. Then, straightening, she turned to Lady Death.

"I am your servant now. Command me."

"Oh, no, no," Lady Death said quickly, going to her and slipping a hand into hers. The woman looked startled to find that Death's hand was warm. "You are my sister, now! I am not alone. There is beauty to be seen, and I will show it to you. Peace to experience. Sorrow to bear witness to, with a full heart. We will run through this world, beholding all. Together."

"Forever?"

Lady Death graced her with a radiant smile. "Until you are ready to move into the Light." She gestured at the chair. "Look."

The woman obeyed, and gasped, to see herself—no, not herself, just her body, just her shell that had once housed the undying soul, lying slumped and still.

At that moment, the door opened and a man entered the sickroom. Lady Death knew his heart and understood that he, like his wife, was a loving parent, a devoted spouse. He bore a bowl of soup, which fell to the floor and cracked into pieces, its contents seeping unnoticed across the stone as he stared at the shell in the chair.

"Papa?" came a soft voice from the bed as the little girl reached out a hand to her father.

The man stifled a sob of joy and tremendous grief. He rushed to the girl and clung to her, unable to answer. His wife stepped forward and tried to touch him, but her spectral hand could not touch his solid, living flesh.

"They have each other," Death said gently.

"Yes, they do," the woman said, her voice thick and sad, but also contented. She turned away from the scene of father and daughter, away from the cares and joys of the living, and looked Lady Death squarely in her beautiful face.

"What now?" the woman asked, steadily.

Lady Death had chosen well in choosing this soul. And she knew what she wanted this woman—the first of those who would soon be her companions, her sisters—to be.

For herself to be.

"We will be women, still. But we shall be something more. There is a beast that humans fear. They are right to fear it, in a way; but mostly, they fear it because they do not understand it. They do not understand that it does not howl, it sings. That the little ones are raised by all. That they live as families. So we will take their forms, you, I, and those who will join with us. We will hunt together and gather souls, and when they are ready for the Light, we will release them joyfully in song."

"That sounds...beautiful," the woman said. "What are these creatures?"

Lady Death smiled. "They...we...are wolves," she said.

* * *

Gillian spoke softly to the crowd, her voice still carrying. "They hunt souls, do the wolves of Lady Death. To this day, they hunt, golden, and glowing, following the shadow-gray form of their sister. They follow her at night, silent beneath the moon and stars, and they follow her at day, unseen; at twilight, and at dawn, at this moment, and the ones before and after.

"They come with purpose to the dying, and swallow the glowing orbs that are human souls. And when that hour comes that the soul is ready to pass to the Light, they throw back their heads and sing to the moon, which is as pale and beautiful as Lady Death. So it is that the soul passes on, joyous and unburdened, at last joining with the Light."

The young nobleman was no longer jovial. The arm that had been loosely draped about his wife's shoulder now pressed her close. And she—her eyes were filled with tears, one hand on her belly. When the young bard asked her, in the hush following the last line, what she now thought of wolves, the future mother said, smiling through her tears, "They are beautiful."

As the spell cast by the tale faded and the crowd began to applaud with great enthusiasm, the performer looked back at her family, proud, happy. They were smiling, holding one another as the nobleman and his wife embraced.

Unseen, a woman with pale skin, white hair, and a long black dress watched from the shadows. Her spirit-wolves sat at her feet. Lady Death had not known that mortals knew the tale, and this rendition of it pleased her. Her gaze moved slowly over the crowd, lingering at last at the happy performing family cheering for their beaming daughter.

They were good, kind people, creative and giving. Their hearts held so much love, they would move swiftly to the Light, Lady Death knew.

She hoped the young bard would remember that.

WEDDING VOWS
Leah Cutter

Present-ish

Wan Ho stood outside of the grand courthouse, waiting.

He didn't know how long he'd been standing there. In the land of the dead, it was difficult to track time. Plus, since he'd died, he'd found he'd lost the impatience of his youth and now could wait contentedly like an old man. He didn't even miss his cell phone—normally when waiting he'd pull it out and play a game, or text his friends, or even watch silly cat videos.

For now, he merely stood. And waited, full of peace. Though every now and again he felt a very brief stirring of chill-inducing anticipation for...what, he wasn't sure.

A misty river ran a few yards in front of him, the riverbed slightly lower than the grassy plane he stood on. The gurgling sound of the water soothed him. The faint scent of sweet incense delightfully filled the air. While Wan Ho suspected the incense wasn't being burned for him, by his family still living in Shanghai, he still breathed it in and felt replenished by it.

Every now and again, the mist on the river coalesced and a figure would form, generally an older man or woman, but sometimes a younger person, like himself. They'd shake themselves free of the river and walk up the soft slope to the courthouse, gaining color and shape as they moved, until they looked like Wan Ho, dressed in their finest clothes and nearly alive.

Wan Ho wasn't certain if any of the new souls could see him. They never spoke to him, or returned his friendly wave. Their attention appeared to be taken up by the courthouse.

Then again, it was a rather splendid building, though it only rose up two stories, and inside, contained a single room. However, brilliant blue-and-green clay tiles made up the slanted roof, living stone sentinels sat on the end of each of the four tilted-up corners, a dazzling golden flag hung from a pole sticking out of the very center of the roof, and colorful murals showing the adventures of the Eight Immortals covered all the walls.

In addition, Ox-Head and Horse-Face, the two guardians, stood on either side of the grand red door leading into the courtroom. They wore magnificent robes of the finest material—blue and green silk embroidered with gold—as well as carried tall shiny halberds and swords.

They didn't acknowledge Wan Ho standing outside of the courthouse, but they permitted him to stand there.

The newly-dead looked to the two guardians for instructions. The guards merely opened the courthouse doors and escorted them before Judge Kan, who would tell them of their next destination: either they would go to one of the various Hells to endure punishment for their misdeeds, or they would pass on to the city of the dead and await rebirth.

No one else had been told by the judge to go and wait beside Wan Ho (and he was starting to suspect that it had been some time, now). And why had Judge Kan asked him to wait? What did he know, that he wasn't telling Wan Ho about? But the judge had kept his own counsel, his bulging eyes lighting up as he made his pronouncement, ordering Wan Ho outside.

So Wan Ho waited, watching the parade of the dead pass into the courthouse. He was glad that the building was far enough away from the Hells that he didn't hear any screams: it was bad enough when a soul received a judgment he or she didn't like and started to wail.

Wan Ho hadn't been afraid when he'd gone to stand before the dark-faced judge. Wan Ho hadn't been alive long enough to be truly wicked. He'd died when he was barely twenty years old, taking an unfortunate fall from a shoddily-constructed balcony in Shanghai.

But what was he waiting for? The judge hadn't told him. Just that he must wait.

The most recent elderly woman who'd come from the river had been escorted inside the courthouse by both guardians. They had treated her with the utmost respect. She obviously wouldn't have to wait long before she would be reborn.

While they were gone, a new soul formed out of the mist.

Only she looked different than the others Wan Ho had seen.

As she left the river, she gained form but not color. She remained as white as a Western ghost as she climbed the river bank. Her eyes looked haunted and she seemed scared as she glanced around. She was beautiful, however, it took Wan Ho a moment to realize that she wore her wedding robes.

Then she focused her attention on Wan Ho.

Shivering, Wan Ho stayed still under her gaze. It pierced him through to his soul, as if she could see all of his life laid bare before her.

It was the same look Judge Kan had given him.

"Wan Ho?" she asked. Her voice sounded much more timid than her look.

"I am he," Wan Ho said.

"I am Ou Li," the woman said, dipping her head in a bow. "I am here to marry you."

Past-ish

Ou Li slowly lowered herself to the hard, concrete floor of the temple. It hurt to bend that way, to make her uncooperative hips and spine move. She did it anyway, stubbornly refusing to accept one of the low chairs that the temple graciously offered the old women who came to pray.

She wasn't old. Barely twenty-one. And her life already ruined.

The statue of Guan Yin towered above Ou Li. The goddess wore flowing white robes that sparkled in the candles lit all around her. She had her left arm draped around a child, a golden-skinned youth who had the flame of enlightenment springing from his forehead. They both sat on a dark-brown *hou*, a proud, mythical creature that looked something like a lion. Beside them stood a second child, another of Guan Yin's close followers.

Ou Li knew that praying to the goddess of mercy would do no good. The doctors had done the best they could, repairing her pelvis as well as possible after it had been shattered by the car accident.

But her womb had also been ruptured. They'd had to remove it.

She would never have children. No matter how she begged and pleaded with each and every deity.

Ou Li couldn't lower her forehead to the cold floor as she should. She still bent her head as far as possible, casting her eyes downward. Then she brought her hands together and prayed for a release from her situation, her struggles, and perhaps, her life.

The smell of pungent incense grew stronger. Ou Li let it carry her away, drawing her up to the planes of the gods. Visiting a temple always made her feel more connected with the spiritual worlds, despite how even her parents denied the existence of anything beyond the physical. However, Ou Li had no doubt. When she prayed, she often felt close enough to touch those other places.

Today, it wasn't merely peace that she sought. She had always tried to be a good girl, to obey and honor her parents. She knew those were old-fashioned sentiments in such a modern world.

So when she prayed, she asked the gods: if not for her, then couldn't there be an heir for her mother and father? Her family line would end with her. Her parents had only been allowed a single child in the current Chinese regime, and hadn't had enough money to pay the fines (and the bribes) to have a second.

Finally, after pleading and praying and begging for what seemed like hours, Ou Li wiped away the tears from her cheeks and started the arduous process of standing.

Her bones sent flaming nails of pain through her hips and lower back. She caught her breath, gasping, but she would not cry out. She ended up on her hands and knees, shaking her head.

Then she tried again. But her legs would not hold her. She could not bend them far enough underneath her to support her weight.

She was just going to have to crawl, leave the center of the temple floor to find a wall to pull herself up on.

Ashamed but determined, Ou Li tried to stand again.

A strong hand caught her elbow as she started to tip over, steadying her until she found her feet.

"Thank you," Ou Li said, turning to look at her benefactor.

He was an old priest. Ancient, in fact, given the wrinkles of his face and the pure gray of his scraggly beard. His robes, too, were old-fashioned and worn, the red faded and the sleeves patched.

His eyes still held life, however, burning like two coals as they bore into her.

"Come," he said, continuing to hold onto her arm. "Let us have tea."

Ou Li nearly objected. What would her parents think if she went off with this strange priest? But Ou Li had always found herself drawn to other places, other spirits and beings.

This priest knew of those things. She was certain of it.

She finally nodded and said, "All right. I will have tea with you."

Besides, what did risking her life matter? She had so little left to give.

* * *

The priest walked with her to a tiny room, just behind the temple complex. Inside, there was barely enough room for the pair of them. Tall bookshelves filled with ancient books, scrolls, and knickknacks rose from the floor to the tall ceiling. A single light clipped to one of the shelves provided the only illumination. The room smelled of unwashed old-man, sour and rank.

Ou Li nearly turned around and left at that point. But the priest pierced her with a sharp look and said, "I have an answer for your problem."

Ou Li paused. She hadn't said anything about her problems, though she supposed the pain in her hips was obvious.

"Oh, really?" she asked. She knew she sounded horribly disrespectful. She still couldn't help herself. "And what do you think is my problem?"

The old priest gave her a sly smile as he picked up a large plastic bottle, the label long worn off. He splashed water from the bottle into an electric kettle sitting on one of the shelves. "Your problem isn't your hips and back, though that is what most would say," he said as he pulled an ancient teapot from another shelf. It looked like something a tourist would pick up—a cheap replica of a teapot from the Tang dynasty, made from beige clay with stripes of orange, red and green.

He unfolded a tiny table and set it in the middle of the cramped space. Two stools followed, allowing Ou Li to almost gracefully lower herself, though her hips still complained at the position she held her knees in.

"Then what is my problem?" Ou Li asked while the priest stuffed the teapot with leaves from an unmarked black tin canister that probably had held rice at one point.

"Tell me, what do you know of the *minghun* ceremony?" the priest asked instead.

Ou Li blinked, surprised. That hadn't been what she'd been expecting the priest to say at all.

"It is an ancient practice of ghost marriage—where either two deceased people got married, or the dead marry someone who is living," Ou Li said.

"Good, good," the old priest said. "I'm glad you know something of our traditions."

Ou Li bristled at that, though she knew he spoke the truth: so many customs had been lost in the generations of revolutions.

"So in addition to your physical ailments, you lack a husband," the priest said gently.

At least he didn't sound as though he was scolding her for her current predicament. Unlike some of her relatives.

"But what good would a husband do me?" Ou Li asked. "Particularly one who was dead?"

"The State would consider you legally married," the priest assured her. "Then, you'd be able to adopt an heir."

"Oh," Ou Li said. "I hadn't considered that." No man would marry her, not unless she lied about her sterile condition. She hadn't thought about adopting, however. She'd never be able to adopt as a single parent.

But if the State considered her married …

Ou Li waited while the priest poured the boiling water into the teapot. He poured the water out of the pot almost immediately, into a bucket. Then he poured in a second batch of water, setting the teapot on the tiny table and letting the tea steep.

"What do you think?" the priest asked. The delicious smell of a very fine black tea filled the tiny room. "You'd be helping not only your family's line, but his as well. Two sets of parents being honored."

"I'd want to be able to meet my husband, at the very least." Ou Li knew she sounded ungrateful, but this was a big step. "I wouldn't want a sham marriage."

The old priest sighed and considered. "I could arrange that," he said slowly.

"But would we be truly married?" Ou Li mused. "Since we'd only marry here, on the physical plane." It wouldn't feel right, she knew. She'd have to be married twice, once for her, here, and once, well, *there*, as well. Plus, she'd have to know for certain that her husband-to-be consented to the marriage, not just his parents.

"I can only marry you on this plane. You'll have to find someone else to officiate in the land of the dead, when you go visit," the priest said.

Ou Li nodded, considering. She'd never imagined the *minghun* as a solution to her problem.

But for the first time, in a very long time since waking up that painful morning in the hospital, after the accident, she felt a sliver of hope.

Present-ish

"And that's why I'm here," Ou Li continued, explaining to the spirit of Wan Ho, her now legally married husband.

At least in the physical world.

"I wanted to meet my husband," Ou Li told him. He looked just as handsome as the pictures his parents had shown her. He had kind eyes, a generous mouth, and hair that she wished she could touch brushing the bangs out of his eyes. "The priest arranged that, bringing me to a wizard who gave me a potion to carry my spirit here."

She hadn't really known what to expect. She hadn't expected the world of the dead to be so colorful. Then again, there was no time here to wear at the brilliantly painted murals on the courthouse, no rain to splash dirt up on the bright green grass.

"Thank you," Wan Ho said. He smiled at her. "Thank you for continuing both my line as well as yours."

"You're welcome," Ou Li told him. "But in order for the marriage to be fully legal, we need to be married on this plane as well."

As her mother always said, something worth doing right was worth overdoing.

Wan Ho's eyes widened. "Oh," he said. "Where will we get married here?"

Ou Li shrugged. "I don't live here. I don't know." Really, was he expecting her to do everything? So like a man.

Wan Ho looked around, as if possibly a temple would have sprung up beside them.

He looked awfully cute, confused that way.

"I know!" he finally said. "Let's ask the judge."

Hesitatingly, he held out his hand for her to take.

Even in her ghost body, Ou Li felt her heart start to pound. She'd never held hands with a boy before, only with her female friends.

Him offering his hand that way warmed her all the way through. The gesture was more romantic than any of the old poems she'd read. Could she touch him? He looked much more solid here than she did.

Ou Li reached out and tried to take his hand.

Her wispy white hand passed through his. "Oh! Sorry!" she said. It hadn't felt bad when she'd done that. She hoped she hadn't given him a chill or something, though.

She smiled bravely at him, hiding her disappointment.

"It's okay," he said, smiling and nodding at her, though his eyes looked a little sad. "Come. Let's go ask Judge Kan. Maybe he can marry us!"

Ou Li gave her husband-to-be her best smile and walked beside him toward the tall red doors of the courthouse.

In her secret heart, she'd really wanted to be able to touch her husband-to-be's hand, be able to connect with him somehow. It would help her feel as though she had a real relationship, maybe even lessen her envy of the couples she saw holding hands as they walked down the street.

It seemed that some things, though, were never meant to be.

* * *

The ancient woman Wan Ho had seen Ox-Head and Horse-Face escort in earlier still stood before Judge Kan. They chatted like old friends.

Perhaps they were. Wan Ho's grandmother, before she'd died, had told him that when he didn't come to see her, death frequently sat in her visitor's chair.

Except that Judge Kan wasn't really death. He was just the judge who weighed people's souls and told the newly dead where to go. Right?

A few people stood at the back of the courtroom. All dead. Wan Ho had the sense that they were waiting as well, possibly for an escort to their new homes. Many doors lined the walls. Did each go to a different hell?

The courtroom itself was just a large single room. Judge Kan still sat behind a large wooden counter at the back. The same brilliant flags stood on either side of him. Wan Ho recognized some of the countries they represented, such as China, Japan, the United States, and Korea. But what did the small brown fox in the middle of a yellow circle mean? Or the proud elephant with its trunk raised, along with one foot?

The judge himself had a dark-red face with bulging cheeks and eyes. He reminded Wan Ho of a school teacher he'd once known, an officious man always spouting Party dogma about family values while he kept not one, but two mistresses in addition to his wife. Judge Kan also had a thin black mustache and a carefully trimmed beard that grew out of the center of his chin and hung down to mid-chest. No one wore a hat like his anymore—tall and flat-faced, with flaps sticking out over the ears. But Wan Ho recognized it from scroll paintings of the judge, knowing that it was the traditional sign of his office.

Ox-Head and Horse-Face stood with their backs to the judge's counter, staring out at the court. Their large, black, animal eyes didn't appear to see Wan Ho and Ou Li, but Wan Ho still knew they'd seen them.

Wan Ho waited with Ou Li a few steps behind the ancient grandmother talking to the judge. Finally, they finished their conversation and the two guards escorted her out a side door.

"So, what have we here?" Judge Kan said as Wan Ho and Ou Li stepped closer. He blinked, then glared at Ou Li. "You don't belong here. Not yet."

"I know, sir," Ou Li said. "I am not dead."

Wan Ho smiled with pride at how bravely his mortal wife spoke to the judge.

"I am only here for a short while," Ou Li continued on. "So that I might properly marry my husband."

"I see, I see," the judge said, stroking his thin beard.

"Can you marry us, sir?" Wan Ho asked, hope-ful.

"I cannot," the judge said, his voice tinged with regret. "That is beyond my jurisdiction, I'm afraid."

"Can you tell us who could?" Ou Li said. "Maybe a priest who is recently dead."

"Perhaps. Perhaps," the judge said. "You should go to the western hills. You might find someone there."

"Thank you, sir, thank you," Wan Ho said, bow-ing.

Ou Li also bowed. At first just her head, then with a gasp, realized she could bend from the waist and give the official a formal bow.

"Thank you," Ou Li said again as Ox-Head and Horse-Face escorted them to a side door.

Wan Ho wished that he could take his wife's hand. All the couples he'd ever seen had done that, even his parents. Or maybe, that he might give her a gentle kiss. That, perhaps, they might even truly live as husband and wife, and share bodies as well as souls.

Such things were not to be.

However, he still was able to stand proudly by her side at the top of a low foothill, overlooking a peaceful valley and hills covered in soft green grass.

"Ready?" he asked.

She nodded, determined.

Wan Ho recognized it as the look of a woman who would not be stopped by a mere detail, such as death. He'd seen a similar look only once, from his mother, when she was determined to get her son into the best school despite the Party officials denying her access.

However, instead of taking the easy trail down the hill, Ou Li turned and looked at the path going up into the craggy mountains. "The priest will be this way," she said.

Wan Ho followed meekly behind, pitying anyone who stood in her way.

* * *

"I won't be able to stay much longer," Ou Li confessed as she sat beside a lovely babbling stream with her husband-to-be. That was how she thought of him. Though the *minghun* had been performed back on earth, she wouldn't consider herself truly married until after being married in both worlds.

It was tempting now to think of Wan Ho as more. Especially since it had turned out that they liked many of the same movies and video games. Getting to know him had just cemented his place in her heart, making her think of their connection as real.

Though how anyone could like that K-pop singer with the long white hair and pretentious English name was beyond her.

Wan Ho nodded, looking sad. "I will miss you," he said.

Ou Li's heart melted just a little more.

The priest had warned her that she wouldn't have much time in the nether worlds. She hadn't thought it would be so difficult, though, to find someone to marry them!

They'd climbed out of the peaceful valley and up into the rocks. She was certain they'd find a hermit's cave up there, or a holy man sitting on a ledge.

But they hadn't found another soul. While it was very colorful and delightfully cool in the world of the dead, Ou Li found that she missed the birds who should have filled the nearby pines, the soft plopping of fish in the creek before them. Even a buzzing insect would have been a welcome respite from the aching silence.

It made her uncomfortable, which, she supposed, was kind of the point, as she didn't properly live here.

"Will you come back? If we cannot find a priest?" Wan Ho asked, not looking at her.

"I cannot," Ou Li said, her voice heavy with regret. "The priest said I could have a single visit. After that, well, I'd be here for good."

"I see," Wan Ho said. He continued to not look at her. "You know, if we can't get married down here, I...I won't hold you to your vows."

"Thank you," Ou Li said, grateful. Though she might try to stick it out, it wouldn't be right for her to only be half married. Her entire life would feel like a sham. Despite how much she thought she might be able to love him, now that she'd met him. "I would still honor you as a relative," Ou Li promised. "Burn incense for you and clean your grave during the *qingming* festival every year."

"Thank you," Wan Ho said. He sounded so sad. But Ou Li wasn't certain what more she could do.

"Wait, who's that?" Wan Ho asked, pointing over her shoulder.

"I can't tell," Ou Li said, raising to her feet gracefully. It was so wonderful to be out of pain! Though the land of the dead bothered her, it was almost worth it to have working hips and knees again.

Off in the distance, the figure resolved into a short monk. He wore deep-red robes over an orange shirt. His bald head looked very round and his skin was tanned golden.

It wasn't until he drew closer that Ou Li realized that the monk was ancient. However, his long years had worn away most of the wrinkles on his smiling face. His neck showed his age the most, with seven deep wrinkles circling his head.

"Good day, children," the monk said in greeting.

"Good day, wise sir," Wan Ho said, bowing deeply.

Ou Li joined him, still thrilled to be able to bend her spine so easily.

"We were looking for someone to marry us," Wan Ho continued.

The monk looked from Ou Li, to Wan Ho, and back again. "That is not normally one of my duties," the smiling monk said. "I generally escort people, such as yourself, my lady, from the earthly plane to this one."

As he spoke, the skin on the monk's face melted, showing white bones and bulging eyes.

Ou Li gasped.

Wan Ho looked at her questioningly. He hadn't seen the transformation.

The priest's bulging eyes stared hotly into hers. "Are you certain that you want Death to marry you, my lady? There's no turning back. No court would grant you a divorce."

"I am certain," Ou Li said. She raised her chin, though she shook inside at the thought of facing Death himself. "This is my husband to be, in this world and all others." She paused, then added, "The gods must have tied a red ribbon to our ankles, before we were born, to draw us together now." She truly believed the words as she spoke them.

The monk looked down.

Ou Li caught her breath as she suddenly felt a cool ribbon slide around her leg. Was a matching one now tied around Wan Ho's?

"Very well, then. I will marry you," Death said. "I had been coming to take your soul," he added, pointedly staring at Ou Li. "You've been here far too long. You would be a permanent resident after only a bit more."

"Thank you for your forbearance," Ou Li said. Now that she'd met Death, though he was a little scary, she knew she'd never be truly afraid of him ever again.

"Face each other. Raise your hands, as if to touch palms," Death ordered.

Ou Li smiled at Wan Ho and did as the priest asked.

Wan Ho did the same, giving her a radiant smile.

"Wan Ho," the priest said. "Do you promise to honor your wife? To fill her nights with sweet dreams, and to turn away any bad luck that might visit her?"

"I do," Wan Ho said. His voice took on a deeper tone, setting the nearby hills to ringing.

"And do you, Ou Li, promise to honor your husband? To burn incense for him to live on? To send him ghost money every feast day? To keep his grave clean?"

"I do," Ou Li said. She heard more bells ringing as the promise took hold.

She would stay true to her husband for all of her days.

"Then by the power of the Eight Kingdoms I declare you man and wife," Death said.

He sounded surprisingly cheery.

"Now, you may kiss the bride," Death said with a wink.

Ou Li blinked, startled. How could she kiss Wan Ho? She was a ghost and he was dead. They hadn't been able to touch before.

Still, she trusted the monk's words. She closed her eyes and leaned forward.

Soft lips touched hers. Sweetness enveloped her. She had the sense of falling into the kiss, all the worlds disappearing as they gently touched each other with their lips, softly exploring, his sweet taste filling her.

Until Ou Li couldn't hold herself up anymore and she really was falling.

Down, down, down.

She landed in her own bed with a start, gasping as real air came back into her lungs.

She was alive. Here, on earth.

And finally, properly married.

* * *

Wan Ho stood alone next to Death at the side of the softly tinkling river.

"What will happen to her now?" he asked. His whole soul mourned her loss. Despite the soft green grass beneath his feet, the beautifully stark mountains around him, the world felt, well, dead, without her.

"She will live a prosperous life," the monk replied. "I see a son in your future. As well as grandchildren."

"Really?" Wan Ho asked. The world seemed slightly brighter. He knew the child wouldn't be of his loins, but his son would carry on the family name, which was more important. His parents would be well pleased. As would Ou Li's.

Wan Ho looked around the valley. "Where should I go now?" he asked. Would Death guide him? Should he go to the city of the dead? Or should he go back and talk to Judge Kan?

"Now, you wait," Death said. "It won't be too long."

"Thank you, sir," Wan Ho said.

Suddenly he found himself standing outside the grand courthouse again. Ox-Head and Horse-Face stood on either side of the door. The misty river flowed and burbled to itself, the dead marching out of it as they saw fit.

Wan Ho settled in to wait contentedly for his wife to join him, again.

He had all the time in the world.

CICADA SONG, IN A COUNTRY SINCE LONG GONE

Aliette de Bodard

On the last evening before they leave the old country, Giang finds Cousin Ly in the courtyard, disconsolately staring at a large, heavy box of sandalwood.

"No space for it?" she guesses.

Cousin Ly grimaces. "No." She lifts the lid; stares, for a while, at the keepsakes inside: all the remnants of her life before she came to live with Mother and Giang, the faded photographs of her dead mother, the letters her parents wrote to each other when her mother was posted in the provinces, cramped handwriting on rice paper that's turned opaque and brittle with age. "I'll have to pack them inside a bag."

Giang kneels by her side. The air reeks of the smoke of burnt flowers, and in the distance is the thunder of bombs falling over the city of Thu Huong. "Want some help?" she asks.

Cousin Ly grins. "Already packed?"

Giang shrugs. There was too much she wanted to take, so in the end she took nothing. She looks up, at the apricot trees in flower—there's the familiar, unrelenting sound of cicadas nesting in the branches: a sign that whatever happens, life goes on.

She so wishes she could believe it. "I wanted—" she hesitates, but Cousin Ly knows her too well.

"Your girlfriend?" she asks.

"She's not—" Giang starts, and then shakes her head, because it doesn't matter anymore, does it? "She left yesterday with her parents." She thinks of Moc Mien's hands gently running on her shoulder, of her breath, quickening so much her lungs feel too tight and cramped. "I don't know where."

"Ah." Cousin Ly's gaze is too sharp, more adult than her sixteen years. "I'm sorry."

Giang shakes her head. "Don't be."

It's nothing, in the grand scheme of things: she should be worrying about the war, about tomorrow and her family's panicked journey to the border; about whether they'll survive, whether they'll find the refuge Mother is so desperate for. Moc Mien leaving shouldn't feel like the end of the world.

But it does.

Cousin Ly says, "What do you think it'll be like?"

"In the Everlasting Empire?" Giang forces her mind back from Moc Mien— as, no doubt, Cousin Ly has intended all along. "I don't know. Mother says everyone wears dresses of brushed silk. And even the peasants have pork and shrimp on the table."

Cousin Ly snorts. "Your mother is trying to make it attractive."

"Can't say it's working," Giang says with a shake of her head. The thought of leaving their home—the courtyard, the cicadas, the petals scattered on the beaten earth—just makes her sick.

"Has to be better than here." Cousin Ly's face is dark. "Safer."

The echo of a blast deafens them—Giang ducks, but it was still too far away. In its wake is only silence, as if the cicadas were hesitant to start up again. She swallows, tasting only ashes in her throat. "I'm sure," she says, rising.

* * *

They leave the city like thieves or criminals: Mother and Cousin Ly and Giang piled up in the back of a covered cart going into the mountains, towards the border with the Everlasting Empire.

The cart wends its way higher and higher on the path, behind a steady flow of others, fugitives all desperate to leave before the city falls.

"Here," Mother says, handing them rice cakes. Her eyes watch upwards, for alchemical fliers and enspelled messenger birds—one will kill them faster than the other, but in the end they'll be dead from both.

Cousin Ly sits, clutching her bag on her knees. "They said the city would fall today or tomorrow. And then—"

"We'll be out of the country by then." Mother's voice is firm.

In Giang's mouth, the rice cake tastes like ashes. "I don't know—" she starts.

Mother pauses, for a moment, in her endless staring at the sky; her gaze intent. "We'll find a house," she says. "Or build one, if we have to. A garden full of cicada songs. And we'll never have to leave it. Promise."

"You can't know that," Giang says.

"They're building a wall," Cousin Ly says. "Between the Everlasting Empire and us. The alchemists and the monks, with cinnabar and peach wood and jade. Shutting us off."

"They are," Mother says. She sighs. It's hard to tell if she's angry or sad. "They're scared. Because the war keeps growing."

If Giang closes her eyes she can still see the marketplace; can still smell the smoke and feel the blood on her hands; the words struggling to get out from a too-full throat. A stampede in the New Year's crowds, the newscast had called it—making it sound distant and without bite. A lie, Mother had said, with more force than usual—hugging Giang and Cousin Ly hard and thanking the ancestors they'd come back safe.

"But—" Giang starts, stops. "But how will we get out?"

"The wall isn't finished," Mother says. "There is still time." She leans back, looking at the sky again. She sounds utterly confident, and in spite of herself Giang finds herself believing her—because when has Mother ever been wrong?

"You sold the shop," Cousin Ly says.

Mother shrugs. "There'll be other shops. Or other people who need clothes sewn." She shakes her head.

"I can help," Giang says. "With the sewing. I'm old enough."

She glares at Mother, daring her to contradict her, but Mother doesn't. She shakes her hand with an odd, soft fondness, and merely says, "Of course. But you'll have your own life soon enough, child. You both will have."

Cousin Ly snorts and holds her bag tighter. "A longer one than we'd have had in Thu Huong."

That shuts up conversation for a while: Mother goes back to watching the sky, and Giang doesn't feel like making the effort of starting up the conversation again.

The cart stops. Mother drops down to speak with the driver; comes back, gesturing at them to come out, to hurry.

There is nothing in the sky but faint black specks and a low, rumbling noise that gets louder and louder as they walk.

Single-file on a narrow path—stumbling over rocks, as clouds pass over the sun, leaving dappled, illusory tracks on the cliff-face—and all the while the sound is getting louder and louder, the black specks resolving themselves into the sharp, tapered shape of fliers, closer and closer, until she can almost count the scars on their hull. Closer and closer—how close do they have to be, to drop their bombs?

They finally reach a plateau where they pause, out of breath.

Mother points to the end of the plateau, where the land rises again to a jagged edge. "That's where the border is," she said. "They're closing it, but they're not done yet. You have to—"

She never finishes her sentence.

A whistling sound, like gas from a pierced balloon—an impact that sends Giang reeling to the floor, filling her world with a piercing thunder. Everything goes black for a fraction of a second, as she kneels coughing in the dirt. Then she's pulling herself upwards, in a rising cloud of dust and smoke—ashes and burnt flowers, a smell that clings to her as if it had claws of its own. "Mother? Cousin?"

"Child." By touch more than by sight, Giang crawls to her; finds her, standing with her eyes on the sky. Mother's voice is low and raspy. She hasn't moved. She—just the way she's standing...

A fist of ice tightens within Giang's guts.

"Promise me, child."

"Mother?"

"You remember where the border is. You have to leave. You—" Her face moves, then, with an expression Giang has never seen. "Make it worth it, child. Please."

"No," Giang says. "I can't see anything. It's just dust. Mother—"

Mother pulls out her hands. They come red, with blood pooling from the wound on her chest. "Never mind me, child." She grimaces; starts singing in a low, wordless voice—something that starts as a song, but as she goes on, even the tune is lost, until there's just a low-level drone, like monks' prayers in the instant before they fall silent. In her hands is something. It takes Giang a moment to see what it is: a cicada, the same ones as in the courtyard, fat and blood-red. Mother moves her hands, and the cicada opens its wings, and flies. Mother crumples then, like a puppet that's lost its guiding will.

"Mother!"

She doesn't look up, or move—and Giang *knows*, with a pain like a knife twist in her chest, that it's too late. Mother's face is slack and unmoving; the blood pooling on her chest sticking to Giang's hands, like tar—to Mother's eyelids as Giang fumbles, trying to close them. There's nothing left in Mother's face: the eyes glazed and unseeing, with no warmth, no hint of recognition or even pain. She's gone. Dead.

Cousin Ly. Where—

All is dust and silence, and the smell of smoke. She finally finds Cousin Ly on the edge of the cliff. Her eyes are closed, her breathing slow and regular; red spreads under her clothes, staining the bag—Giang snatches it away before she can think, trying to save the letters and photographs in it.

"Cousin."

She's not moving. Giang fumbles; tries to find the voice of the heart. Breathing, she's still breathing.

Above them, in the cloud, a low buzzing—the fliers, coming back for a second pass.

Giang tries to lift Cousin Ly, passing one hand under the back and one under the legs and pushing upwards. She might as well be pushing at a wall—she gains one, two hand-spans away from the ground, and then falls back, her whole body shaking.

The low whine is becoming a thunder.

There's no time left.

The cicada buzzes, heedless, heartless. Waiting, in a world that's blurred and become meaningless.

If she waits, they'll both die here. And she wants, so very much, so desperately, to live.

"I'm sorry," Giang says to Cousin Ly. She rises, stumbling away, and starts running. Behind her is the thunder of fliers—and then the sound of more bombs dropping, obliterating the plateau where Mother died. Where she abandoned Cousin Ly.

* * *

The cicada moves away, step after step, through smoke and death and the smell of charred meat—and as Giang walks away from the ruins of the plateau, tottering on unsteady legs, it blurs and widens, and becomes the shape of a woman—a tall, shadowed silhouette wearing the fine-panel clothes of some old dynasty, the kind you only see in theatre plays. She wears a large, conical hat, its brim shadowing her face, and her bloodied hands are wide open, though Giang never manages to run into their embrace.

Giang stumbles towards the cicada woman—towards the border, never looking back.

* * *

Giang turns seventeen in the land of the Everlasting Emperor.

She's finally found work in a restaurant, one of the rare places that will take in poor and unskilled foreigners: cutting up chickens and cooking rice for rich refugees, those who had the foresight and means to flee earlier. She sleeps in a courtyard with a dozen other kitchen hands, her mat under the red lacquered eaves of an old pavilion, tossing and turning with nightmares in which the song of cicadas follows her around in empty streets choked with dust and grit.

In the kitchens, the only talk is of the wall: that the Everlasting Emperor will finally seal off the old country, making sure no bombs and no alchemical weapons can cross over. The ceremony is scheduled in three days.

Giang keeps her head down, cutting up onions until the smell closes up her throat; tries to think of the future—like standing at the edge of a cliff with nothing to hold her back.

When she comes back to her corner of the courtyard, there is a letter on her sleeping mat.

Who could be writing to her? She knows no one in the city: she came on foot and alone with no money, and the other refugees are kind in a distant way, knowing nothing of her or her family.

The letter is written on thin rice paper. It's been carefully slit open, stamped with the vermillion seal of the Imperial Censorate.

Giang kneels to pick it up. The paper rustles under her fingers. The handwriting on the letter is as familiar as her own.

It's from Cousin Ly.

The world wobbles and crumples, and she hears once again the buzzing song of the cicada in the dust of the mountains.

Cousin. I hope this finds you well, though in truth writing this is like floating a coconut shell downriver and hoping it reaches a particular fisherman's village—I don't know if you're still alive, or how you have fared.

But I know people have found refuge in the Empire, and one of the traders who came back swore blind that he had seen you in the capital.

I am well.

Alive.

She's alive.

Giang sits down, struggling to breathe. There are holes in the letter, where the imperial alchemists removed entire sections. Cousin Ly was found by the rebel army. She doesn't say, but she has to have been taken prisoner; has to have been sent to work camps—but her tone throughout is matter-of-fact, telling her not to worry—food is tight but she survives, and she would be glad for any news Giang can spare.

She doesn't mention joining Giang. Of course by now it's a fantasy: the wall is merely the latest incarnation of the Empire's rejections. There are more than enough penniless, hungry refugees in the streets, and no place in those gleaming, clean cities for any of them.

"You all right?" A voice cut through the buzzing of the cicadas in Giang's ears: Lan Anh, one of the sous-chefs—the youngest one, with a muscled chest and small, almost invisible breasts that Giang envies.

Giang folds the letter, feeling small and ashamed. It's too little, too late— she's not even sure any answer she writes would ever get back to Cousin Ly in time, but she has to try. "I'm fine."

Lan Anh stares at her, her broad face expressionless. Then she moves away—Giang breathes a sigh of relief, turning back to her pallet, and the difficult task of composing a reply—but a clatter of plates announces Lan Anh's return. "Here," she says. She's holding out one of the midday spreads: concentric circles of shrimp, crisp five-spice pork belly, and diaphanous square noodles—and two bowls and two sets of chopsticks, precariously balanced atop the plate. "You can't—" Giang says.

Lan Anh shrugs. "They won't miss it." She grins; for a moment Giang finds her breath catching in her throat, and it's not out of sorrow. "All right, all right, maybe they will. I'll tell them it's on me."

"They'll fire you—"

Lan Anh settles down, holds out an empty bowl and chopsticks to Giang, and takes one set for herself. "Would be surprised. Many refugees, but not so many that can cook to local taste." She grins again, irrepressible. "Come on. You're too thin anyway."

Giang takes the bowl; feels the warmth of Lan Anh's hands on hers; fights the urge to look away. "You've been here long."

Lan Anh's face is grave. "Five years," she says. "Mother sent me abroad before the war broke out. They'd been saving money the entire time."

"How—"

"The signs were there," Lan Anh says. She shrugs, again, and the cicadas' song all but drowns her voice.

Giang asks, because she has to. "Your mother—"

Lan Anh shakes her head. "Only enough money for one journey. I send part of my earnings back." She grimaces. "Hard to know what will happen, after the wall. Word's been that they won't allow money out of the Empire, either—no point in wasting it on a doomed country."

Giang opens her mouth to protest; to say that she can't say that this casually; and then sees Lan Anh's bruised, haunted eyes. "Who knows," she says, finally. In her ears, the old country's cicadas buzz.

Lan Anh doesn't ask about Giang's own mother; but then she's seen the band of mourning on Giang's arm, and she knows it's only for deceased parents—a one in two chances of getting it disastrously right. Instead she says, "You get used to it, you know. Not being there." She lays a hand on her chest, where the heart is. "It'll always be home to us—the place where we grew up; but it doesn't mean we can't be happy here."

Giang says nothing, for a while. She picks up one of the pork belly pieces, letting it crackle under her teeth—the sharp taste of five spices filling her mouth to bursting. "While others suffer elsewhere?" She tries, so very hard, not to think of Cousin Ly; of stumbling away from her, bloodied and panicked. Of leaving her to die.

"You do what you can, with the gifts you've been given," Lan Anh says, at last. She picks up a square noodle, holds it to the light, thoughtfully. "I don't think anyone can claim more than that."

Gifts. A cousin close enough to be a sister, on the other side of a wall that won't allow anyone out. "I don't know," Giang says.

Lan Anh smiles, and there's very little of joy in it. "No. Neither do I." When she speaks again, her tone has changed. "You should apply for a sous-chef post. The pay is better, and there's less risk of being dismissed when they find someone cheaper to hire."

"Me?" Giang snorts. "I can't cook."

"I couldn't either." Lan Anh shrugs. "I can teach you, if you want. In your free time, of course. There's no room for dawdling, here."

"Why would you bother—" Giang starts, and then she catches Lan Anh's burning gaze. She holds out her hand, slowly, carefully; and when Lan Anh doesn't protest, runs it on Lan Anh's cheek, feeling the warmth of the other's skin under hers, a tingling fire taking over her entire body—and the cicadas in the background fall blessedly silent, leaving only the barely familiar song of desire.

* * *

"First mommy, first mommy, there's a letter!"

Giang is trying to paint: paralyzed by the idea that her brush should move in a slow, assured line and create the first hint of a mountain crest on the rice paper.

"Give me a moment," she says.

The paintbrush slips. It always does, and her mountain becomes smudged—not in a way that artfully suggests fog, but simply looking and feeling wrong. She sighs, looks up.

Her eldest daughter Hai Ngan is holding a folded sheet of paper—a familiar shape that stabs at her heart, with the vermillion shape scrawled across the back. "Where did you find that?"

"It was on the terrace," Hai Ngan says. She frowns, stares at it. "Are you going to put it with the others?"

The others. The thin thread still tying her back to a life she left a lifetime ago: Cousin Ly's handwriting, speaking of life in Thu Huong; of her own wedding, of living with distant relatives Giang only dimly remembers meeting. "I will," Giang says. "But I have to read it first." She hesitates, and then says—because Hai Ngan has been asking, again and again, about the letters— "You can help me if you want."

Hai Ngan pulls a chair and effortlessly clambers on it, settling down at the table with the eager seriousness of a five-year-old. "All right. What does it say?"

"It's from the old country. Where Mommy was born." She unfolds the letter, carefully. There's a sound at the edge of hearing, getting louder and louder—one she hasn't heard in a while, the low humming that becomes the buzzing of a cicada. Her hands feel stiff, as if with blood. But from the kitchen comes a loud noise as baby Chau repeatedly bangs a wooden toy against the floor; the laughter of Lan Anh, egging Chau to show her again—and the cicadas and the blood both seem to go away, leaving just a tightness in Giang's chest, as if she'd been running for too long.

Cousin. More things floated your way—who knows, these days, what gets out and what doesn't. I hope you are well and prosperous.

"Who's writing?" Hai Ngan asked.

Giang thinks, for a while, of what she can say—of dusty mountains and blood, and cicadas in a courtyard. "Your Second Aunt. She—she grew up with Mommy. Like you and baby Chau."

Hai Ngan makes a face. "I don't like baby Chau."

"She's your sister."

Hai Ngan's face is set in that stubborn way and doesn't move. Giang scans the letter: more holes, entire passages removed by the imperial censors, inappropriate sentences—what could Cousin Ly have to say, that doesn't fit in with their view of the world?

The letter is short, with its removed fragments. Cousin Ly married and is expecting a child of her own. She jokes about the difficulty of getting white rice; about the fish in the market that's all gone from fresh to dried, all the meat going for prices dearer than they can afford. Not prosperity, then, or at least not for her.

The sound of the cicadas is like thunder in Giang's ears.

Cousin Ly has enclosed a portrait of herself at the spring festival table, with the others of the family behind her—half as many cousins as Giang remembers, and far too many blurred pictures on the ancestral altar behind Cousin Ly. The table is spread with food, an abundance that seems almost obscene in a country wracked by war, but of course Giang knows all about appearances, and saving the best to honor the ancestors.

"Is that Second Aunt?" Hai Ngan, peering over the edge of the table at the portrait. "What is she writing?"

"She's giving news," Giang says. "Of herself, and your other aunts. And your ancestors."

"Oh." Hai Ngan pops her thumb into her mouth, frowning at Cousin Ly. "She doesn't look happy."

"I don't know," Giang says. She folds the letter, carefully—she'll set it on top of the other in a portrait of her desk. She'll write an answer, too; though she suspects it won't be delivered. No letter she got acknowledged her previous ones. She's about to put the picture away, too; but Cousin Ly's face stares back at her, and she can't bring herself to bury her a second time. So instead, she sets it on the bookshelves, on the left side of the ancestral altar.

"First mommy?" She turns, to find Hai Ngan has dragged an atlas larger than her to the table. "Show me."

Oh.

"The old country," Hai Ngan says, with a touch of impatience in her eyes—always commanding, in spite of Giang and Lan Anh's best efforts to teach her otherwise.

Giang kneels, opening the book to the right page—slowly tracing the circle of the old country, the sea on the east, the Everlasting Empire on the west; and the shape of the wall. Slowly, carefully; ignoring the sound of the cicadas in the background, faint and almost indistinguishable, drowned out by the rustling of the pages and Hai Ngan's voice. "Here. That's Thu Huong, where I used to live. And here." She points, carefully, to a place north of the city. "That's where your ancestors are buried." She avoids, studiously, the other place—the plateau where Mother crumpled and died, where she failed Cousin Ly. "You can't visit—"

"I know." Hai Ngan snorts, and rolls up her eyes. "The war."

"It was bad," Giang says. She feels ashamed, circling around a subject she's never quite sure how to broach. "But we're safe now."

"Mmm." Hai Ngan's fingers are tracing the lines of the rivers at the southern edge of the Everlasting Empire. "When I'm grown up, I'll travel the world." Her face is set—looking, in that moment that clenches around Giang's heart like a fist, oddly like Cousin Ly when she was younger, when they both sat in a cart waiting to cross a border since long closed. "Like you did, first mommy. Finding new things."

"That's not—" Giang opens her mouth to say that's not why she left, and closes it. Does she really want to encourage curiosity and attachment to a country there's no going back to—even though it's her home and her ancestors' home, and her mother's last resting place? She flexes her fingers again, trying to banish the memory of the cicada's sound from her ears. "I'm sure you'll make a tremendous traveler."

"The best." Hai Ngan grins, tapping the atlas with a proprietary air. "I'll make you proud."

Behind her, baby Chau screams—they're so easily frustrated, at this age—and Giang can hear Lan Anh whispering soothing sounds, singing the words of a lullaby about coming home at the end of the day—again and again, until the baby's howls fade into restful silence.

* * *

The nightmare starts in the year of the Wood Rooster, just as Giang turns fifty-nine.

Lan Anh died a year ago, and the letters have stopped: Giang goes out on the terrace every day, half-hoping to catch a glimpse of a vermillion seal, but there is nothing. The last letter she had from Cousin Ly mentioned the birth of a grandchild, and Cousin Ly's worries about the baby's health, in a country where medicine is scarce and doctors charge a fortune for the least service.

Giang doesn't know if the lack of letters means anything—if Cousin Ly has grown weary of Giang's silence. The house is empty now, both her daughters grown and gone, and Giang is more lonely than ever.

The nightmare always goes the same way: Giang wakes up gasping in an empty house, listening to a distant sound like fireworks. The bed is cold and hard, the paintings sharp and painfully garish, the landscapes of mountains and rivers arranged in unfamiliar configurations.

She wanders into the kitchen, desperately looking for something familiar—and something crunches under her feet. For a single, heartbreaking moment she thinks it's dry bones, but instead it's a desiccated cicada with the faintest suggestion of folded wings on its back—the shriveled husks left after their last, desperate molting and lovemaking, after they've sent their children to the safety of the darkness below the earth. But when Giang kneels to pick it up, it moves, spreading its wings and flying away from her.

It shimmers and shifts and stretches, and the ghost of the cicada woman coalesces into existence—the five-panel tunic, the broad-brimmed hat, the face in shadow, and every detail Giang remembers from that long, long stumble to the border of the Everlasting Empire. On the hem of her wide robes, two faint shapes—half-open wings—and the hint of a segmented body on the front panel of her tunic, except that on her chest is a large red smudge, the color of blood, and when she holds out her hands they're stained the same red. She gestures towards Giang, the imperious movement of someone used to command.

Come.

Behind Giang, the sound of fireworks rises and swells and fill the entire world; and she realizes, all of a sudden, that they're not fireworks at all, but an older, more frightening memory: the bombs going off, and the cloud of dust, and

Mother's still face, and Cousin Ly lying in the dust—and blood on Giang's hands, hardening into a dense, opaque shell.

And then Giang *really* wakes up, with the taste of burnt flowers in her mouth and on her clothes. When it doesn't go away, she rolls out of bed, over the space where Lan Anh used to sleep, and pours herself tea from the teapot in the kitchen. She stares at the portrait of Cousin Ly, in its old spot on the bookshelves, trying to guess at the pictures on the ancestral altar behind her cousin, at which one could possibly be Mother's—but all the faces are dark and blurred, and indistinguishable.

* * *

By the time Giang's daughters come to visit for the spring festival, the cicada woman has moved from nightmares to daylight—haunting the hearth and kitchen, a translucent shape that no neighbor seems to be able to see. Giang isn't really surprised that neither of her daughters see her, either.

Giang has pulled out all of Cousin Ly's letters—the fragmentary, fragile news of the old country, rereading them in the dim light of a lantern, trying to discern meaning in holes and patched-up words.

"You don't look well, First Mother," Chau says. Behind her, the ghostly cicada woman shakes her head and gestures, once again, for Giang to come to her.

"You can talk," Giang says.

"Only to be expected." Chau shifts in the chair with a grimace, the large mound of her belly protruding under the silk tunic she wears. "At this stage of the pregnancy—"

"You shouldn't even be travelling," Hai Ngan says, a little more sharply than warranted. But of course she's the eldest, and she's always had a tendency to boss Chau around, even before she started being in charge of trading expeditions. "Where did you hide that husband of yours?"

"Dinh Toan? He's coming later," Chau says. "He had something to finish at the tribunal, a case that dragged on longer than foreseen."

"Hmm," Hai Ngan says. She's never much liked Dinh Toan and the feeling is mutual. But that's just Hai Ngan being bitter: Chau married above her station to a county magistrate, and she's herself a graduate of the provincial examination, a steady, bright future that is everything Giang could wish for; Hai Ngan, for all that merchant is a profession without much prestige in the Empire, has been growing wealthier and wealthier, and it's her money that's paying the rent on Giang's house.

Hai Ngan goes to the kitchen and comes back with three filled cups on a tray and the food Giang has made. There's always something infinitely comforting in the familiar gestures, the ones Lan Anh taught her—the feel of the knife coming down on the wooden board; the smoothness of mushroom slices; the stubborn stickiness of courgette skins needing to be scrubbed away until the sides of her fingers turn ruddy and raw.

"Here." Hai Ngan rummages in her sleeves, withdraws a package wrapped in oiled paper. "I brought some sweet cakes from the east."

Chau eats in silence. Hai Ngan, who can't sit still, wanders over to Giang's desk, the cicada woman following, desultorily floating in her wake. Too late, as Hai Ngan bends over the papers, Giang realizes she hasn't put away Cousin Ly's letters, or the old portrait. "I remember that letter," Hai Ngan says. "From Second Aunt Ly." As she rises, the cicada woman becomes visible behind her—but it's not to Hai Ngan that she holds out her bloodied hands.

Giang ponders, for a split second, what she can say; and the only thing that comes to mind is the truth. "I've been thinking about the old country."

Chau nods, putting away her teacup and carefully rising from the chair to join her sister at the desk. "Because of the memorial?"

"Don't be silly," Hai Ngan says, quick and lithe. "First Mother's never kept that custom."

No, because there was no point in keeping anniversaries of cities' falls. Because the old country was dead and shut off; her last letter sent without answer; her cities lost, Giang's cousin and her first adolescent crush since long gone silent, a youth that ended without a chance to flower.

"Ssh," Chau says—and in the silence that follows, Giang hears the buzzing of the cicada woman, rising and rising until it seems to erase everything else.

"First Mother? First Mother?" Hai Ngan is shaking her, her face creased in concern.

Giang forces herself to move, though all she can see is the blood on the cicada woman's hands. "It's nothing. I'm just tired."

"Just tired. Second Mother said she was just tired too," Hai Ngan's face is stern, an expression Giang knows all too well, one that masks fear rather than annoyance. "Before the diagnosis."

"I'm fine," Giang says. "Don't worry on my account."

Chau shakes her head. "Of course we're going to worry. We're your daughters." She doesn't ask about the papers, but that's only because she's more polite than her elder sister.

"You're going to have a child," Giang says, shaking her head. "That's what should matter." She stares at the cicada woman, and finally says, "I've been having nightmares. About what happened in the old country." They never name it—none of the refugees do. Superstition, as if it were a dead person that shouldn't be recalled.

Chau's face is grave. She opens her mouth, shuts it again. "I don't know what it was like. No one does, not in our generation."

"No trading expeditions go there." Hai Ngan pulls a chair, stares at Giang—but doesn't sit down. Of course. She prefers being in control. "We could get in—that would be easy—but getting out would be all but impossible."

"I know," Giang says, curtly. "But—" She's told them their grandmother died getting her out of the old country, but not about the cicada woman, or what it meant—if she can even be sure of what it meant at all. "I've been thinking about my cousin, lately. Your Second Aunt Ly." She hesitates again; hears only the relentless buzzing of the cicadas. "She survived the war, but not through anything I did. I left her behind when Mother died. She'd fallen to the ground after the bombs hit, and I couldn't carry her. Too much—" she takes a deep, shaking breath, not looking at her daughters. She could say she was following Mother's orders, but that's never been anything but the flimsiest of excuses. "There were fliers and they were coming back, and I thought we were going to die. I—"

Silence. Chau looks shocked. Hai Ngan shakes her head. "Second Mother always said that there was no shame in surviving."

"Isn't there?" Giang asks, staring at the cicada woman.

"Don't be silly," Chau says. Her voice is slow, careful. Controlled. Still in shock, then; as if this utterly changed what she thought of Giang. "You can't turn back time."

No. She can't. But—

But Lan Anh is dead, and her children are grown; perhaps it's time for all debts to be finally paid.

Hai Ngan's gaze is sharp again. She holds out the plate with the sweet cakes. "You should eat."

As if she was a child, and her own daughter the parent. Giang snorts. "I'm not senile yet."

"Of course not," Chau says, smoothly, but she doesn't say anything as Hai Ngan holds out the plate again.

Giang takes a cake, bites into it, keeping her eye on the shadowed face of the cicada woman. It tastes, not of sugar or honey, but acrid like smoke, like burnt flowers.

* * *

That night, Giang has the nightmare again—waking up in an unfamiliar house, going into the kitchen to find only the cicada woman staring at her, and the sound of fireworks filling her entire world. She wakes up gasping for breath, swallowing the acrid taste in her mouth—and is halfway to the kitchen for a cup of tea before she realizes there's a lantern burning there, and the faint sounds of a conversation.

"She's too stubborn."

"As if you didn't know what that was like."

Hai Ngan and Chau sit at the table, around two cups of tea. They look up, startled, when Giang wanders in—and fall silent, as if it wasn't perfectly clear what they'd been discussing. Between them, the cicada woman stands, a ghostly, uncannily still shape—the bright red stain on her clothes gleaming in the dim light, sharp and more focused than all the rest of her. "I'm sorry," Giang says. "I couldn't sleep."

"Nightmares again?" Hai Ngan's voice is disconcertingly sharp.

Giang stares at them—at the curve of Chau's belly, at Hai Ngan's rich silk pajamas, her face for once free of the dust of the trail; at daughters she's raised from infancy, now safely grown into adults of their own, earning their own living, expecting a child—and finds the words welling like blood out of a wound. "I need to go back. To the old country."

Silence. She's expected to hear the buzzing of cicadas, but everything is mercilessly clear, as sharp as broken glass. Hai Ngan's gaze rests on her, and Chau moves, shifting positions with deliberate slowness.

"You live *here*." Hai Ngan's words are clipped and precise, the way they always are when she's angry, and every one of them is a fist beating against Giang's chest. "You've always lived here. This is your home. You just can't— for Heaven's sake, Chau is expecting a child. If there was ever a time—"

"To stay?" Giang looks down at her feet, small and shamed. "You don't understand."

"No, I don't! You always said it was the past. You always said there was no going back. You—" She stops, breathes; starts again more slowly, words used as tools and as weapons, as she's always done. "You always said we were safe here."

In a way that Giang wouldn't be, in the old country—even if the war is over, what kind of welcome can she expect, in a country devastated by battles, where her cousin all but starves? "I have to."

"No," Hai Ngan said. And, more softly, "I'm sorry, First Mother. It just makes no sense."

A shifting sound from the chair: Chau, slowly pulling herself upwards— giving up, and rolling sideways until she can stand up. She stares, for a while, at Giang—with the same wide eyes she had, as a toddler, when she clung to tables and chairs and plates, and broke all the cups of Lan Anh's best tea set. "I can't understand either," Chau says, slowly. "But I don't pretend to." And, to Hai Ngan, "She carried us this far. You can't possibly think to set boundaries now."

"She's our mother."

"Yes," Chau says.

"Your child—" Giang starts, and Chau shakes her head.

"You worry too much about us, and not enough about yourself. You'll eat yourself to the bone."

"There's no coming back, if you do this. Not for a while." Hai Ngan looks at her cup of tea, bites her lips. "There's talk they might reopen the wall, but that would be in years."

Giang knows. "I don't know what to say—"

"Then don't. Just stay. Please."

Giang walks closer. She hugs her eldest daughter, as she did when Hai Ngan was very small, coming barely up to her waist, as stubborn and as fearful of change as she is now. "I failed your aunt, in the old country. And for years she's been living there in the hell it's become, while I had everything I could possibly dream of here."

"Life is unfair," Hai Ngan says. "It's none of your business."

"It is," Giang says. "I stole that life from my cousin, and I have to make amends for it. You know what debts mean."

"I don't want to know."

Chau says, from behind Giang, "Let go, big'sis."

"Like you find this easy?"

"No," Chau says. She sounds exhausted again. "I'm not happy. Why should I be?" When Giang turns, she catches sight of Chau's hands, clenched so hard blood has fled the knuckles. "But I'm not going to tell my mother how to live her own life."

"I—" It sounded so easy, so certain when she walked into the kitchen, and now Giang finds that words have fled her. The price of going back is like that of going into exile: there is no clear path, nothing that is painless or without cost.

"Do you want me to stay?" she asks.

Hai Ngan pulls herself away, watches her; watches Chau. "Yes," she says, and just as Giang's breath catches, "but Chau is right. It's your choice, First Mother."

Between Giang's daughters, the cicada woman raises her head, to the light of the lantern. Giang half-expects to see Mother or Cousin Ly, or some half-insectile monstrosity she'd recoil from—but there's nothing of that, merely an impenetrable, featureless darkness, with only the barest suggestion of a human face. She hears, again, Mother's voice, humming that tuneless song—her voice faltering, scattering into the low buzzing of cicadas, a sound that pierces Giang's heart as surely as the tip of a knife.

* * *

Seen from afar, the old country looks almost peaceful. The wall stands on the edge of an expanse of deserted mountains on either side, slowly curving away like the body of a great dragon: the cities and countryside all lie further in, and there's barely anything that seems to reflect the broken, starving land of Cousin Ly's letters.

An illusion, though one that brings no ease or comfort.

Giang stands on the border of the Everlasting Empire, at the gates of the wall. Besides her is the cicada woman—her five-panel tunic whipped around by the rising wind, her hands bloodied as Giang's were, forty years ago.

In her mind is Hai Ngan's voice, clipped and precise and careful. *You know there's no coming back.* And Chau's: *you'll eat yourself to the bone*—and further on, Lan Anh's words, about doing what they could, with the gifts they've been given.

A wife and two daughters; and some measure of happiness—all bought for her because she ran away, because she abandoned Cousin Ly. Because she wanted to live so much, so selfishly, that she never looked back.

You've carried us this far, First Mother.

The cicada woman doesn't speak. She merely holds out her hands, offers a choice. To turn back, to where Hai Ngan is waiting, forever fleeing that dusty plateau where Mother died and where Giang left Cousin Ly; or to walk away from her children and the life she's built, and finally go back to Cousin Ly and everything she left behind.

Giang takes her first step forward, onto the dry, rock-strewn soil of the old country, feeling its warmth under the soles of her feet like that of a hearth.

DYING ON STAGE

Andrew Dunlop

Sunday

"Did you hear about the church that burnt down? Holy smoke!"

Ray O'Connor awoke to a bad comedy routine on his front drive. A *loud* comedy routine. Somewhat morbid, too. There were probably worse ways to start a Sunday morning, but none sprang rapidly to mind.

"What did one skeleton say to the other? I've got a bone to pick with you!"

After some internal debate, Ray decided that investigating the cause was more important than his morning cup of coffee. Even before his retirement, he had treasured weekend mornings. As a high school teacher, they had been his sole indulgence in the field of sloth. That he could rise at whatever hour pleased him any day of the week, now that he was fully retired, was a trivial fact. Weekend mornings—Sunday mornings—still retained a special quality.

He flirted with the idea of calling the cops, for public nuisance and trespassing, but couldn't bring himself to do it. At his retirement party, the other teachers had told Ray that his curiosity would be the death of him someday, and it was difficult to argue the point. If the would-be comedienne was dragged away, he'd never find out what this was all about.

"You know, they have to keep a gate up around the cemetery—people are dying to get in!"

As Ray opened his front door, he saw the woman standing on his driveway, spouting corny one-liners. If she was at the wrong address—if this was just some oddball way of harassing a friend and she had gone to the wrong place—then his appearance at the front door hadn't persuaded her of it. She was of indeterminate age, in full mourner's clothing, complete with veil, and was shouting jokes through a megaphone.

Ray furrowed his brow. He was coming to regret skipping the coffee. Years of indulging that single vice had made him a creature of habit, and it was distressingly difficult to face…whatever this was, without it. He had at least set the machine to percolate away, before striking out to investigate. Better to rationalize the coffee as a reward, then; a pat on the back for resolving the oddest problem that he had faced in the last few years.

Ray tossed the Sunday paper into the house and shut the front door, going down the few steps of the front walk and following the small path to the driveway. He walked up to the woman and crossed his arms. "Well?"

The woman turned to him and he noted that what he had first taken to be black clothing was actually dark reds and greens. She was, perhaps, in her early twenties, fair of countenance, with emerald eyes and a mane of auburn hair. She looked distantly familiar, but the connection eluded Ray and he discarded it.

"Ah, the man of the hour!" She hadn't put down the megaphone, although she did turn to greet him. He grimaced. It hadn't been hard to get her attention, at least.

With great effort, Ray forced a friendly demeanor. "Do you mind keeping the volume down a little bit?" He put a hand to his temple. "It's Sunday morning, after all, and most of my neighbours are enjoying a little lie-in. You understand."

"Sorry, but I can't be doing that." Despite her words, the young woman did shut off the megaphone, apparently realizing the patent absurdity of bellowing at someone a few steps away. "It's my job to mourn your death, y'see." She gave him a winsome smile, evidently convinced that the matter had been settled, and held up the megaphone again, with every apparent intention of resuming.

Ray's brow crinkled a little bit. He looked down at himself. He certainly *felt* fine, a mounting headache notwithstanding. "I suspect you may be a little early. Hopefully by at least a few years, although I suppose accidents happen." His tone was dry, but he scowled at the young woman anyway. Perhaps this was some sort of obscure threat? "Who hired you to do this?"

"You are an O'Connor, aren't you?" The young woman lowered the megaphone again, apparently annoyed at the continued interruption. "Ray O'Connor? Of the Dublin O'Connors?"

Ray ran a hand through his thinning hair. "I'm certainly Ray O'Connor, miss…although not of Dublin for at least four generations at this point." He was never certain if he was supposed to count the first generation, so he erred on the side of caution. "Why?"

"Well, it's only fit that an O'Connor, be he noble of spirit and goodly of mind, be mourned by his family bean sidhe, isn't it?" The woman huffed. "Spend a few short generations away from home and you forget the old ways. What do they teach in the schools here, I ask you? Can't even recognize a household spirit of mourning when you see one."

Ray bristled. True, there hadn't been a comprehensive comparative mythologies class when he had been teaching, but there was nothing wrong with the education system… "Wait, bean sidhe…" his voice trailed off, as umbrage was replaced by confusion. "You're saying that you're a banshee? A wailing woman that sings a lament in front of the house of one who has died or is soon to?"

The self-proclaimed banshee gestured to herself, as if presenting as evidence her presence, garb, and megaphone. "The same. I can think of a thing or two I'd rather be doing on a Sunday morn myself, comes to that. Duty called, however, and you'll not be finding me or mine wanting in answer to such a summons." She gave a mock curtsy with the long dark skirts she wore.

Ray frowned. He did recall some tales saying about as much, taught on his grandmother's knee. On the other hand, a great deal of his heritage had been left on foreign shores, with every effort to assimilate for years before his birth. Beyond an abridged family tree and a few special observances around St. Patrick's Day, he was familiar with few traditions observed by his ancestors.

"I...have some questions." He wasn't a superstitious man, he knew—he reassured himself of that, firmly. Good and bad luck were just probability and causality, and neither magic nor faeries had a place in his set of beliefs. Still, there was something curiously compelling to this visitor's surety, and that alone was enough to keep his curiosity piqued.

"Well I don't have answers for you! I'm a supernatural mourning spirit and a psychopomp, not a reference book!"

Ray's frown deepened. "Now see here, miss. If you're here to mourn my death, what is it that I'm supposed to have died of then? As I said before, I'm remarkably healthy for a dead man." A good head of indignation built up behind him. "In fact, if you're supposed to lament my death, I rather feel like I should protest the stand-up routine, too. You're not exactly singing, are you?"

The woman bristled at that. "Well pardon me. Not all of us are blessed with beauteous singing voices. You're getting mourned, as is your due, but don't get snippy with me just because you didn't warrant the next great voice of Ireland." Ray felt it possible he had touched on a sore point. "And if you must know, you're to electrocute yourself when you take the coffee pot from the machine. Unlikely, really, but a freak chance of wiring and there you go."

Ray blinked, bemused. "Do you think there's a good chance of that happening at this point?"

The self-proclaimed banshee closed her eyes and breathed out deeply through tightly pursed lips. "I don't suppose I can convince you that you didn't hear that?"

Ray turned and headed back into his house. "No."

Just to be safe, he unplugged the coffee maker before drawing the pot from its cradle. That afternoon, he went shopping for a new machine.

* * *

Monday

If bad comedy was an unpleasant way to wake—or, Ray chuckled to himself, to have at one's wake—then having a distressingly authentic Punch and Judy show set up in front of his house added little to lunchtime. He hadn't seen the strange woman claiming to be a banshee for over twenty-four hours, and while he hadn't been—quite—ready to write it all off as a prank or similar, neither had he elected to let it trouble him. Life was, after all, what you made of it, and by seventy, he was pretty good at putting a positive spin on every day.

It was that or become salty and crotchety, another old man that hung around the local barbershop and groused about how life had been better before all these young people had shown up to ruin the concept of youth. Ray shuddered at the thought. He wasn't a polyanna, but if you were only as old as you felt, then those men must have been in their late second century. Feeling young and vital by comparison and inspired to prove it, he'd decided to go out for a jog.

He rounded the corner to home and frowned on seeing the small puppet theatre that had been erected on his driveway. So, she was back. If it was a prank, it was an unusually committed one—if it was something else…well, he wasn't entirely sure just *what* it was. Weird, definitely.

Ray had seen a Punch and Judy show once before, when he had been much younger. It hadn't been well received. They had never had the same popularity outside the UK, and by that point the themes of domestic abuse hadn't exactly been the last word in comedy. The puppeteer had been skilled, but there was something profoundly creepy about abusive puppets.

Both of which were dressed as mourners. And—yes—even the crocodile had a small piece of black crepe covering its eyes.

Ray came to a stop in front of the stall. "I'm pretty sure that puppet shows aren't a suitable lament either." Punch turned to him, his swazzled voice incomprehensible in reply. Ray tried again. "And I don't talk to the puppets. Get out here."

The young woman emerged, frowning. "Look, do you have any idea how hard it was to lay hands on this stuff? Especially on short notice."

Ray folded his arms over his chest. "I'm fairly certain that's neither my fault nor my problem. What are you doing?"

The banshee huffed. "Well, since you didn't like the stand-up routine, I'm exploring alternate venues of oral expression in an effort to lament your upcoming death. It so happens that I did a paper on Punch and Judy shows when I was pursuing an arts degree and I knew someone who had a setup I could borrow."

The puppets said nothing, but the banshee still held them tense and Ray squirmed a little. There was the disquieting feeling that remaining silent was their own choice, rather than the result of their puppeteer not giving them words. The carved faces were ghoulish and mocking.

"Look, I'm not sure I buy your premise," Ray found himself very carefully *not* thinking about the short that he'd discovered in his old coffee machine, "but if you must insist on pretending to be a banshee, and you feel this strange need to harass me, then why don't you just sing? It's traditional, and at least people would have some idea what you were doing."

Ray couldn't make out the woman's reply—her usually strident tone was all but a whisper, and he strained to hear her muttering.

"I beg your pardon?"

She scowled. "I get performance anxiety, alright? I don't have a very good singing voice and I get worried that I'll be judged harshly for it." She didn't meet his eyes. "And…well, I'm doing my best. When you cork it, you'll be mourned, and I'll have done my bit for your branch of the family tree, or what's left of it at any rate."

Ray was bemused. "When I cork it? Going to die again, am I?"

The woman nodded. "Noon on the dot. You make yourself a tuna sandwich and choke on a bone that wasn't removed."

Ray frowned. "Well, there are two problems with that." He gestured at the house. "Now that I know the dangers of my canned tuna, I think I'm going to have the ham. No offense, just not looking to snuff it right at the moment. Two, it's already five minutes past."

The banshee closed her eyes and let out a deep sigh. "Not again." She gestured at him. "Look, everyone dies sooner or later. Nature of being a mortal. From the Greek, I think. Mort. To die. Al. One who does. Get on with it, already!"

"I'm pretty sure that wasn't exactly accurate etymology."

The young woman ground her teeth. "Spirit of death. Psychopomp. These are things that I am. Reference guide? I am not. Dictionary? Not that either. Why won't you just die? It's your time! I checked, believe me."

Ray was getting frustrated. "Just take your damned puppet stage and get off of my property." He gestured at his home. "Nobody in this house is dying today. Not for your convenience, not for your entertainment, and not for your stupid puppet show."

As he stormed into the house, he could swear that he heard, in the back of his mind, a tiny, tinny voice cheering.

That's the way to do it!

* * *

Tuesday

There was a one-man band on his driveway.

Ray groaned. Strictly, it was a one-banshee band, being played inexpertly. She hadn't been a bad puppeteer, and the banshee had the panache, if not the material, of a decent comic, but he didn't care to speculate what had inspired this particular bit of foolery. Apart, of course, from his ever present oncoming death.

A brief flash of imagination had him wondering if he'd have to put up with this every day if he lived another thirty years. He shuddered. His copy of Bullfinch hadn't said anything about being annoyed to death.

His first couple of attempts to get the woman's attention were unsuccessful, due in no small part to the massive bass drum on her back, beating out what he presumed to be the polka equivalent of a requiem. Eventually, he walked in front of her and waved his hands, managing to get her attention away from the sheet music on a small stand strapped to her shoulders.

The banshee spat out the harmonica. "Yes?"

He gestured at the entirety of her outfit. "Really? A one-man band?" His gesture continued, frustration exaggerating his movements until the question described by them became existential in scope. Ray sighed, running a hand through thinning strands. "Why?"

"Well, you didn't like the puppet show, and you weren't a fan of the stand-up comedy, so I figured I'd go musical this time." A shrug, accompanied by the clanging of a top hat cymbal. "Since you seem to have this obsession with singing. Plus, I included the traditional element of wailing on the harmonica! Pretty clever, huh?" There, for a moment, was a hopeful smile, familiar from dozens of students that had hoped a moment of cleverness could make all the difference.

Ray snorted. "Words fail me." This was proven false as he continued in the same breath. "So if you're so self-conscious about doing a poor job with the singing, how can you play this array so badly without shame? I feel like I should also point out that I have no intention of dying, but if you didn't listen the first two times, I can't imagine why you would now."

The banshee carefully unstrapped the rig—the main part of it at least—and set it on the ground. "Alright. First of all, rude." She frowned. "I don't control the times of death. I merely come to herald it and serve to ease the pain of passing. That you will die or not is not something of which you must convince me, but the world." There was a moment's pause, as she composed herself and organized her thoughts. "The thing is...nobody expects that a bean sidhe should be good at being a one-man band, or a puppeteer, or a comedian. You have no idea the kind of pressure that comes from the expectations."

Ray's heart softened a little at that. As a teacher, he'd seen too many kids trying to live up to expectations that they hadn't felt ready for or been able to face. Sometimes they had powered through it, and sometimes they had been broken by it, but every time he'd seen it, he'd known that it was one of the hardest things in the world to face. On the other hand...

"Look, you can understand my attitude. You might not be a mortal..." and here he wasn't certain if he was simply humoring her, or if he'd come to believe it himself, "but portents of death don't exactly put one at ease. What's supposed to happen to me this time?"

The banshee's eyes narrowed. "Oh, no. You're not going to get me with that old trick this time. Every time I tell you how you're going to die, you then go and avoid it. If I tell you, you won't even get *into* the shower."

There was a pause. She closed her eyes. Ray, familiar from long experience with the appearance of someone slowly losing their patience and possibly their mind, heard her slowly counting backward.

"Five, four...Aw, crap."

"Right. I'm...going to go to the gym, maybe. And have a shower there." He glanced at her. She made a gesture of dismissal. "Should I be calling the exterminator or the electrician?"

The banshee had bent over to collect the discarded pieces of her one-man band outfit, but rolled her eyes. The moment had unquestionably passed. "Just put down a non-slip mat."

* * *

Wednesday

Ray disliked yard work, but was also strongly against plant detritus cluttering his lawn or garden. The conflict of values ultimately lead to the distasteful chore being done as quickly as possible, so that more pleasant pursuits could be undertaken.

It was late afternoon and Ray was not a little on edge. The banshee hadn't shown up yet, and there was a certain hesitating anticipation in the air, like waiting for the other shoe to drop. He didn't wish to jinx it—not that he believed in jinxes *per se*, but it didn't hurt to be careful under the circumstances—but perhaps she had finally given up? It was bittersweet, that possibility. He had friends, but no close ones. He didn't dwell on the prospect of death—he tended to try to keep active—but it was comforting, somehow, to think that when he was gone, he would be mourned.

Inexpertly, but still.

And, as if on cue, the sound of loud declamation from the front yard. It sounded like blank verse, but it was impossible to be certain at a distance.

"The evil men do lives after them; the good is oft interred with their bones..."

Ray wasn't sure where the banshee had gotten a ruff. It wasn't like one could just buy one these days. Still, given her usual dark costume, it didn't look entirely out of place. Definitely eccentric, though he was coming to expect eccentric from her.

Then again, she didn't seem to have any difficulty sourcing unusual props and costumes. He wondered if it was a banshee thing, or if she was particularly suited to set and costume design. It was impossible to tell without knowing other banshees and he didn't know *anyone* quite like her.

"Hold it, Brutus."

She looked over at him, voice faltering slightly as her concentration was broken. "Marc Antony, actually." She gave Ray a sheepish grin. "Maybe not the most flattering passage for you to walk in on, but ... not bad, right?" It was that same hopeful smile again.

She was persistent, obnoxious, and not a little macabre. She had undertaken what could be described by the uncharitable as a campaign of harassment and she had persisted for days. And yet some online research had revealed that banshees weren't bringers of death, but heralds of it. Beings intended to ease the transition from life to death, to mourn the passing of a life, and to ease the moment of a painful transition.

It was odd. If the neighbors had taken offense, they had said nothing—and that was definitely not the style of the neighborhood association. They were happy to squawk about any number of other issues, and he was quite certain that a great deal of pearl clutching would have occurred. Another sign that this might be the genuine article, a herald of death—there was nothing like a community of pensioners for whistling past graveyards and being wilfully blind to a manifestation of the Reaper.

Or perhaps it was all a coincidence. Stranger things, he was sure, had happened, although he found himself hard-pressed for examples when put on the spot.

He turned back to the banshee in Elizabethan garb. "I stand corrected. Marc Antony." He tried to remember Julius Caesar from his college years. "If you say you're going to read my will next, I'm going to have to direct you to my lawyer."

She actually cracked a smile. "Well, 'tis good to have one. Especially," she gestured at him, "under the circumstances."

He rubbed at his eyes, pointer finger and thumb pinching the bridge of his nose as he did so. "The circumstances being my imminent demise from...something?"

"Allergic reaction to a bee sting in the back garden." She said absently. There was a pause. "You know, I'm starting to wonder if I'm actually doing this on purpose, on an unconscious level."

"I have noticed a surprising uptick in the number of fatal accidents I'm supposed to have." Ray said wryly. "No strong correlation with actual accidents suffered, mind you, but it's still a disturbing trend."

The banshee shrugged. "It's your time?" She shook her head. "I don't know how it works. I'm part of the system, but not the whole of it. I can tell when someone is going to die. A banshee comes to mourn for them, and they cork it. I don't know why it isn't working now. The theory seems to be pretty sound, and by all accounts it's always worked before." She held up a hand. "And before you even start, don't ask me about free will. I don't know, alright?"

She slouched off, looking for all the world as if she was in search of a theater to star in.

It hadn't been a bad question, Ray reflected, as he gathered up his tools and studiously avoided the flower beds which were receiving due attention from the buzzing bees. But then, perhaps this was it; him exercising free will. And if the Neighborhood Association came by to complain about his messy yard work, then he could tell them about the banshee and they could ignore him too.

* * *

Thursday

A few local stores offered discounts to seniors on Thursdays—probably following some obscure sales algorithm—so as much as possible he tried to pick up the essentials while the better prices could be taken advantage of. Shopping around for the best prices made for busy Thursdays, but a fixed income meant that it was necessary. As he wandered around the grocery, he paused briefly at the canned tuna, before thinking better of it.

It didn't hurt to be a little extra careful, considering.

He supposed that, accepting the premise, he'd had several close encounters with Death, or near enough as made no difference. For some reason, he'd bought in to the mass-media interpretation—a tall, gaunt, pale figure with the black hood and scythe—all of his life, but now it was hard to imagine anything other than the…well, pale, yes, but neurotic and not particularly skeletal woman in the role. He had been skeptical—still was—but the fact of the matter was, there was the ring of truth to her demeanor. He didn't wish to believe that he was slated to die, but it wasn't impossible to believe that the *banshee* believed what she was saying.

And it had influenced his life, as well. He'd been trying to do more healthy activities, and trying to distract himself, while simultaneously waiting for the herald of death to show up again. There was a metaphor for life if he'd ever heard one.

Lost in thought, he nearly wandered into that same vision of Death, currently in the process of setting up what appeared to be a grocery samples stand. He raised an eyebrow. "Free samples of death? A little on the nose, wouldn't you say?"

She scowled at him, clearly irritated. "Well, if you must know, I was *planning* to give a sales pitch, continuing in the theme of 'the oral tradition.' Now I wonder if I'll even bother." She glanced down at the table, where she'd set up a hot plate. "Also, this is the longest I've spent in a single place. It's not as if I need a job, but it's useful to have something to do while I wait for whatever horrible thing is due to happen to you next."

Ray gave the banshee a bemused look. "Your confidence in my ability to survive is rather underwhelming." He shook his head. "I'll admit, I don't know what to make of you." She gave him a sharp look, but he held up a hand. "I don't know why, but I believe you are who you say that you are. It's just … difficult to make sense of. Beyond the obvious, I mean. If you're the Death of my family, why are you struggling so much with this?"

She gave a faint, sad smile. "Do you really want to know?"

He nodded and the feeling of familiarity returned, stronger and different than before. Initially, it had been the sense that he had met her somewhere before. Now, it was clearer, and yet more opaque; as if he had walked with her every day of his life and yet didn't even know her name. She suddenly seemed very old indeed and he felt very young.

He nodded again, uncertain of himself now. "I do."

She took a sip from one of the cups of water in front of her. "I am your

Death, Ray O'Connor. And the Deaths of your ancestors, and the Deaths of hundreds of others besides. But here, and now, in this place, I am *your* Death, and this is who I am. And I am young because you have not brushed with Death before, and I am inexperienced because you are far from the bones of those who came before you. And I am frightened to sing because I am the only Death you get." She gave a rueful smile. "And I don't want to make a hash of it. I only get to sing once, and I worry that my song will not be enough. So if I half-ass it, I haven't yet reached the point of no return."

Ray had slipped into a liminal space, of sorts; no one acknowledged the two of them, because they were in that twilight zone that was between here and there. The eyes of passing shoppers had slid by her automatically; death was the ultimate threshold, and to acknowledge her was to stay there longer than anyone felt comfortable doing. He had ceased to exist to the world outside. Real, and yet unreal.

He started to speak, but the moment had been intimate and now it had passed. A minute before he had seen something vulnerable and it had changed the world, at least a little; now they were back in the store, if a step apart, and if there were anything to say, he didn't know what it was.

He tried anyway. "I'm sorry..." but it rang hollow and was ash in his mouth. Sorry for what? He had prided himself on living his life as fully as he could; was he sorry he wasn't resigned and salty, like his neighbors, or living in the shadow of his own death, so that she would have more confidence?

The banshee shook her head and began to pack up her things. "I need to go." Ray watched her leave, not sure what he should say or do, and so saying and doing nothing.

Ray didn't buy all that much that day after all, excellent discounts notwithstanding. Somehow, parsimony seemed less important right now. He was polite, but curt with the clerk, and left quietly, deep in thought.

* * *

Friday

The banshee didn't come to Ray on Friday, although he looked for her. It left him a little sad, although he had no idea why. He worried that he'd hurt her, and he worried that she had said things that she wished that she hadn't. As he went to bed that evening, he wondered if she had given up. He fell asleep wondering what that might mean. Sleep was long in coming, and by the time it arrived, he had no more satisfying an answer than when he first retired for bed.

* * *

Saturday

Ray saw the banshee outside of his house, once more. No props, that he could see from his window, no elaborate costumes, just her, in dark veil and garb, almost exactly as she had been when they had first met, although strangely silent now. There seemed to be no time like the present, and he went down the short path to the driveway, and down to the street, which was also strangely quiet for this time in the morning.

His initial impulse was to begin with a joke, but something within him strangled the notion in the cradle. It seemed inappropriate, and besides, he was mostly just happy to see her, whatever her presence foretold.

He offered the second cup of coffee he had poured to her. She tilted her head and took it. "Thank you."

"It seemed the least I could offer. New machine and all." More than he probably should have spent, but it was the top of the line model. Good for entertaining, for all that he scarcely ever entertained.

"I'm sorry about the other day," she began. "It wasn't particularly fair of me to unload all of that on you. No offense, but in terms of the cosmic balance of the universe, you're most certainly on the user-end, not particularly to be bothered with the provider's troubles. It's not f—"

Ray cut her off, holding up a hand, shaking his head. "Three words that are always true and hardly worth finishing." His voice caught in his throat a little bit, but it had been a week that had forced him to consider some unpalatable things. "Look..." he caught himself pausing again, and then forced himself to continue. "I've been considering what you said. About your concerns and your problems. I just wanted you to know..." it was hard to keep going, but he knew that he had to. "Well, the world can be a harsh and cruel place. If you've seen—been—as many deaths as you said, you don't need me to tell you that. Often things come at us faster than we can handle them, when we aren't expecting them, and not in the way that we would have chosen. I'm not in any rush to shuffle off this mortal coil, but if it comes to it—when it comes to it—sing. It doesn't have to be perfect. Life never is. But you never take a second step if you never take a first."

As a teacher, he'd given similar speeches to students struggling with problems that were felt bigger than they were. In a sense, it gave a strange sort of perspective to realize that problem didn't stop beyond the human level. It just scaled upward.

She smiled, sadly. He tried his best to smile reassuringly. And then she opened her mouth and sang.

It wasn't beautiful. It was a little haunting, but not in sublime majesty; it moved the heart and the soul because it was genuine, not because it was perfect. Here and there, the wordless tune cracked and faltered, but nothing was withheld and nothing was forbidden. It was a balm upon the wounds in the world and for a moment, nothing hurt, and the weight of age fell from Ray like dew from a leaf. He wasn't young again; not even comparatively. But all of a sudden he wasn't old, either. He wasn't Ray O'Connor, Old Man, and he wasn't Ray O'Connor, Frequently At Odds With the Homeowners Association. He was just Ray O'Connor, as much and as loud as life could permit, standing in the street with a young woman who might or might not actually be there.

The song came to a pause and the world flowed in again. Somehow, it wasn't as harsh as it had been. The colors were vibrant, but not gaudy; the noisy world pronounced, cacophonous, but not obnoxious. The aches and pains of age were back, but they were familiar, not demanding. For a moment, there had been nothing but the song, imperfect though it was. Now, everything else was back, but it was a world where the song had happened and the imperfections of the world seemed less demanding, somehow.

The banshee tilted back her head and sang a final, trilling note, high and mournful, great, terrible, and magnificent.

It came at Ray faster than he could handle and when he wasn't expecting it. He never saw the truck coming.

A Constant Companion

JULIET E. MCKENNA

"Wait till I get hold of Anil Deker, spreading tales like that," the young woman muttered wrathfully. She strode through the market square rather faster than was ladylike, though thankfully the townsfolk were too busy with their own affairs to notice.

"Oh, don't look at me like that." She shot a glance at the enormous black hound loping at her side. "I won't betray him to Inky Jerban. But he won't go around clucking like his aunt's chickens by the time I've finished with him."

They approached a light carriage waiting by the public water trough. The chestnut horse in the shafts pricked its ears, looking over the edge of its nosebag. The driver was dozing on his seat, his russet livery coat unbuttoned. As the horse whickered, the gray-haired man sat up, concerned.

"Lady Dalria? Is something amiss?" Carden asked as he buttoned his coat.

The young woman curbed her anger. This was hardly Carden's fault. "I'm sorry. I've changed my mind about visiting the market. There's some new rumor that my brother's alive and returned to claim his title, along with the castle and all the estate."

The coachman's expression darkened as he jumped down to open the carriage door and unfold its step. "It's been, what, six years since the last time someone turned up spouting such nonsense?"

"Quite so." Dalria paused as she plucked up the green fabric of her skirt to avoid treading on the hem.

"Well, your grandsire drove that scoundrel off with his tail between his legs. We'll soon be rid of this one."

Dalria smiled as if she shared Carden's confidence. Inwardly, she sighed. She well remembered her grandfather ripping that last imposter's claims to shreds, even though she'd barely been thirteen years old. Now though,

Grandfather was dead and gone like the winter that had claimed him, and his loss was still so recent, so raw, that grief could still overwhelm her without warning.

She must maintain the composure he had taught her, essential to fulfill her duties as his heir. Essential if she was to challenge the lawyer who handled the business and legal affairs of her birthright—Master Jerban's letters already indicated that he assumed she would follow his instructions, rather than him taking hers.

"Indeed, but I fear it may not be so simple this time," she said as she settled into the coach. "It seems that Master Jerban has brought this particular claimant to Harles himself."

"My lady?" Carden gaped at her.

Dalria took a moment to make sure her voice stayed calm. "You remember Anil Deker? Nephew to Mistress Warin, the egg seller?"

The coachman nodded as he secured the door. "Proud as one of her own roosters she was, when he went off to clerk for the castle in Bastrys."

"It seems he was quick to share such juicy news with his family when Jerban's coachman stopped to water the horses," Dalria said tartly. "And his aunt is already spreading it in the market."

"We must have just missed them on the road." Now the coachman was looking pensive as he climbed into his seat and gathered up the reins.

Placidly, the horse headed out of the little town and towards its stable. It gave no sign of noticing the great black hound trotting at its side.

* * *

As they reached Harles Castle, Carden drove into the inner courtyard, drawing the carriage to a halt in front of the grandest entrance.

Ordinarily they'd have gone to the stable yard on the castle's far side. Dalria would have walked in through the kitchens, pausing to wish Mistress Zante good morning. They'd have shared a glass of cordial and a honeycake as they discussed the housekeeper's daily concerns.

Dalria could pretend that life continued as it had done before her grandfather died. But everything had changed.

* * *

As Carden jumped down to open the carriage door, Dalria took care to descend with all the poise she could muster. Wide windows on either side of the ornate doorway overlooked this inner courtyard, and she could guess who would be watching for her arrival.

Carden bowed low as she exited, just as he had always done to her grandfather.

No, she must not remember that. She must keep her grief at bay until she had dealt with this challenge.

The great black hound growled softly, deep in its throat, as it stalked up the steps at her side. Comforted, Dalria felt her courage returning.

"My lady." Harbon was waiting to open the carved oak door. "You have visitors."

The door to the reception room on their left opened. Dalria turned, her expression calm and composed. Grandfather had taught her the value of never letting any adversary think you were taken unawares.

"Lady Dalria." Mistress Jerban advanced into the magnificent entrance hall. Her gown and adornments were doubtless the finest that Bastrys merchants could supply. Ochre silk, elegantly accented with gold and amber jewelry, was entirely fitting for these opulent surroundings.

Dalria could see the older woman's disdain for her own plain woolen gown. As for going out in public, even in this warm spring weather, without a suitably decorative and decorous shawl? Mistress Jerban would sooner walk barefoot through soiled streets. That was merely one of the lessons the woman had chosen to share on her first visit, offering endless, unwanted advice in that dark week of the old Margrave's funeral.

Dalria smiled. "You may address me as 'My Lady Margravine,' or Lady Reole, if you prefer."

Mistress Jerban curtsied, perfunctorily. "That title awaits the Paramount King's confirmation." She turned to summon the young man standing with her husband by the window.

Dalria forestalled her, turning to Harbon. Turning her back on whoever was loitering with the lawyer, uninvited and unwelcome. "I will see Master Jerban in my grandfather's—" she coughed "—in the muniment room."

Without a backward glance, she walked past the lofty staircase leading to the upper floors and took the passage heading for the castle's oldest regions.

She heard Master Jerban's footsteps hurrying after her and quickened her pace. Striving to keep her breath even, she found the key to the muniment room on the chain at her waist.

Master Jerban arrived as she was taking her seat at the table where her grandfather had worked long days in the service of Harles Castle's tenants and dependents. All those people were now her responsibility.

He cleared his throat. "My lady."

Dalria sat straight-backed in the ancient oak chair and studied him in the dim light filtering through high, narrow windows. "Explain yourself, if you please."

"I would not have brought this young man here unless I believed his claim warrants serious consideration."

He looked at the high shelves packed with books and scrolls and document cases, the oldest records dating from hundreds of years ago. "Your brother's unknown fate was your grandfather's deepest sorrow. That his grandson could not be laid to rest beside his son and his wife—"

Dalria smacked the table top so hard that her hand stung. "Do not presume to lecture me on my family's grief. I remember the full depth of our loss—"

She screwed her eyes tight shut against treacherous tears. Feeling the comforting pressure of the great hound's body against her thigh, she buried her aching hand in his wiry fur.

Jerban was shaken. "You were not even five years old—"

"Old enough for that vile day to be engraved on my memory." She glared at him. "What makes this fortune-hunter any different than the others who tried to deceive my grandfather?" She scorned Jerban's surprise. "As his health failed this winter past, he told me to expect them with the spring finches. He knew how fraudsters would flock to prey on a young woman inheriting such an estate."

Her wave encompassed the muniment room with its generations of records, the sprawling castle beyond and all the lands from this hillside town of Harles down to the river port of Reole where her ancestor had won a Margrave's coronet by fighting at the King's side.

"Quite so. I have already sent the constables to haul several such scoundrels before the Justiciars. This young man's situation is quite different." Jerban laced his bony fingers together.

Dalria had noticed he always did that when he was about to lecture her, from her earliest days sitting quietly in this room at her grandfather's side. But Grandfather was dead and life had changed beyond recall.

"How so?" Beneath the table, she felt the black hound rest its head on her feet.

Jerban cleared his throat again. "His name is Keresh Rowle and he was raised as an orphan in the Sanctuary in Eridanse. When he was fourteen years of age, he was apprenticed to a papermaker and no one thought any more about him. These past months, though, news of your grandfather's death has spread along the rivers."

He paused.

"Whether it was by chance or the Moon God's will, that news reached the Sun Goddess's temple in Eridanse. Idle talk revived memories of your parents' fate and your brother's loss."

Dalria raised a hand to interrupt him. "Did such gossip recall how all enchantments in the Sun Goddess's gift failed to find him alive?"

"True, but even the Moon God's magic could not find his body," countered Jerban. "A priestess remembered the child Keresh had been brought to them a few months after that tragedy. She checked the precise date in their records and discovered he had been wearing an amulet which had been kept in case anyone ever claimed the child. If they could describe it, as proof of good faith—"

"What of it?" Dalria demanded.

"It shows a stag-horned sheep." Jerban reached for the inner pocket of his plain brown coat and produced a polished bronze rectangle, pierced and hung on a chain.

Even in the dim light, Dalria saw the unmistakable outline of her family's crest. She fought to keep her tone level. "And what does this Keresh say?"

"Very little," Jerban said with unexpected frankness. "He remembers nothing of his life before the Sanctuary. He knew nothing of this amulet, until the priestess discovered it and the Temple sent him to my office in Bastrys."

"My brother's name was Rechen, not Keresh." Dalria pressed her lips tight together. She felt the great hound stir beneath the table, rubbing its head against her legs.

"The child was brought to the priestesses sick almost to death with onion-skin fever. When he recovered, he didn't even know his own name." Jerban shrugged. "Keresh was the name of the priest-physician who saved him while Rowle was the family name of the grain merchant who found him abandoned, unconscious, in the street."

"In Eridanse?" Dalria shook her head. "My parents' vessel hadn't even reached Stannar when the squall sank it. How could a child not yet seven years old travel, what, five hundred leagues?"

"We assume the child was taken there by some unknown person," Jerban said testily.

"You can assume he was carried there on a winged horse," Dalria retorted, "but you have no evidence. That amulet proves nothing."

"He is of the same age—"

"Really? You've studied his teeth?" Dalria challenged. "You can be so certain when even the best horse-dealer can only tell a beast's age to within a few years?"

"I have the evidence of my own eyes," snapped Jerban. "I am not a complete fool, my lady. Your father and I were much of an age, and I was already clerking for Master Therind, who was your grandfather's man of affairs before me. I was honored that your father counted me as a friend. This young man, Keresh—" he groped for the best way to explain "—the resemblance is beyond striking. You must see for yourself. Do me that much courtesy, my lady."

Dalria felt embarrassment reddening her face. Grandfather had told her often enough that rank didn't excuse rudeness. "Very well," she said with all the dignity she could muster. "I will join you shortly." She reached for a piece of paper, any paper. It didn't matter what might be written on it, as long as looking at it meant avoiding the lawyer's eyes.

"My lady." Master Jerban bowed and withdrew, his shoulders stiff with indignation.

Grandfather would doubtless have told her the man was only doing his duty as he thought best. Just as his irritating wife doubtless thought she was helping a provincial, motherless girl. Dalria pressed ice cold hands to her flaming cheeks and closed stinging eyes.

The great black hound crept out from under the table and laid its head in her lap. With a questioning noise between a whine and a whimper, it looked up at her with liquid, deep brown eyes. She bent over to embrace the fearsome beast, pressing her face into its fur.

Silent moments passed. Dalria drew a shuddering breath, her resolve returning. She sat upright, her eyes dry. The great hound stretched its neck to brush her check with a flick of its long tongue. She patted its shoulder. "I suppose we'd better go and see, boy."

Returning to the newer building, she found Harbon in the entrance hall, looking anxious. The door to the reception room stood ajar. "My lady, your guests—"

"Where have they gone?"

"To the gallery." He gestured towards the stairs. "Should I have bedchambers prepared?"

"Thank you." Dalria smiled. "Please inform Mistress Zante there will be four to dinner. Meantime, you may go about your usual duties."

She went up the stairs, head held high. The great hound padded along at her side. The gallery was on the uppermost floor, light and airy and running the full width of the building. The long room offered a generous space for guests to gather in, or for small children to play endless games when wet weather forbade adventures out of doors. Dalria and her grandfather had spent countless such days together here. Then as she and he had both grown older, they had spent their time discussing the portraits hung in tiers two and three high.

Jerban was escorting the young man. "This is Lord Savalris, fifth margrave, who rebuilt much of this castle after the civil war."

"The family resemblance is undeniable," Mis-tress Jerban observed.

The young man, Keresh, stared at the paintings, astonished.

"Have you shown him Lord Lyelen?" Dalria asked as she entered. "My great uncle," she explained. "He travelled up and down the kingdom's rivers on my great-grandfather's business and left bastards the length and breadth of the realm."

She felt a qualm as she looked at this pretender for the first time. The angle of his dark eyebrows and the sharp beak of his nose were strikingly familiar, while the velvet mystery of his brown eyes reminded Dalria of her grandfather.

He bowed low. "And the dog?"

Dalria's heart pounded and her mouth was suddenly dry as dust. For an instant she truly feared she might faint. "You can see it?"

Keresh straightened up and looked at her, puzzled. "It's in all the pictures."

True enough, the fearsome hound stood next to every man and woman who had ever held the Reole title. Long and lean, its shoulders were level with even the tallest margrave's hip. Beside some of the women, its head rose higher than their waist.

"It's a crag hound," Jerban explained. "This family's prosperity was initially founded on flocks of stag-horned sheep grazed on their hill country estates—"

"Can you see it now, here, in this room?" Dalria demanded.

Beside her, the great beast pricked its ears, fur-plumed tail wagging, all its attention focused on the young man.

"What do you mean?" Keresh looked around, bemused.

Dalria found she could breathe again. His gaze swept past the hound at her side with no flicker of recognition in his eyes.

"Local folklore—" Jerban began hastily.

"It's of no consequence," his wife insisted in the same breath.

"That hound you see in all these portraits is Death," Dalria said baldly. "Our family's Death, at least, and if you cannot see that self-same black hound large as life and standing beside me, that proves beyond all doubt that you cannot be my brother. You are not my grandfather's heir."

"What?" The young man gaped at her.

"Magic extends beyond the temples and shrines, even if such things are seldom spoken of." Dalria met his gaze unblinking. "I have seen this great beast ever since that foul night when my family drowned. My grandfather saw him ever since his own grandfather died and he became the heir to his mother the Margravine. This is how our family's magic works."

"However sincerely meant, such stories prove nothing," Master Jerban insisted. "As far as the law is concerned—"

"Do you think we would come all this way without testing the witnesses and their testimony?" His wife was affronted on her husband's behalf. "We brought them all before the Justiciar in Bastrys, with a priest and priestess in attendance. We have sworn affidavits—"

"The Sun Goddess's magic proves that someone is telling the truth *as they know it*." Dalria clenched her fists, hidden in the folds of her skirts. "The Moon God's magic warns his priests when someone tells a *deliberate* lie. Neither reveals matters of *fact*."

"Validating such testimony rules out deliberate fraud." Jerban's courtesy was growing strained. "I have the Justiciar's authority to search the records here for mention of this amulet. For any indication that your brother could have been wearing it when your parents' boat was lost."

"Will you look for records of other trinkets bearing this house's insignia?" Dalria snapped. "Which could have passed through any number of hands before being hung around some pauper brat's neck?"

She regretted those words as soon as she saw the young man flinch with humiliation.

"Forgive me," she said curtly. "I did not mean to insult you."

He didn't acknowledge her apology, still looking up at the portraits. "How can an artist paint this hound, if only those who will inherit can see him?"

"That's merely one of this fable's contradictions." Mistress Jerban shot Dalria a venomous look.

She ignored the woman, addressing her reply to Keresh. "Other people may see him when there's a death in the line of succession. Ask the servants here. A few remember him appearing when my parents were lost. Several saw him when my grandfather died."

"They might wish to think so, because some shadow set their imagination running riot," Mistress Jerban scoffed.

"Artists work from the descriptions given to them by those sitting for the portraits." Dalria colored again as she recalled the polite skepticism of the urbane artist who had commemorated her last birthday. Once more, she blinked away tears. Her grandfather had died scant days after seeing the picture finished.

"They're remarkably consistent." The young man walked slowly along the gallery, studying portrayals of the hound. At Dalria's side, the beast sat on its haunches, long red tongue lolling from its open mouth.

"Hardly surprising." Mistress Jerban waved a dismissive hand. "Crag hounds are still bred in the hills."

Infuriated, Dalria stepped forward, any willingness to think the best of the woman's motives evaporating.

"My lady." Master Jerban bowed hastily. "With your permission, I will begin my search of the muniment room's records. The sooner we have some indication of —" he hesitated "—whatever might be firmly established, the better."

Though he didn't wait for her dismissal, turning to head for the stairs as soon as he finished speaking. Dalria saw his wife's barely veiled satisfaction. She also saw the embarrassment which Keresh was valiantly trying to hide. Whatever he had been led to expect, this confrontation was none of his making.

"You will excuse me." Dalria fled, barely able to avoid running in her haste to escape.

* * *

She made her way to the walkway built into the thickness of the old castle wall. Reaching the tall tower to the right hand of the outer gateway, she climbed to the ancient vantage point built for watchmen. She and her grandfather had come here ever since she was a small child. She had grown up with him telling her that all these lands would become her responsibility, together with the livelihoods and wellbeing of every man, woman and child who dwelled there.

The climb wasn't without its difficulties. The hound kept trying to squeeze past her in the narrow passage. Dalria recognized the displeasure in his low grumbling growl. He had been content for her to make this ascent with her grandfather, but since the old Margrave's death, the hound had made his misgivings clear. When Dalria pushed open the topmost door, the great beast seized its chance and forced its way past to stand between her and the low parapet.

"It's all right." Dalria sat down on the mossy slates. Asserting herself over the great hound was one thing. Stupidity was quite another. The wind up here was strong enough to pluck at her hair and clothing. Any sudden gust might well test her balance.

The great hound lay down with a huff of satisfaction. Its bulk still barred her from approaching the edge nonetheless and while it rested its muzzle on its forepaws, its dark eyes remained watchful.

Dalria gazed out over the countryside. The rooftops of Harles were just visible in the distance. To her right hand, the hills grew steeper and sharper, darkened with distant forests, while to her left, the land softened to the rolling green pastures of the downs.

"What happens now?" she challenged the dog. "Will Master Jerban find something to prove his theory? He really wants this boy's claim to be true." She bit her lip. "I never knew he and my father were friends. True friends, it seems, if he's so desperate to do the right thing by his memory."

She couldn't accuse Jerban of any ulterior motive. He hadn't gone looking for this unforeseen claimant. He had tested the youth's story as far as he possibly could.

"Why does his wife want this to be true?" Dalria drew up her feet hugged her knees. "To see her husband's influence increased? To see him earn the commissions and emoluments that will keep her in the style to which she's accustomed?"

She shook her head. "No, that's not entirely fair."

Doubtless Mistress Jerban had an interest in her husband's continued prosperity, but the woman was equally concerned with the best management of Dalria's inheritance. She had identified a handful of miscreants abusing the castle's customary charity shortly after the old Margrave's death.

What the woman found incomprehensible was Dalria's determination to take up the burden of her legacy. On her previous visit she'd made it clear she expected the girl to defer to older and wiser heads. If not, then she doubtless thought that an heir who did would make a far better margrave.

The great hound lay with its head on outstretched forepaws, watching intently as Dalria contemplated this conundrum.

"If Jerban can make a plausible case that this Keresh could very well be my long-lost brother, then the burden passes to me to prove that it is impossible. How am I supposed to do that? You're the only proof that I need, but I'm the only one who can see you here."

The black dog thumped its feathery tail on the slates.

"What then?" Dalria stared into the distance, unseeing. "Will Inky Jerban go to law to challenge me? Go to the Justiciary, waving his affidavits? Must I find myself an attorney to challenge him? How much of my time will this waste? How much of this family's income will vanish into lawyers' pockets? How far will the story spread? How soon before people choose to believe it, whatever the truth may be?"

She knew how uneasy the local townsfolk and farmers were, to see the Margravate resting on one unmarried young woman's shoulders. Her father had been an only son and his sisters had married into noble families many hundreds of leagues away. If this great inheritance was passed backwards to them, if her aunts chose to divide the family's holdings among their children's distant lineages, who knew what might befall the people here?

"Can my Aunt Rabesa see you?" Dalria looked thoughtfully at the massive dog. "Can you somehow be at her side all the way away in Chalus as well as with me here? Should I write and ask her? But what if she can't see you, because she's so far away? What if she can see you but denies it, for fear that her husband's family will think she's mad? Then everyone will call me a liar and say that our family's magic is no more than a myth. Surely that will strengthen this claimant's case?"

The hound whined, its brows hooded with concern.

"The sooner we resolve this, the better for everyone. But how can I prove I'm not lying?" Dalria drummed contemplative fingers. "Who else has seen you, and when?"

The great black dog didn't answer. He simply lay there, watchful and silent.

A few moments later, Dalria pursed her lips. She sprang to her feet. The hound leapt up and barked. She ignored him, heading down the spiral stair. As she followed the dank and shadowed walkway back to the newer reaches of the castle, the great hound was nowhere to be seen.

Dalria paused beside the muniment room door and knocked firmly. "Master Jerban! Come with me!"

She strode into the magnificent entrance hall and yanked the bell pull that would summon the servants. She flung open the door to the reception room, to reveal Mistress Jerban surprised into an inelegant gape.

"What is it?" Keresh, over by the window, was equally startled.

"Wait there," Dalria ordered.

"My lady?" Harbon appeared from the corridor leading to the kitchens, Mistress Zante hard on his heels.

"Wait there," Dalria repeated.

She climbed the broad sweep of the staircase but did not turn towards the library on the left, or to the withdrawing room on the right. Instead she climbed onto the marble balustrade overlooking the hallway's tiled floor. She swung herself around so that her feet dangled over the perilous drop.

"My lady, what are you doing?" Mistress Zante was horrified.

"Where are you?" Dalria called out. "Show yourself!"

Master Jerban appeared in shirtsleeves, clutching a sheaf of paper. "What's going on?"

He saw his wife's trembling hand pointing and looked up. Seeing Dalria on that perilous perch, he was lost for words.

"Show yourself," Dalria shouted, "or do I have to do more?"

Her words echoed back from the unyielding marble and tile. Everyone else was dumbstruck.

"Very well," Dalria said grimly.

She got gingerly onto her knees. First she set one foot beneath her, and then the other. Gathering all her courage, she rose to stand on the balustrade. She swallowed hard and stared straight ahead. Perhaps it would have been wiser to remove her shoes before trying this. The marble felt treacherously slick beneath her leather soles. She didn't dare look down though.

Stretching out her hands should improve her balance. She tried, only to find that didn't help. If anything she felt more unsteady. Cold dread clutched at her heart. Dalria stood, frozen. This folly would be the death of her. If she moved a muscle, even to try to get down, she would surely fall.

The hound appeared. It seized her skirts in its mouth and hauled her away from the drop. Dalria screamed as she fell backwards: for one heart-stopping moment, she had thought she was toppling forwards. The carpet did little to soften her landing. Her elbow hurt so fiercely that she feared she'd broken her arm.

"I'm sorry." Tears trickled down her cheeks. "Don't you understand? They had to see you."

The great black dog showed no sign of paying any heed. It stood over her, its baying deafening. When it heard footsteps running up the stairs, it whirled around, defiant with shoulders hunched and hackles bristling, barking at the intrusion.

"It's all right." Dalria managed to sit up, wincing as she realized how badly she'd bruised her tailbone. "Now, all of you, tell me that you can see him."

"I can." The young man, Keresh was looking warily at the great beast.

"But you couldn't see him before," Dalria said swiftly. "Not until everyone else could just now."

"Get back." Jerban tried to put himself between the snarling dog and the young man. "It may attack."

"Where did it come from?" His wife stood at the top of the stairs, wide-eyed. She recoiled with a yelp as the angry hound snapped at her. In the next breath, it vanished and she gasped. "Where did the creature go?"

"Madam." Harbon took a step forward, quivering with indignation. "That was the Hound of Harles. I saw it on the night this winter past when the old Margrave died, and so many years ago when My Lady Dalria's parents and brother were lost. I will go on oath before any priest or priestess whom you may summon."

"As will I!" Mistress Zante narrowed her eyes at the silk-clad woman.

"It has gone because as the rightful margravine, I am no longer in mortal danger. The hound need no longer alert you."

Despite all her aches and pains, Dalria grinned. "So you believe me now?"

Keresh turned to Jerban. "I have no claim here. You will withdraw my name from all proceedings before the Justiciary."

"I only—" The lawyer protested.

"Enough." Dalria managed to get to her feet without wincing too visibly. She was gratified to see everyone fall silent.

Let them try denying what they had seen. If they did, she'd apply to the Justiciary herself, to have their testimony sworn before the Sun Goddess's servants and the Moon God's too, for good measure.

"Mistress Zante, please ensure our guests have everything they need for their night's stay. They will be leaving first thing in the morning. Now, if you will excuse me," Dalria nodded graciously, "I have estate matters to address."

She turned around and walked away, towards the lesser stair that led up to her own bedchamber. She forced herself not to limp. At least with her back towards them, she could support her injured arm with her other hand unseen. She only hoped she could keep this up until the following day.

The great black hound padded along beside her, expressing his displeasure at all this upset with gruff whuffing and head shakes.

* * *

The following morning, Mistress Zante startled Dalria awake with a peremptory rattle of the curtain rings. "Good day to you, my lady."

"What—?" Dalria sat up in bed and instantly regretted it. Then she saw how bright the sky was. "How late have I slept?"

"Late enough, and you needed the rest after yesterday's dramatics." Loyal servant she might be but Mistress Zante narrowed her eyes in rebuke nevertheless. "Master Jerban and his wife have already set off home."

"So soon?" Dalria felt guiltily relieved that she need not face them over morning pastries. She had intended to, truly, especially after ducking out of dinner the night before to avoid any further arguments the lawyer or his wife might have mustered. "What did they say, when you told them I had gone to bed early with a headache?"

"Nothing. I don't think any of them said two words beyond 'please' and 'thank you' as we served them." Brisk, Mistress Zante began tidying the bedchamber.

Dalria watched her bustling about. There was no hint that the woman could see the great black dog sprawled across the end of her bed.

Satisfied for the moment at least, Mistress Zante turned to her. "Now, do you want your breakfast on a tray?"

"I'll take it in the south parlor, if you please. But there's no hurry. I want some air before I eat." Some air and some time to think how to write a conciliatory letter to the lawyer. The estate still needed his services and Jerban didn't deserve to have his reputation smeared by scandalmongers sniffing for gossip if rumors of a breach between them spread.

Dalria got cautiously out of bed and was relieved to find her bruises and stiffness were less than she initially feared.

The hound raised his head and looked at her, expectant. Did that mean she was forgiven? She fervently hoped so.

The dog was waiting by the door when she emerged from her dressing room. Taking the back stairs, Dalria cut through the castle's older courtyards to reach the family's burial ground. As she rounded the small shrine, she halted, startled. "Oh!"

Keresh was studying her parents' graves, beyond the fresh earth that marked her grandfather's burial. He was as taken aback as she was. "Forgive me," he said hastily, "I'll go."

"No, wait." Dalria was outraged, though not at the young man's presence. "They left you here? Master Jerban brought you all this way and wouldn't even give you a seat back in his coach?"

"He would have. I didn't want it." Keresh broke off, as though he'd said more than he intended.

Dalria wasn't going to let him get away with that. "Why not?"

"I have nothing to go back for." Keresh's casual shrug was unconvincing. "It doesn't matter," he continued, resolute. "I'll find work easily enough. I can turn my hand to most things."

Dalria couldn't think what to say. At her side, the great hound stiffened, nose questing towards Keresh. Dalria braced herself for his barking, but instead the black dog whined and walked over to lie down between the scars of those twin graves in the grass.

Oblivious, Keresh continued to contemplate her parents' headstones. "I never sought to take what wasn't mine. I only came here because Master Jerban was so certain. Truly, I have no idea who my family might be. I just wondered if this was where I might belong. But now we know the answer to that."

"I'm sorry." Dalria winced, and not only because of her bruises.

"Is he here?" Keresh looked at her. "The hound?"

"He is." Dalria gestured towards the graves. The dog's long black tail wagged. "Just there, in front of you."

"I'll leave." Keresh stepped hastily backwards.

"No, wait. I know none of this is your fault."

"That never saved an apprentice from a beating." His attempt at levity fell flat. "Tell me one thing though. How can you stand it? How can you live with Death sniffing at your heels every day?"

"That's not how it is." Dalria looked at the great hound, who was rolling onto his back, broad shaggy paws waving absurdly in the air. She smiled fondly.

"Crag hounds are guard dogs, and so is he. He will be my lifelong guardian and my guide. He's been my comfort ever since my parents died. I saw him in a dream of their boat as it sank in that awful storm. I saw him dragging their bodies to the riverbank, so they could be found and brought home to be buried. I saw him diving, searching, frantic to find my lost brother. Then I woke to hear him howling, broken-hearted. He appeared to the whole household that night, standing in the center of the inner courtyard. For a few moments at least." Dalria drew a steadying breath to banish those painful memories.

"I don't doubt it," Keresh assured her with a shiver. "Not after yesterday."

How could she make him understand? "Believe me; I have nothing to fear from him. I know that when my end comes, the hound will shepherd me to whatever lies beyond this life. I know that as he guards my heirs and descendants, my legacy will be remembered, just as I honor and remember my ancestors whom he's walked with in generations past."

"Yet you were ready to throw your life away?" Keresh challenged. "Risking your neck yesterday?"

Did she owe him an explanation? Dalria decided it could do no harm.

"I couldn't think how to convince Master Jerban until I remembered the very first time I saw the hound. That was before my parents died, when my brother was sick with mulberry fever. But he recovered, and yesterday, I realized that must mean the heir need not always die for others to see the hound. They just have to be in mortal danger. So I decided to see if I could make him show himself." She couldn't help a shudder at the dizzying memory. "And yes, it was a reckless thing to do."

She looked up to see the spring sunshine gilding the castle's ancient stonework. "Every man, woman, and child walks with death every single day. From the first moment when a baby draws breath, the sands in their life's hourglass are running downwards. Those in my bloodline can see death as their companion, that's the only difference. Believe me, it's a gift. It's how we know sooner than most that the key to living your life to the fullest is understanding and accepting that it will end. Then you can make the most of every day in the meantime, for yourself and for others."

"You truly believe that?" He was torn between disbelief and curiosity.

"I do," she assured him.

He looked around at the mighty castle walls rising on all sides. "Perhaps that's easier done in comfort than cold and wet on Eridanse's streets."

Dalria could see he didn't mean to insult her. She also saw the great hound sit up, floppy ears pricked. She could tell that he approved of this young man.

"Why don't you stay here and find out?" she suggested.

"What?" Keresh was taken aback.

"If you can turn your hand to most things, there's always work to be done, in the castle or in the town. Besides, Master Jerban wasn't wholly wrong. You saw those portraits for yourself. You surely have Reole blood in your veins and however it may have got there, that means you do have ties to this place."

As she saw tentative hope in his eyes, she offered Keresh an open hand. "You may not be my brother, but perhaps we can be friends?"

THRICE REMEMBERED

A. Merc Rustad

The first thing he remembers: cold water, silted and salty. Weeds in his mouth, a clay bank under his hands. Crocodiles. Yes, he knows the crocodiles, and that the great beasts should have eaten him.

The second: a knife against his spine. Blade pressed into skin as he retches water and his body convulses. Blood on his throat, an invitation for flies.

The third: a chain around his neck, colder than the river. Metal links smeared in blood.

All else has fled, for the chain steals all memories. Only these three pieces remain, gifts of iron and teeth.

* * *

Slaves don't speak.

Slaves obey.

Slaves owe nothing to who they were before.

The masters tell him this as he stands on the churned bank, watching the crocodiles twist and snap in blood-frothed waters. A river, but it isn't cold. The body thrown to the beasts—what is a body?—should have been his. He almost remembers why, until the chain sucks away the thoughts in each link.

Zuaar is what they call him, the masters in jewel-toned suits with golden skin. He looks no different than them, except he is dressed only in chains. The name means dirt, they say. Because he is dirt.

Odd how his skin feels like fire.

* * *

"What do you remember?" the slave keeper asks every night.

"Nothing," he says. It is true every night until it's not.

He knows the way out of the compound, drawn by instinct, through the barred window slats, across the roof and down to the canal. To the river. It shines black and silver-blue in the night. Deceptive and still as a crocodile's eye.

Raaushar, the crocodiles whisper. Fire.

Not dirt.

But water turns dirt into mud, and fire turns mud into brick, and bricks seal the fire in kilns. Makes it a slave.

When he returns to the compound, the chain bites deeper into his skin. But one link is weak. The memory seeps back into him, an ember from the kiln ashes.

* * *

By day, Zuaar serves crystalline wine and fish stuffed with honeyed olives. He waits on the masters who sit on high daises under silk shades, while acrobats and flutists entertain. Lesser slaves wield dragon-feather fans and shy away from his gaze. Men and women with bright bracelets and rings in their ears and lips watch him the way they watch the crocodiles.

"This is dangerous," the court whispers, and the masters—no, the first master, the god-king himself—dismiss the rumors. The king smites those with wagging tongues.

"There is no danger. It is chained."

Soon the court watches him as if he is a scorpion with its tail severed and its pincers crushed.

There are nights the courtiers want him in their beds, and he obeys. They are empty vessels and they give him no satisfaction. The chain tries to swallow what he sees, but there is still a weak link.

On a night like all the rest, the queen summons him. Sandalwood incense fills the room; a breeze off the river lifts the sheer curtains around her bed. Her eyes are dark-lashed and brilliant as fire.

His breath stops. This is passion. He remembers.

"Come," says the queen. "Speak with me."

He is silent.

"Do you remember, Belruuvaw?" she asks, threading beads along a silken thread. She creates a bracelet, or perhaps a collar, with smoke-dark glass that mirrors her eyes.

He does not.

"My husband the god-king is wrong," she says. He ignores her blasphemy. "Do not forget I opposed him in this."

On another night, she weaves the beaded collar about his ankle, the glass like the river's kiss on his flesh. She never takes him into her bed.

There are days the court wants him whipped and tormented for their pleasure.

The pain: he remembers blood. So much blood, the river became fat and red. The whip: he recalls what it was to hold it in his hand. Perhaps that is why his palms are so callused.

The god-king watches him, unblinking like a dragonfly. Zuaar remembers what fear looks like in another's eyes.

* * *

First: the sun is less bright every day. The astrologers wail and their prayers are empty. He thinks them fools.

Second: the god-king does not sleep. His advisors whisper in his ear, but he hears nothing. The god-king only watches the chains.

Third: the crocodiles starve, for there are no bodies thrown into the river.

When Zuaar watches them, they weep. He cannot ease their hunger or their grief.

* * *

The queen lies sick under the fading sun. She no longer speaks with him, nights he sated himself on the timbre of her voice, the caress of her words against his skin. He yearns for her. He waits, but she does not summon him, until one night she does.

"Belruuvaw," she says.

He savors being in her presence, even faded. The chain eats at his knowledge, yet through the weakened link he knows she reminds him of someone he once loved.

"We must ease her suffering," the doctors say.

Zuaar kneels at her side as the doctors give her asp venom in honeyed date wine. She reaches out, her hand empty against his forehead. Her reed-hollow voice dims as she whispers: "Remember, Belruuvaw."

But she does not die.

The doctors wail, sending him away.

* * *

The god-king calls him to an audience. "What do you remember?"

"Nothing."

The chain is still cold. But two links now are weak, worn down so they will snap if he tugs against the metal.

The sun did not rise today. The court is silent. There are no whips and there is no wine.

"Can it be undone?" the god-king asks. "If it is unchained, can it be undone?"

"It is possible," the advisors lie, as smooth as river eels.

The god-king throws his gold scepter and it strikes Zuaar in the face. Blood trickles from his jaw.

"Undo what you have done," commands the god-king. "Undo this, Belruuvaw."

And at the final word, he who is not Zuaar and who is not Raaushar feels the third link crack. The chain is undone.

* * *

The first thing he remembers: his name is Belruuvaw. Raaushar was his twin sister, the sun.

The second thing he remembers: he is the god of death. When the king slaughtered half the world to summon him from his kingdom below the river, he came. He is Belruuvaw, and such a sacrifice he could not ignore.

The third thing he remembers: he killed his sibling. She left him for the god-king of the land; none other than the life-bringer would speak to the bringer of death. Enraged, he fed her heart to the crocodiles, and so the sun faded until it can rise no longer.

He remembers the river where he fed the crocodiles his sister's heart, where the king bound him as a slave. And so nothing left in the world could die; when he did not remember death, death did not exist.

The king wished Belruuvaw imprisoned for murdering the sun Raaushar. The king thought if Death did not remember her, his lover Raaushar would come back to him.

The mortal knows nothing.

Belruuvaw remembers all, now.

The chain, undone, snaps free from his neck. He surveys the trembling court. He remembers rage. He remembers the whips and the pain and the nights in his cage. He fingers the broken chain, its links crumbling into rust through his fingers. Even metal dies.

"We have done you wrong," says the king. "We beg of you, restore the sun and let death come again."

That was his other name: Hauushar, the bringer of mercy. But there are scars around his throat where a chain once clung, and they make it so easy to forget.

"No man nor woman can die, even when in agony or despair," the king cries. "You murdered Raaushar, and now my wife lingers yet, undying. Must you deny her as you do so many?"

Belruuvaw remembers loneliness, but he will not restore his sister's heart. The sun will never rise. Let the mortals know darkness eternal, as he does now that Raaushar has gone

"What will you do?" asks the king, who is only a man.

"Nothing," he says, and he turns towards to the river, to the crocodiles.

Around him, the world pleads for release. For death and for the sun. Belruuvaw does not answer.

At the bank of the river, he watches the crocodiles. They whisper their greetings while they beg him to nourish them once more. If he does not allow death to return, they will always starve.

"Belruuvaw," the queen says behind him.

He turns. She walks with liquid grace, and she has wrapped an asp around her shoulders. She strokes its head as she approaches him.

He does not call her sister even as he allows her near. She is not Raaushar.

She touches the beads wound about his ankle with her toes. "Remember, Belruuvaw. I opposed my lover." Her skin is like fire against his flesh. "Do not punish the world for one man's weakness."

"Why should I not?"

She regards him with contempt. "Then you are no better than the god-king."

He raises a hand, though he has no whip to hold, his fury checked by the scars. "Do not speak of him."

"I will speak of whom I please." She lifts her chin and lays a hand along the side of his throat. "You will continue this cycle, and for what purpose? Did you learn nothing?"

"Nothing," he says bitterly, a word uttered too many times. Two crocodiles crawl onto the bank and lean against his legs, rough skin and smooth teeth pressed into his flesh. "Leave me."

She smiles, a challenge. "You can do little, Belruuvaw, when you fetter your power so. I am not dead. What can you do to me?"

He places his fingers over hers, her flesh hot as the dawn against his scars. "I will give you release."

"No." She withdraws her hand, and her smile. "Unless you restore what you have taken, I will not come with you to your kingdom." She uncoils the asp and lets it glide away. "Did you willingly forget compassion? You knew that once. I spoke with your sister Raaushar, you know. We were friends. I asked her not to forget you when she loved the king. I told you this, each night you came to me, but you could not remember. I grieved for her. I helped my husband plot your undoing, my rage unsated. But then you were mine, and she was still *gone*."

Belruuvaw hates her words. He has no collar to blame. The beads grow cold around his ankle. She turns once more for the wailing court, and the despair of her people.

"Raaushar," he says, and she does not answer. That is not her name, and she will not answer to a lie. "Wait. I would speak with you, my queen."

She looks over one shoulder at him, all the chill of a desert night hardening her expression.

He remembers pain, rage, betrayal, but he has not forgotten what it is to please, or to love, as he loved Raaushar. He cannot abandon his children the crocodiles. They should feast, not starve. He can do nothing for only so long.

The first choice he makes: Belruuvaw reaches into the bellies of his crocodiles and withdraws his twin's heart. He gives it to the woman who is not Raaushar.

"If you carry this heart, my queen," he says. "You will burn unending." But he will always remember her. "You will become the sun. You may light the world or burn it to ash, as you please."

Her hand trembles when she accepts it.

The second choice: he undoes the beaded string from around his ankle, the gift the queen gave him. He does not need the beads to remember, now. He killed his twin because he watched her fall in love with the king of the land; he watched her abandon her place in the sky. He will not stand by and merely *watch*.

The queen examines the sun's heart, then swallows it whole and smiles at him one last time. She burns and she rises against the darkened sky.

Crocodiles splash in the cold river as he sends them to fetch the dead—all those who should have died while he forgot. His children will bring him the souls and they will suffer no more undying.

The third choice: he must return to his kingdom, allow the world to balance itself once again, and so he throws himself into the waters—cold, silty, full of salt—and crocodiles devour him.

CHARNEL HOUSE

Ville Meriläinen

The wasteland opened before us, cold and bleak like we'd stepped inside a predator's eye. Blue Girl sat on Huntress' back, shoulders drooping, the hem of her dress ripped at the knees. She'd be fine tomorrow. Until then, the wolf would gladly ease her burden.

Blue Girl had a smile to cut glass and enough heartache to kill a man, but we liked each other well enough and were useful to one another, so we journeyed together. Huntress and I cared for little else but staying alive. She had lost her cubs when escaping the fire that took her mountain and now wandered the earth looking for them. My reason was more selfish: I simply enjoyed living, even when there was nothing to live for. Blue Girl helped by letting us eat her arms before we lay to sleep, knowing the flesh would regrow by the morning. In return, I had promised to bring her to Charnel House, the one place where she might find the end of her own search: Blue Girl wanted to die.

"I see nothing but burnt earth for days to come," Huntress said. Our paws raised clouds of dust and ash with every step, but to the omnipresent smell of smoke clung an undernote of a coming storm from the clouds at horizon's edge. "Are you sure this is the way?"

"Positive," I replied. "I can feel it in my bones."

Huntress hummed, a growl deep in her throat that never failed to make me uneasy. The great wolf was a kind creature, but murder remained etched deep in the grooves of her face.

"I think I can walk now," Blue Girl said. Her voice was hollow, legs crusted with dry blood. She'd cut them coming down the mountain and bled so much I'd fretted a rock would give her the surcease we could not.

"You stay where you are," Huntress said. "Maybe you *can* walk, but it doesn't mean you should."

"Won't you carry me as well?" I said. "I could sit on her lap. I'm far smaller than she."

Huntress returned a sideways leer. "Careful, fox. If you're so lazy, I could carry you with my teeth."

I bared mine into a grin, though her comment nearly coaxed a whimper out of me. "I thought it a sensible suggestion. Your stride is longer than mine, and swifter without me slowing you down."

"Were that a problem, I'd sooner leave you behind."

"Now, now. How would you find Charnel House without me?"

"I'm not convinced we'll find it *with* you. You might as well be making us run in circles to keep getting fed."

"Don't be wicked, Huntress," Blue Girl said.

"She's only teasing, dear. We've grown inseparable, she and I."

Huntress snorted at that. "I'm more attached to her than to you. We'll part ways at the House as agreed."

"Don't be wicked," Blue Girl said, more firmly. "Promise me you won't abandon him when I'm gone."

"I've not given up on my cubs, girl. I doubt he wants to join my search once he has no feeding hand to bite."

Huntress glanced at me, as though expecting a remark, but I saw no reason to antagonize her. She was certain the cubs lived, could feel their closeness in her marrow the same way a murmur in my own pulled me towards the demise the girl yearned for.

It was ironic that, out of the three of us, I was the one drawn to Charnel House. I would have been thrilled to be deathless like Blue Girl, but she wanted nothing more than to escape. Huntress and I had found her after she jumped off a cliff so high she'd been a dot atop it. She came down like a falling star with a tail of silk, but got up from the crater as though she'd only tripped.

She spoke in her sleep sometimes, blaming herself for the way the world was, but that was an absurd notion to entertain. How could someone who'd gained the trust of two wild beasts through the virtue of her kindness have caused a calamity this vast?

I gave the girl a look from the corner of my eye. She met it with a wan smile, cutting through fur for a pluck at my heartstrings. I refused to believe she was guilty for the way the world was, but the child *had* seen something that had broken the spirit within an unbreakable body. When she smiled, none of the defeat lacing her bearing showed.

Wind drove along the drifts of ash around us, and as we climbed a mound, I noticed the broken ribcage of a small beast poking out of it. For a moment, I felt sorry for Huntress. I was sure her cubs were gone, starved by now even if they'd somehow lived through the end of the world. I caught her glimpsing the bones as well, and set my gaze ahead when our eyes met and I saw the bared pain in them.

"Fox," said Blue Girl, interrupting my musing. "Would you tell me more about Charnel House?"

"What do you want to know?"

"I want to hear you speak. It's too quiet."

"Hmm. Have I told you how grand and beautiful it is?"

"You have."

"What about the lands surrounding it?"

Blue Girl tapped her lip in thought. "You say there's still grass and that the milk on the leaves makes you forget your worries."

"Then what of the people who used to live there?"

"They were as grand and beautiful as the house, but turned it into a home to death, and now only an old crow dwells there."

I smacked my mouth. "Sounds like you know as much as my stories do."

"Oh." She fell quiet for a minute, then asked, "Would you like to play a game?"

"Are you after my name again?" I chuckled. It was a difficult sound to produce, but it made her smile a little brighter. "Go on, then."

"Is it…Redtail?"

"No."

"Whitepaw?"

"No."

"Firefur?"

"You've tried that."

"Nuisance?" offered Huntress. She earned only a flat stare for it.

Blue Girl went on to fill the silence with her guesses, but I rejected them all. Truth was I didn't have a name, never knew I was supposed to until I met her. With only the three of us, "fox" was just as good, but I had decided to claim she'd guessed correctly once she landed on one that sounded nice in my ears. I thought she'd done the same; we'd started calling her Blue Girl because she was a girl and her dress was blue, but Huntress had told me it wasn't a proper name.

I suppose I understood some of her desire to learn mine, as names seemed to have power of which I hadn't known either. It was only after we named her that we learned to understand her, though we had walked together for some time by then.

"One of these days," she huffed, after her tone reached the peak of vexation, "I'm going to learn it, you know."

"I'm sure you will," I said with a chuckle. Annoyance lingered on her features, turning the ensuing smile impish.

We came to the bank of a dry river. A stream still ran through the bottom, but if we went down, the sides would be too steep to climb back up. Even so, Huntress leapt off the ledge without hesitation, padded to the stream and lapped from it with such vigor she might've been trying to drain it altogether. I hopped after her, and once we'd drunk, looked around for a way out.

"Should we spend the night here?" Blue Girl suggested. "I'm tired and you could drink as much as you want."

Huntress said, "A sound plan. I'm parched."

"Well then," I said with a yawn, "make us a fire, dear. I can do with some shuteye."

She headed off to gather scattered pieces of wood. The wood was charred, violently splintered; the wasteland's birth had created a storm unlike any before, and fire and lightning had decimated the lush forests once ruling the lowlands. Everywhere we went, we found nothing but gray earth, as though it had been sucked dry to the last drops of life. We had passed no other beasts on our way, only skeletons so fragile they turned to dust when we tried to gnaw on them.

Left to her own devices, a somber air soon overcame Blue Girl. Huntress noted it as well and went to join her, tattling about this and that to pull her out of her thoughts. I sat on my haunches, watching them pick up and pile the wood.

Once she was warm, Blue Girl would let us eat. I wasn't hungry enough for it not to sicken me, and so I watched them in brooding silence. What did it say about us, helping her towards a fate neither felt she deserved, using her body as sustenance on the way? Yes, the limbs would regrow—but that only meant we fed on her pain.

These thoughts passed as the flame grew and drowsiness settled in, as they did every night. I was a firm believer in one's own freedom, and so it was not my place to deny her any choice concerning herself. Huntress felt much the same. Besides, we could do nothing but follow her: finding no one else meant we had none to rely on but each other, and the wolf's kindness wasn't limitless.

Thus, in order to help each other for another day, we ripped the flesh of Blue Girl's arms until she passed out, and when they were picked clean, nestled against her in an effort to balance the suffering we inflicted with affection.

I woke up to raindrops pummeling my nose. Blue Girl was still asleep, mended hands folded under her head. I stretched out of the nook of her bent knees, jowls shaking with a yawn. Huntress was gone. Blue Girl was easily upset if we weren't here when she woke up, so the wolf often used the early hours for scouting and returned at dawn. I suspected she'd left to look for a way up.

I returned to Blue Girl after drinking. The rain had washed her feet; the dress had mended with the skin, dampened from periwinkle to a deeper shade. She shuddered when I lay beside her.

"Forgive me," she whispered, still asleep. "I have mothered ruin."

I reared my head for a look at her. Poor dear. She was too young to have mothered anything, much less anything this awful.

She might've cried in her sleep, or maybe it was rain. I didn't dare lick her face for the risk of waking her, and so I only nuzzled against her throat for some more rest. It was always strange to be so close to her; her body looked as soft as a child's was meant to be, but her meat was sinewy and her stomach taut with muscle. She pulled me closer and cradled me in her arms until I dozed off.

My dream took me to Charnel House. Mist hung over pale grassland, where the house sat amidst a copse of skeletal trees. I had overstated its beauty. Maybe it had been a place of splendor in the past, but now it was like its lone inhabitant, scraggly and diseased, so far as a house could look diseased. Cracks ran over windows like cataracts in the crow's eyes, pillars were chipped and thin like his legs, murals on the walls had faded as his feathers had lost their luster. It was where dead things went to die, so the story said, so why not Blue Girl?

"Hello. Are you bringing a visitor?" cawed the crow when I approached. He perched atop the open door. It was too dark to see what was inside.

The crow's familiar tone seemed odd, but, being fully aware I was dreaming, I decided to pay no mind to little lapses in logic. "I don't think I should."

"Your task is only to guide her here. She will decide whether to enter or not."

"She is misguided."

"That, ultimately, is irrelevant," said the crow. He swooped down onto the porch and pointed his wing towards the dark house. "This is where she belongs. This is where she'll be happy. You know this."

"Do I?"

The crow nodded. "You only don't know you do. You would if you knew her name."

"Do you?"

"I know all names."

I cocked my head at that. "Do you know mine?"

"Of course."

"Ha. You don't even know I don't have one."

I thought I read a grin in the way the crow's beak parted. "You think yourself clever, my friend, but every creature has a name. Come to Charnel House and I will tell you. You may then enter as well, should you wish to follow her."

I awoke then, startled by the crow's horrid offer. The dream faded as I blinked in light and shuddered away its memory.

"Good morning," said Blue Girl. She had propped her head against a restored arm and scratched the nape of my neck. "Did you have a bad dream?"

"I dreamt of Charnel House."

"Is that a yes or a no?"

"Neither, I think."

She moved to scratching behind my ear when I fell into silent thoughts. "Is something the matter?"

I let her pet me for a moment. "Blue Girl," I said, pausing when she found the good spot. She hummed to spur me on. "If you go inside Charnel House, you will die."

She smiled. "I think you've mentioned that, yes."

"I won't come with you."

"I didn't think you would."

"I need you to know that."

Her brow furled, though she still smiled. "What on earth has come over you, silly?"

"I don't want you to go inside alone."

"Everyone goes to death alone, fox."

"But you've done nothing wrong. You shouldn't have to go at all."

"Oh, fox," she said, sighing as she stood. "Not this again. Won't you come find Huntress instead? With that, at least, you can help me."

"Is she not back yet?" I said with surprise. It was unusual for the wolf to stay away for this long.

"She left just before you awoke," Blue Girl said. "She found a way up, but that was a while ago. We should catch up."

Blue Girl and I jolted when a howl reached us. She faced me with fright. "That must've been her. Come! She may need us."

We hurried down the ravine, Huntress' howls growing more panicked as Blue Girl started running out of breath. The bottom turned muddier and muddier until we found the wolf—neck deep in it. The wall had crumbled; rocks formed a path gradually submerging as it reached her.

"Help me," she whimpered. "I tried to climb up, but the wall couldn't carry my weight. A stone pushed me in and my foot is stuck beneath it."

I dashed for her, but stopped when she cried, "Be careful! There's a pit. My feet reach the bottom, but it's too deep for you."

"Can't you push the rock aside?"

"I'm not strong enough."

"You're too far for us to reach," Blue Girl said, face twisted with worry. She picked up a stick, poked the ground until she found a way around the pit and held the stick out for the wolf. "Here. Maybe I can pull you out with—"

The stick crunched and broke when Huntress bit for hold. Blue Girl raised the splintered end and frowned before tossing it away. She hemmed, felt the mud with her foot, then reached out her arm. "Bite down. I have a good foothold here."

"You'll break like the twig."

"I'm stronger than I look."

Huntress hesitated. I had no wisdom to offer save for, "It'll grow back."

The wolf said, "It is one thing to hurt you to live, but I don't want to do so for nothing."

"Do you think you'll never sink?" replied the girl.

Huntress gave a whimper before parting her jaws. Blue Girl cried out when they closed on her forearm, groaned as she gritted her teeth and leaned back. She held herself up with her free arm as her feet sought the hold hidden under mud. Blood spurted onto Huntress' nose, but the girl persevered. Her wail rose into a scream until Huntress let go and Blue Girl tumbled backwards.

"Why did you—?" she shrieked, cutting herself off when Huntress climbed up and shook mud off her fur. She limped to Blue Girl, rear leg twisted, and licked the row of puncture wounds on the girl's arm

"Thank you," said the wolf.

Blue Girl smiled through tears. The smile wilted when she faced me, and I realized horror must've shown on my features. "What's wrong, fox?"

"You've said nothing when you let us eat. I thought you were used to the pain."

She pressed her lips together, averted her eyes, and shook her head.

Huntress looked away from her, at me. "How far to Charnel House?"

"Three days."

"I can go without eating for three days."

"You don't have to," Blue Girl said. "It's fine, really—"

"I will do you no more harm, girl," growled Huntress, "and I've half a mind to turn around, carry you to the mountains, and raise you as my own, away from this awful place."

"And what would that solve?" I said. I did my best not to cower when she swung towards me. "You'd leave one wasteland for another, and sooner or later you'd hunger again. All you'd do would be to prolong her suffering, making a home above the valley of cinders where you keep the last living creature as your pet and prey."

Her growl deepened. "Are you saying you accept her resignation now?"

"It's not our place to decide her fate, Huntress."

"No," she admitted, after a long, long spell of consideration. "But it *is* my choice not to eat her. I will not be used for penance any longer."

"Nor will I," I said, and faced Blue Girl. "And I stand by what I said before. You've a good heart."

Blue Girl bowed her head, placed her healthy hand on the side of Huntress' neck, and whispered, "Thank you."

We were able to climb up over the pile of rocks Huntress' fall had made. Her injury did nothing to our pace. She'd already had to slow down for us to keep up—now she merely had to do so a little less.

* * *

The wasteland turned from an even plain into an uphill climb. On the plateaus we found more skeletons, human instead of animal, as though a necropolis had been unearthed. The ground was soft, once fertile, perhaps, and I wondered if they'd been field hands who'd worked the lands around Charnel House.

Every time we passed such boneyards, Blue Girl kept her gaze fixed on the overcast and allowed Huntress to carry her. The wolf never complained for the added weight on her leg wound, just as Blue Girl tried to hide the wounds on her heart from us.

On the third morning, we found the first signs of life since our journey began. Grass grew thick on the slopes, wet with dew.

"Don't touch it," I said, when Blue Girl fell behind to inspect the pearls of milk gathering on the leaves. "It'll take away the pain in your arm, but also everything else. We're almost there."

Charnel House waited atop the final climb, where the land leveled and the grass grew taller. The cooling evening raised the milk into mist, making even Huntress complain of feeling lightheaded. It was cold here; the chill of death wafted from the house like exhalations from the netherworld.

"Girl, I don't want you going nearer," Huntress growled. Her fur bristled. "You don't belong here. Turn away."

"Please," I tried. The mist numbed my thoughts, making my feet pad on by their own accord. "She's right. I've made a grave mistake. I never should've brought you here."

"But I see it now," Blue Girl said, voice drowsy. "It's beautiful."

I saw it too, the shimmery gloss appearing on the house's surface, how it seemed to radiate in the glow of a waning sun. Even I felt an attraction to the place, so much greater than before. The gentle hold in my bones hummed a gentler invitation, asking me to cross the threshold.

"Please don't go," I whimpered. "You are a kind creature, sorely needed in this world. If you went, there might be no one else left but Huntress and I. Neither of us have half the heart you do."

"But, fox," said Blue Girl. "I made the world this way. I don't deserve to dwell in it. Don't *want* to—"

"You cannot have!" I snapped, steeling my mind to dash to her and step in her way. "My dear girl, why do you say these things? Why do you not see how sweet you are? We are beasts—had we been alone, I would have abandoned Huntress to drown in the mud. And she? If we had stayed together this long by the two of us, nothing I could've said would've deterred her from eating me. Is this not true?"

"It is," Huntress said. "You have tamed us, girl, made us caring by caring for us. If you wish to step inside, it is your right, but I will not bid a fond farewell. I will grieve for a life thrown to waste."

"You don't understand," Blue Girl said, with chilling patience. "This is my share. Remember me as a fool if you must, but move out of my way."

"A fool is the last thing I'll remember," I said.

The girl did not reply, only stepped past.

"Ah, hello," said the crow sitting atop the open door. "How good to see you, at long last. Come in."

"Thank you," said Blue Girl. She turned, folding her hands over her front. Warmth pulsed in my breast and I feared her smile had cut so deep if I spat the grass would turn red. "Fond or not, I bid goodbye, my friends—"

"Not you, silly chit," said the crow. He swooped down and hobbled past her to Huntress. "Come, come. It's time to go."

Dumbfounded, Huntress stared the crow down. "I'm going nowhere. It's the girl you want."

"She?" The crow darted a look at Blue Girl. "She couldn't come in if she wanted. She's alive."

"So am I."

"How could you be, when the forest burned around you?"

"I survived."

"How?"

"I..." Horror flashed on her face, then fury settled in. In a snarl, she said, "Step back, crow. I will not be tricked. I must find my cubs."

"You did, Nastasha. You found them in your den, where their charred bones rest with yours."

A pang boiled the blood Blue Girl's smile had freed. My chest was afire, as was Huntress'—afire and worse, by her look. She turned to me with an expression of desperation, and I met it with some of my own. "Her name is Huntress," I said, words rolling off an unfeeling tongue.

"'Huntress' is no name. It is a title."

The wolf whispered, "Nastasha."

I whispered, "Nastasha."

"That is her name," said the crow, "and now she remembers."

Nastasha took in a deep breath she released as a long, wailing howl. Her fur seemed to give off mist. To my shock, I realized it was smoke.

"My friends," she said, voice frail and ethereal. "I do remember. I must go. I don't belong here." She came to us, gave Blue Girl's face a lick. "My cubs *were* gone—but they hadn't moved. I found them slain when I brought them food. When the fire came, I could not bring myself to leave them."

"I'm so sorry," Blue Girl said, scratching the wolf's jaw.

Nastasha came to me, prodded my nose with hers. "You guided *me* here."

The crow studied us with an amused twinkle in its eye. It hadn't spoken of Blue Girl in my dream. That blasted fiend had told me I was leading the wolf to her doom, and I'd been too much of a fool to understand. "I'm sorry. I didn't know."

She looked long at me, until I thought a smile appeared in her lupine features. "I forgive you."

"It's time to go," said the crow. Nastasha nodded and padded towards the open door, stopping at the porch to face us for the last time. Her fur had burned off by then, skin melting, bone showing. She did not make it all the way inside; a gust of wind blew her ashes into the darkness.

When she was gone, the murmur within my marrow calmed. The pull, however, forced my legs into motion, and it took effort to force them rigid and keep myself standing in place. Blue Girl still regarded the empty space Nastasha had left, but the crow noticed my struggle and said, "Your duty is done. You can go as well."

This drew a gasp from Blue Girl and made her wheel about. "Not you, too?" she sniffled.

"Dear girl, no one loves being alive as much as I," I said, with a scolding look at the crow.

"You remember why you had to guide her, yes?" said the crow.

"That does not mean I belong here."

"No," the crow admitted with a nod, "but—"

"Stop."

He cocked his head.

"Are you about to tell me my name?"

The crow nodded again, and I went to the weeping Blue Girl. She knelt to rub my ear, brushed her nose with the side of her palm.

"Would you like to guess first?" I said.

"Is it..." Her voice came out creaky. She cleared her throat and furled her brow. "Huntress' name was Nastasha."

"It was."

"Then yours might be something closer to mine than one from a fairytale, too."

"It might."

"Is it... Phillip?"

"It is not."

"Is it Henry?"

"One more try."

She sucked on her lip, brows knitted, inspecting me as though trying to see it hidden somewhere on my face. "Is it Ichabod?"

The tiniest grunt fled a chest gone perfectly rigid. I was flushed with memories, how I had tried to plead the wolf to spare me—because, with a full stomach, I was unable to escape her.

I forced on a smile, straining muscles that weren't meant to move in such a way. "See? I knew you'd guess it eventually."

"Ichabod," she whispered, wiping her eye. "Ichabod, Ichabod, Ichabod."

I licked her fingers before facing the crow. "Do I have to go? She would be all alone."

"You've atoned," he said. "It's your choice, but you know you don't belong here."

"Atoned?" said Blue Girl.

"We are beasts," I answered, "and beasts are cruel to one another."

"I don't think that's true. You've been nothing but kind to me."

"Why are you so quick to believe the best of us, when you don't see the good in yourself?"

She licked her lower lip, straightened herself. "Crow," she said. "When I named him in my thoughts, I could hear him speak. When I learned his true name, I saw the bite marks on his throat. If he knew mine, could he see me as I do?"

The crow nodded. Unease tickled my neck, as though a wraith petted me where Blue Girl had a minute ago.

"Dear Ichabod," she said, sitting on her knees. "My name is not Blue Girl. It is Evelyn."

Between blinks, Blue Girl grew from a sweet little creature into a woman so beautiful I thought her radiance might blind me. I gasped for breath, unable to move my gaze from this sun with a hand resting on my ear. Her voice had deepened, each phrase flowing like a song.

"Charnel House was my home," Evelyn said, "before we befouled it, my family and I, with our desire to become everlasting. We ate the shine of the sun and it turned into a pale remembrance of itself. We drained the earth of verve to enhance our own. We stole the lives of creatures to stretch mortality into eternity. And I, I am the worst of us all."

"Why?" I said, though I didn't want to hear the answer. I wanted to hear her voice again, heart aching from being deprived of it for only a pause.

"I am a kinslayer," she said, calmly, as though stating any mundane fact. "My family became the death of a planet, but I became the Death of Deaths and took from them their shine and verve and long lives to reach true immortality. When I left to enjoy my newfound godhood, I learned its price. In my desperation to find something still alive, I wandered so far I could no longer find my way home." She closed her eyes, shuddered a sigh. "I lost my way for countless lifetimes, but wherever I went, I found nothing but ruin. Sometimes, I came across animals who had survived—though I now suspect they all were like you and Nastasha, tied too closely to this world for me to devour. After I had let them eat, I woke up alone. None of them were as devoted to living for the sake of living as you, I reckon."

She trailed off into a hum, scratching the good spot. Her touch sent shivers through my body. "I thought I'd have to live alone until I met you," she went on, quieter. "I'm glad we did meet, though neither of us got what we wanted. It seems that, in the end, I stole what was dearest even from you."

"I don't believe you. You are my friend. If you had the powers you claim, you would have used them for good."

"If you were a cruel beast," she said, and her smile eviscerated me in a way it hadn't come close to before, "why do you cling onto the good in me?"

"I couldn't go to my demise knowing you, too, were a wicked creature."

Her hum turned inquisitive. "Ichabod, I've confessed to you *because* I want you to go to your demise without burdens."

I pricked my ears at that.

"I sought to die here because I was weak and lonely, and afraid you'd leave me like all the rest," she went on. "Now that I know I cannot do that, I have something else in mind. I will walk the earth and return everything I took. I will give away my shine so that stars may glow at night. I will let rivers run wild and unrestrained. And," she tapped my nose, "I will make sure every forest I raise has a fox as its little prince."

"You can do that?" I said with surprise. "Do you promise?"

She hugged me tight. "It will be difficult, but I swear it on this good heart of mine."

"Then," I said once she let go, "I think it is time I left."

"Goodbye, Ichabod. I won't forget you."

"Goodbye, Evelyn. I'll try not to forget you."

I padded towards the house, no longer frightened. At the porch, a ghost of uncertainty crossed my thoughts, and I paused for one last look at her. "Please turn away. I don't want you to see me change."

"Won't you feel lonely, with no one to see you go?"

"Everyone goes to death alone, Evelyn."

Evelyn bowed her head with a mirthless laugh. "Of course." She spun, and when the crow glanced at her, I dashed into the shadow a pillar cast. After a minute, she asked, "Ichabod?"

They couldn't see me hiding, and the crow said, "He's gone."

Evelyn turned, gazing up at the house. "Good. I don't want him to see me, either." She lowered her gaze, looked towards the entrance for so long I thought she had spotted me, but then asked, "What did he atone for?"

"I don't know," said the crow. "He did something that caused the wolf to resist you, something that bound her soul here, and theirs together. It left them half-eaten; you took their lives, but left their bodies walking. Every creature yearns to find where they belong, but she was too distracted by the grief of her last moments to find her way here, and he could not be free until she was."

Evelyn wrapped her arms around herself and looked at her feet. When she raised her head back towards me, even from a distance, I saw her tears.

"Did you truly not notice your companions were spectres?" the crow went on.

She brushed her face and hardened her expression before turning. "Don't be snide. Your eye was always sharper than mine. It was the one thing I couldn't take from you."

"Mm. I will go as well, now everyone is accounted for."

My heart sunk when she replied, "I think that's for the best. No creature should have to walk this earth anymore."

"But you will. If you went through that door, nothing would happen. Death herself can't die."

She sighed. "I feared as much, but my feet are tired. I think I've earned some rest."

"I see," the crow said, sweeping a look at the house and the plains. "For what it's worth, I forgive you."

"Thank you."

"Goodbye, Evelyn."

"Goodbye, Tristan. Bring my love to mother and father."

The crow hobbled away from her. When his claw touched the threshold, I witnessed him shed his feathers and turn into an old, withered man. As he stepped inside, he grew younger, handsomer, until he faded into the darkness.

Evelyn had sat down to inspect a blade of grass she'd plucked. "Please, don't," I whimpered to myself when her lips parted. She did not hear me; the bead of milk rolled off the leaf to touch the tip of her tongue. She began to hum softly, plucked another and drank its milk. A dull iron cloud took away the lustre of her eyes.

Head hanging, I approached the door. Evelyn's only lie was one of kindness, and it made her prior honesty regarding her vileness hurt all the more. She *had* taken what was most precious from me, but it was not my life. I had lost both my friends.

As the shadows sheltered me, I began to feel lighter, at peace with all the deeds I had come to feel shame for when I learned kindness from Huntress and Blue Girl. I wondered if Huntress' forgiveness was for unwittingly tricking her into coming here, or if she knew I had killed her cubs. It wasn't an act of evil, only self-preservation. I was hungry, and thought to kill them young so they wouldn't grow to hunt me.

At the precipice between this world and the next, I stopped to listen to Evelyn's humming. I heard no beauty in her voice anymore. It had turned into breathy, discordant notes, and ceased altogether when I walked into Charnel House, where dead things went to die.

HOW DEATH CAME BY HIS SOUL
Amanda Kespohl

He was tall, pale, and lean, like the willow trees that gave him shade. His somber dark eyes suggested that he was likewise made for weeping. His shape pretended to be human, but the spiders gave him away. They skittered in and out of his sleeves, running along his pale fingers like the strands in a web. The holes in his moth-eaten silver robes offered glimpses of the bare bones of his rib cage, and beneath that, a pulsing red glow.

The only eyes that saw him arrive in the forest were the kind that saw nothing else. Flat and empty, they offered him only his reflection from above slack mouths filled with protruding purple tongues. He walked to the bodies, hanging from the apple tree like rotten fruit, and touched them, one by one. As his fingers rested upon bare, dirty feet, the spiders scuttled up to dance across their flesh, trailing threads like cracks in a frozen pond. Around and around they wound, in a dance of a thousand tiny feet, until a spectral wind inflated the silken silver strands. Like gauzy bubbles, the bits of webbing drifted away, bearing glowing, translucent treasure, and left the dangling vessels the emptier for it.

"Where will they go now?" a voice inquired.

The spiders went about their business, but their master balked, unused to being interrupted. No mortal eyes could see him, not unless they belonged to the dead or dying. He lifted his face toward the forest canopy and eyes the color of magnolia leaves looked back at him. Not mortal eyes, and dripping with curiosity like dew.

"Where will what go, nymph?" the Prince of Ash and Bone asked. The weariness in his voice was the kind that had no cure. No matter what may come and go in this world, death is a constant. There were only moments of respite to be had before he was called again.

Slim, nut brown hands pushed aside the foliage. She shimmied down the trunk, landing lightly on a root. "The souls, I mean. Where do the souls go, when you pack them off like that?"

"The only way to find out is to follow them." The Prince raised an elegant eyebrow. "Do you wish to follow them, nymph?"

"Oh, no, my tree has many years before it returns to the soil." She squatted, wrapping her arms around her knees and propping her chin on her kneecaps. "That is, unless some human's ax cleaves my trunk. Then I suppose I'll find out a lot sooner than I'd like. Does Death come for ones like me?"

"Not usually. Spirits like you know your own way back to eternity. You're much closer to it than humans."

"Oh. So you won't be back again? At least, not unless soldiers catch more bandits and hang them in my branches?"

"No, nymph. I won't."

Her lips pursed. "You keep calling me that."

"Is that not what you are?"

"I'm a *dryad*. The least you could do is call me by my proper name."

"Then you should call me by mine."

"So few here dare to speak of you at all. I wouldn't know what to call you."

"I am the Prince of Ash and Bone."

"Blech." Her face puckered. "Terrible mouthful, that. Give me something easier."

"What would you call me?"

Unfurling like a flower, she offered, "There was a shepherd who used to doze beneath my tree, ducking honest labor. Funny little fellow by the name of Cassius. I like that name."

"Then to you, I will be Cassius," the Prince said. Spectral lines thrummed, summoning him back to work. He ignored them, choosing to follow his namesake's example. "And what do I call you?"

"Oh, those who know I exist call me the Dryad of the Apple Tree."

"Terrible mouthful," the Prince said. "Give me something easier."

The dryad grinned, rocking onto the balls of her feet. "If we're exchanging names, then I've already given one. It's your turn."

He studied her, taking in the curling dark hair that twisted around her willowy body like vines, and her pert, heart-shaped face. "Idonae. I name you Idonae."

"And where did you come by that name?" There was a teasing note in her voice, but the song was friendly.

"It belonged to a princess who once waited in a tower for her true love. She doesn't need it anymore."

"Oh." She sank down to sit on the root, looking sad. "He didn't come?"

"He died along the way, so she followed him, instead." Hesitating, wondering if he had said something wrong, the Prince added, "She was the loveliest thing I've ever seen, so you reminded me of ..." His words stopped, dispelled by the sudden wanting in her eyes. He cleared his throat. "In any case, that is the name I would give you."

"I accept it." Idonae toyed with a strand of her hair. "So, you were saying that you won't be coming back?"

"It may be," the Prince said, "that I misspoke."

* * *

The following spring poured through the forest in a shower of pollen and petals. Nodding like ringing bells, blossoms hung heavy in branches and crowded together in sun-kissed grasses. All around their stems, little creatures chattered and scolded, while above them, the birds sang love songs to one another.

In the shade of her apple tree, Idonae sat with long legs crossed at the ankle, weaving stems together with deft fingers. Her tongue stuck out from between her lips as she concentrated. Dark head pillowed in her lap, Cassius watched the birds flutter from tree to tree above them. There was a time when they had scattered upon his arrival. Little by little, they had become accustomed to him. It made him feel strangely grateful. It was unusual for creatures with any sensitivity to his presence not to fear him.

"I wish I could give them something," he murmured.

"Give who something?" Idonae asked, worrying at a troublesome stem.

"The birds. I'd give them seed, if I could. So few have offered me such sweet song."

"Give them my seeds."

"Your seeds?"

"From my apples. My apples have the sweetest seeds."

"I have no doubt. But if I pick your apples, won't you miss them?"

"I'll grow new ones." She glanced down at him. "Besides, I like to see my fruit nourish life. Be it a new tree or a little bird, it makes me happy. It's what I was meant for, my tree and I."

"Unfortunately, I was not meant for the same."

She tweaked the tip of his long, thin nose. "Of course you were. Go pick apples, silly. This will only take a moment longer." She returned to her work.

The Prince rose to his feet, drifting around the apple tree with his odd, gawky elegance. Plucking down a ripe piece of fruit, he let his fingers seep into its flesh. Beneath his touch, the fruit withered away until it was no more than a thick, pulpy liquid, which dripped down between his fingers to feed the earth. All that remained in his palm were bits of core and a few brown seeds. He reached up and took another apple.

By and by, the seeds he had collected nearly overflowed his cupped palm. Deeming his offering to be sufficient, he walked over to stand before a tree where birdsong wove in and out of the branches like bright ribbons. The birds hushed at his approach. Awkwardly, he held his hand out toward them.

After a while, he said, "They won't take the seeds from me."

"And no wonder, after seeing what you did to those apples." The soft pat pat

pat of footsteps crept up behind him. Her hand took his, guided it down to the earth, and coaxed him to spill the seeds into the grass. "One step at a time, love. There's no rushing the affection of wild creatures."

"So I've noticed," he murmured.

She retreated back to sit in the cradling roots of her tree. "Don't be ridiculous. I loved you from the moment I saw how delicately you handled your spiders."

He returned to her side, letting his head sink back onto her thigh. Out of the corner of his eye, he saw a sparrow land in the grass to investigate the pile. "You are a strange sort of nymph."

"I wouldn't know." She shrugged, her eyes on her work. "I'm the only one I've ever known. There's only one in each forest, you know."

"Don't you ever get lonely?" More birds flew down to the ground, following that first sparrow's brave example. They hopped closer, stealing seeds from the pile and flying away to eat them in safety.

"No. I have the birds, the deer, the wolves, the cranky black bear that lives down the hill, the ants that crawl up my trunk, and the gnats that hang in the air when it's thick enough to drink. I am connected to a great web, and all the life in it hums in my veins."

"As am I. But when I feel the lines thrumming, it's not to protect what I love. It is a call to take a life, like a spider creeping toward a moth struggling in its web."

"It's what you were made for. You can't help that anymore than a spider can help eating bugs. Besides, you do protect what you love. You protect me."

"How so?"

"There is a rumor that Death himself favors this apple tree. No man in the world would dare to harm it now."

"Oh?" His dark eyes slid back to study her face. "How do they know that?"

"Not all birds find Death's company so unsettling." She nodded to the break in the forest canopy. The flash of blue-black wings caught the light as they circled.

"Ah, yes. Where I go, the crows do tend to follow." *Sometimes spying*, he added to himself, darkly.

"That they do. Even mortals know that much. So your presence keeps me safe, and I can go on keeping my forest safe. How could my birds not love you for that?" She fussed with a final stem, and then gave a cry of triumph. "Ah-ha! I've done it." She proudly displayed the product of her labors. "A proper crown for a proper prince."

At her prodding, he sat up and allowed her to settle a wreath of red, yellow, and white flowers around his brow. "I'm sure I've never looked more regal."

"I certainly think so." She adjusted the crown, then crawled into the circle of his arms and pressed her warm lips against his sallow cheek. His eyes closed.

The spectral lines thrummed, calling for the Prince of Ash and Bone. But he was Cassius now, and could not answer. So he turned his face from the endless work that lay before him and toward the sweet nymph in his arms.

* * *

After that spring, he was a long time gone from the apple tree, much longer than he meant to be. The summoning threads were always so much heavier for his inattention. Five summers hung heavy on the vine, softened into fall, and shriveled into winter, only to be reborn as something sweeter in the spring. By the time his weary feet padded through the grass to her tree again, the spring blossoms marked five years of his absence.

She said no word of rebuke, nor remarked upon the passage of time. Instead, she greeted him with eyes as bright as new leaves, and brought him to rest against her tree. They talked until the sun began to flicker like a guttering candle and he told her of all the places he had been since they parted. As night poured like wine between the boughs, turning the forest black and silver, they walked together, arm-in-arm, serenaded by a hum of crickets.

"It's useful, that heart of yours," she remarked.

"Oh?"

"Yes, the light it gives is much handier than any torch."

"And you dislike torches?"

"Well, fire makes me nervous."

"Naturally." He looked at her, and the shadows hung on her profile like a widow's veil. "I would frighten all the flames away, if I could."

She patted his hand. "It's enough that you frighten the mortals. It makes them careful of how they tend their campfires here. As long as you keep visiting, I'll live as long as any dryad can."

"Then I shall."

* * *

The next decade, plague wrapped greedy fingers around the world and squeezed it in much the same way that Death had once squeezed an apple. Wading through mass graves, scattering spiders like a farmer might scatter seed, the Prince of Ash and Bone wondered how the dryad fared. He thought of her smile, of the light in her leaf-green eyes, and his heart gave a sick, wet thump. Part of him wanted to walk away, to turn his back on the dying and return to her quiet green haven. To leave the place where no one saw him, and let the world rot away without his help. But there were so many souls trapped in pain and misery. They called to him, caught in the web, struggling to break free. He could not leave them to suffer. He didn't think that she would want him to, even for her.

Soon, he promised himself. *I will go to her soon.*

He kept his promise, in a manner of speaking. "Soon," to an immortal, is sometime before the world crumbles into dust. As one who did not fear death, the prince was likewise unmindful of his accomplice, Time. So it was twelve years from the last time their fingers parted that he found his way to the shadows beneath the dryad's apple tree.

She was quieter than she'd been when he saw her last, and wan. Her dark hair looked brittle, and she moved as if her body pained her. Speaking to be heard above the harsh, wet lurching of his heartbeat, Cassius asked, "What has happened?"

"My tree was sick. It's better now. I'm getting stronger every day." She pulled him down beside her, leaning gratefully against his shoulder. "I've missed you."

He put his arm around her, smoothing her wilted tresses. "I shouldn't have left you so long. I should have been back sooner."

She shook her head against his shoulder, her eyes closed. "No. No, you have things you must do. I only wish sometimes that I could go with you. I'll never see any of the world beyond my forest. I cannot leave my tree."

"I'd gladly take you if I could. I might take some pleasure in the world, myself, if you walked through it with me."

She tipped her head back and opened her eyes to look at him. "It's enough for now that you're here. I saved seeds for you. So that you can feed the birds."

He smiled and took the little packet from her hand. "That was kind, but I didn't bring anything for you." He thought a moment, then lifted his fingers to her hair. Small gray spiders trickled across his hands to scatter in her hair like furred jewels. Weaving and dancing, they worked their way from her head down to her shoulders, trailing a silver veil behind them. Fine and delicate, it cascaded down over her dark hair like gossamer lace. Idonae turned her head to and fro to admire it, and it shimmered like starlight.

"You look like a princess," Cassius mused. "Like your namesake."

"I look like a bride." Idonae grinned, as wild and fey as she'd been the first day he met her. "Careful now. Wrapped in your webbing like this, some spectral wind is like to blow me away."

"I'd never let—"

She put her finger to his lips. "I don't need vows from you. I'm not truly a bride, you know. What I need is for you to feed my birds."

He pressed his cold lips to her warm cheek, then twisted to his feet to pour the seeds into the grass at a safe distance. They sat down against the trunk of her tree, as comfortably intertwined as the tree roots that surrounded them, and watched the sparrows feed.

* * *

Even as the world began to weave back together in the wake of the plague, war raked it apart again with poisoned talons. The Prince walked through battlefields with the unwanted company of crows screeching above his head, crying praise for the clash of arms that left them such sweet carrion to feast on. In the bloodiest part of the battle, a beautiful white-haired woman reclined in the branches of a bare white tree and smiled at the men watering its roots with their blood. The Queen of Crows. He ducked his head, keeping tattered banners and armored men between them. His mother would have no kind words if she saw him slinking around with sad eyes, his shoulders hunched as if beneath a burden.

"A god should find some joy in his purpose," she'd tell him, as she often did. "That you do not shows your weakness."

Clever though he was at avoiding the Queen's black eyes, only a little darker than her heart, the crows' eyes missed nothing. Even as he escaped into the shadows of the trees at the edge of the field, their mocking voices called after him, *She knows. She knows. She knows.*

She knows what? he wondered idly. But the lines were thrumming, hanging heavy with souls, and he had no time to dwell on the jabbering of crows.

When he returned to the dryad's forest, it had only been a year since he'd been Cassius to her Idonae. Still, it had been too long.

There was no smell of smoke to warn him. The flames had long-since been extinguished. There was only silence, as if all the birds in the forest had forgotten how to sing. Charred twigs crunched beneath his feet in lieu of the tickling of grass. No soothing shadows greeted him as he came to the place where he'd left her. No graceful tree, swaying its limbs as if dancing with the breeze. Only ash and ruin.

He knelt beside the blackened, twisted bits of what used to be an apple tree and sank his fingers into the pile. Fumbling, sifting, he tried to find some piece that he would still recognize as her. Lifting his cupped palms, the soot slid between his fingers, leaving them empty. Staccato splashes brought out patches of moon pale skin as tears dripped onto his hands. He stared at them, and he hated them, because all they could do was take, and never give back what had been taken.

A wingtip brushed his face. A mockingbird chirped in his ear, sharing a fragment of a song. A whir came from his left, the light pinch of feet landing on his other shoulder. A bluebird gave him another piece of song. By and by, his arms, wrists, and shoulders were crowded with birds, some as bright and shining as jewels, and others clad humbly in gray or brown. But every one of their voices was fine and sweet. They sang to him, and all he could give back to them was the sharp, ragged sound of his breathing.

A sparrow settled on his fingertips. She did not offer him a song. Instead, she opened her beak and dropped into his palm a small brown seed. An apple seed. For a moment, he stared at it, uncomprehending. Then he knew what it was, and where it had come from. The sparrow left him, and he curled his fingers into a fist.

What to do with this last piece of her? He could plant it, but some part of him recoiled at the thought of giving her to this wretched charred soil. Anywhere else, there would still be axes and flames and disease. There would always be death.

In his mind, she said to him, "I like to see my fruit nourish life. Be it a new tree or a little bird, it makes me happy. It's what I was meant for."

Numbly, he raised the seed to his lips. As he swallowed, the birds scattered in every direction, leaving him in the midst of a sudden hush.

As the seed settled into the bottom of his stomach, his heart shone down upon it like a pulsing red star, warm with the weight of her memory, bright with the sympathy of birdsong. With a sudden tickle, it began to sprout roots. They grew and stretched, wiggling down to tangle in his guts. Once they had found their footing, they thrust up through his chest to push branches between the gaps in his ribs. New leaves tickled against his bones. He unfastened his robes, letting them sink down to his waist so that he could see the tiny apple tree nestled inside his rib cage, cradling his heart in its branches. From behind him, gentle fingers reached out to touch his shoulder.

"And now I will follow you," Idonae whispered.

From that moment on, Death was never lonely, because ever after, he was never alone.

THE TAB

Mack Moyer

The gravel crunched under his wheels as he parked the rig in an unpaved parking lot outside the motel. From the driver's seat, John watched Clara strut into the motel room. She was young, not even thirty-five yet, with bouncing blonde curls, and a blue satin dress that clung to all the best parts. She gave him a quick, smirking glance over her shoulder before she went inside.

John's ring finger felt naked. He stretched his fingers but it didn't help. He wanted to follow Clara into the motel room, but not yet. There was a bar across the road, a ramshackle joint with a neon Budweiser sign in the window.

He heard a crash as he got out of the cab. He staggered and almost fell, with a sudden bout of dizziness taking him unaware. Must have been his blood pressure acting up; the doctor had put John on new hypertension meds and warned they could make him lightheaded if he stood up too quickly. The dizziness passed. John looked for signs of a wreck. It sounded close, yet the scant traffic whizzed past unabated.

John went to the bar. A sign hung over the door. BARATHRUM, it read.

Inside he found the bar empty except for the bartender and a tall, skinny man in black sweeping the floor. The lights were dim and every surface was covered with a layer of dust.

The bartender had pronounced crow's feet and a warm smile, slicked back hair, and a salt-and-pepper chinstrap beard. He wore blue jeans and a dark fleece zipped up to his chin with a goat's head stitched into the breast.

"Have a seat pal," the bartender said. He wiped the dust off the bar.

The skinny man in black paid John no mind.

John sat. "Little slow?"

"Business comes and goes," the bartender answered. "Let me guess, Jack and a lager?"

John laughed. "You're good at this."

The bartender popped the cap off a bottle and slung a double shot into a tumbler. "I've been here awhile, what can I say?"

John put his money on the bar.

The bartender slid it back. "Your money's not worth anything here, John."

John almost choked on his beer. "How'd you—"

"I'm good with names."

It must have been Clara. She knew him well enough to know he'd stop for a beer before hitting the motel room. "Did a blonde women pay for my drinks? Blue dress? Mid-thirties, roundabout?"

Flashing red lights outside caught John's eye. The crash, he thought. He looked through the window, but there was a haze, fog perhaps, and he couldn't make out what was happening.

"How's the beer?" the bartender asked.

It was thick and hoppy and strong. John couldn't remember the last time a beer tasted so good.

"I thought so," the bartender said. He lit a cigarette and took a long drag. "Now John, we need to talk about your tab."

"You said my money's no good here."

"That's not the tab I'm talking about." The bartender punched some keys on the cash register and a long receipt snaked out of it. He studied it for a moment. "It's not the biggest I've ever seen, but you owe more than you've paid."

John got up from his stool. He wasn't one to leave a free beer unfinished, but his gut told him to get out. "Alright," he said. "I'm done."

The skinny man watched silently as John made for the door. John turned the knob but it wouldn't open.

"Let me out," John said.

"Not until we talk about your tab."

John was grinding his teeth. "I don't know what you guys are doing, but if you don't open this door I'll split both your heads open."

The skinny man swept a cigarette butt into his dustpan.

The bartender examined the receipt. "You are pretty good at splitting heads open. January 1982. A parking lot in...whazzat? Ink's a bit smudgy. Oh, the River Wards in Philly. Pleasant neighborhood, from what I hear."

John froze.

"Don't worry," the bartender said. "That one doesn't count against you. The whole 'turning the other cheek' thing is great in theory, but in practice, not so much."

The memory flashed across his mind's eye. It had been cold that night when the bar let out and the mood was sour in the neighborhood after the Birds dropped another game. He couldn't remember why that guy came at him with a baseball bat, but John had never regretted what he did to him.

His throat felt dry, his stomach queasy.

"Finish your drinks," the bartender said. "Trust me, you'll need them."

Seeing no other option, John sat down. He downed his Jack. Just like the beer, it was strong and good. "You guys have a bathroom?"

The bartender pointed across the room, next to the pool table.

John squeezed into the cramped bathroom and pissed into the shit-stained toilet bowl. As he washed his hands he caught sight of himself in the mirror. He cried out when he saw his face had been crushed, with one eyeball dangling from the socket and liquefied brain matter dripping from a crack in his skull.

He fell as he backpedaled out of the bathroom. The skinny man looked down at him, expressionless.

John touched his face with trembling fingers but felt no deformities. An illusion, but even so, the fear coiled in John's gut so tightly he thought he might vomit.

"I should have warned you about the mirror," the bartender said, shrugging. "My apologies."

"I was…" John couldn't catch his breath. "I was…"

"Not yet." The bartender patted the bar and grinned. "Come on, drink up."

The red lights screamed through the window as John returned to his stool, lit a smoke, and threw back the remainder of his drink. "Alright," John said. "My tab."

The bartender refilled his mug. "Your tab."

His heart felt heavy in his chest.

"Some of this shit, geez," the bartender said.

Somehow John already knew. "Teddy."

The bartender nodded. "That poor prick. If it makes any difference, you're not the only guy who owes for Teddy. I know boys will be boys, but Christ."

"So the guy in the parking lot doesn't count."

The bartender shook his head.

"But picking on some kid in high school does?"

"I don't make the rules, John." He squinted as he looked over the receipt. "All because of a speech impediment and a weight problem."

John remembered Teddy well. "He lived with his aunt, an older lady from what I remember," he said. He felt a lump form in his throat. "He'd go to bingo with her at the church annex. We used to laugh at him."

"And you know what Teddy did to himself once she died, I assume."

"I don't want to talk about it." He finished his mug. "Another."

"Gotcha, pal."

"I need to piss again. Any way you can cover up that mirror?"

The bartender turned to the skinny man who was sweeping dust from under the pool table. "Can you cover up that mirror?"

The skinny man scowled and shook his head.

"Sorry. Just try not to look."

John averted his eyes from the mirror in the bathroom. He wiped sweat from his brow as he emptied his bladder.

He stepped back into the barroom and his feet sank into a moist earthen floor. The lights had been replaced with candles burning along the walls. Bloated worms slithered past and stalactites bit down from the ceiling with skulls—some human and others not—impaled on the points.

The bartender read the receipt line by line. He frowned at John. "It's not looking great."

John stroked his beard. "Why all this for me? I never hurt anybody on purpose."

The bartender raised his eyebrow and for a moment his teeth looked brown and cracked and there was a hint of red in his eyes. "Lying counts too. More than you'd think. So do not lie to me, pal."

The skinny man hovered over John's shoulder.

"Back off," John barked. That same sense of self-preservation he felt back in 1982 kicked in. John leapt off the bar stool, fist cocked, but the fight drained right out of him when he saw what the skinny man had become.

The skinny man wore a long black robe now with the hood pulled back, his broom a scythe with dried blood caked onto the blade, his face devoid of flesh save for a thin green film across the forehead, his eyeless sockets dark pools of absence.

John sat down.

"So," John said to the bartender, "is that it, really?"

The bartender tucked the receipt into his pocket. "You tell me. Our records can be dodgy at times. Personally, I think we should upgrade to a more streamlined system but you know how these big operations can be. Bureaucracy and whatnot."

"Another please," John said.

The bartender obliged. "Drink fast."

"Fuck."

The skinny man placed his skeletal hand on John's shoulder. John tried to ignore him, but knew that at any moment those fingers could tighten and pull him away forever. He looked at the bartender, who just shrugged, as if to say, *Forever is right, pal.*

"I always give money to the homeless kid at the intersection," John pleaded. "The one with the bum foot."

"Seriously? John, you're talking about pocket change."

"I'm just a regular guy."

"Most people are. Doesn't change the tab."

"Am I that bad?"

"In my opinion, no. But the scales are tipped just enough in the wrong direction. I don't know what to tell you."

"But I'm good to my family, my mom and dad. I would have been good to my kids, if we ever had any. I'm good to…" he paused, thinking of Evelyn. "I'm good to my wife."

The bartender's eyes flared red again. "Are you, now?"

John covered the naked finger on his left hand.

"Where's your wedding ring, John?"

He swallowed hard. "I had to take it off."

"And why is that?"

John scrambled to dig the ring out of his pocket. He could feel it through his pant leg but couldn't squeeze his fingers inside. The pocket was too tight, and growing tighter. "I can't get it," John whimpered.

"At least you had the decency to take it off before you came here," the bartender said.

"Evelyn would never know."

The bartender nodded. "You would."

John's beer mug was now a crude stone chalice filled with blood, thick with clots. A dead roach floated in the center.

"You don't know shit," John said. "I would never try *that* with Evelyn, not now."

"That's your excuse?" the bartender said. He looked to the skinny man. "Can you believe that?"

The skinny man remained silent.

"John, this is on you and you have to pay for it."

John pushed the chalice away. "I'm surprised you didn't mention the accident."

The bartender leaned on the bar.

"It was my fault." He changed his mind about the chalice. He took a sip. The blood didn't taste as bad as he thought. "It's been years since we—"

"Fucked?" the bartender asked. "Your old lady just isn't into you anymore?"

John glared at him. "Watch your mouth." Another sip. His shoulders slumped. "It was my fault. Getting the house was my idea, even with that fucking mortgage."

The bartender looked over the receipt again as he listened.

"I could only swing the payment with extra overtime," John went on. "And that was with Evelyn already working her ass off. Then one month the money stretched a little too thin. I picked up three double shifts in a row."

The bartender watched John closely.

"It was my fault. I shouldn't have been driving after that last shift but I thought I could make it." John sighed. "I picked up Evelyn from work. I didn't see the stop sign. I was…"

"Drunk?" the bartender asked.

"Tired," John answered. "I'd *never* drive drunk with my wife in the car."

The bartender scratched his beard for a moment. "And the woman at the motel?"

"Evelyn can't do that for me anymore, so I talked to Clara." John took a long drink from the chalice. "I'm still wrong. I know I'm wrong." He wiped the blood dripping from his upper lip. "Anyway, do what you need to do."

The bartender folded the receipt then tapped it on the bar. "None of that was in our records."

The skinny man was sweeping the floor again, not the earthen floor but the linoleum John saw when he first arrived. The stalactites receded into the ceiling, skulls and all.

"Like I said," the bartender continued, "we don't have the best record keeping system. I mean, I do my best, but it's not always enough."

John's hands were shaking.

"I guess you can go," the bartender said. "That is, unless you want a quick one for the road."

The skinny man looked at the bartender.

"What? I like him."

John ran to the door. It opened this time. He disappeared into the haze outside.

* * *

John awoke in pain, strapped to an unyielding backboard with a neck brace tight under his chin.

His rig was upturned. A dump truck had rammed it from behind. Two paramedics hoisted John on their stretcher as police and firemen and bystanders looked on.

He saw Clara in the crowd.

John sobbed.

"Take it easy, pal," one of the medics said.

The world was all flashing red lights and the smell of spilled diesel as they lifted him into the warm confines of their ambulance. John reached into his pocket for his wedding ring, desperately thinking of Evelyn, his poor Evelyn, and what would happen to her if he was gone.

He checked both pockets. The ring wasn't there.

One of the paramedics loomed over him. He had wrinkled eyes with slicked back salt-and-pepper hair and a matching beard. John's vision grew bleary, distorted, and the medic's face shifted into that of a red-eyed goat with twisted horns and brown teeth.

But only for a second.

"I found your ring near your truck," the medic said. He slid it onto John's finger.

"Thank you," John croaked.

"Don't sweat it," the medic said. "I'll put it on your tab."

DEATH AND MY MENTIONS

Fran Wilde

Kryssamit paid the captain of the rusting vaporetto to take her all the way up to the Hotel des Bains' half-sunken second floor. She clutched her worn messenger bag as the boat creaked precariously over the waves. Below the hull, shadows of windows gaped open like startled fish. Everything in Venice smelled like sewers and rot, even out on the Lido.

They didn't pay her enough for this.

Wouldn't, either. Not until after the company's public launch in twelve hours.

Instead, Aeterna, Inc. gave interns like Kryssamit discarded hearts and souls. Those were the company's terms for the digital equivalent, anyway: lost photos, deleted experiences, personal histories scraped from dating profiles. Meant for personal use only, but on the black market, those went for good money.

Aeterna had been the first to realize: everyone wanted immortality. Or at least the guaranteed server space that came with it.

That's why interns, at least, worked for no money until the launch. That's why they'd sift through discarded files, looking for footage—hearts and souls, that proved connections with celebrities, geniuses, with Ms. Lavin, with any of the immortals Thoth might potentially select.

Buyers with just the right amount of insider information were particularly keen on making themselves more interesting, perhaps gaining Thoth's attention, pre-launch.

A seagull cruised the blue sky above the boat. Instead of taking a photo, Kryssamit thought back to her last conversation with Aeterna's AI. Thoth, once a non-player god in a moderately popular video game, had laughed at various investors' efforts to game Aeterna's first pre-approved immortality list. Meantime, Krys worried aloud. "No one's putting down a deposit, just angling for your attention."

"Our boss isn't worried; you shouldn't be," Thoth had said in Krys' ear when it finished laughing. The AI gave Krys and the other interns their work orders, but Thoth's boss was Aeterna's aging CEO, Merienne Lavin, whom, until today, Krys figured she'd never meet.

"Thanks to BethAnn Plantagenet leaping on deck to become the first immortal, everyone's watching and waiting," she'd shot back. "But everyone still wants to see how she fares."

Graceful BethAnn, mediocre singer, dark hair, tea-colored eyes that just ate up the camera, young starlet already struggling to find work after her newly-discovered status wore off. She'd wanted to make sure her legacy didn't get wiped. "I want to last," she'd told reporters. She'd signed on. For all of it.

For the right to be first more than anything.

"If there are no glitches, people will pay all sorts of money for a spot on the list. For all the extra heart and soul mods too." Thoth was right about the latter already, but not just for the mods. Krys couldn't sell second-hand hearts and souls fast enough.

"Not diving today?" The vaporetto captain asked, breaking into Kryssamit's thoughts.

Krys shook her head. "Here for work."

The captain looked about to ask more questions, so Krys dug in her bag, even though the only things inside were a satellite screen, some files, and a crumpled chocolate bar wrapper.

People hungered for information and advantage everywhere. At Aeterna, the interns' public mentions flooded with asks for footage of the burn room, of Thoth, of BethAnn. Anything. Some of the interns faked data to turn a quick profit and got canned. But Krys never had. She'd stuck to hearts and souls.

Until Thoth put her on a boat headed for the worst network zone in the world, on the day of Aeterna's public launch. To deliver a report to the only other person besides BethAnn that the company had guaranteed immortality: Merienne Lavin, Aeterna's CEO. Who'd retreated to sunken Venice to watch the birth of the first immortal, to die of old age herself, and then to reappear with the help of Aeterna's software.

But in order for Aeterna's version of immortality to succeed, Ms. Lavin had to stay alive for a few days more and BethAnn needed to die.

And then BethAnn needed to come back.

But BethAnn had only managed to do the first thing so far.

The details were in the report Kryssamit carried to the Hotel des Bains.

As the boat bumped over the Adriatic's chop and what was left of Venice crested the horizon, Krys cursed her luck and wished she'd done a lot more hustling. The company's future could go either way. All Kryssamit's invested time could go either way too.

"Don't worry," Thoth said in her earbud. "You'll be fine."

That was easy for the AI to say. "Why didn't you send a VP? A manager?" Kryssamit whispered so the captain wouldn't hear. She wasn't sure how many VPs there were at Aeterna.

"You're much less expensive," Thoth whispered back.

Less Expensive: *more expendable.* Less connected. No one at Aeterna Inc. or anywhere else wanted to be disconnected for too long. When social profile ranks impacted your credit *and* the popularity of opinions drove down the price of goods, you stayed on the hook. Downtime could wreck you. Worse, once Aeterna launched, downtime could limit how deep your afterlife went.

Who deserved immortality? That had been the big question in Krys' mentions and everywhere else lately. What no one knew to ask yet was: *Who'd get thrown off the servers later to make space for the future?*

That was insider info even the biggest hustler wouldn't sell. They knew they were expendable already.

There was a time when there'd been enough storage to go around. But everyone logged everything now. Cradle to grave. In sepia and full color. Artistic, with font overlays, music, and straight up raw. Too much data, and companies had begun deleting things wholesale to make room for new. A few mistakes here and there, lifetimes lost, and Aeterna was born to standardize what would be kept and what would be discarded.

Whatever. Krys had always wanted to travel, see things firsthand. She'd just never had the cash. Now, Venice shimmered beneath her, on the company's dime.

Ms. Lavin had the cash. Had paid Krys' way. Lavin would make it all back and more after the company launched. But the CEO didn't want anyone to know she was dying, not until after. So, secrecy, and an intern to hand-carry a report to a wifi slow zone. Less risk of damaging information getting out last minute.

And Thoth trusted Kryssamit. That meant a lot to her.

> Find a pipe or a metal frame to boost your signal once you're in the hotel.

Thoth's messages in Krys' mentions came through even as the AI's voice faded with the last of the network.

Kryssamit cursed softly. Thoth had said of the whole trip, "You won't be alone."

She'd believed the AI. It would have been reassuring, too, except Thoth had let her listen in as it said the same thing to Death, the assassin hired to take BethAnn over to immortality. That gave Kryssamit chills. Thoth didn't seem to mind.

The vaporetto chugged to a slow halt. No one waited on the balcony to catch the tossed line, so Krys jumped the short distance to the ledge and clung there. "I'll call when I'm ready," she shouted, hoping the captain could hear her over the engine.

The elderly captain didn't even look back as Krys struggled over the railing, the salt-wake licking at her jeans and soaking her sneakers.

She made it over the ledge and then climbed the makeshift ladder to the third floor. No elevators here in the shell of the old hotel. No entrance either. Merienne Lavin had taken the entire floor for herself and her secretaries and no one had cared to stop her. Boxes from numerous drone deliveries lay scattered around, their packaging gutted and spilled across the scratched parquet.

"Everyone's out diving the city," Ms. Lavin's voice echoed against the high ceilings. She coughed softly into her sleeve. "Come in."

Krys did as told. The wide settee the CEO lay on was the only soft thing in the room. Lavin's skin was nearly transparent as ice. Swathed in a thick cream turban and robe, she looked like a has-been twentieth century movie star. A walker waited beside the settee. A box of health-shakes, two dozen, sat half-opened on the floor beside it. Bottles of pills, too.

"Ma'am." Krys fussed with her messenger bag. "Still no sign of Ms. Plantagenet."

The CEO waved her forward. "It's true then. She might be gone for good?" Her hand shook.

Kryssamit nodded. "Death kinked the job."

She'd practiced saying it on the flight from London. Thoth had said it first.

"How? We had a contract." Lavin sounded truly amazed, but her outrage clipped each word short.

Krys waited. When Lavin didn't continue, she said carefully, "The evidence was hard to find. Just a few bits of footage." She swallowed hard. The footage was Aeterna-owned, but she'd made the copy. Risky for an intern, an employer's misdirected blame. "This is so far above my paygrade..." She let her voice trail off. Krys was pretty sure Lavin didn't know she was selling hearts and souls, but was it worth antagonizing her boss?

Thanks to the black market, Krys had paid off all her debts before she left. She'd banked some credit in the bank-of-mattress, too. Bought a better camera for her phone, more filters. But it wasn't enough. Immortality or adventure. One or the other.

That's why she'd gone to Venice when Thoth said go.

Now her funds were halfway around the world. And she was here, in a sunken hotel on the submerged Lido, with no network. Lavin cared about secrecy, and Krys could see why. But a few strands of footage shot here might make her famous enough for even a wayward AI to consider her worthy of immortality. Some day.

Better that than a data-wipe when a server ran out of space. That's what BethAnn had told all the reporters, every chance she got. Aeterna was betting that, tomorrow, everyone would agree.

But if Krys and Lavin couldn't beat Death, the bet would fail. No BethAnn, no launch.

"Show me," the ailing CEO said. "Show me everything."

> Sali, this guy just tried to pick me up in a bar by quoting my Aeterna page.

But he's got nothing on his profile. He's a blank.

The soon-to-be immortal's voice sounded like water over rocks in the cavernous hotel room. "BethAnn Plantagenet, last known conversation," Krys whispered. "Seven billion followers."

Lavin nodded, turning her ear to listen harder. "As it should be."

> Dick.

"Sali's her personal assistant—an AI. Foul mouthed thing."

"That I know," Lavin said.

"Locked down right after the murder. Won't talk to anyone."

"That I didn't."

> No, really, it's a problem. He said I'll be wiped. That it's just marketing. A blank said that to me.

> Aeterna promised. We're good for it.

> I'm making copies anyway. I want your help.

Krys pulled out a sheaf of logs showing BethAnn's attempts to copy her data. Each time she reached for an image, shifts happened. Footage disappeared, replaced by other shots, different angles. Pieces of stories appeared with a new name added here, a shade-dimmed silhouette appearing by her side.

"Who is that?" Lavin whispered. But Krys had watched her face. She'd said the words as if she was being recorded, for effect. Lavin knew who the silhouette was.

She'd seen the same silhouette in her own Aeterna-locked footage.

Krys swallowed dryly. "Your assassin? Freelance, right?"

Lavin waved a frail hand. She reached for a shake on the table beside the settee. "There's water in the bathroom in gallon containers. And some snack bars. Help yourself. We can get more delivered."

Grateful she wasn't being offered a shake, Krys rose and turned until she spotted the bathroom behind peeling doors. Her footsteps squelched on the parquet. In the bathroom, six jugs of water, a clean plastic cup with her name Sharpied on it, and a dozen snack bars were set up on the ornate sink next to rows of pill bottles. "You won't be alone," Thoth had said. She shivered. She drank two glasses of the room-temperature water and pocketed one of the bars before heading back out.

> Sali, I think he's following me. I just took my boat to the dive area, and there's another boat already here.

> If already there, he's not following you, he's ahead of you.

> Sali. Cut it out, I'm frightened. I know the contract said to act happy, but this—

> You can film that. We don't have a lot of footage of you frightened. Could come in useful.

A final image. BethAnn's face. A smile. Not frightened. As if she recognized a friend. And then nothing.

* * *

"When they found BethAnn's boat, her dive gear was still onboard. She's down there, in the sunken city," Lavin said softly.

"Beneath the Bridge of Sighs," Kris added. The report was poetic, at least.

A tourist had found her, on an excursion dive. Left her there, too. No matter how many times Thoth washed the system, more images of BethAnn appeared. Venice and the dead immortal: one caught the other. The sunken limestone arch, her splayed form pressed against it, cargo pants filling with fish, long, dark hair strung with kelp.

"Now we know where she is," Lavin snapped, her voice like crumpling paper. "Soon, everyone will know it. My mentions are already filled with her. And still, I can't get her back." The old woman's voice held a deep longing.

Krys shuddered. "There's more."

"Tell me. I'm not paying you to hesitate." The fear in the old woman's voice came as a bit of a shock. Krys couldn't weigh it—was it fear for Aeterna? Or fear for herself?

"Death sent a ransom note." Now Krys' voice wavered. If Merienne Lavin was afraid, Krys had a right to be, too.

On the screen, a silhouette appeared. "You'll forgive me if I don't show my face," a voice said. "I'm trying to build my own portfolio, and, well, this is not something I want remembered for eternity."

Lavin leaned forward, reaching for the screen. "I know that voice. I'd only contracted with him on paper. I didn't realize. Robert."

The voice sounded as old as Lavin's own. Still. "Thoth wasn't able to trace him to a name. He's got no records."

An almost-face. Shadows. "I've done other things like this for you over the years, Merienne. Now it's done. Now you'll give me a life. As promised, but better. More experiences, more background. More hearts. Souls. All of it, if you want to see BethAnn again."

"That's impos—" but Lavin stopped. "No. It's possible. Especially if Sali's helping him."

Of course. And now Death wanted a profile.

Krys shook her head. He wanted it badly enough to murder the first immortal, permanently. Withholding BethAnn's files was almost as bad as wiping them.

"This is a disaster for the company," Lavin whispered. She began coughing. "Ten hours until we go public. You have to help me, Miss…"

"Kryssamit." She didn't give a last name. Lavin was just being polite.

"Thoth likes you. Said you were the brightest of the catalogue interns. The best with mentions and backstories."

Krys blinked. "That was kind."

"So you must help me. BethAnn's gone, I'm ill. Who knows if we can satisfy Robert? We must find her, or fake her, on our own."

Krys froze. Lavin wanted to use her hearts and souls, too? Impossible. Not for a starlet as well known as BethAnn. "Nothing to fake," Krys dodged, and cursed under her breath.

So much for getting paid.

"Now what will you do?" Krys asked. No immortal, no IPO, no company. No company, no pay.

"We wait," Lavin said.

"For Death."

The old woman nodded. "He'll come here next. I'm ready." Lavin reached for her walker. She withdrew a small pistol from the handle.

Krys swallowed. They were absolutely not paying her enough for this.

* * *

"I'd rather get a boat back to the mainland," Krys muttered. "Now that I've brought what you needed."

"I'll call you a boat when it's over," Lavin whispered. Her eyes were on the balcony doors. She looked younger and more awake than she had when Krys entered. "This is for posterity."

Krys didn't speculate what "it" and "this" were. She was trapped in a half-drowned hotel with an immortal, waiting for Death. That was obvious enough.

What she wanted was to be back at home, sitting on her own mattress, working on her own footage. Getting a stronger profile.

"Can I film while we wait?"

Lavin waved a hand dismissively. "You can film the whole thing. Consider it a bonus."

Krys frowned. "Really." Lavin and Aeterna had been all about secrecy.

"Really. I want the whole world to see Death for who he is."

The change in her posture shocked Krys. "That will make him famous. He'll be immortal, too."

"He's a killer who wants to be more." Lavin was already weakening from her momentary rally. She lay back on the divan. "Someone who spent his entire life trying not to be photographed or filmed. And now he worries that he doesn't exist at all. I'll fix that."

Her words rippled against the walls of the room at the Hotel des Bain, even as the sound of a distant motor approached.

"Krys, dear, would you get me a glass of water?"

"Now?" She'd hoped to get a shot of Death coming through the French doors.

"Yes." Lavin said. Her eyes were on the balcony. "Unless you don't want to get paid."

The boat sounded louder. She went to get the water. Maybe Death would give her a ride back to the mainland.

* * *

Krys lingered in the bathroom, trying to get a signal. There was one corner that had a small flicker of hope, in the decrepit shower. She touched the wall over the pipes. The signal grew. Bless Aeterna for getting even the interns satlinks.

Her mentions were packed. People looking for her. Her last footage had been hours ago. Was she okay?

Nothing from Thoth.

Should she let him know what was happening? How much signal did she have? She uploaded the footage she'd taken of her reflection on the water, but the footage of the Hotel des Bains ruins and Lavin would take too much time to upload now.

Krys pulled her hand away from the wall and lost the network.

Shouting, from the room.

Opening the door a crack, she looked out. A man stood on the worn parquet. Lavin had risen and was leaning hard on one of her walker handles. Her robe hung down in folds over her bony shoulders.

"You cannot be serious, Robert."

"Dead serious, Merienne. When you started this company, it was to track online activity, not make a profit from people's memories. You warned all of us to stay out of the limelight. What choice do we have now? If we want to buy a home, get a job outside, we need a social presence. I don't have one. I'm a vampire. No reflection. Doomed to a half-life."

There was a pause. Death cracked his knuckles. Krys braced for a shot.

"I tried the black market, but no one would credit me. I thought if I could get through to one of your employees—to BethAnn, even, or the AIs—then maybe they'd help me. But no one talks to someone without any history. BethAnn certainly wouldn't."

Krys smiled ruefully. That was true. She'd sold baskets of souls cheap as ghost followers for just those reasons. She'd needed the cash, but she still felt a twinge of guilt about selling other people's memories.

Robert kept talking, turning so that Krys could see his profile. "And then you called with the job. Same old Merienne."

"Different now," she coughed. Krys stepped out of the bathroom.

Death—Robert looked at her. "Who are you?"

"Just an intern."

"They couldn't even send a manager."

"No."

"Because you're disposable."

"Maybe so are you." Krys said it fast, but Death frowned. "You have no past. So no future."

The assassin nodded. "True." The way he said it made Krys wonder if he worried about getting paid, too.

She relented. "If you want, I can help you build one. I have a pretty good hand with creating a construct." She couldn't build a new BethAnn, but she could help Death. "I just need your face on film." She held up her camera again. He looked right at her. Captured him.

Merienne glanced at her with a hint of gratitude, but kept the pistol ready.

They had five hours before the company went public.

> Death footage. A text message from Thoth.

She went back to the bathroom and put her hand against the pipe. A stream of images. Snippets of BethAnn's last footage. A grainy low-res of him in the cafe. Not as the silhouetted Death, but as Robert. And again alone on a boat near the popular Venice dive site that BethAnn had visited. Zooming in, Krys saw a satellite phone in his hand. He'd been filming himself near the immortal, too. Maybe trying to surf BethAnn's mentions later.

Krys sifted through adventure tourists' footage—some had found enough wifi to upload from Venice's warren of abandoned upper-floor rooms. She saw Robert again and again, watching BethAnn.

A chill ran up Krys' arms.

One camera caught a profile and a flash of BethAnn's dark hair. Talking, in the shadow of a doorway, but not to Robert.

"Got you." Krys burst out so loudly both Lavin and Robert turned as she emerged from the bathroom. Thoth pinged her. Hard.

> Get him to release BethAnn's personal assist-ant.

"I'll clear your name, just release Sali—the PA/AI," she said. "Give Merienne what she wants."

"Merienne wants absolution." Robert said. "A Legacy. Not immortality. They're different. Sali promised me both if I sequestered her final data." Robert said. "Plus options."

That was kind of cheap, Krys thought. "I've sent footage to your profile. Enough for a start." She'd sent him more than that. She'd given him a wideband link.

Death tapped his satphone. "I've released them."

Kryssamit could see it on the network. BethAnn had reappeared, her final moments burned through her AI's connections. BethAnn's last words flooded the networks. "It's you," she said. Her face filled Krys' screen.

She didn't look scared.

>> We're sending the boats from the dive site.

"Thank you, Sali," Lavin said. But her voice sounded strained. She gazed at the screen.

>> BethAnn also.

Lavin sputtered. A wave slapped against the hotel balcony.

>>> "I'm back." BethAnn's face, with Sali's assist, all across the networks. Her first whispered words; the birth of immortals, of Aeterna, too.

Lavin's face transformed, softened. "We did it." She reached out to touch the screen.

BethAnn smiled too, just like she had in the last frame before she died. That last "it's you" had bothered Krys so much she'd made a copy.

Sali came online in Krysamit's ear, private channel. "Hello, Krys."

> I didn't think you'd mind.

Thoth's soft echo. BethAnn's voice saying hello also.

The silence around their greetings echoed, nibbling at Krys' thoughts.

They were powerful, these AIs and the immortals with them. But they couldn't go out into the world like Krys could. Or Robert. Or, possibly, even Merienne Lavin.

She narrowed her eyes. It was almost morning in New York. The whole world had just watched the emergence of an immortal. By this afternoon, Aeterna would be public and Lavin would be very rich.

"You don't pay me nearly enough," Krys said. She turned the camera to her own face. So that everyone would see her, too. "Not to cover for you." That "it's you" hadn't been Robert. "You killed BethAnn, not Death."

"It's true, I don't pay you enough. I'll change that once you leave," Lavin said, lying back on the settee. "I'd like to go in peace."

"Murder was your marketing plan, and dying your escape clause," Krys finally said. The first of the boats threw a line up to the balcony.

With a slight incline of her head, Merienne acknowledged it. "Robert spoke to her. Wanted to warn her. The rest of you? You were willing to go along with it. What's changed?"

"You would have been immortal anyway. Who will run Aeterna now?" Krys asked. "How will you make good on your promises if you're really dead?"

Lavin frowned and nodded to Krys. "You'll fix it for me. With Sali and BethAnn. You're promoted."

"What about the mangers? The VPs?"

Lavin waved her hand. "We never had any. Just interns. Kept overhead low. Fewer questions, too."

Expendable. Overhead. Not low enough, by far. Questions, not enough.

Krys wondered, if she weighed Lavin's heart, would there be too much guilt, or not enough to move the scale. "Maybe you'll live instead," she said.

Lavin's eyes shut tight against the thought.

"That would be interesting," Death said, an eyebrow raised in Krys' direction. He turned to his former employer, smiling. "Consequences are for the living."

As Merrienne Lavin was carried onto the vaporetto from the balcony, with Robert following, Thoth made a change. Krys' network flooded with credit, with connections. Her mentions filled with congratulations.

Krys swore. She saw everything now. She let the world see it too.

> You did well.

> How many memories, how many people, Thoth? Is it worth it?

> It's all data. And this way, the best people never die.

The best. Who judged?

The hearts and souls she'd sold on the black market. That last look from BethAnn. "It's you." It *was* her. All of them. As much as Merienne. It was everyone doing a small job that made the bigger jobs so easy.

"Don't," she said aloud. She looked around the abandoned room in the drowning Hotel des Bains. She didn't want to film it, or share it on the network. She wanted to let it disappear below the waves in all its forgotten glory.

"Some things are best let go." She could travel. She had the credit. Her back pay. The money in the mattress, too. See some things firsthand.

She wide-banded her last words. Sent them out as vid, as image, as word.

> I quit. You can keep your hearts and souls.

Krys closed her connection with Thoth, closed the network. Her mentions went silent as she watched the sun sink into the submerged windows and bridges of Venice.

A SHIFT IN MOOD

Kathryn McBride

"Mum, I have to go now." Death twirled the telephone cord between his fingers.

"Not until you promise me you'll get the time off."

"Yes, I promise, alright? I just have to find someone to cover my shift, but I've seriously got to hang up. You know I'm at work."

"Well, 'til later then. Love you."

"Ok. Bye."

"I said, 'I love you.'"

"Yes, I know." Frustrated, Death peered over the top of his cubicle and scanned the room. It was an endless maze of gray partitions and modular desks, each workspace dotted in the center with a fleshy bit of humanity not unlike himself. Cupping the receiver for privacy, he whispered, *"Love you, too..."*

"That's my boy. Chat soon."

"Bye, Mum."

Death hung up and turned to gaze out the skyscraper's wall of windows. He pulled out the latest Corporate Directory and quickly assessed each possibility. It seemed logical to start with the most likely candidate. Death grabbed his Employee of the Month coffee mug and made his way to the break room.

The overhead fluorescents spotlighted a table in the corner, piled high with a pyramid of coffee filters, sugar packets, tea bags, and boxes of tiny plastic stirrers. Barely visible behind the mound was a balding man with comically large eyes.

"Hey, Greed. How ya' doin?" Death leaned awkwardly against the wall.

"I'll be better once Maintenance responds to my request. I've asked them to bring me a stepstool."

"Is there something you need to reach in the upper cabinets? Perhaps I could help."

"Don't be ridiculous. I emptied those cupboards ages ago. The stepstool is for my personal collection." Growing impatient, Greed came from around the table and looked Death in the eye. "We both know you're not one for small talk. Get on with it."

"Well, let's just say I have something to give you."

"Give it already, then. Right here, on top of the pile." Greed patted the stack of goodies with barely a tremor to the structure.

"It's not a *thing*, per se. More of an opportunity. I would like to give you my shift tonight. Now before you say anything, understand that there's a lot of people who would snatch that offer up in a heartbeat, but I wanted you to have first crack at it, because I know you would be the one to most appreciate it. What do you say?"

Greed scrunched up his face. "Thanks, but no thanks."

"Ah, Greed. Why not? It's the opportunity of a career. A once in a lifetime chance to be Death for a night."

"You know what I do, don't you? I collect things."

"Exactly! Tonight, you could collect an actual human life. Exciting, isn't it?"

"Perhaps if I could keep it. But I can't, can I? No, I must hand it over almost immediately. No profit in that."

"You're looking at this offer from the wrong angle, my friend. It's not about the keeping of the soul, but the important part you'll play in the journey."

"Downright communist attitude, that is. No matter. I have plans tonight anyway. Maybe Gluttony is free." Greed motioned to the refrigerator.

Protruding from its gaping doorway was the bottom half of a grotesquely large figure. The other half was immersed head first in the refrigerator, gorging himself on other people's sack lunches. It happened every day. Death failed to understand why his co-workers kept packing them.

"What do you say, Gluttony? Wanna have a stab at becoming Death tonight?"

Gluttony's mottled face peeked out of the fridge. A long piece of romaine coated in egg salad dangled from the corner of his mouth. "Quite a nice offer, but no thanks. I got plans."

"I will leave you two to the rest of your day, then. Have a good one, gents."

Death backed out of the room, still holding his empty cup.

* * *

As the lift rumbled down to the thirty-seventh floor, Death took the opportunity to tweak his appearance in the mirrored interior. He smoothed out the creases in his trousers and tried with little success to flatten the cowlicks in his dull charcoal hair. He had to pass the Vanities Department on the way to his next destination and he never failed to capture their notice.

As usual, Beauty was the first one to pop out of her cubicle, stepping directly into Death's path. "I thought that was you, Death. Been a while since you've come visiting." She really was delightful to look at, all fiery red hair and high cheekbones.

"Yes, well, this is more of a professional call. I'm on my way to see Pain and it's rather important, so if you don't mind, I'll just squeeze on by."

"Please don't squeeze by anything," Style yelled from behind his desk. "Go around the long way, through the Character-Building pool. You've been here thirty seconds and the air already reeks of sulfur."

"Now that is just a hurtful stereotype." Death took a discreet sniff to make sure it wasn't true. "The longer you sit there and harass me, the longer you'll keep me in your precious airspace."

Style swaggered out of his cubby to Beauty's side. He was a skinny tangle of pointed shoes, pegged trousers, and vest buttons. He tilted his head and with one perfectly manicured finger, swept a lock of blond hair to the side. He gave Death a critical side-eye as he spoke.

"You know I'm only teasing. In fact, there are moments when I think your look is absolutely meta. At times gothic, a little anti-establishment, all in all, highly editorial. With the right resources, you could really take your whole 'hood and scythe' vibe to the next level."

"Style, I appreciate the positive feedback, and I will absolutely keep you in the loop if I decide to, you know, *next-level* it." Death emphasized "next level" with air quotes.

"Never mind. I'm over you now. I'm sure Pain can smell your funky Death musk approaching, so don't keep him waiting." In a flurry of dismissive hand gestures, Style threw himself down at his modernist desk.

Beauty stayed put and stuck out her pouty bottom lip further than Death thought possible. "Sorry, Death. Maybe I'll get to see you outside of work sometime. You should call me."

"Yes, alright. Maybe." Death turned to leave, then looked back. "Are you sure?"

Beauty nodded her head as she shifted her weight from one lovely silk-clad hip to the other, playing with her hair and parting her lips just so. Death could hear Style hissing at her as he walked away.

"I do not get it. What do you see in him anyway?"

"I dunno. Death has that sexy bad boy thing going on. Like it's probably dangerous to go out with him, you know?"

Death moved through the rest of the Vanities Department with a little spring in his step. Beauty thought he was sexy. Before the promotion, back when he was just wishy-washy old Coma, she never looked twice at him. Hardly anyone did. Try ignoring Death, though. Not so easy. He had more attention than ever, but still not much of an idea about the proper thing to do with it.

* * *

The Unsavories Department was always a bit of a let-down after Vanities. Although the Vanities were undoubtedly taxing on one's self-esteem, at least they were a lively bunch. Death cut through the gloomy corridors and stained carpet to find Pain, hands massaging his ample forehead, pouring over reports.

"Pain, Pain, Pain, my man, Pain! How are you, Mate?"

Pain jumped up and embraced his old friend. "Look at you! It has been an age since I've seen that face." He took a small step back to take in the full breadth of his visitor. "I thought you might've forgotten all about us down here in the trenches. How are you?"

"I'm alright, I guess. Same old, same old. Could be worse, y'know."

"Oh, I know. Trust me, I know. Just yesterday, assignment comes across my desk for this bus accident. Driver gets flipped out of the cab, and his own bus, out of control, runs over him. Then a second vehicle comes 'round the bend, shatters both of his femurs, then a third guy in a minivan who witnessed the whole thing decides he needs to stay behind for the accident report—noble thing right? Except when he goes into reverse to park, he misjudges the scene and completely runs this poor bloke over again!"

"What? I didn't hear about this. It never came across my desk."

"Right, I know. Because he didn't die, mate. The guy gets run over three times and lives! Been absolutely mauled. Nothing but blood and bone and pavement. Disturbing, even by my standards. Literally exhausting work. Could barely get back to the office on my own power."

"Geez. I'm sorry. That is a rough day."

"You better believe it. Soothed myself with a fifth of whiskey last night and Drunk ended up coming over to keep me company."

"Did it help?"

"You bet your britches it did," Pain patted him on the shoulder, then let his grip linger there, "You've been letting me go on and on, but you are clearly here for a reason. What's up?"

"I do need a favor. Mum called and there's this silly family thing happening and I need the night off. I'm looking for someone to cover my shift."

"Oh man," Pain slumped back down in his chair, "I can't. I'm so sorry."

"It seems everyone I ask is suddenly otherwise occupied. Tell me, is my job really that terrible? Particularly in relation to what everyone else in this building does."

"No, no. It's not that. I mean…" he paused for dramatic emphasis. "I'm Pain. And although I fully understand that I just finished complaining about a particularly difficult workday, in the end, Pain is kind of my thing. I inflict it, rather well I might add, and there is only one type of person I cannot affect. Do you know who that person might be?"

"A dead one?"

"That is correct. A dead one! You are brighter than you look, Death." As the edges of Pain's lips began to curl upward, he appeared increasingly distraught. "Is there something wrong with my face? Look at my face. Is it a stroke? I'm having a stroke, aren't I?"

"Pain, calm down. It's a smile, alright. You told a little joke and then had a smile about it."

"Oh, brilliant! That is a relief." Pain's face settled into its usual grimace. "Just because I was smiling, that doesn't mean I'm not sorry about your shift."

"I know and I don't want to push you out of your ... *comfort zone*, if that's what we can call it. I really do understand. But can you think of anyone who might cover me tonight? Mum's all excited and I don't want to let her down."

"Have you tried Apathy?"

"Pain, you're a bloody genius."

"I know!" Pain picked up the telephone and rang Apathy's line. The friends looked at each other expectantly while they waited for her to answer. "Damn, went to voicemail. She doesn't even care enough to pick up. Her level of commitment is right impressive."

Death rushed back toward the lift. "I'm off to ask in person. Wish me luck!"

"Luck called in sick today. I'll wish you Success instead."

* * *

Death found Apathy in the Parking Garage. There she perched on a stool in the scratched plexiglass toll booth, resplendent in her ill-fitting uniform. Her nose was buried in a worn paperback adorned by a windswept couple embracing on a plain, or perhaps it was a farm. Hard to tell through the glass. He knocked gently to get her attention.

"Apathy, my dear. So good to see you."

She barely turned to acknowledge Death's greeting before shoving the metal drawer out for payment.

"I'm not here to pay for parking. I'm not even in a car. See, it's just me. Death. On foot. I've come to have a chat with you."

"What is it then?" Apathy set the book down on her lap.

Death absentmindedly brought a finger to the plexiglass window and began making fidgety figure eights. He fixed his gaze on Apathy's nametag as he carefully chose his words. "Would you...*care*...if I...gave you...my shift tonight?"

"Why would I care?"

"Yes!" Death's took an excited step back and threw both hands in the air. "Why, indeed? So, it's a deal, then?"

Apathy placed a yellow slip of paper in the metal drawer and pushed it back out to Death. "I guess so. Just get that signed first."

Death took the form and considered it. In bold letters at the top, it read "Shift Transfer Request." Not one to take time off, Death wasn't sure what to make of it.

"I've actually never filled one of these out before."

"I have. Loads of times. It's why I keep them in the booth. You Upper Floor gits love to have me cover shifts for some reason."

Death arched an apologetic eyebrow. "Ah yes, well, on behalf of all us gits, we are grateful. Who signs off on it?"

"The Guardian."

"You can't be serious!"

"Very serious. Take a look at the fine print." Apathy grabbed her own copy and read aloud to Death: "*No shift transfer shall be effective without the signed consent of The Guardian. Unapproved transfers will result in pervasive and ceaseless Punishment.*"

He was in too deep to quit now. Death gave Apathy a forced smile and placed the transfer request in his pocket.

"Thank you, Apathy. I will get this signed and see you in my cubicle at 6:00pm sharp."

* * *

Death had only been to the Executive Penthouse once before, shortly after he was promoted from Coma. The Guardian invited him upstairs for a congratulatory drink. It had been an intimidating encounter. Death was ill-equipped to handle The Guardian's barrage of questions, so he took a long slow sip of brandy to calm his nerves. Forgetting to swallow, Death attempted to say, "*Yes sir, I do prefer blueberries,*" but instead poured forth the contents of his mouth. The resulting cascade of liquor pooled into a sort of murky crotch pond atop his khakis. The two men stared at each other for a longer period of time than seemed appropriate before The Guardian finally stood up and thanked him for coming.

Death hoped The Guardian's assistant would take the high road and not bring it up.

"Well, as I live and breathe, look who it is. Death in the flesh. What brings you here today? Thirsty Trousers? Parched Pants? Dehydrated Dungarees?"

"That last one was a stretch, even for you, Sarcasm."

"I'm sorry. I couldn't help myself. I live for these moments." Sarcasm adjusted her cat-eye glasses and began flipping through a large, leather-bound volume atop her desk. "I don't see you on the calendar, Death. Is The Guardian expecting you?"

"No and I'm not really sure I need to see him," Death pulled the transfer request out of his pocket and unfolded it, placing it on the desk in front of her. "Maybe you can just take care of this for me."

"A Shift Transfer Request? Certainly not. Well above my pay grade. Wait here while I ring him. I'm sure he'll want to see you."

Death took a seat and pretended to sort through some magazines while she rang The Guardian on the intercom.

"Mr. Guardian, I have Death in the lobby. He needs a Shift Transfer Request reviewed."

"Who?"

"Death, sir."

"Death...It's not ringing any bells. Which Department?"

"He's sort of a Department unto himself."

The other end of the intercom was silent. Sarcasm lowered her voice.

"You remember Death. The Brandy Fountain. Loose Liquor Lips. Death."

"Oh, of course! Death! Send him right in."

Death shot Sarcasm a look. "That's how he remembers me?"

"Honey, that's how we all remember you." She pressed a button and the double doors to The Guardian's office swung open.

* * *

The office was larger than Death remembered, the walls covered in a jumble of oil paintings, oversized books, and gold filigree. The Guardian motioned for him to have a seat in front of the marbled desk.

"Death, I must say you are looking well, taking into consideration the nature of your daily duties, that is. Looking well, as graded on a curve you might say, but looking well nonetheless." The Guardian's smile seemed exceptionally bright against his artificial tan. "I understand you've come here with a Shift Transfer Request."

"Yes, sir. I have it right here." With trembling hands Death placed the form on the marble's edge.

"It's just for one night, sir. Tonight, actually. I've got this family thing and Apathy said she'd cover. I've never asked anyone to cover for me before, so I didn't realize the approval level was this high. I hate to bother you, but if you'll review my file, you'll see I have perfect attendance. It's just tonight. So, if you wouldn't mind signing it, I'll be on my way. Back in the morning. Working hard. As usual. Back to it in the morning."

The Guardian placed an outward palm across the desk to stop Death's inane chatter. Leaning back in his throne, he considered the request.

"Absolutely not."

"Did I hear you right? Did you say, 'Absolutely?'"

"You heard me. Absolutely *not*. Death does not take a holiday. It's a dangerous thing you're proposing."

"Well, I wouldn't exactly call it a holiday. It's just a few hours. And I've got coverage lined up."

"Who? Apathy? That young woman excels in her line of work which makes her entirely unqualified to do yours. Can someone with so little resolve commit to the kind of work you do? I think not. You received the promotion because you've got what it takes to rip a soul right out of its flesh and that is a rare quality indeed. I won't hear any more of it. Now chin up. Get back out there and do some slaying."

"With all due respect, Mr. Guardian, I'm not sure you understand my job description. I'm not a slayer. I am the transporter of the slain. All Apathy needs to do tonight is shuttle the souls from Point A to Point B. For a short time, I think she's capable."

"You don't slay?"

"No, sir. You have an entire Department dedicated to that. War, Hunger, Accident, Murder, Suicide, Disease, just to name a few, and they are all lovely at what they do. Such finesse."

"Enlighten me. What do you do again?"

"I'm Death, sir. I take the freshly disembodied souls and bring them to the other side."

"Like a trolley?"

"Well, that's a bit simplistic, but yes, I suppose like a trolley."

"How far do you take them?"

"It depends really. Generally, not far."

"Couldn't we just put up signs then?"

"Signs? What kind of signs?"

"Simple signs. If all you do is escort souls 'generally not far' to their next destination, we don't even need signs with words. Well-placed arrows should do the trick."

"What are you getting at?"

"If I'm being honest, I'm not sure your services are relevant anymore."

"Of course they are! If you get rid of me, who's going to take all the souls to the other side?"

"I may just have the slayers do it themselves. It couldn't take that much more time out of their workday. We'll cross-train them."

"Terrible idea. The souls won't follow their slayers into the beyond. They need a neutral party."

"You mean like a well-constructed sign with arrows?"

"No, not like a bloody sign. More like a caring transportation professional who can tailor the experience to their individual needs."

"Give me examples. How do you appear to the souls?"

"Well, sometimes it's complex, like getting all dressed up and navigating the River Styx to the Underworld while other times I simply beckon lovingly from a tunnel of light."

"Who still goes across the River Styx?"

"It was very popular with the Mesopotamians for a while."

"As in *ancient* Mesopotamia? So not at all anymore. Forget about that." The Guardian leaned over the desk towards Death. "How about the tunnel of light thing? What does that entail?"

"There's a trick to it. See, I represent a loved one who has already passed, so I must remain far enough away from the newly deceased that my features aren't visible. I appear as a dark, but familiar figure against the light, motioning for them to come through."

"Motioning how?"

"You know, like..." Death rose awkwardly from the overstuffed chair and began to make long sweeping gestures with his arms.

"We could use an inflatable for that. The kind you see outside car dealerships. We'll hook a generator to it."

"You'd use an inflatable to summon souls to the afterlife?"

"If it got the job done, why not?"

Death had run out of arguments.

* * *

"You're late." Apathy was sitting in Death's task chair spinning around in circles.

"I know, sorry. This transfer request turned into a whole *thing*, but it's done now." Death had The Guardian's reluctant signature on the yellow slip, buying him time until he could pull together a formal slide-show presentation on the Importance of Death as a Viable Mode of Transportation complete with spreadsheets, statistics, and the results of customer satisfaction surveys.

"Apathy, I can't thank you enough for this. I've got detailed instructions in the binder on the top shelf and the phone is automatically routed to voicemail, so you won't have to answer any of the special-order calls, like reincarnation or intergalactic travel. They're generally very patient, anyway, happy to wait. All you need to worry about is what comes across this fax machine. You'll pick the faxes up off the machine like so, look up the Transportation code in the binder and just follow the directions next to that number. Got it?"

"Sure, I guess. Seems pretty easy."

"Yes. Wait. No! It can be incredibly complex. If you happen to get any faxes referencing the River Styx, just put them in a pile in the corner and I'll get to it in the morning."

"You still get requests for the River Styx?"

"Well, not lately. But a resurgence could happen at any time. You know, *everything old is new again* and all that. It's a very retro point of view. I think I heard Style mentioning it was poised to make a comeback."

"Did Style really say that?"

"Yes, of course he did. Pass the word."

"I probably won't."

"I know." Death threw his scarf around his neck and headed out to his Mum's.

* * *

There were cars lined all along the block leading up to the house. Certainly more cars than he had family. It began to look to Death that he nearly got fired for trying to attend his own surprise birthday party. Walking up the path, he could see the buffet table through the Dining Room window. Gluttony had taken up residence on the far end, repeatedly filling his plate while Beauty was picking through the appetizers, presumably bemoaning the multitude of carbs present.

Shortly after Mum yelled an unnecessary "SURPRISE!" she excused herself to check on Greed. So far that evening, she'd caught him twice in the cupboards and once in her jewelry box. As she hurried off, Pain gave Death a warm hug and handed him his birthday gift.

"You bastards." Death was not immune to the irony of the evening. "I practically killed myself to cover my shift just so you assholes could come and have a party at my expense."

"Correction: a party *in your honor.*" Pain laughed. "Besides, I'm the one who hooked you up with Apathy. Before that, you were just spinning your wheels. Never would have made it here on your own. Face it, you need me."

While Pain was talking, Death ripped the soiled wrapping paper off his gift: a flask of whiskey.

"I'm telling you, after a tough day, this will take care of all that ails you, my friend. Speaking of, I think I saw Drunk around here somewhere. I'm going to go have a look for him." Pain disappeared into the recesses of the house.

Enjoying his new flask, Death wandered the crowded rooms greeting family and co-workers alike. Even Style had come. Granted, he was curled up on the corner of the couch, rolling his eyes and hating everything, but he was there and that counted for something.

As Death wandered up to the makeshift bar, he caught a familiar sight. Perched precariously close to the counter's edge was a paperback novel, splayed nearly in half, presumably marking the reader's place. He cautiously lifted the book with two fingers to inspect it. Taunting him from the cover were two impossibly good looking individuals which he could now see, up close and personal, were indeed on a farm.

"Oh, no." Panicked, Death spun around searching the room. "No-no-no-no-no-no-no…"

"Hey. You found my book."

In the moment it took to turn towards Apathy's voice, Death still hoped beyond reason that it wasn't actually her speaking. But there she hunched, right before his eyes.

"Tell me you have a twin. And that you are she."

"Can I have my book back?" Apathy reached for her novel.

Death quickly shoved it behind his back. "No! Not until you tell me why you left the office."

"Your job is so boring! Even for me. Some folks were getting on the lift and I heard them talking about this bash that everyone was going to. Just thought I'd have a look see. Fair to say I didn't expect to see you here."

"It's *my* birthday, Apathy!"

"I did not know that. Well, then—Happy Birthday, Death."

Death pondered his fate. No one was covering his shift, the transport would be behind schedule and increasingly backlogged with each passing minute. The Guardian would no doubt unleash Punishment upon both of them, if he even got to keep his position. The last thing Death could stomach was the thought of going back to Coma.

"Apathy, I need your help to make this right." Death feared he sounded as desperate as he felt, "Can you do that for me?"

Within five minutes, they had rounded up enough volunteers to expedite the work. Nurture drove the carpool back to the office and passed out little baggies of snacks.

Once inside, they all dutifully took to their assigned tasks. Death had done a fair job of impressing upon Greed that a safety deposit box combination or two might be revealed in one's last moments, and Beauty was flattered when told her presence would make the transition more appealing. Pain was placed in charge of rounding up the stray souls leaning toward haunting, while Apathy stayed her course of pointing the affable cases in the right direction, much like a well-constructed sign. Not one to be left behind in the excitement, Mum came along too, and was promptly put in charge of the River Styx.

Death looked out from the tunnel of light to gaze upon his, dare he say, *friends*. Channeling the inflatable of The Guardian's dreams, he put his lanky arms to work while humming a faint tune that sounded to the incoming parade of souls much like the happy birthday song. It was regarded as an utterly charming touch and several made a mental note to report it later in their satisfaction surveys.

FINDING THE DANCER

Andrija Popovic

I knew my day was fucked the moment I saw Death's Jester perched outside my window like a vulture. This vulture, though, wore a full tuxedo with tails and a red flower in his lapel. His bright yellow mask flashed a saw-toothed smile as he sat atop one of branches of the old oak tree.

Phantoms lived by specific rules. The first one is that the Jester will be the first face you see after you die, and the Dancer will be the last before you move on to whatever follows this existence. It's in the book. At least, it's in the version I wrote. Aspects of Death appear at moments of pain, trouble, and transition.

The Jester always followed pain and trouble.

Pain and trouble phased through my door in the form of Alicia, friend and ghost road trader.

"Trish! Thank gods you're here." Alicia dropped her backpack on the floor. Brick-like cell phones, 3.5 inch floppy disks, and 35mm film cartridges tumbled from the half-open flap. "I need your help."

"Alicia. Dammit!" I banged my knee against my desk. My typewriter let out a plaintive ding. "Hi. Good to see you. Help how? Guidebook writer help? Or…" I looked over at the Jester in the trees while Alicia cleaned up her backpack. Her peacoat spread out around her like a black, woolen dress.

"Maybe 'or.'" She flipped open a cell phone, circa the late '90's "Bill's gone missing. I tried finding him, tried calling him and texting him. He was supposed to meet me when I got back. None of the other traders have seen him in a week."

"He's not a newborn phantom, Alicia." I stood up, deliberately blocking out the window.

"He was my *apprentice*." Alicia frowned and glared. "I have a responsibility. You know this."

Once upon a time, Alicia was a newly dead phantom. I took her on as my apprentice, teaching her the ways of unlife the way someone taught me. We traveled together. I helped her adjust. She found a career trading in old, memory-soaked objects—the only kind phantoms could use—and traveling the ghost roads. I found a friend who kept my more *unusual* skills close to her tweed vest.

Eventually, she took on her own apprentice, Bill. I settled down in one spot to write my guidebooks and histories for phantoms. When Bill fell in love with a local phantom, Simon, I was overjoyed. My apprentice passed an important milestone in our society—her charge was now an integrated and functioning phantom. I gained more friends, and another neighborhood trader to boot. It was comfortable and safe until now.

"I'll help. But, I think Simon's a better person to ask."

"I did ask him. Simon just swore at me, called you a sorcerous bitch." Alicia stood up, leaning against my bed. Tattered notebooks spilled from the rumpled covers. "He said 'Bill's gone to find the Dancer, and I hope he does!'"

"Wait—he said what?" I pulled my heavy jacket closer. Phantoms never feel totally warm. Fingers and noses always remain cold to the touch, even in the height of summer.

"He said he's finding the Dancer. But you can't do that. It's not how it works. It's—" I stepped away from the window. The Jester tilted his head like a curious bird and waved to Alicia. Alicia covered her mouth and backed away, almost falling through the door again.

"It's not right. I know. *He's* not right. But there he is, outside my window like a turkey vulture." I reached under my desk for a worn Jansport backpack, stuffing in a box of typewritten pages, unopened packages of blank bond paper, and the smallest SmithCorona typewriter ever made. "Let's go to Bill and Simon's. How's your ride these days? Bill was supposed to fix mine."

"Don't worry. I'll get us there."

"Good, because we might have to outrun him."

* * *

The Jester followed us as we drove into town in Alicia's massive Ford F-150 truck. He ran along the treetops, keeping pace as the truck pushed one-hundred miles per hour. He never missed a step, hopping from branch to branch. The grin on his mask seemed to get bigger and bigger as we got closer to Bill and Simon's house.

For the living, Kent Hills is just another sleepy little town in rural Maryland; lots of antique stores, a quaint downtown, and nice restaurants for anyone relaxing after winery hopping. Its better years are behind it, though. Along the road you can see abandoned homes, old barns, and shuttered schools.

For phantoms, Kent Hills is a thriving metropolis. Buildings drink in memories as readily as objects do. In our world, one step removed from life and reality, everything old is actually new again. We can build a life from the leftover memories of the living.

This is important. We need to keep occupied. This is the first lesson any old phantom passes to their apprentice. Travel, trade, explore, but do *something* to keep focused. I wrote travel and guidebooks. Alicia traded on the ghost roads. Phantoms still have a little life left inside them—just enough to resonate with the real world and keep them going. When that dissipates, there are worse things waiting for a phantom than a visit from Death's Dancer.

Simon stepped out of his house the moment Alicia's truck pulled into the driveway. Deep black circles ringed his eyes. His hair, last seen in a trim cut, was now bristled and uneven. Dust covered his button-down shirt and once crisp slacks—the same outfit I'd seen him in one week ago. A rusty demolition hammer dangled from his fingers.

"This is your fault, Red. And yours, Chica." Simon gave everyone nicknames, even if they didn't fit. Alicia is a thin blonde lady. I haven't had red hair since I died.

"Simon…" Alicia slowly stepped down from the truck.

"He was happy here!" Simon smashed the hammer into driveway, cracking the asphalt. "Got off the road. Settled in with the local markets. Got this place with me! He was happy!"

"That's what we thought." I took a step closer.

"You thought wrong!" Simon pointed the pry bar end of the hammer right at me. "Those traders you hooked him with? The computer guys? They fucked it all up!"

"It was just mechanical stuff," I said. "He was helping them find parts, keep newer machines running. Getting ribbons for my typewriter. That's all."

"Not lately! Started getting shit from out west to clean up and sell. Hard drives. Tape drives. ZIP discs. *Memory* devices, Red!"

"Memory devices?" Alicia glanced at me. I grew cold again. Salvaging and restoring old technology keeps a lot of phantoms busy. Computer resurrectionists, though, do more than keep old technology going—they salvage and sell data. Hard drives stored memories along with files, photos, and programs. Phantoms are nothing if not voyeurs, and it is far too easy to become obsessed with the world of the living. Hard drives give some a dangerous window into the past.

"He'd go up into his workshop and when he'd come back—" Simon sniffed and rubbed tears from his eyes. The hammer fell from his fingers. "The last few weeks we'd fight every other night over the same thing: What's going on? Why aren't you talking to me? Tell me something! But, no, he'd be all about those damned shipments from out west and how he needed to print shit out."

"Print out?" Alicia stepped closer, putting a foot on the hammer and a hand on Simon's shoulder. "Print out what?"

"Mostly photos. When he left, he had a big box of those under his arms." Simon fixed me with his eye. "And he had pages. Typewritten pages, with marks all over them, like a draft copy. Found one after our last fight. Looked like your guidebook shit, but corrected. With parts scratched out. All about the Jester and the Dancer…and the City."

"Oh, no." I crossed myself out of habit and fear.

"Yeah. That's right, Miss Sorceress. So what did you give him, huh?!"

"Nothing!" I shook and slumped against Alicia's trunk. "Not deliberately. I mean…"

"Did he have a workspace?" Alicia reached down and grabbed the demolition hammer.

"Yeah. Up in the attic. Tried to get in. He locked it somehow. Can't pass through." Simon sat down on the driveway. "Tried smashing my way in. Didn't work. But, if anyone can get in, she can." He pointed right at me.

"Thanks, Simon." Alicia nudged me in the shoulder with the hammer head. "I'll get the bags. You go inside and see what he's done."

Numb, I nodded and walked to Simon's front door. It opened before I could touch the knob. The Jester stood inside. He swung the door wide, bowed, and motioned me upstairs.

* * *

"I never understood why you used haiku to break down barriers." Alicia stood behind me, arms crossed, watching as I typed the final draft of my seventeen syllable poem onto a fresh sheet of paper. The Jester watched as well, gloved fingers on the chin of his mask in pantomime fascination.

"It's different for every one of us. Pages and ink are my style. It helps me—"

"Connect, I know." Alicia leaned close as I pressed the page, ink first, against the door. Bill had poured a little of his own essence in the lock. Even at a distance, he held it closed by force of will. "But haiku?"

"Small and impactful. It's a verbal breaching charge." The locks clicked open, and I pushed the attic door up and over. Bill's workshop was a museum of obsolete technology, broken down and catalogued by manufacturer, part number, and region.

"Yeah, this isn't it." Alicia fingered the bins of hard drives—all dismantled, and disconnected. "Parts, but nothing he can read it with. And no printer, either. Where's the real workshop?"

"I think I have an idea." I frowned as The Jester pointed to a blank wall. It cut the attic in half and felt wrong. New construction from old materials give off a strange vibe. You can sense the ghost world trying to reconcile the paradox.

Alicia smashed the hidden door apart with the demolition hammer. Within we found walls of CRT screens all hooked into a series of beige computer towers. A keyboard rested on a small bench, white cord leading into the back of one of the computers. She started booting everything up. "Some of this is relatively new, but those ZIP drives are mid-90's, at best. And I think those are tape drives."

While Alicia focused on the computers, I rummaged around a work desk flanked by an old laser printer and a copier. Mounds of printed pages, all liberally covered in notes, obscured sets of hand-labeled three ring binders. Atop it all was a single printed photo of a smiling blond man in a bright yellow shirt. His curly hair and beard were a stark contrast to Bill's straight, black hair and clean shave.

Who's this?" I asked. "Old boyfriend?"

"Yes." Alicia snatched the photo out of my hand. "Daniel. His boyfriend from before he died. When I found Bill out west, he was still in a shroud. Our smiling friend was standing over him. Daniel's name was the first thing he said when I pulled the shroud free."

"Oh, shit." I spun Alicia around. "The computers."

The screens were on and humming now. On the left, every screen was a mosaic of photos featuring Bill and Daniel together. The photos belonged in any couple's album: dinners out, vacation photos, and holidays. A few were portraits of Bill holding notes: "Miss you. Can't wait until you're back from Texas." Bill dressed a bit square in life, while Daniel seemed ready to go clubbing at any moment.

But as the photos progressed and the 'miss you' images grew more frequent, the smiles on Daniel's face were less genuine. He looked just off camera, as if mentally elsewhere. Bill, for his part, seemed intent on smiling twice as much and twice as wide, as if to make up for Daniel's lack of enthusiasm.

On the right-hand screens we saw where Daniel's enthusiasm went. He obviously traveled for work, but didn't always share his adventures with Bill. There was a large set of photos from various nude beaches showing Daniel's tan, fit figure lounging with handsome companions of both sexes.

As the photos progressed, they became more explicit, featuring a wide variety of partners in a wide variety of carnal escapades. I tugged at my shirt. The memories in the photos radiated electric life. If phantoms always feel a little cold, then strong emotions warm us. And passion—well, that's like a mug of hot chocolate by the fireside.

"Oh, Bill." I looked back at the left-hand gallery. "Why didn't you let this go?"

"I thought he had. When we traveled together on the ghost roads, when he was my apprentice, he talked about Daniel less and less. Then he met Simon. I thought he would be happy." Alicia dropped the photo onto the floor. "What's this?"

Before I could stop her, she grabbed a binder from under the pages. The sheets fell onto the floor, covering my feet, almost sticking to my legs. Alicia opened it to the first page. Her jaw set. She flipped the binder round and showed it to me.

Hidden Rules & The City. It was an exact copy of the manuscript I was revising when the Jester first appeared outside my window, down to the ink smudges. I looked at my feet. All the pages were mine—copied from my home.

"Well? What is this?"

"He copied it. He must have copied it when I was out traveling or—"

"That's not what I asked, Trish." Alicia shoved the binder into my arms.

"It's mostly stories. Histories I'd picked up about phantoms and the City. A few rituals, maybe. But just a lot of stories about the Jester and the Dancer.

Where they show up and what they do—"

"And how to summon them?"

I steadied myself against the desk, clutching the binder. Alicia crossed her arms, her expression halfway between screaming and weeping. Behind her the Jester casually read through a few scattered pages, tossing them to the ground when done. "Yes."

"Gods, Trish." Alicia grabbed at her hair. "Can he do it?"

I nodded. "Yes. He has to be back where he died, back in Van Nuys, but if he has all my notes he could." My legs gave out. I fell onto my scattered writing. "Oh, God. I told him about the book. Told him I was writing it. I wanted to make a real history of the phantoms. So it all went in there. The City. The Dancer. The Jester. Sorcery. All of it was there. And I just left it where he could see it. I left a loaded gun where a depressed man could find it."

"He hasn't pulled the trigger yet." Alicia grabbed me by the jacket. "Get up. He may know what you know, but he isn't a sorcerer. He has to travel by the ghost roads. That takes time. But we've got another road we can take, don't we?"

I stood up. My hands shook, so I grabbed the edge of the desk. "I haven't done it in years. Not since you were my apprentice. And not this far."

"But you can still do it." She walked over to the computers and yanked out the power. The monitors went dead, one by one. "And we need to do it. Now."

"OK." I took a deep breath. I didn't breathe, but I needed it. I needed the memory of breath, and life, for what I had to do next. "We'll head to Van Nuys through the City."

The Jester just politely applauded and waited for us to head downstairs.

* * *

If phantoms are echoes of people, the ghost roads are echoes of highways. Traders travel long circuits around them, finding memory-soaked items from all over the country, setting up markets, even delivering packages. For phantoms, they are UPS and the mail and Amazon all bundled together.

Why not send it by air? Good question. Airplanes don't work for the dead. Folks who try end up lost.

Any phantom can travel from Maryland to Van Nuys, if they find the memory of a good car. But it's a week's worth of driving across country. It's safe, but slow. And being well out of the rat race due to death, we tend to be OK with it.

Every now and again, though, you need to be somewhere fast. You need a shortcut, a way to quickly connect disparate places together. You need the City.

People aren't the only ones with memories. Places have them, too. Since the first human built a permanent shelter against the elements—a home—and created the first temple to the gods, the memories invested in those places have accrued. Eventually, they grew together, building one atop the other, until a City arose.

The City connects all cities, both in space and in time. It is a living record of human existence, stretching from today into the distant past. In the City, the walls not only talk, but they scream and sing.

There is power in the City. If you can reach it, you can travel anywhere, or see any event. You can alter the world by changing its memories. It's a dangerous thing, but possible if you find the right key: words of power scrawled on the ground or chants spoken while meditating or photos that capture old memories and souls alike. With that key, a person can travel, they can manipulate, and they can survive when the City begins to defend against manipulation.

In life, I was one of those people: a sorcerer. Death did not change that.

I connected to the City through writing. My little bits of typewritten paper were infused with memories and places, thoughts and dreams, and with them I built spells. This time, I was building an on-ramp, one page at a time. I walked four paces from the truck, sat down, and used my typewriter to describe our destination in a brief prose poem. Once two pages were done, I would drop them six feet apart, weighed down with stones, to mark our lane.

And then I'd repeat the process, until some ten pages later I could feel the road underneath me touching the City's streets.

Alicia kept the truck running while I worked. I'd taken her on short trips through the City as an apprentice, so she knew the process. She added bits of my writing to the truck's front and back, anchoring it to me and through me to the road. When I hopped into the passenger seat, the Jester was lounging in the truck's bed, waiting for the ride to begin. He gave me a thumbs up and lay back, hand under his head.

I wanted to blame him. I wanted to lay everything on his grotesque, smiling face. But none of this was his fault. I'd given Bill the tools to break how the world worked. The Jester was just another consequence of my pride and carelessness.

"You ready?" Alicia revved the engine, eyes fixed forward.

"Yes." I stowed my typewriter in my backpack and pulled out a box of pre-written haiku.

"Will you need them?" Parking brake set, she spun the tires until smoke billowed behind us.

"I hope not. But just in case." I laid the box in my lap. "Punch it."

Alicia dropped the brake. The Ford surged forward, roaring. At the end of my typewritten on-ramp, the green countryside of rural Maryland gave way to a kaleidoscopic cityscape. Buildings—from massive skyscrapers to mud huts— grew and shrank alongside us. The road shifted from advanced solar highway to simple beaten dirt track and back again every time the wheels spun.

We were in the City with a day's worth of driving ahead of us. I crossed my fingers, and hoped no one would notice one lonely truck on the road west.

* * *

We were just short of Van Nuys when the wraiths swarmed us.

Moments before, Alicia and I were talking like friends again. She hadn't quite forgiven me, but the constant rumbling of the truck crossing an infinite variety of road surfaces only added to the silence in the cab. So she asked me: "Did I do something wrong with him? When he was my apprentice?"

"What? No, God, no." I sat up. "Alicia, you were a better mentor than I ever was. You gave him a chance to see the world, meet people, and find a home. You taught Bill so much. All I ever did was put you in constant danger just so I could write my damn guidebooks."

"What's a little danger to the dead? No, I'm glad you found me and pulled my shroud off. I would have driven any other mentor crazy." And then she smiled. "Like that one guy in Boulder City? Crazy feet?"

"Jeez. Haven't thought of him in years. Is he still there?" The conversation spun on like that for hours, until we saw a tiny disc of California sun ahead, showing the way out. The City began to resemble Van Nuys. Buildings flattened out. Houses went from dark brick to light beige, with Spanish tile roofs. We were almost there.

And then the Jester pounded on the back window. We yelped. I turned around and saw him pointing to the buildings on our left. Gray figures darted across the manicured lawns, office parking lots, and hotel railings.

"Shit. Drive faster." Alicia caught sight of the figures and floored it. The City's wraiths had found us.

Like us, they were dead. But unlike a phantom, wraiths carry a deeply human anger into the afterworld. They are so hung up on their deaths, and the bitter memories they harbored, that they became ravenous for life. Any life.

Alicia kept her speed up. The wraiths threw themselves in front of the truck, a swarm of sentient locusts. Every one bore horrifying scars—broken faces, gutted bellies, shattered limbs—and from those wounds sprang ghastly features. Empty eye sockets sprouted barracudas. Hands became the rancid beaks of scavenger birds. The wraiths clawed at the truck, holding on even as the tires splattered their bodies along the road.

I grabbed a handful of typewritten pages from the box, folded them into strips, and held them like throwing knives. Every one carried three haiku. My breeching charges became anti-personnel mines. I opened the back window and slid out into the truck's bed.

The Jester waved. A wraith snapped at him with a set of alligator jaws spilling from its crotch. He ducked. His assailant, unbalanced, fell over the side. It hit the road with a wet splat. The Jester raised his hands and offered me the rest of the wraiths.

"Thanks a fuckload." I threw haiku bombs at the angry dead. The pages knew their purpose. They plunged into wraith skulls, one after another. The wraiths howled and tore at their faces. My words burning them, they leapt for the safety of the City's shadows.

"C'mon Alicia. I'm not a haiku machine!" Another handful of wraiths fell, faces disinter-grating

"It's a fucking truck, not a super car!" She tried to power through the swarm, but every wraith Alicia hit slowed us down.

For the second time in the space of minutes, I was happy the Jester was there. When the last of my haiku bombs cracked a wraith's face in half, he took over. The Jester sent wraiths off the truck with flicks of a finger. I may call them locusts, but to Death's Jester, they were literal insects.

"Almost there!" Alicia pounded the truck's roof. The end of the road, Bill's old house, shined like a stained glass window. She howled, as if her voice would push the truck further. I kicked a wraith from the cab. The Jester dusted off his suit and sat down once again.

When the truck hit the gateway, the last of the wraiths dissolved into a howling wind of blood and bone. Behind us, the door to the City closed, pulling the wraith remnants with it. Alicia slammed on the brakes. We skidded into the driveway of Bill's old home.

I hugged Alicia through the open window, laughing like an idiot. "Welcome to California…"

* * *

Bill's old house looked like an advertisement for Southern California living. A split level home resting on a small hill, it had two garages and a side parking lot—a shrine to the American automobile. A red tile roof, now faded from years under the sun, topped the beige stucco walls.

For all the visual warmth, the air was blisteringly cold. Thin films of ice grew over the house windows. Frost collected on our clothes. The normal numbness in my fingertips crawled up my arms. Even the Jester shivered when the wind picked up.

"Fuck." Alicia pulled our backpacks from the cab. She threw me mine. "He's here, isn't he?"

I nodded. "Inside. Quick."

We phased easily. Bill was in the living room, seated on a black office chair. A mandala of photographs surrounded him. Each picture was carefully arranged and annotated. Bill was shirtless, so cutting himself open and bleeding on the photos was easier. Phantom blood—thick as printer ink and just as black—trailed in a circle around him. It wept from dozens of hateful words cut directly into his skin.

"Hey, Alicia." Bill waved. Blood dripped down his hand like wax on a candle. "Guessed you'd be coming after me, but I figured you'd be too late. I forgot about Trish, though. Hi, Trish." He smiled an exhausted smile. "I'd have finished days ago but it was hard to find the chair."

"Bill. Please—" Alicia stepped forward, but Bill whipped a line of blood into the air. It sizzled and boiled when it hit the edge of the circle.

"Sorry. This is a private dance." Bill laughed when the Jester stepped past us and sat on the couch. "He's here, too?"

"Of course he's here," I said. "Bill, please, this won't work."

"Yeah, it will. I found the key. It's the chair. I need this specific one." He looked to Alicia. "You know how I died?"

"You said it was an accident."

"Yeah. In this chair. A manufacturer's defect. Daniel was at a 'conference' in Hedonism II. He thought I didn't know. So I sat down, started to write him how I felt. And I leaned back. Boom!" He laughed, wiping bloody tears from his cheeks. "The cylinder exploded. Drove a sliver of metal into my spine and killed me, instantly. Well, sort of killed me. I just need to finish the job."

"Bill, please." Alicia knelt on the floor. "Why? Just tell me"

"I can tell you. He couldn't let it go." Bill blinked when I spoke up. "The fact Daniel kept cheating on you, over and over, and you never got a chance to say anything. At most, what, he read your half-finished letter? That wasn't enough, was it? It lingered with you."

And then he laughed. He laughed, shook his head, and said, "Nope. Well, half-nope. Yeah, I couldn't get over it. I knew Daniel was living two lives. I saw the club membership bills. I knew the extra days on the road were spent swinging with his friends. I knew all of it. But I said nothing."

"No one wants to believe they're being cheated on—" said Alicia.

"No, no! I didn't care about that! The thing that hurt was Daniel never *asked me* if I wanted to join him. And I never got up the guts to tell him I knew, and *I wanted to be there with him*." Now the tears outpaced the blood on his face. As he wept, the ice on the windows cracked. "We said nothing. I said nothing. Years of missed opportunities. And that's why I'm here.

"You were wrong." Bill jabbed the knife right towards me. "That first guidebook you wrote. What was the first line? 'Life is wasted on the living?' No. Not the living. *Us*."

Bill jabbed the knife into his palm with every word. "Life was wasted on *us*. On phantoms like us. That's why we're here, aren't we? We wasted our lives and this is our punishment. We subsist on memories and suffer, while the rest of the world *lives*."

"Bill…" Alicia pleaded. By now, only the Jester wasn't crying. Every time Bill hurt himself, the windows and doors shuddered. My skull ached. It felt like a tornado drawing close, about to rend the house to pieces. The sound system kicked on and dialed itself to an old tune. I knew it: John Coltrane and Duke Ellington playing "In a Sentimental Mood."

"It's too late." He spun in the chair. Blood dripped from the red words in his arms. It spiraled about his feet. "She's here."

The door opened. The Jester stood up and doffed his hat, bowing like the gentleman he pretended to be.

The Dancer had arrived.

* * *

My descriptions of the Dancer had all been secondhand. While writing my guides for phantoms, I met only one person who had seen her. At first, I thought he was exaggerating. But I was very, very wrong.

Death's Dancer was painfully beautiful. She wore a bandeau-style dress. The silken fabric, rose petal red, flowed around her like splashes of water frozen in time. A sheer scarf, sparkles woven into the fabric, covered her bare shoulders. Frost spread from her bare feet when she took a step.

The Dancer also wore a mask, but it was night black and Venetian in design. Tiny crystals, bright as ice, spread from the mask's eyes in a damask pattern. They matched the jewels in her wavy black hair.

Bill sobbed. He held out his bloody hands to her. The rivers of inky life around him spun like leaves in the wind. They rose and circled him. Drops drifted up towards the ceiling. Physics gave everything a pass because it was distracted by the Dancer.

She reached out her hand.

"No!" Alicia dived for the Dancer. I grabbed her...and so did the Jester. He held onto her shoulder, smiling mask now nothing but compassion. He put a finger to his mouth, whispered "Shhh."

"Please..." Bill sniffed, wiping his nose with a gore-streaked hand. "Please."

"No." The Dancer reached up and touched one of the droplets of Bill's blood. It froze; a floating chip of onyx. All the other droplets followed suit. One by one, they fell. Not onto the floor. They all fell back onto Bill's skin and into his wounds and through his veins. The blood he spilled for her was returned. And when the last drop vanished, she faced him.

"You have other dances on your card. So many other dances." She wiped away his tears and drew him out of the circle. "Our dance is yet to come."

"Then why did you come?" I shook, hands bound into fists, and growled at the dancer. "Why bother with any of this if you were just going to say no?"

"Because he needed to know Daniel wasn't his only real dance. And he wouldn't believe it from anyone else." As she spoke, the Dancer took the Jester's hand in hers.

"And because she needed to stop blaming herself." Now the Jester spoke, voice low and resonant. "Teachers are not responsible for every choice their students make."

"You, though..." The Dancer looked right at me. "You stopped the dance." The sound system went quiet. Ellington and Coltrane vanished with a squeal.

"You do not get to be careless with your words." The Jester's mask cracked, and shifted. The smile contorted into a deep frown. "You should know better. You need to do better. And you would not have believed it from anyone else."

"Now, go back to your dances, and leave us to ours." The frost under the Dancer's feet grew, stretching out over floor and furniture, crawling up the walls until the living room became a ballroom cut from ice. The Jester took the Dancer in his arms, a smile returning to his mask. The sound system, now clear as crystal, sprang to life. Leonard Cohen crooned "Dance Me to the End of Love."

"After all," said the Jester. "Not everyone gets a second turn on the dance floor."

I could set my watch to their steps. They were precise, but never mechanical. There was nothing but comfort and love here. The Dancer and the Jester knew this waltz well and adored dancing it together.

We piled our coats onto Bill, helped him off the floor, and took him out into the sun.

* * *

"So, what do I do now?" Bill sat on the truck's tailgate, Alicia's coat draped over his shoulders.

"Same thing as the rest of us." I looked back at his old house, now completely covered in ice. "Live. And learn. You were right. Life was wasted on us, and we knew it. But we got lucky. Someone gave us a second turn on the dance floor. We can't waste it this time."

"So let's dance." Alicia looked round her. "We're in Van Nuys, aren't we? Let's crash a porn shoot. One of the parody ones! They're still filming those, right?"

"Or we can go to Deep Creek." I rubbed my hands together. "It's a clothing optional hot spring, just outside Los Angeles. Nude hikers by the ton—"

"How about I just start by heading home?" Bill ducked his head. "Seeing if Simon will forgive me a little?"

Alicia nodded. "Sure. Let's get you home first. You can decide what you want to do from there." She stopped and looked at the page of my writing still taped to the truck's bumper. "Um, shall we take the short cut?"

I reached down and tore the page off, crumpling it into a tight ball. That was all the answer they needed.

"The ghost roads it is," said Alicia, and hopped into the driver's seat. Bill let me get into the jump seat before taking shotgun. I lay back with my backpack—typewriter, paper, and all—held close like a dance partner.

"It'll take a while." Bill buckled in, glancing back at me.

"What's the good of being dead if you rush everywhere?" The truck rumbled to life, pulling out of the frozen driveway. I closed my eyes, listening as the music faded into the distance. "We have time. Let's enjoy the dance while we can."

...For Leonard. Hallelujah...

THE FALLOW GRAVE OF DREAM

Jim C. Hines

Every birth casts a chain about Death, an obligation and a promise. For some that chain stretches a century; others receive but a single link, ephemeral as moonlight on a pond. The fragility of new life calls to Death like the Earth pulls the moon.

At your birth, as you linger on the boundary of death, so too does Death linger. Not because this is your time—Death knows, even if your parents and the doctors don't. Something else holds Death's fascination. Not pity. Potential, perhaps. A grain of stolen power. Kinship.

Sterile hands hurry you from your mother to a place of piercing lights and razor-edged sound. You're isolated from human contact, nourished instead by plastic tubes and stiff wires. While other infants nurse at their mothers' breasts, you stretch your deformed limbs toward Death, suckling that mote of power.

Doctors whisper words like *ataxia* and *skeletal malformation* and *febrile seizures*. You wave a hand as if to collect the sounds from the air. Death watches in silence as your stiff, flailing movements brush death across your parents' dreams. Over visions of smiles and laughter and perfection, you paint stick limbs and misshapen features.

You're too new, too distracted by bright lights and the pinching of needles and the flutter of idly passing dreams. Your power is as fragile as your infant bones. And so your parents repaint their dreams with defiance and hope. You are theirs, and they will care for you. They will *fix* you.

But Death recognizes and names you, giving your power form and purpose. Cold, dry air carries a whisper, unheard by any other.

You shall be the Death of Dreams.

* * *

If you are a painter, your parents are crude sculptors. Month after month, you endure their hammers and chisels. Surgeons carve your young bones into new shapes and emboss scars into your soft skin. Metal braces stretch and reform your limbs. Sickly-sweet medicine replaces mother's milk.

You're four years old when you walk for the first time. Butterfly stickers decorate the aluminum bars of your tiny walker. Each clumsy step across the living room strains your tight, fragile muscles. You know nothing but determination to reach your parents' outstretched arms.

When you succeed, you sound your triumphant yawp and collapse against them, giggling. In those moments, your family is one in pride and triumph and hope…

Their hope soon turns to a flood that threatens to drown you. Their dreams grow stronger, smothering you like dirt and clay. Gone are nights of sitting together, marveling at the glowing fireflies beyond the windows. Gone are days of collecting fallen leaves for your room, decorating in red and yellow and brown. Each day the hammers strike harder, the chisels drive deeper. The more they wring your body, the more tears you shed.

We should strengthen the core.

The neck muscles aren't strong enough.

We need to do more walking to build strength in the legs.

The pain is to be expected.

The feather-touch of your brushes never stops. You push back against their hope, painting with the hallucinations of every fever-induced seizure. Every cry of pain rousing you from your sleep. Every infection, another layer painted over the glow of their dreams for you.

Two years after those first steps, your mother walks you like a dog up and down the length of the driveway. Sweat prickles down your curved back. Your heart pumps acid through your muscles. When the fireflies emerge, the sweat burning your vision turns them to dandelion-shaped blobs of light.

You grasp your brushes in your cramped fingers and deliberately ease your grip from the walker. Pain and power bloom like a rose, scattering petals of blood across the cement.

Another visit to the hospital.

Broken nose.

Fractured cheekbone.

Abrasions to the chin and forehead.

You pretend not to notice your mother's tears, just as you pretend not to hear her arguing with your father later that night.

Why weren't you watching more closely?

I was!

Not closely enough.

It was an accident.

It wasn't.

The rain washes your blood from the driveway the following morning. No more will they torture you with their impossible hopes. Those dreams died when you left the hospital, painted over with blood and your mother's tears.

* * *

Marriage is a dream rooted in love and happily ever after. For years, you've watched death spread through the heartwood of that dream. Kisses wither and fall. Arguments sprout from the tiniest of seeds: a dirty dish left out, a receipt misplaced, a grocery forgotten.

All I asked was for you to pick up diapers on your way home.

I forgot, okay? I'll go right now.

Don't bother.

You're drunk, aren't you? Jesus Christ. You've been drinking while you were watching our kid?

Their words uproot memories of another night, one that began with a bout of choking and aspiration and ended with pneumonia and a feeding port carved into your stomach. You could have died, but you claimed another death in your stead. You painted over your mother's dream of career with helplessness and love and obligation and fear.

Their resentment grew and spread from the grave of that dream. Resentment of each another. Resentment of you.

I'm trying to keep this family from going broke!

This is no family. It's a goddamned hospital and I can't run it alone. You hardly even show up for visiting hours.

You flee to thoughts of your new school, of half-days surrounded by new friends and their dreams. Donovan wants to be a pro football star. Jaylen an astronaut. Skyla a veterinarian. Cassie a doctor. Hunter wants to be a pilot for the Air Force.

When the teacher turned uncertainly to you, you tapped out your answer on the bulky voice synthesizer mounted to your wheelchair. *A lepidopterist.*

The teacher beamed, showering you with praise for knowing such a big word, never suspecting the lie. You love butterflies, but you know your future leads elsewhere.

I used to think you were cheating on me, but you're not. You're just working late so you can avoid coming home. So you can avoid us!

Why the hell would I want to come home to this?

It goes on for hours. Screams alternate with sobs. Accusations with apologies.

The glowing stars on your ceiling remind you of fireflies frozen in flight. Your anger builds like a fever as you listen to their barbed words tearing at each other. At last, your brushes lash out without thought or control.

Soon, the front door slams and the car pulls away, tires spinning in the gravel. For a time, silence fills the house. When your eyes are heavy and your mind straddles the border of life and sleep, your mother enters your room.

You feel the angry heat of her presence, smell the drunk of her breath, and try not to move.

We were happy before, she says, her words salty with grief and pain.

You keep your eyes shut. She reeks of rotted dreams.

You did this. He isn't running from me. He's running from you.

She's your mother, so you believe her. You swallow her words like chunks of ice that lodge in your chest.

She keeps talking. Maybe she believes you're asleep. Maybe, like so many others, she simply forgets you're capable of hearing and understanding what's said around you. Maybe she simply doesn't care.

She talks of dreams and plans, of futures she'll never see. Love and hope and career and happiness, all stolen. And then, before stumbling away and leaving you to cry silently to yourself, she gives you a gift.

All those dreams, and you *killed them.*

She's your mother, and you believe her. You accept your role. You are the Death of Dreams.

* * *

You develop a fascination with obituaries and funerals. You begin lying to your mother, claiming complete strangers were the parents of friends at school or volunteers you'd met at the hospital, all for an excuse to sit amidst those solemn crowds, embraced by silence. In that stillness you learn to touch the dreams of those gathered to say goodbye. Dreams of conversations they'd never have, of misunderstandings never clarified. One way or another, everyone dreams of more time.

Instinctively you pluck those dreams, tossing them one by one like dried rose petals onto a sinking coffin. With each one you take, you feel…not relief, exactly, but movement. A letting go, like a stream thawed and unblocked after a long winter.

You're fifteen when you first feel Chris' stare through the funeral gathering. At first you ignore it, as you have so many others, but as you complete your work, you see in him the rough strokes of a new dream taking shape, fanciful and fragile. Your slightest touch could collapse it to dust, but as you look deeper, you see yourself reflected in his dream. You wheel closer, offer a cautious hello.

Chris doesn't flinch or look away. He whispers an inappropriate joke about a dinosaur and a lonely chicken. When your fragmented laughter bursts free, Chris lights up like the sun.

From then on, it becomes a challenge to make each other laugh. Jokes and puns and clever wordplay. You read together—Erma Bombeck and Terry Pratchett, Mark Twain and *MAD Magazine*, every collection you own of *Calvin and Hobbes*…

The first time you use your updated voice synthesizer to share a dirty joke, Chris laughs hard enough to spill tears.

Chris is a year older, able to drive you on short trips. Your mother's nervousness is nothing to the glow of her joy at seeing you happy. You know she uses these short reprieves to drink, but you avert your eyes from the empty bottles and the hangovers, just as you've learned to blind yourself to her dreams, afraid of what you'll see. Afraid of what you'll do.

You and Chris explore and hold hands and read and laugh at bad horror movies. You go to a park, where Chris arranges blankets and sleeping bags and hand-cut foam blocks to support you as you lay together and watch an August meteor shower. Between streaks of light, you point out constellations and the red dot of Mars.

You kiss Chris for the first time that night.

I love you. You hate the cold of your synthesized voice, but the answering whisper raises bumps on your skin, sending tingles from your chest to your groin.

You dream of warm nights, of lips and hands and skin, of companionship and love and security and adventure.

But you are the Death of Dreams.

Four months after that first kiss, Chris carries you through the butterfly exhibit at the county fair—a cramped trailer full of plastic plants and monarch butterflies. One lands on your knee.

I love the way your eyes light up when you see something new. There are so many places I want to show you.

Death grows in your chest as you force yourself to look closer at Chris' dreams. Dreams of a future, of the two of you together. Dreams of love, yes, but also of purpose and duty and self-worth and obligation.

Chris dreams not of being with you, but of *saving* you.

You paint burning tears over Chris' dreams, and in killing them, save you both.

Your mother holds you that night, the taste of beer on her breath. It's the most connected you've felt to her in years. You bury your dreams of Chris, wondering how long it will take them to blossom into something new.

* * *

You're nineteen years old. Your mother stands numb, holding an umbrella over you both against the drizzle as you watch the gleaming coffin sink into the earth.

This was an acquaintance of your mother. Her grief is distant. Weary and cold. You turn away from her, afraid of the damage you might do.

Afterward, you gather with strangers in a church basement that smells of macaroni and Jell-O. You make sure to talk to Father Perez for a few minutes. Of all the funerals you attend, Father Perez's are your favorite. He talks to you as he does anyone else. His deep voice is both soft and powerful, and his black moustache is bushy as a squirrel's tail.

Soon, he moves on to greet and comfort others, leaving you to sit and watch and listen for any dreams you might have missed.

You were careful. Thorough. Collecting dreams like your younger self collected leaves. Your mother stands alone by the wall, hiding behind a

Styrofoam cup of red punch.

Pained, self-deprecating laughter tugs your attention toward a quiet corner. *I was jogging in the woods. Tripped over a root.*

Mhm. Is this like the time you fell in the bathtub two months back?

Neither of them pay attention to you. You wear your wheelchair like a cloak of invisibility.

It's not like that.

Why do you stay with that asshole?

He's not...

One dreams of violence against the man who hurt her friend.

The other...fear. Escape. But beneath it all, dreams of hope. Of the man she thought she knew, a man who was once charming and kind and attentive. Protective and passionate. She dreams of changing him, of finding that man again. Saving him from what he's become.

She took a vow: for better or worse. The worse things become, the more tightly she clings to dreams of better. The more tightly those dreams bind her.

By now, painting death over a dream is easier than breathing. Her tears capture the gleam of the fluorescent lights. You listen to the sudden hitch in her words. You watch her dream wither.

As she and her friend hurry away, you see something more—a new dream taking root in the ashes of the old. And for the first time, you understand. You embrace who and what and *why* you are.

* * *

Without Birth, there is no need for Death. Without Death, what need is there for Birth?

For years, you've avoided the husks of your mother's dreams, walled them away with bricks of guilt and fear. Guilt over the dreams you'd killed. Fear of destroying what remained.

You told yourself—believed, even—that it was to protect her.

Later that night, as she pores over bills and prescriptions and insurance letters, you return to that long-hidden landscape beyond the wall. Her dreams are fragile. A single inadvertent touch could send cracks spiderwebbing through them.

One dream calls to you. Buried beneath grief and denial, you find your own death. It's both dream and nightmare. She stands over your grave, her soul gutted from her body. She imagines the emptiness to follow. Deeper yet, shrouded in guilt, she imagines relief. Freedom.

She imagines you flying free of your broken body. Free of the pain and struggle. An angel finally released from this cruel, earthly prison.

She thinks your fascination with funerals is your way of preparing for death.

How long has she been buried with that dream? How long has its poison leached into her vision, distorting her world?

Swirling anger and pity on your brushes, you sweep the dream aside, leaving an empty canvas in its wake. And you ask—whisper—beg—for her to see you. To see that you don't need death to fly.

Other dreams and memories begin to surface. In one, she reaches to stroke your bangs from your eyes. Your head lolls to the left. In another, you wear your favorite T-shirt, with the butterfly dressed as Wonder Woman, and laugh at two young squirrels chasing one another outside the window.

She looks at you, and a smile eases the tension of her mouth.

As her vision grows clearer, so too does yours. You can see Death's dreams for you, now. Dreams of growth and love and life and purpose. You are partners. Collectors. Family. As eternal as life and dream.

You are the Death of Dreams, and the Birth of Possibility.

WHAT HAPPENS IN VEGAS

Stephen Blackmoore

"The fuck did you get into, Jimmy?"

"Something bad," Jimmy says, his voice tinny through the cheap phone.

"You need bail?" I don't tack "again" onto the end of that sentence. Considering that the phone woke me up into a hangover headache like two steel spikes shoved through my eyeballs I think that's pretty good.

"I got backroomed at the Gold Rush."

The Gold Rush is one of those shabby little places way way *way* off the strip. The Bellagio it's not. Though, like all casinos, I'm sure it's loud, smoky, and stinking of desperation.

"For fuck sake, Jimmy." Getting backroomed is when casino security thinks you're cheating and insists—politely—that you follow them into the back room for a "friendly chat"—or maybe a broken nose, so rumor has it. In Jimmy's case they'll either give him a stern talking to and dump him on the street, or call the cops and have him tossed into the North Las Vegas jail for his bi-monthly visit. There are worse things, so I'm not real clear on what the big deal is.

Jimmy Freeburg is a fuck-up. One of those guys who's always got an angle that doesn't pan out. Horse tips, blackjack strategies, poorly thought out scams and cons—nothing big. I've bailed him out a good, five, six times…? After a while it all blurs together.

As roommates go I've had better. He's really kind of a pain in the ass. So why do I go to all that trouble?

Magic. Some people have it, some people don't. Jimmy does, but he doesn't know it, and he couldn't do anything with it if he tried. His magic's like a badly tuned radio. All static, no signal and it's twisted around just enough that it shrouds him in a sort of psychic fuzz. Makes him hard to get a read on, hard to track. Extends to the places he spends most of his time, even when he's not there.

So our apartment's something of a black hole, magically speaking. As are three strip clubs, four bars, and unsurprisingly, the North Las Vegas jail.

Magic camouflage is useful. But it doesn't always work.

A noise on the line. Somebody else comes on. "Eric Carter." A man's voice I don't recognize. It's smooth and oily and even if he didn't know my name I wouldn't like him. "Necromancer. Left L.A. under a bit of a cloud. I understand you murdered Jean Boudreau."

Like I said, it doesn't always work.

"Technically," I say, "the ghosts I fed him to murdered him."

There's silence on the other end. I'm not sure what this guy was expecting, but I don't think it was this. Another mage? That or he's looped into our world enough to know what I am just by knowing my name. I'm a nobody, but I'm a rare nobody.

Everybody's got their own weird ideas of what necromancers do. Sacrifice rams, drink blood, eat babies. We don't eat babies. Well, I don't eat babies.

The reality is that we're keyed into the dead and dying. We see ghosts, talk to them, pull out their secrets like we're yanking teeth.

This does not make us popular party guests.

"I see," he says. "I'd like to see you here at the Gold Rush. I have need of your particular talents."

"Pass, thanks."

"If you don't, I'll be forced to shoot your friend Jimmy, here."

"Knock yourself out," I say and hang up the phone. I consider going back to sleep, but I know I can't. I pissed off a lot of people back in L.A. when I killed Boudreau. Now somebody's found me and I can't afford to stick around and find out who.

I knew Vegas wouldn't last forever. Now it's time to head for somewhere else. I roll out of bed, throw on some clothes. Everything important I own fits in a leather messenger bag. I've got a clunker downstairs with a glowing check engine light that'll get me to Utah before it catches fire. I'll steal another from there.

The phone rings again. I grab my messenger bag. Phone keeps ringing. Sorry, you're in the shit, Jimmy. I get it. But honestly, you and I, we've never really been friends. You were useful. Now you're not. And I'm not going to answer that phone.

I answer the phone.

"I take it you didn't shoot him."

"Consider that a poor opening gambit," he says. "My name's Sebastian McCord. I own the Gold Rush Casino. I would still very much like to meet you."

I rummage through my messenger bag, make sure I've got everything. "No," I say, checking that the Browning Hi-Power I keep in there is loaded. "I really don't think you would."

"We've gotten off on the wrong foot."

"Seemed pretty clear to me. I don't come by, you shoot Jimmy. I'm not coming by, so shoot Jimmy." I hang up.

A few seconds later the phone rings again. I let it go a couple times before picking up. Before I can speak McCord says, "I'd like to hire you to kill a man so that he'll live forever."

Okay, *now* he has my attention.

* * *

Death is everywhere. Arbitrary, capricious, but honest. It makes one promise and it keeps it every time: no matter how we get there, sooner or later, we all die. Even people like me, for whom death is more of a gray area.

Death in Vegas is like a clot in an artery, bunched up along the strip stretching back decades. The usual Haunts and Wanderers, ghosts born of trauma either trapped in one spot or walking freely. But it's the Echoes, mindless recordings of murders, accidents, suicides playing over and over that really stand out.

Been a lot of years since the first casinos went up. In that time a lot of people have stepped in front of cars, gone through windows, jumped off balconies. A waterfall of bodies pours from the top floors of casinos that aren't there anymore.

At five stories the Gold Rush is too small to have jumpers, but some Haunts and Wanderers roam around the parking lot.

Inside the décor is old west saloon—dusty wagon wheels, wood trim, peeling paint, and threadbare carpets. Half the slots are out of order. I was betting this McCord guy's another mage and now I'm sure of it.

Gaming tables and slot machines are arranged with the kind of feng shui that would give a Buddhist fits. Ventilation keeps the smoke from a hundred dead cigarettes curling over tables, screwing players' luck. Cards have custom rune-etched backs. The house should have one hell of an edge. So why's it all so shabby?

I wander the floor, magic prickling across my skin. I'm sure McCord knows I'm here. Besides cameras and run-of-the-mill security, I can feel the magical surveillance.

Probably how he found Jimmy. Scrying spells slide off him like water off Teflon. But when somebody notices a Jimmy sized hole in a sea of color, one thing leads to another, questions are asked, answers are given and, voila! Here I am. I'm worried about Jimmy, sure—he doesn't know what's happening—but I'm here because of McCord's little immortality request.

I go to a security guard in a mauve blazer and khaki pants—Jesus, who comes up with these uniforms?—and tell him I have an appointment to see Sebastian. He radios it in and soon he's escorting me to the fifth floor.

"Mister Carter," McCord says as the doors open on what I assume is his private apartment. "Thank you so much for coming."

Thick guy, early fifties, way too tan, muscle gone to fat. Got a Rat Pack vibe that fits the apartment. Ten-foot-wide picture window showing a view of Vegas where if you squint you can see the Strip. McCord, his casino, even this apartment, screams "trying too hard." He's got a view. He'd rather be in it.

The thing that does stand out is the girl. Curled up in an easy chair reading a thin, leather bound book about the size of a paperback. Early twenties, maybe? Skin like ebony, black hair in cornrows. She's got long legs in skinny jeans and a top tight enough to get anybody's attention. Which is probably the point.

McCord steps aside. I don't move. "Ah," he says. "I can see how you might not trust me."

"Whatever gave you that idea?"

"He's onto you, Daddy," the girl says as she turns a yellowed page. "I told you. You should have just talked to him, first. You never listen."

"She's smart," I say, stepping into the apartment.

"Baby, please," Sebastian says to her. "Not right now." His smile strains through gritted teeth. "That's Nicole. She's...a handful. I'd like to apologize for earlier. I'm used to business negotiations where that's an opening bid. I hope you can forgive me."

"Probably not," I say. "Speaking of, where's Jimmy?"

"In a suite on the fourth floor," he says. Cooling his heels until I agree to do this thing for him, no doubt. "Can I get you a drink?"

"No, I'm good." I claim the only other chair in the room. It's under the window next to Nicole and facing a couch.

McCord fidgets, clearly bothered I've taken his throne in front of his...girlfriend? Sugar baby? Finally, he sits on the couch facing us, squinting into the desert sun that's peeking down from the top of the window.

"Interesting layout downstairs," I say. "Everything's arranged just so."

"Thank you," Sebastian says.

"So how are you fucking it up so badly?"

"Excuse me?" he says. Nicole lets out a laugh that she quickly tries to hide.

"It's designed to give you every edge imaginable. But this place is falling apart."

"We've had hard times," McCord says. His face looks about to pop.

"So, you called," I say, backing off. "I came. Now what?"

"We need you to raise a guy from the dead," Nicole says, before McCord can get a word in. "But you have to kill him first."

"This just any guy?" I ask. "Or did you have one in mind?"

"Oh, it can be any guy," Nicole says, closing the book with a snap. McCord winces at her carelessness. "You, me, Daddy over here. Doesn't really matter. But the spell starts while the subject's alive. Finishes after he's dead."

"Volunteers are gonna be a little thin on the ground," I say.

"Something like that," McCord says. "Nicole?" She casually tosses the book at me and McCord winces again.

The leather's tanned. Little too thin. I realize why once I turn it over and see a nipple off to one side of the back cover. Human skin. I've seen three necromantic grimoires besides this one. They're all bound in human skin. One was written in 1994. Necromancers don't have a bad reputation because we're creepy, it's because we're a bunch of medieval clichés.

I flip it open, scan a few pages. The ink has gone that shade of brown you only get when you write with blood. Like I said, clichés.

"It's a spellbook," I say.

"By some medieval monk or something," Nicole says. "There's no name, but it's been dated to around the twelfth century."

It's in Latin, of course. Easy enough. But the trouble is in the diagrams and charts. Any mage can read the spells, but if you don't know the dead it won't make much sense. About two-thirds in I spot it. This whole conversation clicks.

"You want to make an Oracle," I say, looking over the page. Complicated spell. Lots of moving parts. I can see half a dozen ways to streamline it right off the bat.

"I do," McCord says.

"*We* do," Nicole corrects.

I've heard of Oracles. Never seen one. They're supposed to be able to answer any question, open any lock. I'm sure it's more complicated—everything with magic is. I'd heard they were a necromancer thing, but never knew how.

"This is fucked up," I say. "On multiple levels."

"Squeamish?" Nicole says.

"I had to French kiss a three-day old corpse one time to bring it back long enough to tell me a safe combination," I say. "So, no. I'm not squeamish. But this? Jesus."

"What part do you object to?" Sebastian says.

"I didn't say I objected to any of it," I say. "Just that it's fucked up. You need a 'volunteer,' you cut their head off with a saw while they're still alive and conscious, and finish up by sealing the soul in the head. A talking Magic 8-Ball for your very own.

"But can you do it?"

"Sure. The question is will I? There's a line about summoning an Avatar of Death. Which one? There are a lot of them. They're all assholes."

Death is a many-headed thing. The gods and spirits that embody it are as varied as the worlds they come from. Bansidhe, dullahan, Oom Hendrik, Azrail, Baron Samedi, on and on. Hard to say whether they came from belief or belief came from them.

Death is death, but we give it a face.

"If it's money—"

"Please. Money is easy." I tap the book with my finger. "I want this."

"Absolutely not," he says a little too quickly.

"All right." I toss the book into his lap and stand up, slinging my messenger bag over my shoulder. "Have fun."

I'll haggle with demons and spirits. They have rules. But other mages will gut you when you're not looking.

"Wait," Nicole says. "You can have the book."

"Nicole—" McCord starts, but she cuts him off.

"It's *my* book," she says. "Neither of us can use it and the only thing we want from it is the Oracle. So, yes, he can have the book."

They glare at each other for a good long while and I wish I had some popcorn to watch this drama unfold. McCord doesn't break eye contact, but his face tells me he's lost. I can see the barest hint of a smile on Nicole's face. Smart money says she shanks him as soon as he's not useful.

"Fine." He tosses the book back to me. Their bedroom talk should be fun tonight. "It's yours."

"Fantastic. Let's get started."

* * *

It isn't until Jimmy and I are back at the apartment that it sinks in. I've agreed to murder a man for a Twelfth Century book filled with death spells, bound in human skin, and sporting a prominent nip-slip on the back.

It's not the skin, the blood ink, even sawing a guy's head off, but the nipple that bothers me the most. Either it's because it's needlessly gauche or it just makes the whole thing a little too real.

"I don't understand," Jimmy says, pulling me out of my chain of thought. "You're a necrophiliac?"

"No," I say. "Necro*mancer*. Big difference. Usually."

Jimmy looks the nerdy type; Buddy Holly glasses, pasty skin, kinked up hair that makes his head look lopsided. But he's not that bright.

"Mages can all pretty much do the same things, but we all do one thing better than others. I see ghosts, talk to the dead."

"So, like fireballs. Healing people? Can you do that?"

"Fire, yes. I suck at healing magic, though."

"But some can," he says. "They can cure diseases."

"Complicated," I say. "It's more like getting really aggressive chemo. Only a lot more can go wrong."

Jimmy gets a weird look in his eye; distant, considering. "Huh. Okay."

Something's just happened, and I'm not sure what.

"I know it's a mind fuck," I say. Learning somebody can change reality with a snap of their fingers takes some getting used to.

"No, I'm good. So, what's with all that stuff?" he says.

"All that stuff" is a can of red Krylon, some bottles of herbs, and a carton of salt laid out on the floor. There's more to the Oracle spell, but the opening is to summon this Avatar of Death.

It could be lot of things. Better I know now than find out when I'm in the middle of chopping somebody's head off.

"It's complicated," I say. "You might want to stand back." Jimmy gets behind the kitchen counter, ducking so only the top of his head and eyes peek over.

I spray-paint a protection circle on the carpet with the Krylon. I make it as strong as I can, pouring the salt and herbs along it, then spray another just to be sure. I drip some blood into each, and use a little power to activate them. The circles glow an iridescent blue.

"I'm summoning something," I tell Jimmy, tapping into the local pool of magic to get enough power to fuel the spell. I could use my own power, but this way I won't be dry if something goes wrong.

"If it goes bad…" I say.

"What?" If it goes bad we're both probably dead and our souls sucked out through our eyeballs.

"It won't go bad. Fifty-fifty. Maybe sixty-forty. Just stand back." I begin chanting lines from the book. It's mostly repetitive nonsense, but there's a kernel of power. Reality twists on itself.

A column of viscous black forms in the circle. Out of it poke arms, legs, ropy appendages that could be intestines, could be tentacles. Eyes and mouths appear, are swallowed up by the oozing black. Talons, wings, sneering faces filled with rage.

"Shit." Of all the things this could have been, this is one of the worst.

Every myth, every monster, every gremlin and goblin story, has a grain of truth. In this case a grain is all you get. This myth is of the Keres, Greek spirits of violent death. Winged women with fangs and talons who hang out at battlefields, ripping out souls of the dying and slurping them down like Hot Pockets.

They eat souls. The rest is horseshit. They don't look like winged women, they don't restrict their diet to the dying.

"Ποιος με καλεί."

But they do speak Greek.

"Dude, English."

"Who summons me? Where is my feast?"

Only an idiot wants to summon a Ker. What makes them so dangerous and unique is that the Keres don't play by the same rules almost every other entity does. Banish one, it comes back. Like that one ex you can't get rid of.

The cost of summoning is a soul. If it doesn't get it, it takes the summoner's. Which, in case you haven't been following along, would be mine.

The book doesn't say why the summoning is important, but knowing it's for a Ker I can see why. Part of the spell feeds the "volunteer's" soul to the Ker. Keres won't let go of a meal and that's where the spell fucks them. Before the summoned Ker can finish its meal, the spell yanks it and the half-eaten soul into the severed head, trapping them both.

"Is it supposed to get…bigger?" Jimmy says.

"Preferably, no." I scan the book for anything that can help. Protection spell, failsafe. Something. What have I learned about Keres beyond 'They're assholes,' and 'Stay away?'

"I invoke the law of…" Fuck. FUCK. What is the word? Adjudication? Adjunct? "Adjournment."

The roiling black freezes. "Adjournment," it says, the word coming out slow and disgusted. It's not happy. "Before the next full moon, then, wizard. I will have my due."

The column of ooze seethes and bubbles like boiling pitch, flickering like a busted blacklight. It disappears back into the void.

"Is it gone?" Jimmy looks intently at the empty protection circle. He didn't do too badly. Most folks, first time they see a summoning, they piss themselves.

"It'll be back," I say. "When it returns, if I'm lucky, it'll only kill me."

"Lucky?" He looks like he's just stepped in dog shit.

"There are so many worse things than dying," I say.

"No," he says. "There aren't." There's venom in his voice. I've hit a nerve.

"You okay, man?" His glare answers my question.

"I have things to do," he says. The door slams shut behind him. Of all the weird shit today, that might be the weirdest. Something's going on in Jimmy's head. Pretty sure it's not good.

* * *

I'm on the balcony getting away from the stink of spray paint and wondering what the hell I'm going to do now.

Mages have one thing in common. None of us know when to stop poking the beehive. I was looking at this whole thing as one big academic exercise. Despite evidence to the contrary I'm not really into murder. I was planning on skipping town before I had to actually chop somebody's head off.

There's a knock on the door. Almost midnight, and I don't remember ordering pizza, so this probably isn't good news. I slip the book back into my messenger bag and pull the Browning. Guns are useful for mages. If it's someone or something that can sense magic I won't give myself away.

I look through the peephole, Nicole's on the other side waving.

"Fancy meeting you here," I say, opening the door.

"I was nowhere near the neighborhood," she says. I close the door behind her. She sees the gun in my hand, but doesn't raise an eyebrow.

She takes in the squalid apartment, sits on the threadbare couch. "This is…quaint," she says.

I join her, putting the Browning onto the chipped coffee table. "It works for me. To what do I owe the pleasure? Checking up to make sure I haven't bailed with your book?"

"Not worried about that. Sebastian is. Had a fit once you walked out the door."

"I don't think he likes me," I say. "Feeling's mutual." McCord strikes me as the kind of guy who beat up kids in junior high for their lunch money.

"He has that effect on people. No, I'm here because I wanted to float an idea by you." I was wondering when we were going to get to this.

"Float away."

She leans forward, looking very earnest. "Sebastian thinks small," she says. "He wants to use the Oracle to get the casino back on its feet, as if it ever had been."

"Does seem like small potatoes," I say. "You can do a lot with an Oracle."

"Exactly," she says. "And Sebastian doesn't see that. We need a subject, right? Why not him?"

"I don't think he'll volunteer."

"Knock him out, strap him down. Start sawing."

"You really hate that he makes you call him Daddy, don't you?"

She laughs. "God, yes. But he's got money and contacts, even if he doesn't have brains or much ability."

"And you do?"

"More than he does. More than half the mages in this town. And they're running casinos on the Strip."

"They're fucking with his business and he's not strong enough to fight them," I say.

"And he thinks the Oracle will give him an edge." She leans in closer. I've seen this play before. One of these days I'd like to be wrong about assuming the worst of somebody.

"How'd you meet, anyway?" I turn away and pick up the gun, slide it back into my messenger bag. Whatever moment she was trying to make between us breaks.

"A dating site," she says. She leans back, visibly deflated.

"For mages?" Seriously? They have those?

"Mages and anybody else in the life. Mostly humans. It's hidden behind a legit site. We hooked up. Got to talking. I had the book, he had the money."

Nothing like murder to attain unbelievable cosmic power to bring a couple together. And they say romance is dead.

"So, how about it," she says. "We use Sebastian. You and me get the Oracle."

"I get the talking head on weekends and holidays?"

She puts her hand on my arm. "We can work out the details." I can feel the charm she's trying to cast, but it won't do any good. I started getting tattooed protection spells before I left L.A. They cover my left arm, part of my back. There's more I want to get, but that takes time and the right people.

"I like that," I say. Better to let her think she's got me. I feel a prickling sensation in my tats as they push against the spell. "But how?"

"Drug him," she says. "A celebratory drink right beforehand." She pushes more of her magic. My arm is getting uncomfortable.

"All right," I say. "I'm in." The pressure eases.

"Thank you, Eric. You won't regret this."

Oh, but I already do.

* * *

I wake to find Jimmy sitting on the coffee table staring at me. Nicole didn't stay long after I agreed to kill McCord, and I'd passed out on the couch.

"You know it's not polite to stare, right?" I say.

"I'm dying," Jimmy says. It takes me a second to register that. I'm still half asleep and he says it as casually as if he's offering me a cup of coffee.

"Congratulations?"

"You need to fix it."

I sit up, rub the sleep out of my eyes. "What the hell are you talking about?"

"This…this thing," he says waving a hand toward the circle painted on the floor. "Magic. You said there were magic doctors."

"Jesus, Jimmy. Magic doctors? You make it sound like My Little Ponies. Yeah, there are doctors who use magic, but there aren't a lot of them, and it's not that simple."

He grabs me by the shirt, eyes wide and pupils the size of dinner plates. "I had cancer. It's back. I can't stop it. I don't have money for chemo again. I'm dead in a year so I need you to tell me where the fucking magic doctors are."

I pull his hands off my shirt. "Okay," I say slowly. "I get it. What exactly is going on?"

It takes a while, but eventually he gets it out. Testicular cancer. It's come back and metastasized into his bones. Pelvis, spine, some in his left femur, and who knows where else. Can't get treatment. Insurance won't cover it and besides he doesn't have any. The one doctor he's seen tells him he's got no more than a year if it's left untreated.

I didn't know any of this because I made a point of not knowing any of it. Jimmy was a useful tool to hide myself. The trouble with useful tools is the moment you see them as real people it gets a whole lot harder to use them.

When it comes down to it, Jimmy cares about staying alive. He doesn't care how he does it. If he can't get a doctor, there's always the spooky, death wizard roommate. Like I said, death is death, but we're the ones who give it a face. As far as Jimmy's concerned, that face is mine.

Jimmy's not looking for a doctor, he's looking to make a deal with the Grim Reaper.

"What do you think I can do, Jimmy? I can't cure your cancer. I can't take your death away. What do you want me to say?"

Jimmy sits back on the floor, deflating. Anger is replaced by thinking.

"What happens when you die?" he says. Jesus, if I had a nickel for every time somebody asked me that.

"Dude, I'm not getting into this without coffee or scotch." I rummage through the kitchen. No coffee, but there are still a couple of fingers in a bottle of Talisker under the sink. I throw it back straight out of the bottle.

"All right. Here's the deal. You ready?"

"Yeah."

"I have no fucking clue."

"But…"

"I see ghosts. They're stuck in this sort of limbo state and slowly fade away. Where do they go after that? I hear rumors. I have stories. But that's it. What I hear is that you go where you think you belong. Heaven, Valhalla, Elysium, whatever. Do I know for sure? No. I'm still learning this shit, man."

He sits back and his eyes fill with tears. "I'm going to Hell, then. I've done things."

I think about telling him some of the shit I've pulled but I know it won't help. If he believes he's going to Hell, then yeah, he's probably going to Hell.

"What if I change religions?"

"I don't think it works that way."

He gets up, paces back and forth. "I can't die. Devil's gonna get me. It'll be fire for eternity."

"You don't know that," I say. Empty words, but I can't think of anything else to say. "Everybody dies, Jimmy. I can't fix that."

"What about that thing you made," he says. "Eats souls, right? But not really?"

"The Ker? Yeah, something like that." I explain the ritual to him again, what it's designed to do, how it does it.

"Whoever's the Oracle, they live forever?"

Cue lightbulb.

"No," I say. "Not just no, but fuck no."

"Why not?" he says. "You said immortality. That's living forever. I'm going to Hell, Eric."

"Did you hear anything else I said? This isn't immortality. This is being a head in a fucking box gathering dust until somebody needs winning Lotto numbers. Forever."

"Will it hurt?"

"Will—? Of course it'll fucking hurt. You get your head sawed off."

"I mean after. When it's done. Will it hurt? Because right now everything fucking hurts. My bones are on fire. I shit blood. I don't have a year. I'm not sure I have another fucking week."

"This is worse than dying," I say.

"How do you know? You just said you don't know where we go for sure. Is it worse than Hell? Is it worse than walking around in Limbo waiting to drain away? And what do you care, anyway? You don't have a goddamn thing to lose."

I don't know how to answer that. I don't know if it will be worse. I don't know what his Hell looks like.

I don't say anything. I've got nothing to say.

"That's what I fucking thought."

"You really want to do this?"

"Yeah, I do."

I feel sick. I should walk away. But I didn't walk away when the phone rang, and I didn't walk away when McCord was threatening to shoot him.

"I'll think about it."

* * *

I meet McCord in his office at the casino. It feels like decay. Rot settled into the very bones of the place. Given what Nicole was telling me, I suspect that's exactly what it is.

It's taken the last couple days to pull everything together. The reagents were easy, but there are details of the spell I'm still having trouble with. I'm pretty sure I've got it now.

"Ready when you are," I say. "Did you get the ritual space?"

"It's good to go. Do you really need that many leather straps?"

"I'm sawing a guy's head off while he's still awake. Yes. We're *really* gonna need that many leather straps. Speaking of which, have you found a 'volunteer?'"

"Yeah, about that," McCord says. Nicole dropped the first shoe. Now McCord's dropping the second. Some people are so predictable.

"Problem?"

"Maybe," he says. "It's Nicole. I think she might be trying to sabotage this."

"I thought you two were solid?"

"I did, too," he says. "But there's distance. She's disappearing at night, won't tell me what she's doing. Could be nothing, but my gut says it isn't."

He might as well be reading from a script. I want to fast forward through this bit so I can just agree to kill her for him and move on. But I play along.

"What do you want to do? Bit late to cut her loose."

"I was thinking of bringing her in…closer."

"You want me to cut your girlfriend's head off," I say.

"Jesus, man. Put it that way it sounds horrible." This whole fucking thing is horrible.

"But that's what we're talking about. I'll be honest, I'm not comfortable with that plan. I like her."

Which I do. She's smart. Can hold her own. She's also backstabbing, manipulative, and not big on ethics. Pretty typical mage, come to think of it.

"Me, either. Really." McCord's pouring it on thick. "But I don't think we can afford not to."

"You think she'll shank both of us." I make a show of thinking about it for a second. "Poison."

"Poison?"

"Yeah. This is a big deal. Before we start we'll have a toast. Only her drink's spiked."

"That would work. But…can you do it? I don't think I can." Oh, McCord, you old softie. Getting somebody else to do your dirty work.

"I understand. I'll handle it."

He lets out a breath, puts a fatherly hand on my shoulder. "Thanks," he says.

"I appreciate it."

I'm sure you do, you lying sack of shit.

* * *

I'm at an under-construction house outside Vegas that McCord has arranged as a ritual space. No water, no power. Nobody for miles.

Nicole wants me to kill McCord. McCord wants me to kill Nicole. Jimmy is scared of dying, so he wants me to cut his head off. One of them is going to get what they want.

When this is over I think I need to take a good long look at my life choices.

The house is mostly framing and sheetrock. Floor's poured concrete. That's where it stops looking like a construction project and turns into a horror show.

Bolted to the concrete is a surgical table with leather straps. Plastic tarps cover the floor, ceiling, hang from the walls. Couple of oil pans at the head of the table. They'll catch whatever blood doesn't spray all over everything else.

Next is a surgical tray holding the reagents and an 8-inch-long bone-saw.

The three of us wear disposable hazmat "bunny suits" with face shields. I've got a barbeque apron over it that says "Kiss The Cook." It's hiding a couple surprises.

In the next room is a table with champagne already poured. McCord picks one of the glasses up as Nicole comes in and I give him a barely noticeable nod. I hand one to Nicole, give her her own little nod.

Neither one of them has said anything about us not having a subject already on the table. I've told them both that I've got somebody ready and prepped, each of them assuming I'm talking about the other.

"To a brave new world," I say, and toss my glass back. They do the same, eyeing each other warily. Within seconds they're grimacing and looking a little woozy.

"What the hell did you do to me," McCord says, grabbing Nicole.

"Me? I didn't—" They both turn. I pour some more champagne, toss it back. Puffs of steam are coming up through my collar.

One of my tattoos makes me more or less immune to a lot of poisons. A wave of dizziness passes over me and disappears. It's not perfect.

Nicole gets it first, panic showing in her already-drooping face. "Take him," she says, voice slurred. "We had a deal." Knees sag and she falls to the floor.

"What do you think, McCord," I say. "Want to be a head in a box?" He reaches for me and I can feel the prickling of a spell, but it fizzles.

"Yeah, one of the side-effects. No magic." McCord lets out a grunt and falls to the floor.

I drag them into the other room and prop them up against a wall. They're not unconscious, just paralyzed. I picked up this recipe from a Bocor in St. Kitts a while back. If I got the dose right they should come out of it at the same time.

"Goddamn, you two are easy." I say. "In case you hadn't guessed, you tried to sell each other out." I pull a straight razor from the apron pocket and nick my thumb. Blood wells up from the cut. I use it to draw a rune on McCord's forehead. I repeat the spell on Nicole.

If I use either of them to make the Oracle, whoever's still alive will try to take me down. If I don't do the ritual, the Ker eats my soul. It's not what you call a win-win.

"The obvious solution would be to kill you both, make the Oracle, go on my happy way. Only I don't want one. And much as I don't like you two, I don't see any reason to kill you, either." I pull two tiny Sig-Sauer P-238s out of the pockets inside the apron, and chamber a round into each.

"That doesn't mean you won't kill each other." I put the pistols in their hands, fingers on the triggers, wrap them in duct tape so they don't fall out.

"You sure you want to do this?" I yell over my shoulder. "Last chance."

Jimmy pushes aside a plastic sheet and comes in from another room. He's wearing his best t-shirt, his cleanest jeans. If you're gonna die and be resurrected as a talking head, go in style, I guess.

"I'll be alive, right?" he says.

"Not in any way you know it," I say. But we've already had this argument.

There are times I'm not sure what the dividing line is between living and dying. A corpse is meat, but a soul goes on. Look at it that way, things get blurry.

Death happens. It's supposed to. I don't understand why. Don't think I ever will.

But it doesn't mean we have to be at its mercy. If this is what Jimmy wants, knowing everything I've told him, who am I to say no?

"I'm ready," Jimmy says. He gets up on the operating table. I turn back to McCord and Nicole, vision blurry. I wipe stinging eyes with the back of my hand.

"Here's how it's gonna go," I say. I put down the face shield, pull on gloves. "Option one is I make your Oracle and you figure out who gets it. Or there's option two." I lift the duct taped guns so they can see them. "One of you walks out of here with Jimmy's head.

"The rune's a minor geas. If you think of coming after me, it will remind you that I'm the one who gave you what you wanted and didn't kill you. Loudly. Repeatedly. Until you stop. It won't kill you, but you'll wish it had.

"Now if you'll excuse me, I have to go cut my roommate's head off."

I strap Jimmy down tight. If I'd known him, really known him, not just for his usefulness to me, but as a person, would we have been friends?

Probably not. I'm not good at friends.

It stings, but it's what he wants. And if I want to survive this, it's what I have to do.

I start the spell. Light candles and incense, deposit reagents in a circle around the table, chant in Latin. The room fills with the stink of the incense, Jimmy's panic sweat, my own fear and guilt.

A thick, black void forms over Jimmy. Faces shift in and out of the roiling sludge. I place the bone saw against the hollow of Jimmy's throat.

"I end Adjournment," I say, my voice almost cracking. I nod down at Jimmy. "This is your due."

The Ker reaches out with grasping hands, tongues, wrapping itself around Jimmy. It sinks into him like a ship slipping beneath the waves.

"I am satisfied," the Ker says.

I start to cut. Jimmy screams. A moment later so does the Ker.

* * *

I sit on a stool I pulled in from another room. It's the only thing in here that isn't covered in gore.

Jimmy's headless body lies strapped to the table, blood still dripping from the severed neck. His head sits nailed to a wooden base with a dowel up the back to keep it from flopping over. I've placed it in front of the two paralyzed mages. Whoever survives this gets the trophy.

"You want to kill them." The voice is sort of Jimmy's, a reverberation that makes my teeth ache. "Don't."

I turn the head around. Jimmy blinks at me, only it's not Jimmy. It's his face, his eyes, but Jimmy's not in there. Not like he was.

"How come?"

"I need one of them." Jimmy's face twists into what I think is supposed to be a smile. "One day, so will you."

Will I now? I wonder how much of him is still there, how much is the Ker. Maybe it's neither one. Both dying to create something new. One thing's for certain, whatever the hell I've made isn't answering to anybody.

I look over at the two paralyzed mages, guns in their hands, mine twitching for my own gun. "Got a preference?"

"I already know who's walking out of here," the oracle says.

"How you feeling?"

The smile shifts, the eyes clear, and it's pure Jimmy. "Nothin' hurts, man."

"Glad to hear it."

"Thanks for this," he says, and then his eyes go flat and whatever bits of Jimmy were floating on the surface have gone back under.

I stand up, head for the next room so I can get these blood-covered overalls off.

"Hey, man," the Oracle says, just the way Jimmy would, but when I look back I see the hungry eyes of the Ker glaring at me. "Want to know your future?"

"I already do," I say. "I die just like everybody else."

DELAYED EXCHANGE DEFERRED

Kiya Nicoll

There is a trick to playing chess with Death.

Not any set will do. Many a well-meaning gambler would set up the board by the bedside of a dying child, waiting to catch Death at work, to make the challenge. Sometimes the child would recover, and sometimes not, but the player never saw Death come or go, and never played the game. Knowing this, some would set up morbid boards, with pieces carved from finger bones, hoping to catch Death's attention. Death did not show for them either. Others would try pieces of gold and silver with ruby eyes, as if Death had ever cared about riches, or found his presence compelled by wealth.

Not any set will bring Death to play, but the sets that do have very little in common. Some are stone and some are wood and some are made of other things. There have been sets that could bring Death to play passed down through generations that have forgotten their power, and there are new ones made, for a special purpose.

This one is made of odds and ends, and barely seems to cohere as a set. The board is scratched into an old table, lines drawn against the side of a book and gouged out with a pocketknife, the pattern of the squares marked out with scars from hundreds of stubbed-out cigarettes. The white's king's rook is a shot glass, the queen's side is a brass cylinder, the knights a pair of erasers shaped like bumblebees, the bishops an orange and white pill bottle and a tiny upright crucifix, the king and queen a pair of chipped porcelain figurines with golden rings glued, a bit crookedly, to their heads. Black's side is just as motley: the rooks are flat metal discs—one oval, one circular—the knights a pair of misshapen lumps of charcoal, one bishop a syringe tube packed full of hair, the other a tuning key for a guitar, with the royals a pair of small dollar-store dolls, each with half a rainbow of colored rings settled on its head. White's pawns are bottle caps—well, seven bottle caps and a cork—each of them different, and black's are a steady progression of folded paper cranes, monotonically progressing from poorly made to roughly competent.

There are seven paper cranes.

Diligent hands work slowly, carefully, to fold the eighth. It is better made than number seven, though still far from perfect, and the creases do not line up quite right, no matter how often she smooths one thumb along each one. The bird takes its somewhat blossom-like shape, and its crafter hesitates for a moment—just a moment—before placing it on the eighth square of black's second row, adjusting its facing slightly, and standing up to go and get herself a drink.

She is both surprised and not that, when she turns back towards the table, there is someone there. She pauses, looks Death up and down, and says, "You're not what I expected."

"You were expecting what, tall and thin and bony?" says Death. "All pale, dressed in black, and carrying something off a farm?"

"I'm not sure what I was expecting." She pauses. "Aside from not this. Would you like a drink?"

"Very hospitable of you," says Death, approving. She is not tall, nor thin, nor bony, nor is she pale or dressed in black. She is a thick-thighed, generously curved black woman whose hair defies containment, she wears sensible shoes and comfortable clothes, and a set of bracelets on her right wrist. She might have been anyone's aunt introduced at the church social, save that her eyes are full of starlight and her voice, though quiet, sounds like faraway thunder.

"I did invite you to join me. I've got a beer, a bit of whiskey left, the last of the milk. Some orange juice."

"Sounds like you're not planning on staying long," says Death, pulling up a chair to the board. "You've got me playing white."

"You always have the advantage, don't you? Did you want a drink or not?"

"I'll have a whiskey, then."

She nods. "So, do you get a pale one if you're white?" she asks, making conversation, as she opens up the cabinet.

"That's an interesting question, sweetie," says Death.

"Does it get an interesting answer?" The bottle is smooth in her hands, its label scuffed at one corner, and she brushes her fingers over it several times, savoring the sensations of it, before she opens it.

"I keep my counsel." Death lets that statement settle with a certain rumbling finality, and then repeats, "Not planning on staying long?"

"I'm playing chess with Death," she says, pouring the last of the whiskey. "There aren't many ways that goes that mean I'll need groceries tomorrow." She brings the drink out and hands it over with a little half-bow. "There you go." She sits, cracking the last beer from the fridge, and lets it hiss.

Death picks up the glass. "Cheers."

"What the hell," she laughs, and taps the glass with the bottom edge of her bottle. "What're we drinking to?"

"What else?" says Death. "Life."

She blinks, and then nods. "To life, then."

Death studies the board, looks up and studies her opponent, then lightly puts a finger on one of the bottle caps and slides it two squares forward. "Pawn to king four."

"It's a classic opening, I will admit." She takes a swig from her bottle and sets it on the table next to the gouges marking the edge of the board, then slides one of her cranes to meet the bottle cap.

"Why a bee?" asks Death, picking up the king's knight and moving it out past the row of bottle caps.

"I met this girl once," she says. "In another lifetime. We lost touch, we both had crazy lives. But she said something to me that stuck with me. Haunted me. How now she left home, there would be nobody would bother to tell the bees she was gone." She picks up her queen's knight and moves it to guard her pawn, the charcoal smudging off on her fingers. "I looked it up, you know? That there's an old custom, or superstition, or something, that you tell the bees when someone dies, if you don't keep them informed they may leave, or stop making honey, or something like that."

"I see," says Death, and advances the pill bottle bishop to threaten the knight.

"I always wondered if maybe, when she left, they told the bees she was gone. Lied to them. I wonder if the bees care, you know? About whether it's true. Or whether it was true enough to count." She pushes the eighth crane a step forward to menace the pill bottle bishop.

"I never paid much attention to customs like that." Death studies the board and takes the knight with the pill bottle bishop. "What's the charcoal?"

"Pretty well dead wood, isn't it? Came from a bonfire. Down on the beach. Don't know anymore if I was drinking to remember or drinking to forget. Kept some of the wood, afterwards, so maybe it was remembrance. I tried to chip them into dogs, black dogs guarding the way, like, you know, Anubis and stuff, but I don't think they came out well." She sighs and advances one crane, claiming the pill bottle and cradling it in her hand.

"The intent carries, though," says Death. She nods at the pill bottle. "What's the story there?"

She puts the pill bottle down next to the beer, turns it to show Death the name. "Do you remember her? She had half a bottle left when she couldn't take it anymore."

Death is still for a moment, then reaches out to take the bishop back into her hand, her thumb smoothing over the label. "I remember." She sets it back down, and quietly castles, tucking the porcelain king safely behind a fortress of bottle caps and holding the shot glass carefully before setting it down to protect him.

She points to the shot glass. "I got that from his apartment. Landlord said anything his friends didn't take would get thrown out. Nobody else wanted it. Drank himself half to death. Everyone thought taking it would be too morbid. Except for me."

"I remember him," says Death. And then, "You didn't tell me why you wanted the game. There's nobody dying here to beg me to spare."

"There's me." She advances a bishop's pawn to defend the lone pawn.

"I don't see any reason I would take you home with me," says Death.

"And that's why I asked you here," she says. "To make a deal."

"Pardon?" Death looks honestly perplexed, her chin down enough to double, her brow furrowing over those starlight eyes.

"Ask me the stories." She gestures at the pieces.

"You've told me a few," says Death. "And I imagine you'll tell me more if we keep playing. But if we're playing for a forfeit, I'd better know the deal."

"Well, we've done your king's side," she says. "The king and queen, they were my grandmother's. She collected little trinkets. I managed to keep a few when she went. Cancer."

Death nods. "And the rings?"

"Wedding rings. I bought them at a pawnshop. Something died, for them to be there."

"Very true. The crucifix?"

"It's hard to keep up any sort of faith like this. In this world. I had one, once."

Death looks at the crucifix, and then at her. "But not Catholic."

"How do you know that?"

"Tastes different, a dead Catholic faith. Yours was some other kind."

"I suppose you would know, you put it that way." She pauses and studies the figure. "Other crosses don't have the death in them," she says, after a little while. "That one, it's got death with it. Can't escape it. Can't run from it. Got to face it, right there."

That appears to satisfy her. "It belonged to someone kept his faith to the end," she adds, conversationally.

"Did Jesus come for him, then?" asked her host, bitterly.

"I did. What comes after's not for the living, sweetie." Death quelled further questioning with her tone. "The other rook?"

"Bullet casing. Nine millimeter Glock. I couldn't get one from the actual scene, it was all roped off, but I snagged one from a range a bit afterwards where some of them went to practice. No indictment."

Death nods, again. "And your side, then."

She lays a finger on the round disc. "I had a dog once. When I was young enough to be, well, you know. That person died a long time ago."

"And I welcomed him," says Death, with a kindness that her hostess does not expect.

The silence, for a moment, is awkward.

"Not everyone feels they leave their childhood behind in a shroud," says Death. "But the ones who do, I welcome those kids home. They need rest and caring maybe more than most."

She says, after another unsettled pause, "He was a good dog." She skips over the other lump of charcoal, to the syringe. "Overdose. We never knew whether or not it was an accident. It was hard times." She skips the royal pieces and lays a finger on the other bishop. "She was a musician. She was amazing. And then she was gone."

"And that?" Death points at the other flat piece of metal, the rounded-off rectangle.

"Joined the Army. Only shot at college, getting somewhere better. Didn't make it home."

Death nods and waits, eyebrows raised, looking at the dollar-store dolls.

"They were the toppers for a wedding cake," she says. "Big thing. Couple years later he got cancer." She rests a finger on the queen. "He didn't make it." Then the king. "He...didn't make it either, but he's still alive. Well, the body's still moving. Not much of him left, from the grief. They wouldn't let him in to say goodbye."

Death closes her luminous eyes for a moment, looking as if she's casting her attention elsewhere, and there is a pause before she clears her throat and says, "The bottle caps?"

"Favorite drinks. The stuff you'd drink to remember someone by, you know. On anniversaries and when you miss them."

"And the cranes?"

"Wishes. Hopes. Struggling on despite the pain."

Death nods. "What's the bargain you want to strike with me, then?"

"You keep taking my people," she says. "I want you to take me, take my life, parcel it up, give it to the rest of us. Give everyone else a little more time. Take me instead."

Death shakes her head, sadly. "Oh, honey," she says. "That's not how it works."

She brings her first down on the table, nearly upending the beer. "I made the board. I called you here. I want you to take me instead of them!"

Death stands, setting her empty whiskey glass down. "Honey, I told you."

"I don't care what you told me! I worked the spell, I brought you here, I want to play the game!"

Death moves around the end of the table and drapes one arm around her shoulders. She elbows Death in the belly and does not even get the satisfaction of a grunt, for Death is as inexorable as her reputation. "Child, let me tell you a thing."

She grunts, curling her arms around herself, folding into a ball.

"Honey, I got your back."

This is, of course, not the expected thing and she looks up, into Death's bottomless, luminous eyes.

"I always got your back. You know it. You've always known it, that's how you knew how to call me. You knew I'd be there for you."

"If you're there for me," she growls, "why won't you take my trade?"

"That's not who I am."

Her brow furrows. "What do you mean?"

"I'm Death, honey, not Killing. I don't make them go. I don't have the power to take a life and give it to another. Your life's yours, nobody else's, and when you're done, you're done. If you're going to buy any of them another day, you've got to do it when you're living. There's no trade."

Her thwarted rage is near tangible. It sinks into Death's hair and barely moves a single strand of it. "So what good are you then?" she shouts, trying to make the locks stir and failing entirely.

"I'm the one welcomes them home."

She snorts, mocking. "Home." The tone is bitter.

"Home's the place where, when you go, they have to take you in. Isn't that right, sweetie?"

"What home have I got, then?" The anger breaks loose in shouting, with her balled fists clenched, but not daring to try to strike, and through all of the fury Death is unswayed and does not move her arm, leaving it draped around those shoulders with a gentle implacability.

"You got me." The thunder in Death's voice was a little louder now. "You and every other living thing. And you know, no matter what you do, no matter how it goes, I'll always be there for you. I'll be ready to welcome you home, as soon as you cross over."

Death's voice is warm, is something like motherly, a voice that, for all its eerie timbre, actually belongs to that generous body and those sensible shoes.

She looks at Death, looks deep into those starlight eyes, looks for something a little less alien than mortality offered as comfort, but Death is Death, at once alien and utterly familiar. Death has never been far away and she has known this better than most, measured it out in chess pieces and funerals and crumpled paper cranes.

She swallows back a sob, looks at Death, and finally closes her eyes.

"It's all right, sweetie. You know you can come rest, as soon as you're done fighting. That's a promise."

"But I have to be all the way done," she whispers. "I have to have nothing left. Because when I go, I go."

Death nods, and strokes her shoulder.

Her lip trembles. "Will I see—"

"Them again?" Death lays a finger on those lips. "Shhh, honey, that's not secrets for the living. Is it enough? To know that you got a home to go to when it's time?"

She closes her eyes, thinks, and Death strokes her hair. Eventually she whispers, "I have a home."

"You got a home. You're just travelling now. Camping out."

The laugh is shattered, awkward, mixed with tears. She goes boneless, cradled in Death's arms, her head resting on soft breasts, the sobs soaking the colorful, comfortable shirt with tears and snot and likely spit. She cries for a long time, wracked with it, and Death is there, quiet, secure. Death has all the time in the world and no need to hurry.

"Pick up your bottle, honey. Drink to life. There's time enough to go home at the end of it." Death gives her a last squeeze and kisses her temple, then returns to her side of the board. "You always got a home with me."

"But you're in no hurry to see me in your kitchen, is what you're saying."

"Time enough for that later. Right now, yours got no food in it, and you've a game of chess to finish before you can go to the supermarket, girl."

She nods, settles in, and says, "Your move."

ABOUT THE AUTHORS

SHAUN AVERY has been published in many magazines and anthologies, normally with tales of a dark and horrific nature. He also has a fondness for penning satirical stories, especially in relation to fame and media obsession. He has co-created a self-published horror comic, available here: http://www.comicsy.co.uk/dbroughton/store/products/spectre-show/ and recently sold his first comic script, details of which can be found here: http://shanewsmith.com/allthekingsmen/contributors/shaunavery/

STEPHEN BLACKMOORE is the author of the Eric Carter noir urban fantasy series with DEAD THINGS, BROKEN SOULS, and HUNGRY GHOSTS. He has also written for the Gods & Monsters series (MYTHBREAKER), the role-playing game Spirit of The Century (KHAN OF MARS), the video-game Wasteland 2 (ALL BAD THINGS) and the television series Heroes: Reborn (DIRTY DEEDS). His short stories can be found online and in the anthologies DEADLY TREATS and UNCAGE ME. He co-hosts the bi-monthly Los Angeles crime fiction reading series Noir At The Bar L.A. He can be found online at http://stephenblackmoore.com
and on Twitter at @sblackmoore.

LEAH CUTTER writes page-turning fiction in exotic locations, such as a magical New Orleans, the ancient Orient, Hungary, the Oregon coast, rural Kentucky, Seattle, Minneapolis, and many others. She writes literary, fantasy, mystery, science fiction, and horror fiction. Her short fiction has been published in magazines like *Alfred Hitchcock's Mystery Magazine* and *Talebones*, anthologies like Fiction River, and on the web. Her long fiction has been published both by New York publishers as well as small presses. Read more books by Leah Cutter at www.KnottedRoadPress.com. Follow her blog at www.LeahCutter.com.

ALIETTE DE BODARD lives and works in Paris. She is the author of the critically acclaimed Obsidian and Blood trilogy of Aztec noir fantasies, as well as numerous short stories which have garnered her two Nebula Awards, a Locus Award and two British Science Fiction Association Awards. Her space opera books include *The Citadel of Weeping Pearls*, a book set in the same universe as her Vietnamese science fiction *On a Red Station Drifting*. Recent works include the Dominion of the Fallen series, set in a turn-of-the-century Paris devastated by a magical war, which comprises *The House of Shatter-ed Wings* (Roc/Gollancz, 2015 British Science Fic-tion Association Award, Locus Award finalist), and its standalone sequel *The House of Binding Thorns* (Ace, Gollancz).
Visit http://www.aliettedebodard.com or @aliettedb on twitter for more information.

ANDREW DUNLOP is a graduate of the University of Toronto, a tabletop gamer, and an avid reader and writer of fantasy fiction. He lives in Ontario with his extremely supportive girlfriend and a couple of house plants, works by day, and writes by night. He is probably not a superhero, but has never been photographed in the same room as Stupendous Man, so you may draw your own conclusions.

Award-winning and eight-time *New York Times* best-selling author **CHRISTIE GOLDEN** has written over fifty novels and several short stories in the fields of science fiction and fantasy. She has written in such franchises as *Star Wars, Star Trek, World of Warcraft, StarCraft, Assassin's Creed,* as well as authoring her own books. Lady Death appears in Golden's novel *King's Man and Thief,* and Gillen Songespynner's tale is told in *Instrument of Fate.* Golden was awarded the International Association of Media Tie-in Writers' Faust Award 2017, conferring upon her the title of Grandmaster in acknowledgment of her contributions to the field.

JIM C. HINES is the author of twelve fantasy novels, including the Magic ex Libris series, the Princess series of fairy tale retellings, the humorous *Goblin Quest* trilogy, and the Fable Legends tie-in *Blood of Heroes*. His short fiction has appeared in more than 50 magazines and anthologies. He's an active blogger about topics ranging from sexism and harassment to zombie-themed Christmas carols, and won the 2012 Hugo for Best Fan Writer. His next book, *Terminal Alliance*, comes out in November 2017. Jim lives in mid-Michigan with his family. You can find him at www.jimchines.com or on Twitter as @jimchines.

JASON M. HOUGH is the *New York Times* bestselling author of *The Darwin Elevator, Zero World, Mass Effect: Nexus Uprising*, and *Injection Burn*, plus a number of short stories including *Turning Point: A Star Wars Story*. He can be found online at www.jasonhough.com or on Twitter via @jasonmhough

New York Times and USAToday bestselling author **FAITH HUNTER** was born in Louisiana and raised all over the south. She writes two contemporary Urban Fantasy series: the Jane Yellowrock series, featuring a Cherokee skinwalker who hunts rogue vampires, and the Soulwood series, featuring earth magic user Nell Ingram. Her Rogue Mage novels are a dark, post-apocalyptic, fantasy series featuring Thorn St. Croix, a stone mage. The role playing game based on the series, is ROGUE MAGE, RPG.

www.faithhunter.net
https://www.facebook.com/official.faith.hunter
https://www.facebook.com/faith.hunter?fref=ts
@hunterfaith
http://www.yellowrocksecurities.com
www.gwenhunter.com

AMANDA KESPOHL is a fantasy writer, attorney, and folklore enthusiast from Jacksonville Beach, Florida. Her short stories have been featured in *Alien Abduction* (Robot Cowgirl Press) and *Sirens* (World Weaver Press). She currently resides in Tallahassee with her beagle, Bailey. Check out her website at https://amandakespohl.wordpress.com/ or find her on Twitter at @amandakespohl.

K.M. LANEY has been writing since childhood. An avid RPG gamer, both tabletop and online, most of her previous work went into character backgrounds and scenarios for her friends and family. In college she studied mathematics and chemistry. She performed a variety of jobs, from opticianry to silicon wafer inspection to proofreading advertising copy. Special interests include archaeology, Star Wars, Star Trek, and music. She lives in Oregon with her husband, son, cats, and guitars. She currently runs a blog for writers, shortfictionweeklychallenge.tumblr.com. She can be found at kmlaney.tumblr.com or on twitter @kmlaneywrites.

KATHRYN MCBRIDE has a deep familiarity with corporate shenanigans having spent years in tidy little cubicles underwhelming her superiors. Born and raised in San Francisco, she is currently enjoying the shores of Lake Michigan in St. Joseph with her partner and rescue pups. Discovering local breweries, making custom dice bags, and freaking out over current events occupies her free time. Kathryn's short fiction has been previously featured in Bop Dead City and 200cc.

JULIET E. MCKENNA is a British fantasy author. Loving history, myth and other worlds, she has written fifteen epic fantasy novels, starting with *The Thief's*

Gamble which began *The Tales of Einarinn.* She writes diverse shorter fiction, from stories for themed anthologies such as *Alien Artifacts* and *Fight Like A Girl* to forays into dark fantasy and steampunk with *Challoner, Murray and Balfour: Monster Hunters at Law.* She reviews for web and print magazines and promotes SF&Fantasy by blogging on book trade issues, attending conventions and teaching creative writing. Visit julietemckenna.com for more or follow @JulietEMcKenna on Twitter.

VILLE MERILÄINEN is a university student from Joensuu, Finland. His short fiction has won the Writers of the Future award and has appeared in various journals, both online and in print. His musical fantasy novel, Ghost Notes, is available on Amazon. He can be found on Facebook at https://www.facebook.com/vmerilainenauthor.

MACK MOYER is a writer from Philadelphia. His novel, *Sketches of the Wigwam,* is available on Amazon. He fancies himself a low-rent Bukowski, but will never admit it. You can find him on MackMoyer.com, plus Facebook and Twitter.

ANDREA MULLEN started out as a voracious reader of fantastic stories, so it was only a matter of time before she started writing them. This is her first short story in publication. She currently lives in the wilds of Central Pennsylvania, where she tends her vegetable garden, plays games with her friends, and works with rescued beagles. She can be reached online at amullen.tumblr.com, and on twitter @AndreaWrote.

KIYA NICOLL lives in New England with her human family, three cats, and a turtle, and on twitter at @kiya_nicoll, and blogs in the writerly way at the uncreatively named kiyanicoll.com. She commits words, art, and theology on a somewhat regular basis, in and around wondering if she ought to be committed. She was raised on stories and bleeds narrative, but she would not win a game of chess with Death, even though she can remember which way the little horse-shaped ones move.

JULIE PITZEL writes paranormal fiction from a geodesic dome south of Houston. She's been involved in the Houston writing community for over twenty years serving on too many committees and various boards, including two years as president of a local Romance Writers of America Chapter. Julie collects eclectic jewelry and shows off her love of the macabre with more than sixty pairs of Halloween themed earrings. She lives with her husband and a pair of overly affectionate cats.

ANDRIJA POPOVIC is a native of the Washington DC metropolitan area. When he is not assisting grassroots advocacy organizations with their on-line campaigns he indulges in a bit of photography, spends entirely too much on books, and writes haiku for his Twitter account, @Andrian6. His stories have previously been published in *Daily Science Fiction* and the Zombies Need Brains LLC anthology ALIEN ARTIFACTS. He can also be found at his blog, Biomechanoid Blues (biomechanoidblues.wordpress.com)

A. MERC RUSTAD is a queer non-binary writer who lives in the Minnesota. Favorite things include: robots, dinosaurs, and monsters. Their stories have appeared in Lightspeed, Fireside, Apex, Uncanny, Shimmer, and other fine venues. Merc likes to play video games, watch movies, read comics, and wear awesome hats. You can find Merc on Twitter @Merc_Rustad, Patreon   (https://www.patreon.com/mercrustad)   or   their website: http://amercrustad.com. Their debut short story collection, SO YOU WANT TO BE A ROBOT, is available from Lethe Press (May 2017).

KENDRA LEIGH SPEEDLING lives in Boston with her partner and a large gray cat with thumbs. Her short stories have appeared in Beneath Ceaseless Skies, Vitality Magazine, and Penumbra eMag. She also does writing and game design for the Pathfinder tabletop RPG. When not writing things, she enjoys reading, baking, playing a wide variety of games, and yelling about history a lot. You can check out her website, klspeedling.com, or her Twitter @KendraLS for general musings, tales of shenanigans, and the occasional burst of wit.

FRAN WILDE is the author of the Andre Norton- and Compton Crook Award-winning, Nebula-nominated novel *Updraft* (Tor 2015), its sequels, *Cloudbound* (2016) and *Horizon* (2017), and the Nebula- and Hugo-nominated novelette *The Jewel and Her Lapidary* (Tor.com Publishing 2016). Her short stories appear in *Asimov's*, Tor.com, *Beneath Ceaseless Skies*, *Shimmer*, *Nature,* and the 2017 Year's Best Dark Fantasy and Horror. She writes for publications including *The Washington Post*, Tor.com, *Clarkesworld*, iO9.com, and GeekMom.com. You can find her on twitter @fran_wilde, Facebook @franwildewrites and at franwilde.net.

ABOUT THE EDITORS

LAURA ANNE GILMAN is the Nebula- and Endeavor-award nominated author of the Devil's West series, SILVER ON THE ROAD, THE COLD EYE, and the forthcoming RED WATERS RISING, as well as the short story collection DARKLY HUMAN, and other series this bio doesn't have space for. Her recent short fiction has sold to *Daily Science Fiction*, *Lightspeed*, and the anthologies LAWLESS LANDS and WEIRD CALIFORNIA.

A former New Yorker, she currently lives outside of Seattle with two cats and many deadlines. Information and updates can be found at www.lauraannegilman.net, or follow her on Twitter: @LAGilman

* * *

KAT RICHARDSON is the bestselling author of the *Greywalker* paranormal detective novels. She is also a freelance editor and the author of the science fiction police thriller *Scattered Objects,* coming from Pyr in late 2017 under the pseudonym K. R. Richardson. She lives in Western Washington, and is an accomplished feeder of crows.

ACKNOWLEDGMENTS

This anthology would not have been possible without the tremendous support of those who pledged during the Kickstarter. Everyone who contributed not only helped create this anthology, they also helped solidify the foundation of the small press Zombies Need Brains LLC, which I hope will be bringing SF&F themed anthologies to the reading public for years to come ... as well as perhaps some select novels by leading authors, eventually. I want to thank each and every one of them for helping to bring this small dream into reality. Thank you, my zombie horde.

The Zombie Horde: Asha Bardon, Simon Dick, Andrew Wilson, Sarah Cornell, J.R. Murdock, Kimberly Lloyd, Bruno Girin, Sharon Wood, Kari Maaren, Heidi Cykana, Nancy Lambert, Vicki Greer, Ash Marten, Diana Castillo, Brian Quirt, David A. Holden, Gabriel Sinclair, Jason M Hough, David Rippere, Kerry Ebanks, Stephanie Cranford, Stephen Goodrow, Kimba Wilson, Jakub Narębski, Gia B., Tina Black, Christina Roberts, Erin Kenny, Ryan Poindexter, Pierre Gauthier, Phil Olynyk, Scott Drummond, Patrick & Sarah Pilgrim, Alexander Gideon, Carolyn Petersen, Elizabeth Belden Handler, April Steenburgh, Aurora N., Marissa Lingen, Veronica, Millie Calistri-Yeh, Jean Marie Ward, Stephanie Cheshire, Christine Swendseid, Fred Herman, Sidney Whitaker, Teresa Carrigan, Jen Edwards, Fred and Mimi Bailey, Cyn Wise, Brenda Moon, Kristin Evenson Hirst, Juli, Jeffery Lawler, Andrew Kinstetter, Petter Wäss, Duncan and Andrea Rittschof, Nick W., Anders M. Ytterdahl, Michael Fedrowitz, Andy M., Susan Carlson, Cate Crowley, Kelly Crowell, Kerry aka Trouble, John Idlor, Claire Sims, Tibs, Steven desJardins, Sheryl R. Hayes, Anna Rudholm, Jake Woodworth, Chuck Hickson, Jill Chinchar, Andrija Popovic, David Bruns, Elyse M Grasso, RKBookman, Tamara Michelle Slaten, Miranda Floyd, Becky Allyn Johnson, dbschlosser, Samuel Kohner, Carol J. Guess, shadow cat, Patti Short, Don Larson, Zoe, Jenny Barber, Michele Hall, Jim and Darla Nault-Tait, Peter

Donald, Mandy Stein, Shawna Jacques, M. E. Gibbs, Scott Raun, Chad Bowden, Mr. And Mrs. Smooth, Rachel Stuart, Sarah Brand, Michele Fry, Lauowolf, Eleanor Russell, Elise Power, Susan Oke, Michele Dainiak, Elizabeth Inglee-Richards, Cathy Green, Debra Stewart, Douglas Park, Kerri Regan, ANDREW AHN, David Hill, Stephen Ballentine, William Hughes, Atthis Arts LLC, Dina S Willner, Ashley R. Morton, James Conason, Jennifer McGaffey, E. Smith, Katherine Malloy, Lace, Leslie Gawne, Sidsel N. Pedersen, pophyn, Elaine (Lainey) Rothman, Lark Cunningham, Helen Cameron, Sachin Suchak, Niall Gordon, Robby Thrasher, Lennhoff Family, Chris Matosky, Jules Jones, Laura Sheana Taylor, Patrick Thomas, Fen Eatough, Jennifer Berk, Jaq Greenspon, Sontaran Empire, Kevin Winter, Marty Poling Tool, Peter Hansen, Cindy Cripps-Prawak, Alan and Morva, Kyrielle, Diana Ramos, SusanB, Matthew Markland, David Quist, Stephanie Lucas, Erin M. Evans, Tony Anjo, Keith Jones, Colleen R. Cahill, Pulp Literature Press, Steven Saus, Cheri Kannarr, Catherine Sharp, Gary Phillips, Tindra Tieren, Gina & Jon Freed, Adora Hoose, Caryn Cameron, Todd V. Ehrenfels, Debbie Matsuura, Rachel Blackman, Jörg Tremmel, Pat Knuth, Simon Niklasson, Yoshio Kobayashi, Yankton Robins, Ferd Burfle, Carol Mammano, Karen Laage, Michael Bernardi, Mark Carter, Andrew Hatchell, Annie Mosity, Chris 'Warcabbit' Hare, Morgan S. Brilliant, Chrissie & Jake Palmatier, Vespry family, Harvey Brinda, Brendan Lonehawk, Sheryl Ehrlich, Tom P. Powers, E.G. Languzzi, Robert Killheffer, Andreas Gustafsson, Thea Maia, Kai Herbertz, A.K. Skelding, Mervi Mustonen, Ed Ellis, Alisha Henri, Merav Hoffman, Gavran, Chris Gerrib, Keith Bissett, Brenda Rezk, Dave Hermann, Richard P Bissmire, Jessica Reid, Jerel D Heritage, Yes, Robin Yang, Pat Hayes, Keith Setzer, Elizabeth Ann Scarborough, Deborah Fishburn, Colette Reap, Revek, Eagle Archambeault, Tory Shade, Katrina Allis, David Rowe, Ivan Donati, KixieKat, Sharon E. Altmann, Rafe Brox, Molly Elizabeth Atkins, Linden Vimislik, Catherine Gross-Colten, Henry W Schubert, Deborah Blake, Julie Hendershott Kovac, Jaime O. Mayer, Alysia Murphy, JE Chase, Karen Grennan, Peter T, Rick D, Cynthia Porter, Tahmi DeSchepper, Anne M. Rindfliesch, Holland Dougherty, David Medinnus, Clara Strzalkowski, Eduard Lukhmanov, Melme, Cheryl Preyer, Gary Clark, Rachel Sasseen, Kathryn L. Whitlock, Annette Agostini, Sarah Liberman, Svend Andersen, Kristi Chadwick, Pam Blome, Betty Law Morgan, Hisham El-Far, Kathy Holzapfel, Jen B, Sofie Bird, Mark Kiraly, Mary Alice Wuerz, Keith West, Future Potentate of the Solar System, Sally Novak Janin, Mary Jeh, Steven Mentzel, S. Worthen, Hannah Maxwell, Curtis Frye, David Drew, Paul Bulmer, Rolf Laun, Jesse Klein, Shel Kennon, Cathy Schwartz, Christina Stiles, Ross Hathaway, Tammy Greco, Christine Ethier, Bruce Shipman, Tibicina, Michelle Carlson, Missy Katano, Donna Gaudet, Danielle Ackley-McPhail, Jenn Whitworth, Jessica K. Meade, Leah Webber, Chris Barili, Tina Connell, Janka Hobbs, Ian Chung, Rissa Lyn, Jonathan S Chance, Gretchen, Cheryl Losinger, Brenda Cooper, Corey T., Anonymous Reader, ARNSProprietor, Thomas Santilli, Heather Kelly, Nancy

Barber, Selwyn, filkferengi, Ron Currens, Lily Connors, Melissa Shumake, Charlie Russel, Jason Palmatier, David Zurek, Connor Bliss, Tomas Burgos-Caez, Natasha A., John Senn, Nancy M. Tice, Andy Funk from Atlanta, Karen Dubois, Nesa Sivagnanam, Paul McNamee, Robert Early, John Green, Echo Mae, Deena Cates, nobe, Janet Oblinger, Jen Woods, Julia Haynie, Andy Miller, Dr.Deb, Julie Pitzel, John Sturkie, Michael Kahan, Jake Parrick, Ronnie J Darling, Jen1701D, Amelia Smith, Samuel Aronoff, Max Kaehn, Ron Hogan, Patricia van Ooy, Kelly J Cooper, Mollie Bowers, Alexander Smith, CGJulian, Leshia-Aimée Doucet, Andrew and Kate Barton, David Eggerschwiler, Ian Harvey, Amanda Nixon, Mark Newman, Rachel Conner-Maling, Mark Gerrits, Smashingsuns, D-Rock, Simba, Hero, and Nahla, Nathan Turner, Lauren E. Mitchell, Maria Lima, Anne Burner, Orla, Lisa Kruse, Colleen Harkins, Tina M Noe Good, Bill and Laura Pearson, Philip Barkow, Sandy, @lenoxartist, Steven Halter, Dan & Chris Brewer, Elaine Tindill-Rohr, Ty wilda, Kaitlin Thorsen, Heather Fagan, Jeremy Brett, Maureen Brooks, Cherie Livingston, Julie Benda, Tris Lawrence, Michelle Palmer, Rosanne Girton, Evergreen Lee, Kate Larking, Jaymie Larkey Maham, Margaret St. John, Kelly Melnyk, Carolyn Mackriell, Jena Marie Klees, Emily Weed Baisch, Freya Jackson, Paul Gunther, Tristan Smith, Karen H, Annastasia (medicinalink) Gallaher, Kathryn A Patterson, R.T. Bryson, Galena Ostipow, Jeremy Audet, K. Hodghead, Phillip Spencer, Jen Bishop, Hedrigall, Cathy Brown, K. McLeod, Jay Barnson, Kathy Bond, Megan Hungerford, Tony F, Amy Streifel, Noah Bast, Ellie, SwordFire, Gary Ehrlich, ChanieB, V. Hartman DiSanto, Holly Daugherty, Kimberly M. Lowe, Barbara Hasebe, RJ Seymour, Erik T Johnson, Patrick Osbaldeston, Anthony R. Cardno, Russell Martens, Jacob Carson, Andy Clayman, Shelly Jones, Elizabeth Kite, Bill Sykes, Erin Penn, Janito Vaqueiro Ferreira Filho, John/Susan Husisian, Aurelia McDonald, Keith E. Hartman, Gustaf B., Ilene Tsuruoka, Linda Pierce, Wolf SilverOak, Gnondpom, Rebecca M, Lucas Santiago, Crazy Lady Used Books & Emporium, Samuel Lubell, Theresa Glover, Annaliese Smith, Bill Emerson, Liz Wyatt, Abi Scott, Cheryl, Chris Fielding, R Kirkpatrick, Jonathan Adams, Stephen Kissinger, Iain Riley, Robert Parks, Erin Kowalski, Michael Cieslak, Mini Lizard, Kitty Likes, Krystina Harrington, R. Hunter, C.N.Rowen, Rachel "Nausicaa" Tougas, Terry D. England, Judith Mortimore, Daria Fox, Bill McGeachin, RBC, Pat Connelly, Zion Russell, Kevin Niemczyk, C. Liang, anne m gibson, David J Fortier, Justin P. Miller, C. Lennox, Pete Hollmer, Sue Shelly, Nellie, Tammy Graves, Kristy K, Aaron R, Matthew Walker, K.G. Anderson, Vancano Smith, Carina Erk, Lauren Wallace, Laura F., Melissa Burkart, Dino Hicks, J. I. Rogers, Gabe Krabbe, Judy Bemis, Dina Barron, Troy Bucher, Margaret S. McGraw, Kathi Schreiber, Carla Hollar, Lyn Godfrey, Kimberly H., Marc D. Long, Donaithnen, Lisa Deutsch Harrigan (Auntie M), Axisor, Gai LaMarche, Cliff Winnig, Janet Armentani, Danny Neimeyer, Belkis Marcillo, Ian Monroe, Lynn Kramer, Crystal Sarakas, Pamela Lunsford, J.P. Goodwin, Wendy Kitchens, Michael Grey, Rhel ná DecVandé, Terri Oda, Judith Bienvenu,

Heather & Zachary Jones, Victoria L Sullivan, Jamie FitzGerald,